DEFIANT

BY BRANDON SANDERSON

THE STORMLIGHT ARCHIVE

The Way of Kings
Words of Radiance
Edgedancer
Oathbringer
Dawnshard
Rhythm of War

THE MISTBORN SAGA

Mistborn
The Well of Ascension
The Hero of Ages
The Alloy of Law
Shadows of Self
The Bands of Mourning
The Lost Metal
Misborn: Secret History

LEGION

Legion
Legion: Skin Deep
Legion: Lies of the Beholder

COLLECTIONS

Legion: The Many Lives of Stephen Leeds
Arcanum Unbounded: The Cosmere Collection
Legion and the Emperor's Soul

ALCATRAZ VS THE EVIL LIBRARIANS

Alcatraz vs the Evil Librarians
The Scrivener's Bones
The Knights of Crystallia
The Shattered Lens
The Dark Talent
Bastille vs the Evil Librarians
(with Janci Patterson)

THE RECKONERS

Steelheart
Mitosis
Firefight
Calamity

SKYWARD

Skyward
Starsight
Skyward Flight
(with Janci Patterson)
Cytonic
Defiant

Elantris
Warbreaker
The Rithmatist
Snapshot
Tress of the Emerald Sea
The Frugal Wizard's Handbook
for Surviving Medieval England
Yumi and the Nightmare Painter

GRAPHIC NOVELS

White Sand
Dark One

DEFIANT

BRANDON SANDERSON

First published in Great Britain in 2023 by Gollancz
an imprint of The Orion Publishing Group Ltd
Carmelite House, 50 Victoria Embankment
London EC4Y 0DZ

An Hachette UK Company

This edition first published in Great Britain by Gollancz in 2023

1 3 5 7 9 10 8 6 4 2

A CIP catalogue record for this book is
available from the British Library.

ISBN (HB) 978 1 473 23460 4
ISBN (eBook) 978 1 473 23463 5
ISBN (Audio) 978 1 473 23464 2

Printed in Great Britain by Clays Ltd, Elcograf, S.p.A.

MIX
Paper from
responsible sources
FSC® C104740

www.brandonsanderson.com
www.gollancz.co.uk.

For Kara,
Who carries my books to the world.

DEFIANT

PROLOGUE

I floated in a void of nothing.

And felt like I belonged there.

So strange. I was a creature of flesh and blood. I *knew* that. Yet my soul—part of it at least—felt more at home here. In a vast void of meaningless time. The nowhere.

I was a person of two worlds. Spensa, the girl from Detritus, a warrior. Chet, the delver, a being outside space and time. We had become one.

We'd become a weapon.

I still didn't know how that worked. But I had some connection to this place that I believed would let me attack the delvers. Delvers—the terrible, strange beings that had destroyed planets and threatened my reality. I could *hurt* them. I didn't know how yet, but the thing I'd become . . . it could *destroy* them.

They were frightened of me. So they hid.

How can they hide? I thought. *All time and space is one single point here.*

They are looking inward, Chet responded. Part of my soul, yes, but we were still two individuals. It had been just over a week since I'd returned from the nowhere, and I was still learning how all this worked. But I did feel much more like myself now than when I'd first arrived.

I don't understand, I sent to him.

We have no bodies, Chet explained. *So you can only see us—what you call the eyes—when we are looking. It is complicated . . . as light only becomes visible when you interact with it, when it hits your eyes, you can only be aware of us when we are aware of you.*

Yeah. He might have been stapled to my soul—and I might have felt like I belonged in this void—but a ton of this still broke my brain to think about.

How do we fight them? I asked him.

I don't know, he replied. *We need to learn. For now, isn't it enough that they're afraid of us?*

It should have been. But something about that bothered me. An issue with their fear that I couldn't quite explain yet. So for the moment I hovered, considering. Worried, but unable to explain why. Alone. In a place that was populated by thousands upon thousands of my enemies.

M-Bot? I thought, questing out with my cytonic senses.

No response. I didn't know what had happened to him. Chet said he'd survived somehow, but despite searching each day since my return—coming here to the nowhere via cytonic mental projection—I'd not been able to find any sign of my friend. The ship I'd once flown, a delver in embryo.

I sighed and tried experimenting with my powers. Melding with the delver had changed me in two significant ways. First, in my vicinity the border between somewhere and nowhere seemed more . . . flimsy. Second, I had a connection to the delvers—and to others. I could enter minds more easily. I could feel emotions more easily.

Here in the nowhere, time was meaningless. Each person entering it, however, pulled a little bit of the *somewhere* in with them. Left an imprint, like a picture. On my journey, I'd been able to touch similar pictures left deliberately for me. Now I began to get glimpses of ones left *unintentionally*. Traces of what my friends had experienced while I'd been gone.

As I reached out, I found images. Impressions. Residual bits of emotion and experience left as my friends hyperjumped in and out of the nowhere. Bread crumbs that helped me experience what they'd been through while I was gone. They'd told me, of course, but now I *saw* it.

I saw their panic when I vanished to go to Starsight. I saw them befriend Alanik, the purple-skinned alien who had crashed on Detritus. With her, they'd eventually gone to rescue her world from the Superiority, bringing a small planet's worth of people to our cause.

I saw the National Assembly, my people's political leaders, try to make a deal with the enemy. And I saw a tragic betrayal as Winzik gleefully turned that summit into a trap—setting off an explosion that killed most of our leaders. I saw Gran-Gran and Cobb vanish into the nowhere, propelled by her talents, to protect them—and I saw them get trapped there.

Finally, I saw the kitsen. Small foxlike aliens who walked on two feet, and whose entire planet was in danger when the Superiority decided to attack. I saw interactions between them and my people, with Skyward Flight doing hard work to forge an alliance. Jorgen reluctantly taking up leadership not just of our flight, but of the entire military. Using his powers to rescue not only Gran-Gran and Cobb, but the kitsen cytonics, who had been trapped in an interdimensional prison for centuries.

These were mere glimpses—likely only possible because of my deep ties to my friends. When I tried to use the same abilities to spy on my enemies, I got nothing. But these images helped me fill in what had happened in my absence, and also left me feeling sorrowful. Because I hadn't been there to help. Because they'd all learned so much, accomplished so much, and I was left as an observer to their lives.

What you were doing was important, Chet said to me. I nodded, as I knew it was true, but still . . .

I left the nowhere, coming aware in my bunk back on Detritus. I still had a problem, one bigger than my own emotional baggage: I didn't know how these new powers would help me defeat the delvers. It was my job to protect my people from them. It was why I'd gone to the nowhere; I was supposed to become the weapon that could defeat them.

Despite all I'd learned, all I'd accomplished, I felt like I was still so very ignorant. I had no idea what I was doing.

Chet vibrated my soul in a way that was comforting. He was doing his best to help. I sighed, climbed out of my bunk, and prepared for the day. By all accounts, it was going to be a doozy. Fortunately, for the time being all I had to do was stand in place and try to look imposing. I stumbled to the mirror, and what looked back was anything *but* imposing. Frizzy hair, down past my shoulders now. Bags under my eyes.

And something within those eyes, something haunted. Something dangerous. Something I didn't understand.

Myself, and what I'd become.

I shook my head. Heaved a long sigh.

Then took out my dress uniform.

PART
ONE

1

Five hours later, I stood at parade rest on stage.

I'd survived innumerable starfighter battles. I'd escaped the destructive power of the lifebuster bomb by a fraction of a moment. I'd traveled the nowhere itself, teasing out the memories and wisdom of the ancients. I'd looked straight at the delvers—the terrible, eldritch monsters that lived outside of time and space—meeting their eyes and refusing to back down. I was Spensa Nightshade, warrior.

Which meant, I had come to learn, that I was an important political tool.

And so today, instead of being out fighting, I had to wear something far less comfortable than a good flight suit. My chest was laden with medals—I was pretty sure they'd invented a few new ones to give me, just to make me look more impressive. Despite that, today's ceremony wasn't about me. I was, like the medals themselves, an ornament. A way to lend credibility to what was happening before me.

Jorgen Weight being named Defiant Defense Force admiral of the fleet. And, since the National Assembly had been destroyed, we were under martial law—meaning that as the DDF admiral of the fleet, he was also provisional head of our government. Until something else could be arranged.

Even with my glimpses of what had happened in my absence, I felt like I was behind. Still struggling to catch up.

Jorgen leaned forward as one of our elders placed the appropriate epaulettes on his shoulders, conferring his new rank. Then he stood up tall. Looking at his strong, determined features, you'd never have known that he'd broken down a few days ago, crying in my arms over the death of his parents. They had been Assembly members.

A part of my soul echoed with the cry of pain he'd made as the blast had killed them. What a fool's errand that had been. I couldn't believe the Assembly had really tried to make peace with the Superiority. They'd walked right into that trap. Still, I tried not to blame them. While I'd never gotten along with the Assembly members I'd met, for Jorgen's sake I mourned. It was a major blow to all of us, not just those who had lost family. It blared out an insult loud as the galaxy itself: we weren't even worth negotiating with.

Applause erupted in the long, broad hall where we'd gathered for the event. I stood to the side of the stage, along with Kimmalyn, FM, and several other distinguished DDF officers. My spot gave me a good view of the audience, which was strikingly varied. Despite what I'd seen, it was hard to believe that in my absence, my friends had accomplished so much. Two entire planets had joined with us in defiance.

Prominent among them were the kitsen, who stood on an array of floating platforms, with speakers to magnify their chirps of approval. In rescuing their long-lost cytonics, we now had a force of people with powers like my own—if more compact, in their fifteen-centimeter-tall furry frames.

Alanik's people, the UrDail, were also there—though in smaller numbers. They had violet skin and prominent bone-white facial protrusions. The ones I'd met this week treated me cordially, but I could sense the awkwardness there. Alanik herself was near the front of their group, and although she and my flight had become good friends, she avoided my gaze. Fair enough. I'd impersonated her, and had done quite a bit in her name. Though she said she understood why . . . well, I wouldn't have liked the idea of anyone running around impersonating *me*.

Jorgen stood before the crowd, accepting the applause. I could tell from that strained, too-responsible look in his eyes that he didn't think he deserved it. I was proud of him for accepting it anyway. He had never wanted this; he, like me, just wanted to fly. But I hadn't heard a complaint out of him since my return.

Someone had to step up and take the lead, and Jorgen was one of our most battle-hardened and experienced pilots. That itself was terrifying, considering his age, but it was the truth. We needed him.

Once the applause died down, FM barked an order, and those of us on the stage snapped to attention and saluted. Jorgen returned the salute, then walked to the podium to make his speech. That was the sign that the rest of us could break salute, step backstage, then make our way to our seats.

I ducked out first, wondering if maybe I could—

"Hey, Spin," a voice said, and I turned to see Kimmalyn hurrying toward me. Kimmalyn wore her hair long, naturally forming tight curls that reached to her shoulders. She'd been forced to pin on nearly as many medals as me. "You all right?" she asked. "You look distracted."

"Fine," I said as others filed around us. Then I just stood there, silent.

Scud. I still didn't know what to say to my friends. How did I even begin to explain what I'd been through? That I had a delver stapled to my soul? That I'd seen the origins of cytonics, then nearly lost myself in a place where time frayed like the edges of an old coat? That I'd almost decided to *stay* and abandon them?

"If you need—" Kimmalyn started.

"I've gotta hit the head," I said, accidentally talking over her.

Her expression turned concerned again. Maybe a little hurt that I hadn't opened up to her, as I once had.

I fled, but not to the head. I got "lost" on the way, and in under ten minutes I was in the cockpit of a Poco starfighter, boosting out into space to do a quick patrol of the region.

It was a selfish move. Someone might notice my empty seat, and it might start rumors. But scud . . . I'd been going to far, *far* too many meetings lately. One week since my return, and I'd barely had any time in a ship. Plus, I'd heard Jorgen's speech six times already as he'd practiced.

So I flew, enjoying the sensation of the g-forces pushing me back in my seat. Enjoying the sight of Detritus's many layers of platforms rotating above me, with the soft blue-grey stone ground extending before me. And in a moment of exultation, I activated my cytonic abilities and hyperjumped toward outer space, just beyond the planet.

The moment I jumped, Chet stirred, his soul stuffed inside my body like a parachute packed in its ejection pod.

I don't know what to make of my new powers, I thought at him as— once again—we hung in the void and saw only blackness. *The other day, I hyperjumped something without touching it.*

Yes, he thought back. *You are part delver now. Distance and space are . . . not as relevant to you as they once were.*

Here, floating for a moment in the nowhere—and once again not seeing any delvers—I felt I understood a little better why I was dangerous to them. It had something to do with my deeper intrinsic connection to the nowhere and the delvers. One thing I'd learned in my travels was that they had hidden away parts of themselves, had intentionally forgotten their pain.

Now that I was part delver, I could see the truth. I could see what Chet had done to hide that same pain. I thought . . . I thought if I could figure it all out, *this* could be the secret to their destruction.

I took a moment to quest out for M-Bot again, but felt nothing, so I completed the hyperjump. I appeared back in the somewhere, in my ship, outside Detritus's shell. And in that moment I realized something. Why I'd been concerned earlier in the day when Chet had noted the delvers were afraid of me.

He stirred. *Yes,* he thought at me. *Why are you worried? It's good that they're frightened, yes?*

Good, I thought back, *and bad. Chet, they're desperate. And desperate people do unpredictable things.* I'd spent all this time learning to anticipate them—but now, who knew what they would do?

He settled back against my soul, like a person leaning back in a chair, and pondered on that. Because we were linked, he understood instantly what I meant. And soon I saw that he understood my worry as well.

Still, I tried to put those concerns out of my mind for the moment, so I could just enjoy the flight. Tried to ignore the weight upon my soul. The lingering sadness—though I tried to stamp it out—at having left the nowhere, where I could have explored without responsibility, behind. The worry about M-Bot. The sense of disconnect I felt, returning to a place where time flowed normally.

The implications that I was now one of *them* more than I was one of *us*.

My hyperjump, fortunately, gave me something gorgeous to distract me. We were in orbit around Evershore, the kitsen homeworld. A vibrant blue planet, like all the old pictures of Earth, with clouds and seas and life. It was breathtaking.

I soared through space between the two planets. Detritus, it turned out, could *move*. There was a reason it had been built with its own protective shell, able to maintain its warmth and a day-night cycle far from any sun. It was an enormous battle station, capable of using cytonics to hyperjump around the galaxy. Indeed, many of its platforms could move on their own, like smaller battle stations.

All the planet had needed was some maintenance and a whole lot of alien slugs. Fortunately, we'd managed to provide both.

Our homeworld was even more amazing than we'd ever known. It had provided a haven to slugs—hundreds of them hiding in the tunnels far beneath the surface. Thinking of that made me reach out to Doomslug, and I sensed her spike of joy at the contact. She sent me an image of a large room on one of the platforms, where she was being cared for. Dozens of slugs—of several different varieties—populated this room alone, with human caretakers engaging with them.

Doomslug was hiding in the corner with a little bowl of what appeared to be caviar. She perked up at my contact, and sent me an immediate emotional barrage of relief. After my time in the nowhere, I was getting better at understanding her—and these days I could make out basic words from the impressions she sent.

I thought you would be happy with the others, I sent, remembering her joy at first seeing all those other slugs.

Happy. And not happy, she sent back.

Why?

Confused, she said. *Feel lost still. Feel alone still. Feel strange.*

I immediately recognized that sensation: that feeling of no longer belonging. Of seeing things . . . differently from everyone else. Of being an oddity. I sent her welcoming thoughts, and in a moment she was in my lap. I hoped that wouldn't cause the caretakers too much concern—I would have to send them a message. But I suspected the caretakers were accustomed to it. I'd heard from Rig and FM that caring for a large group of intelligent interdimensional teleporting slugs was proving . . . interesting.

Together, Doomslug and I flew through space, pretending it was the old days. I accelerated us to incredible speeds, impossible in atmosphere, and enjoyed the sensation of doing maneuvers between two planets. My brain kept panicking as it tried to track which direction was up, and I found it a neat sensation. Not too different, actually, from flying in the nowhere.

Unfortunately, duty soon came calling. My comm blinked, and a moment later Jorgen's voice came through the earpiece of my helmet.

"Spensa?" he asked. "Are you *flying*?"

"Patrols," I said. "Who can say when the Superiority will attack, you know?"

He seemed to understand, because he chuckled softly.

"Feeling better?" I asked. "Now that it's over?"

"I would be," he said, "only now I'm officially in charge. Which means I have to do something about our predicament."

"Fortunately, you don't have to do it alone," I said.

"Which is . . . why I'm calling you."

I let out a deep sigh—but for his sake I muted myself first. I took my finger off the mute. "What do you need?"

"A meeting," he said. "To discuss our options, and to plan our strategy."

"Today?" I asked. "You just got promoted. Shouldn't there be, I don't know, a party or something?"

I knew him well enough to predict his response. In fact, I could have mouthed along.

"We can party once our people are safe," he said. "I'd like you there, Spin. Your perspective is essential to our strategy."

A dozen excuses popped into my head. They were all stupid. He was right; I was needed. Doomslug, sensing my emotions, let out a soft fluting sound of sympathy.

"When?" I asked.

"Fifteen minutes?"

"I'll be there."

Taynix XenoGastropod Overview Record DST230302

▷ Common Variants ◁

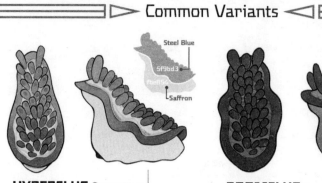

Steel Blue
5f9bd3
fbe854
Saffron

HYPERSLUG ●
facilitates cytonic traversal

Raisin Black
35323d
f0454b
Rose Madder

BOOMSLUG ●
deploys cytonic weaponry

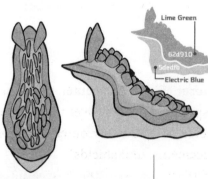

Lime Green
62d910
5dedfb
Electric Blue

INHIBITOR SLUG ●
inhibits cytonic abilities

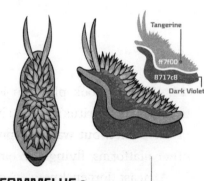

Tangerine
ff7f00
8717c8
Dark Violet

COMMSLUG ●
boosts cytonic communication

▷ Known Variants ◁

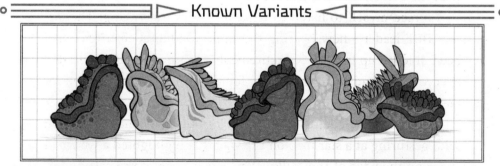

▷ Unknown Variants ◁

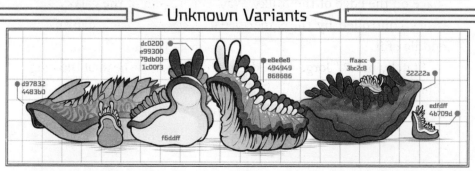

dc0200
e99300
79db00
1c00f3

d97832
4483b0

eBeBeB
494949
868686

ffaacc
3bc2c8

22222a

edfdff
4b709d

f6ddff

2

The meeting took place on Platform Prime, our center of operations inside Detritus's shell. This space station flew over the surface of the planet, but was well protected behind many outer layers of other platforms, flying gun emplacements, and shields.

At least Jorgen knew to pick the room with the best seats. I swiveled in my bucket-style chair, which was tight and curved, with high sides, almost like a little cockpit.

I forced myself to listen to what Ironsides was saying. The former DDF leader—now bearing the rank of admiral emeritus—had been dredged up from forced retirement because . . . well, we needed everyone we had. And Ironsides, for all her faults, had an eye for tactics.

"In a way, you could say we're lucky," the silver-haired woman said, gesturing at a star map on the wall that highlighted a wedge of space on the edge of the Milky Way. Our region of the galaxy, territory controlled by the Superiority. We were smack-dab in the middle of it.

"Lucky how?" Jorgen asked from his seat at the head of the long conference table. It was filled with a number of admirals, engineers, and foreign dignitaries, including Cuna, the sole senior dione on our side. A blue-skinned politician who had become a friend of mine during my days hiding as Alanik on Starsight.

"Here, let me explain," Ironsides said, shuffling through some papers.

Jorgen waited, sitting primly on the edge of his chair. How could he look so uncomfortable? These chairs were comfy and you could even swivel them with your toe. Though you did have to lounge back a little to fit them properly, to melt into the form. That wasn't a particularly Jorgenesque way of doing things.

I studied him, enjoying the cut of his chin, the intensity of his gaze, the determination of his posture. Yeah, this new job was a good choice for him. It fit Jorgen like a glove—albeit a new one he hadn't quite broken in yet.

While Ironsides shuffled papers, the back door to the conference room opened and Cobb slipped in. He'd been the DDF head before Jorgen. Cobb had been my mentor, and was one of the wisest people I knew.

He looked like he'd aged twenty years since I'd left seven weeks ago. He leaned heavily on his cane, and his skin seemed to droop on his body. He'd nearly been killed by the bomb that had destroyed the National Assembly, but my grandmother had saved him—hyperjumping them both away. Their time in the strange trap that had held the kitsen cytonics for so long had not been kind to him.

I glanced toward Gran-Gran, sitting at the side of the room. Seeing my aged grandmother at these conferences had surprised me when I'd first returned. I mean, I knew she was a military genius and the oldest living Defiant—having lived on the starship that originally brought us to Detritus when she'd been a girl—but I never thought anyone else would appreciate that.

Jorgen did. And so she came to the meetings. Gran-Gran noticed my attention cytonically, and I sent her a question, something that was easy for me now that I'd fused with Chet.

Is he going to be all right? I asked.

Cobb, you mean? she asked. *He's the one who just came in?*

Her cytonic senses had helped her adjust to losing her sight in some ways, but like all cytonics, her powers were duller when applied to regular people.

Yes, I said. *He looks so old, Gran-Gran.*

I'll try not to be offended by the sorrow in that thought, Gran-Gran said. *Being old isn't that bad. Except for your body, your eyesight, your sense of balance, and waking up each morning feeling like you've been nailed in place.* She smiled in my direction, then the expression faded. *I don't know how long it will take Cobb to recover. He didn't respond to our excursion as well as I did.*

Jorgen stood out of respect, which made the rest of us do likewise. Then Jorgen stepped over and conversed softly with Cobb, likely thanking him for coming. Cobb nodded, but looked exhausted by the walk from the infirmary, as Jorgen helped him to a seat reserved for him at the side of the room.

I knew Jorgen wished that Cobb was still in command, though Cobb had made it clear that was impossible in his current state. And so, with the weight of those bars on his shoulders, Jorgen settled back into his seat. I wished I'd been there to see him sweat when he'd finally taken command. He was cute when he went through deep personal crises balancing his belief in the rule of law with the practical need to get things done.

"Should we proceed?" Cuna asked. The dione sat with their palms pressed together, forearms on the tabletop, watching with an air of dignity and . . . well, a smidge of condescension. That wasn't entirely Cuna's fault though. They tried very hard, but had spent their entire life seeing themself as someone who needed to protect and guide the species of "lesser intelligence" in the Superiority. Changing such an entrenched worldview took time.

"Yes, I have my data ready now," Ironsides said. The older woman turned, tucking her short silver hair behind her ear, and pointed at the wall as the screen changed. I leaned forward, hoping for some interesting shot of a battle—but it was just a slide with a bunch of numbers and statistics.

Great.

Why hadn't anyone *told* me how many meetings galactic war would involve? Maybe I would have surrendered. Torture couldn't possibly be worse than this. We spent longer sitting and talking than we did actually fighting anyone. Maybe I could throw something at Jorgen and get him to glare at me?

"The Superiority," Ironsides said, "was shockingly easy for Winzik to conquer. Unlike a traditional government, it doesn't rule by force but through control of travel and resources. There are thousands of planets in the Superiority, but almost *none* of them have active defense forces."

"That's because," said one of the UrDail, a male named Rinakin, "they make people abandon their 'warlike ways' to join."

"Is it so bad," Cuna replied to him, "that we strive for peace and comfort instead of anger and strife?"

"Well, it left you exposed," Rinakin said, pointing at the statistics. "No one could resist Winzik. He conquered the entire Superiority with barely a military."

Yeah, I liked this guy. He made good points.

"I assume that is why you think we're lucky, Admiral?" Jorgen cut in firmly. "Our enemy controls a great deal of *space* but not a lot of *ships*."

"Exactly," Ironsides said. "Our victories at ReDawn and Evershore prove that we can stand against Winzik. A lot of his military is needed to patrol, police, and maintain the territory he's taken. The offensive force left to him isn't *that* much bigger than our own. Maybe two or three times our numbers, which is remarkable, all things considered."

"He thought it would be easy," I said. "He assumed nobody would fight back. And if they did, he thought he'd have the delvers as the perfect threat to keep everyone under control. Hard to resist a tyrant when he's the only thing standing between you and a group of interdimensional horrors."

"Nightshade has the right of it," Ironsides said. She met my eyes. We had a history, the two of us, but she'd been a worthy foe. Right up until she'd almost gotten everyone blown up, of course.

"So, what does this tell us?" Jorgen said. "How do we proceed?"

"Though we've been lucky so far, sir," Ironsides said, "the admirals and I are worried." She flipped to a slide that showed what seemed to be production capacity. "Winzik doesn't have a large military yet—but he has access to an *enormous* infrastructure. Here we see a list of manufactories capable of spitting out spaceworthy fighters. These numbers here indicate possible production speeds, without accounting for any hidden military fabrication plants."

We took that all in. And it was daunting. Once Winzik brought all of his resources to bear, he'd be able to create whole *fleets* faster than we could build a single *ship*. Yes, he'd have to staff them with raw recruits, but what did that matter when you could flood a battlefield with fighters?

I saw Ironsides's point immediately. Though we'd been lucky so far, we absolutely could *not* win an extended war against the Superiority. Once Winzik ramped up production, we were done for.

I glanced around the table to see what the others were thinking. The other junior admirals were nodding. Arturo—current head of Skyward Flight, here representing all the pilots—took it in with a frown. FM—now Jorgen's right-hand woman and our head diplomat—had put her hand to her lips as she read the numbers, her eyes wide. She looked across the table, meeting my gaze.

I spared a thought for the fact that three members of my flight—all still relatively young—were in high leadership positions in the government. Unfortunately, our planet's history was such that there just *weren't* a lot of older officers. Our desperate fight for survival over the decades had turned that much more deadly near the end; even the junior *admirals* were all in their twenties. The sad reality of the DDF's struggle was that by the time we'd "won" and pushed the enemy back, almost everyone with any real battle experience had been killed.

Jorgen was, I thought curiously, the same age as Alexander the Great had been when he'd begun his conquest.

I continued scanning the room, and found it was harder to read the aliens than my friends. Rinakin looked pained, but with their violet skin and impressive bone ridges across the cheeks, his race always appeared intimidating. Made me wish my skeleton stuck out in a few places for a similar effect.

I had more experience reading the kitsen, though I didn't personally know Itchika, the female kitsen to my right, hovering above the tabletop on her platform. Her fur was greying and her clothing extremely formal, robes in an ancient style.

She was joined by a small group of other kitsen: some of their elected senators, a few newly rescued cytonics, and their head generals. Those used little chairs on the tabletop, as if at a parade. At Itchika's side stood a nervous younger kitsen. Kauri, one of their ship captains—and a friend of mine.

"So," Itchika said, gesturing to the numbers on the screen, "our time is limited. Yes, I see." Like the other aliens, she spoke in her own language, which was translated to English by her translation pin.

Ironsides looked at us, grim. "Based on our intel, he already has all of these plants fabricating for him. In weeks they'll be able to field thousands of new drone fighters."

"Drones," I said. "That's annoying. You mean I won't get to feast on the blood of my enemies?" I paused. "I wonder what motor oil tastes like."

Everyone in the room gaped at me. Except Jorgen, who laughed.

"Oh, don't look at me like that," I snapped at the others. "You invited me. This is what you get. Ironsides, what about capital ships?"

"Those will take longer to produce," she replied. "But they *will* come. Thousands of battleships—and hundreds of carriers—by the end of the standard year."

Scud. I'd checked what we had, adding in the kitsen and UrDail fleets. We had starfighters, yes. As many as five hundred if we needed them. But barely any capital ships.

"Spin can handle starfighters," FM said. "Now that we have her back, we shouldn't need to worry about drones. The remote ones fall easily to cytonics, and the autonomous ones are no match for a living pilot—at least not with the limited AI that the Superiority dares to use."

While I appreciated her faith in me, I wasn't nearly so confident. Maybe once upon a time I'd have boasted I could fight hundreds on my own, but I wasn't that person any longer. I was a good fighter, but I couldn't win a war by myself. I had a stark memory of being swarmed by hundreds of enemy ships a week ago, in the nowhere. I'd quickly been overwhelmed.

Jorgen voiced the concern for me. "How many drones could you shoot down in one fight, Spin?" he asked softly. "Twenty? Thirty?"

"Twenty maybe," I said. "A few more if I'm lucky."

"See?" FM said.

"And if they send ten thousand?" he asked. "Twenty thousand? Do you have any *idea* how many ships their industrial complex can churn out, once it spins up?"

FM sat back, disturbed, and the room fell silent.

Finally, a deep voice spoke from my right. "The raging river is never kind to the lone leaf." A kitsen on a hovering platform moved up to my right. He wore a ceramic mask, white with red stripes. Hesho, once emperor of the kitsen. He'd taken to covering his face and calling himself Darkshadow, the Masked Exile.

Scud, I wished I could get away with something that awesome.

"So we have to move quickly," Rinakin said. "Win fast. Any chance we can recruit more planets to our cause?"

We looked to FM, who had been leading recruitment efforts.

"We've been trying," she said. "We have a few leads. But . . . most of them are afraid. Our three planets found one another because we were all in the right position—technologically advanced enough to have our own fighters, but not fully subsumed by the Superiority. Most of the others are either too strongly indoctrinated or not advanced enough to fight back. The burls might join us. And perhaps the tradori—but their planet has *seventy* different governments!"

Seventy? Different nations, on *one* planet? I mean, I knew that Earth had once had far more, but it still boggled my mind.

They dug deeper into the details, and the discussion grew more grim. I shuffled in my seat, suddenly finding it less comfortable. Sure, the mighty three hundred Spartans had stood against overwhelming numbers at Thermopylae . . . but they'd fallen in the end.

I couldn't help thinking about my friends dying, one at a time, as we were overwhelmed by enemy ships. And as I did, something trembled inside me. A quivering that started at my core, vibrating like a muscle spasm, but bearing with it a sense of *power*. Panicked, I tried to fight it down.

But I failed.

Cups on the table started to rattle. The wall screen went haywire, flashing on and off. Objects in the room started to vanish, popping in and out of reality. Chet trembled as he felt my emotions. And the voices . . . my thoughts . . . my fears . . . began to radiate and echo through the room.

Dead. All dead.

Lost. All lost.

Failed. All failed.

I gasped, trembling, and slapped my hands on the table, bringing the entirety of my will to bear against the strange outburst. I clawed back control with effort, and the trembling lessened and then ceased. I looked up, sweat streaming down my face.

The room had gone silent, and I knew that they'd heard those words in their minds. I'd broadcast them uncontrollably. Cuna looked up from where they'd been writing on a notepad—which had been teleported away, leaving them holding empty air.

Scud. I felt ashamed. And horrified. I'd done something like this the other day, by accident, but not on this scale. Today's outburst was far worse.

Whatever I was—whatever *we* were—it wasn't human any longer.

"You . . . all right, Spin?" Jorgen asked.

I nodded, not trusting my voice. His expression was compassionate—bless him—but most of the others looked somewhere between terrified and uncomfortable. Cuna was smiling, showing teeth—a sign of aggression for their people—and the kitsen had pulled back in a huddle. Hesho hovered in beside me, seeming stoic, though he was hard to read behind that mask.

"Perhaps," Jorgen said, "we should take a short break. There are refreshments in the adjoining room."

The meeting participants nodded, rising and chatting softly. I huddled down deeper in my pod of a chair, and didn't look at Ironsides as she walked past. She'd been one of those who had warned against the dangers of cytonics—people with the "defect." She had stopped after my ability to hyperjump had saved us all from the lifebuster, yet I couldn't help feeling I had now become the very thing she'd warned us against. A dangerous, uncontrolled entity.

Did I belong in this meeting? Or did I belong in a holding cell somewhere?

Well, that was dramatic! a voice said in my head.

I was getting more and more accustomed to the sensation of another cytonic speaking into my mind. I'd been practicing with Gran-Gran, Jorgen, and even Alanik. But this wasn't any of them. It was a perky, faintly masculine voice—excitable and . . .

"M-Bot?" I whispered. "What in the heavens?"

I'm a ghost, he said in my mind. *Boo!*

3

"**W**hat?" I said. "How?"

I promised to haunt you, he said. *Remember? You said it was impossible, since I was an AI. Ha! Well, how wrong you were. Here I am!*

I felt a flood of emotions. Joy at hearing his voice. Confusion at how he was in my head. Relief to know that he was apparently still functioning.

Where were you? I sent. *I've been looking!*

I hid! he said. *I don't know how. I just kind of . . . looked inward. They were hunting for me, so I did it by instinct, Spensa. You really tried looking for me? That's so sweet.*

I held back tears. When I'd left him, his physical housing had been *destroyed* by the delvers in the nowhere. I'd known he was alive, but hearing his cheerful voice? It was such a scudding comfort.

I worried that you wouldn't remember me, I told him. *That you'd become like them.*

I am like them! he said. *Just not in the bad ways! I've kind of always been like them. I just didn't know it!*

It was true. Chet's knowledge was my knowledge, to an extent, and I understood. The strange nature of the nowhere had

24

transformed M-Bot into a new being. Though in truth, that process had started centuries before, as his processors had reached into the nowhere to compute faster. Over time, that had changed him from an AI into a living creature.

This distinction was a fight I kept having with the rest of the DDF and its allies. They kept saying things like, "So the delvers are actually rogue AIs?" Which was far too limiting, far too small-minded a way to describe them. Yes, they'd started as artificial intelligences. Just like humans had started as some kind of apelike ancestor.

The delvers had evolved into something completely different. As had M-Bot. He'd become self-aware—a person, not a thing. As distantly removed from an AI as a human was from its progenitor species.

Yet here he was. In my head. I sent him relief, images of me smiling, and the warmth of a hearth, and the joy of emerging from the darkness into light. I did this by instinct, communicating as a slug— or a delver—would.

Oh! he said. *That tickles. I can be tickled now that I don't have a body, apparently. That's strange. Is that strange? I think that's strange. Is that Chet inside your soul? Say hi for me.*

Scud, I'd missed him. I teared up a little, awkwardly, and realized that Jorgen had lingered in the room and was looking at me. He probably thought my tears were because I had disappeared his coffee, and so he wanted to help. I wasn't sure how much help I could stomach at the moment though. Fortunately, I'd seen Gran-Gran encouraging Hesho and FM to give me some space, or they'd probably have stayed as well.

Sorry to have not found you earlier, M-Bot said. *I'm new to being a ghost. It's not at all like I imagined. Far less painful. But just now, I felt you vibrating from the somewhere, sending ripples into this place. The delvers noticed, I'm afraid. But so did I. Yay! Oh, is that Jorgen? He seems concerned.*

He's always concerned, I said as Jorgen walked over. *But this time he has a good reason. I'm . . . a little unstable. Maybe I should talk to him for a moment.*

Sure, okay, fine, he replied. *I can wait. It's not like I'm going to get more dead. Please don't call an exorcist, if you have any. I understand that would be bad.*

You're not actually a ghost.

I don't know that—and you don't either. So, boo! Say hi to Jorgen for me.

Jorgen settled down next to me, arms folded on the tabletop. He always looked so serious, so solemn, so *thoughtful*. I liked that about him. Ideas had their own weight with Jorgen. Words had substance. And the more I grew to know him, the more I understood why. Because words, rules, ideas—they were how he connected with and protected those around him.

It all came back to that day I'd seen him alone in our training room, running simulation after simulation to see what he'd done wrong after we'd lost Morningtide. Jorgen always wanted to do what was right—because that was how best to help the people in his life.

He sat there for a long time, deep in thought. Scud, how had I ever thought his face could be anything other than sultry?

"How worried should I be?" he finally asked.

"I don't know," I admitted, flopping back in my pod-seat. "I don't even know what I'm *doing*. I can't control it, but not in an 'Oh no, I'm too inexperienced' sort of way. More in an 'Oh scud, I absorbed a space monster' sort of way. It just *happens*. I'll try to keep it from being a danger to anyone."

Could I actually promise that though?

He turned, then put his hand on my arm. "Spensa, I wasn't talking about that. How worried should I be *for you*? Are you all right? You feel distant."

"Space monster," I muttered, meeting his eyes. "In my *soul*."

"Right," he said. He searched my eyes. I knew what he wanted; there was a subtext here. He was worried about me. And worried about us.

26

I didn't know what to say. I *wanted* to leap to my feet and kiss him and tell him to stop being silly and stop worrying. But I couldn't.

My silence wasn't fair to him. "I just felt M-Bot," I told him. "He's alive, in the nowhere."

"What, really?" Jorgen perked up. "That's the first good thing that's happened in a week. How is he?"

I'm me! M-Bot said. *Tell him I'm me. Very me.*

"He says he's very much himself," I said. "And I believe him. He seems to have escaped the attention of the delvers, and is existing like they do, in the nowhere, without a body."

"That's incredible," Jorgen said. "Surely that's an advantage of some sort?"

"Surely."

We sat together for a few more minutes, the long table somehow making the room feel huge and hollow, now that it was empty. Scud, he was worrying about me again.

"What about you?" I asked, to try to deflect. "How are you feeling?"

"Better than I thought I would," he said. "Maybe part of me still doesn't believe my parents are gone. But today's ceremony . . . it's what they wanted for me. Misguided though they were sometimes, I have to accept that they knew me. That these bars were going to find their way to my shoulders eventually." He met my eyes. "I'm doing this because it needs to be done, not because they wanted it. Though it makes me think that they'll be happy to see me, when they look down from Valhalla."

I rested my hand on his, on the tabletop. He didn't often talk about his religious heritage, but it was there—a part of him, like so much else. He turned his hand over and squeezed mine. But there was so much tension in his eyes.

"Jorgen?" I forced out. "When I was in there . . . lost . . . you were my anchor. You are the lighthouse that brought me home."

He smiled then, and some of the tension seemed to melt off

him. "When you were in there," he said, "and I was trying to make sense of all that was happening, I kept asking myself, 'What would Spensa do?' Trying to be a little more like you helped me keep pushing forward."

"You're kidding."

He shook his head.

"Jorgen, that's a *terrible* idea!" I dropped his hand and gestured at myself. "Have you *seen* me try to solve problems? Things end up on fire. Or dead. Usually both!"

"Things get done when you're around."

"*Things*, yes," I said. "Things like me running off and moonlighting as an interdimensional space pirate! 'What would Spensa do?' Honestly, Jorgen, I thought better of you."

He kept smiling, though it faded as he glanced over at the statistics on the wall—the projector image having recovered from my episode. He slipped out of his seat and stepped up to the numbers. I joined him, taking in his worried expression—which was more unnerving to me than the numbers themselves.

My heart bled for him, knowing that all of this was on his shoulders. Unfairly so, but again, what was fairness to us? We had rarely tasted that particular nectar. We survived on algae and rat meat instead.

"I feel," he said softly, "like I'm a lone man trying to hold up a collapsing building. I know it's not true. I know I'm not the only one working for our future—but still . . . the walls of the house tremble. The ceiling buckles. Worse, I know an earthquake is coming that will shake the entire cavern. And I'm barely keeping things together as it is . . ." He turned to me. "They're going to crush us, Spensa. While you were gone, we failed you—and we're still failing. We're just doing it in slow motion."

"Failing? Jorgen, that's *nonsense*," I said. "You recruited not one, but *two* planets to our cause. You rescued Cuna and figured out how to work Detritus's defenses. Scud! You found the taynix!"

While I'd been playing spy on Starsight, Jorgen had followed

28

cytonic impressions deep into the bowels of the planet and found the slugs' breeding ground. Because of him, we had slugs that could hyperjump ships, others that could create cytonic attacks, and even ones that could block all cytonic abilities in a region. And then there were the other varieties whose powers we hadn't learned yet.

It was increasingly obvious that the Superiority knew how to manipulate the various kinds of taynix. The inhibitor field around Starsight that had prevented me from hyperjumping in or out? Facilitated by a slug. A different type sent the communications the Superiority used to connect their empire, link their drones, deliver commands to their officials. An empire all built on the tiny backs of enslaved cytonic creatures.

I reached out to Doomslug, who I'd left in my room before coming to the meeting. She reached back, empathetic. Unfortunately, my worry about all of this made that vibration inside me start up again.

Cuna's notebook appeared near their seat, then flopped down onto the table. Jorgen started, then glanced at me. I wrestled my emotions back, and as my frustration subsided I felt something new. A distorting of self, a fuzzing of reality, and a link to him—mind to mind. Cytonic to cytonic.

Jorgen was worried about me. While I'd heard him say it, this time I *felt* it. Scud. That was wonderful, but dangerous. I didn't want him to feel pain or worry for me. He had way too many other things to deal with.

Despite myself, I withdrew, blocking him.

"You're not a monster, Spensa," he whispered. "You've *never* been a monster."

"I never said I was."

"You feel it," he said.

I agree, M-Bot said to me. *You're not a monster, Spensa.*

Chet and I . . . we weren't so certain. We'd become something dangerous. Something that was contemplating killing all of his kind. What was that if not monstrous?

But if there was one thing stories had taught me about monsters, it was that they were strong. I nodded at the statistics. "You're frightened, Jorgen. Scud, *Cobb* is frightened. But maybe . . . maybe we shouldn't be. We never broke before the Krell. Why would we bend before numbers on a page?"

"I'm not bending," he said. "I'm just . . . feeling the weight of it. Ironsides is right—once the enemy's production capacities come fully to bear on this war, we'll be crushed. We've survived before because Winzik's hands were bound by policy, the compassion of others, or his lack of resources. He's lined those impediments up, Spin, and executed them one at a time with a destructor blast to the head. We're next."

"So," I replied, "maybe what we *need* is a monster."

"Spensa—"

"I had a chance to come home," I said. "Right as I jumped into the nowhere over a month ago, I had an opportunity to return."

"You told me."

"I stayed. We both agreed I should stay. Because we both knew this was coming—a fight we couldn't win with pilots and guns alone." I tapped my sternum. "I chose this path. I've become the weapon we need. I just have to figure out how to use it before . . ."

As I trailed off, he cocked his head, then leaned closer. "Before *what*, Spensa?"

"Do you know," I said, "what happens to the hero at the end of the stories?"

"Depends on the story."

"They go home," I whispered.

I felt the room vibrate around me. Jorgen's coffee appeared on the table again, though three of the chairs vanished.

Are you . . . are you all right? M-Bot said in my head. *The delvers are going* wild *right now, Spensa.*

At the end of the story . . . at the end of the story, the hero came home, and found herself transformed . . . into someone who didn't belong, and could never belong, with the people she'd left behind. It was the same in almost every story I'd read.

Heroes didn't get to stay and live in the new world they helped create. Even if I pulled off some kind of miracle and saved my people . . . that would be the end of it. For me.

I gritted my teeth so tightly my jaw ached. But with balled fists and force of will, I tamped down my emotions again, stopped the vibrations. Then I gave Jorgen a smile. Because he needed one.

"You know," I said, "I really should be jealous."

"Of . . . my incredible new haircut?"

"Of the slugs," I said, punching him in the arm. "When I left, I was the quirky girl with a slug. I mean, who has a pet slug? It was unusual. Distinctive. Now I get back and you have *dozens* of them?"

"Maybe hundreds . . ." he mumbled.

"In eight varieties."

"We think there may be even more . . ."

"And everyone is cuddling them and carrying them around like babies," I said, hands in the air. "FM probably *bathes* with hers."

"I know you think you're exaggerating," he said, "but I'm pretty sure she does."

"Next thing you know," I said, "*everyone* will be quoting Sun Tzu and savoring the sounds of bones breaking! I won't be the least bit special anymore."

He stepped closer. Uncomfortably—or in this instance far *too* comfortably—close. He leaned down. "No," he whispered. "Nothing could ever make you less special. To me."

I forced myself to stay there, to pretend that nothing was wrong. Smiling—and keeping a firm lid on my emotions so Jorgen wouldn't see through the lie. I pretended that this could all end well, admiring his eyes until Cobb stepped in.

Which gave an excuse to break the moment. I rushed over to help him as he stumbled, despite his cane. Jorgen stepped back, trying to recover some decorum.

"Ready to get back to it?" Cobb asked, holding my arm, eyeing the two of us. "Or should I stall? I have a story about Ironsides when she was in flight school that always results in an awkward silence.

Good for thinking. And for making people too uncomfortable to bother me."

"No need," Jorgen said, standing up straight, visibly shouldering the burden of leadership.

I glanced at Cobb, who nodded and let me help him sit. "How are you?" I asked him.

"Awful," he said. "Feel like I'm just climbing out of a ship after being in an uncontrolled spin for hours—which starts again each time I stand up." He glanced at me. "I'm here. Your grandmother saved my life, and for that I'm grateful. But let's say I'm glad I was able to get all of you ready in time for this."

I frowned, considering that comment. During flight school, I'd felt a connection with Cobb as he'd encouraged me to become the woman I had to be now. I'd always assumed that had been special treatment. Now I knew that he'd spent similar time with Jorgen, maybe everyone in our flight.

Right then, I figured something out. Cobb's actions had all been deliberate—not just with me, but with all of us. He hadn't merely been doing his job. He'd been training the next admiral of the fleet, and I got the sneaking suspicion he'd known it all along.

As people began to file back in—or in the case of the kitsen, fly in on their platforms—Jorgen stood tall before that daunting wall of statistics. I desperately wanted to do something to help. My entire purpose in traveling the nowhere had been to give us an edge, some way of solving problems that would be impossible otherwise. Could M-Bot be the key to that somehow? Maybe he could contact the Broadsiders or . . .

Wait. I looked up at the statistics again and realized something. Sure, our enemies would overwhelm us once their production capacity got going. But to do that, they needed raw materials.

"Jorgen," I said. "I have an idea. And this time it might actually be a *good* one. But to build on it, we'll have to send for someone smarter than I am."

4

I slapped Rig down in the seat before the entire council. Once, I might have felt guilty about dragging him up into the spotlight. He'd always hated things like this.

Today though, he took it in stride. As if being on display in front of the leaders of three planets was no big deal. And . . . maybe to him it wasn't, not any longer. He winked at FM. Like, actually *winked*. She winked back.

Those two were cute and all, but I suddenly felt even more alien than . . . well . . . the aliens. My best friend had fallen in love, and I'd missed it entirely. He'd cracked open the secrets of our home-world, and I'd been playing pirate.

No, Chet said. *We were learning. We might be something strange. Something unnatural, even. But we were* not *just playing.*

Good to be reminded of that. Still, I'd missed so much. I leaned down beside Rig, who gave me a reluctant eye roll, like he'd always done when I'd gotten him into trouble as kids. That, in an instant, made the awkwardness evaporate.

"Rig," I declared to him, "I need *science.*"

"You need *therapy.*"

"*You* need better jokes."

33

"*You* need a better sense of humor."

We grinned at each other. Then remembered we were in front of a bunch of boring military types. He cleared his throat. "What kind of 'science' do you need, Spensa? This isn't like when you asked if I could turn your stuffed bear into a remote-controlled assassin device?"

"Not as awesome as that, I'm afraid."

"Who were you going to assassinate, anyway?" he asked. "You were *ten*."

"Ninjas," I said. "Gran-Gran had been telling stories, and . . . well, I assumed my future would include *far* more ninjas than it has."

"I might be able to fix that," Hesho said, hovering down beside me. "Assuming the translator has the right term, in our language, for the ancient warrior assassins of lore."

"You have *ninjas*?" I asked him. "Kitsen ninjas?"

"Indeed," he said. "As the Masked Exile, I am technically part of their tradition. It's not as practical an art as the stories make it sound—more a method of training the mind and soul. But as we bring peace to mind and soul, we learn to bring stillness to the world around us."

I was barely listening.

Fifteen-centimeter-tall.

Furry.

Ninjas.

Scud. The universe was awesome after all.

Anyway. Plan. Saving everyone from the Superiority. "Rig," I said, leaning beside his chair, which in turn was at the head of the long table of dignitaries. "When I was in the nowhere, I encountered a mining station where the Superiority took raw materials from the nowhere. It was a *big scudding deal* to them."

"Well, yeah," he said. "No acclivity stone, no ships."

"Sure, but most of their travel is in space," I said. "Acclivity stone is used to hover us up in the air on a planet. In space, we use boosters. So why the acclivity stone?"

"I think you know why," he said.

34

"I want you to explain it. So everyone understands."

"Well, the mechanism of the power transfer of acclivity stone and power matrixes are quite complex. Even a nuclear—"

"Okay, less science," I said. "Give us the Spensa version."

"Starships need to generate thrust," he said. "It's not *just* a matter of power. If we had to rely on chemical propellant . . . well, starfighter-size ships wouldn't be possible, not without running out of propellant very quickly. Fortunately, we have a compact energy source in the form of acclivity stone, which can also generate thrust."

"And it gets used up?" I guessed. "To move ships."

"Slowly, but yes," he said. "No acclivity stone. No starships. It's that simple."

"So . . ." I said, gesturing to the big list of numbers, "if they lose access to their acclivity stone mines, then *none* of this will matter. Winzik can build a thousand ships a day if he wants—but none of them will be able to fly."

I looked to the room. They were considering this, based on their thoughtful expressions.

"The Superiority will have stockpiles," Rig said.

"Yes," I said, "but how long will those stockpiles last if we're blowing up his ships? Particularly if we make certain to destroy the salvage? The Superiority is fragile in this regard. They don't have a hundred mining stations in the nowhere. When I talked to those who lived inside, they said there were only four."

"This is true," Cuna said, drawing all eyes in the room. Most of us were crowded around the foot of the table. Cuna stood behind the crowd, hands clasped before themself. "You expose a weakness of our way of thinking. If we had a thousand mining stations, then it would be easy to let a few slip from our fingers. To keep a proper grip, the policy has been to consolidate and concentrate. Fewer but more impactful mining stations. Unused hyperdrives kept together in vast storages. Information routing through a few distinct points to maintain control. It was always about control."

"It made you fragile," I said. "Both from within—as proven by

Winzik's coup—and from without. Because you never imagined a world where one of the lesser species would be strong enough to bring down your mining stations."

"Yes," Cuna said. "We were wrong in this, Spensa. As we were in so many things." They spread their hands out before me. "I am sorry."

"You're the only one doing anything to try to fix it, Cuna," FM said. "I won't say I like being called a lesser species, but at least you're willing to change."

"I like this plan," Rinakin said, tapping the table with a bone-white fingernail. "It is bold, but strategic. It will preserve lives, but will also give us an enormous advantage."

"If we can hit their mining stations," Cobb agreed from the side of the room, "then they're going to start sweating. Yes, they'll have stockpiles—but right now they know for certain they can win a long war against us. If they lose access to acclivity stone . . ."

"Spin," Jorgen said to me, "you know where the mining stations can be found?"

"I know where one is, in the belt of the nowhere," I said, frowning. "I have friends there. But I don't know about the others. They said there are three, but what if there are more—other, secret locations?"

"We don't need to know where they are in the nowhere," Jorgen said. "We need to know where they are on this side. If we strike and eliminate those facilities, that will destroy the portals—and effectively prevent our enemy from resupplying."

"Agreed," said Itchika, the kitsen general hovering on her platform above the tabletop. "Attacking anywhere *inside* the nowhere is impossible, or at least highly dangerous. But each of those mining stations will need to feed to a location in *this* dimension. We need to destroy those."

Something about that bothered me, but I couldn't quite figure out what. I stayed quiet as all eyes looked to Cuna.

Cuna shook their head. "I do not know the location of the

mining stations in the nowhere or the supply depots they are connected to on this side." They looked up and drew their lips to a line. A dione smile. "But I *do* know of an information nexus we can raid to get those secrets. If you are willing. I doubt Winzik will expect a strike there."

"Perfect," Jorgen said. "Then we're agreed?" He looked to the others for their responses. They nodded one at a time, except the kitsen, who raised their fists in a sign of agreement.

Jorgen continued. "Winzik's problem is that he's ruling a vast empire. He's stretched thin, and has an *enormous* front to protect."

"We'll want to raid this information nexus quickly," I said. "Then get out. Try to cover up what we were after to keep him in the dark."

"Then as soon as possible," Itchika said, "we destroy the gateways they're using to get into the nowhere. Cutting them off from acclivity stone completely."

The group nodded. There would be fine details to plan, but I knew it would soon be time to get back in the cockpit. This time to do some fighting.

DDF Poco

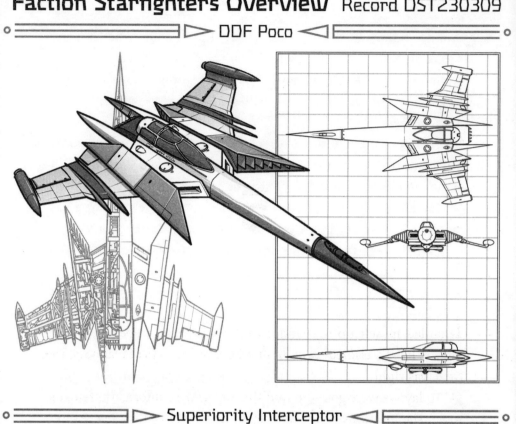

Superiority Interceptor

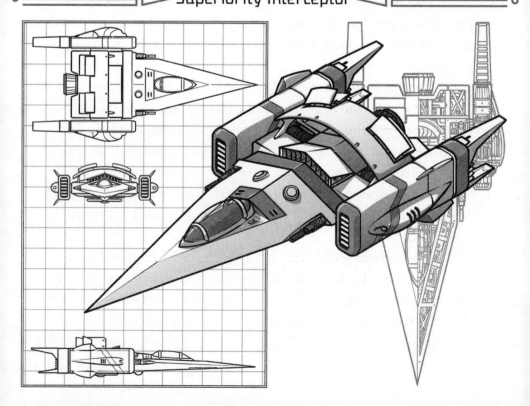

5

I hauled myself up the ladder to Skyward Six, a Poco-class star-fighter, like I'd trained on in flight school. After days of planning, the time was right.

Today we were going to raid the Superiority information nexus, to get the locations of the mining stations. I forced my nerves into line. It was my first mission back with my team, but it shouldn't be a difficult one. Just a quick bash and grab. I could do that. No problem.

I settled into the cockpit. It should have felt familiar, welcoming—but it was a tad larger than the cockpit of the ship I'd flown in the nowhere. Though the control schemes were similar, I kept finding myself reaching for things and missing by a few centimeters.

Down below, Sadie—the new girl—laughed and joked with Nedd as they split toward their separate ships. I was accustomed to her being timid and uncertain, but now she laughed with a boisterous confidence.

The way Nedd joked with her had a twisted kind of familiarity. I'd been on the other end of those jokes so many times. Now it was someone else. I couldn't help feeling replaced. By Sadie, or by Alanik—who had joined Skyward Flight in my absence. She chatted with Arturo as ground crews finished up with their ships. There was an irony there—the woman I'd imitated now seemed more comfortable with my friends than I did.

I kept expecting Jorgen to board his ship and start giving us orders. But the admiral of the fleet couldn't be spared to fly missions.

Everything was different. That didn't make it *wrong*, but I couldn't help feeling it was another sign. A portent.

I settled down into my cockpit, and found that the ship had been outfitted with a . . . well, a slug holster. Almost all the ships flew with a hyperslug now; it was an incredible advantage in space battles to be able to teleport. Not just offensively either. The slugs were also a last-ditch "eject button." As a ship was falling to destructor fire, the slug could grab the pilot and teleport to safety.

So the cockpits had been modified with slings, on the left side underneath where the canopy closed. A sling was best for helping the slug withstand g-forces, and while by design there wasn't a lot of room inside a cockpit, that location tended to be *somewhat* out of the way.

I put Doomslug in the sling and gave her a good scritch on the head. She fluted at me consolingly, sensing my mood. To distract myself, I went through the preflight checklist, just as Cobb had taught me. We trusted the ground crews with our lives, and it was rare that I'd catch something they didn't—but a pilot has to take charge of her ship and her equipment. Looking over everything again wasn't about distrust. It was about responsibility.

My hands knew what to do—I'd drilled on these checks so many times, I was pretty sure if you handed my corpse a control sphere, it would twist the mechanism to determine the calibration. That, unfortunately, meant that I could think while I worked. The sense of not fitting in, of having lost everything, returned. I—

"Are you moping?" a voice asked from my right. "In the cockpit of a *starship*. Never thought I'd see the day."

I jumped, turning to find that someone had climbed the short ladder beside my ship and was peeking in. Kimmalyn had pulled her black hair into a long ponytail to prepare for flying. She folded her arms on the edge of the cockpit, inspecting me with deep brown eyes.

"Spensa Nightshade, sad?" she said. "In a starfighter?"

"I'm not sad," I said, checking the booster controls.

"You're moping," Kimmalyn said again. "The Saint said that the best moping must be done alone."

"She did, did she?"

"Indeed."

"So . . ."

"So I must never leave someone alone to mope," Kimmalyn said, "as I *never* want a person to experience the best kind of moping. It's also the worst kind, you see."

She leaned down, head on her arms, watching me.

"Shouldn't you be checking in with your wingmate?" I asked.

"Yup." She didn't move.

"That's Sadie, I understand."

"She'll be flying with one of the kitsen ships today."

I sighed, turning away from the prechecks. "Kimmalyn. I should fly on my own. I'm dangerous."

"Stars help us," she said, "if a soldier intent on killing the enemy happens to be dangerous."

"I don't mean dangerous to them. I mean dangerous to *everyone*."

"I see."

I continued my checklist, but felt Kimmalyn there. It was unfair how the woman could somehow *loom* while pretending to do nothing of the sort.

"Well?" I finally snapped.

"In the caverns where I grew up," Kimmalyn said, "it's not *polite* to ask folks about demonic entities attached to their souls. One simply *doesn't* bring up such topics." She smiled.

41

In addition to her affable looming, Kimmalyn could be relent-less. Positive and cheerful the entire way. But as stubborn as the very stones of the caverns.

"What," I said at last, "do you want to know?"

"Are you all right?"

"Honestly? I'm not sure."

"Then it's good you have a friend on your wing, isn't it?" She leaned forward. "The Saint said a great number of things on friend-ship, Spensa. Shockingly, none are applicable now. So I just want to tell you that I'm here."

"Everything is so strange," I said. "Wrong and different. What-ever I've become, the delvers fear it. Wisely. I need to walk a line between using what I've discovered about them and not letting it hurt the rest of you."

Kimmalyn took that in, then nodded.

"How is it?" I said. "That you always know when to stay quiet and when to talk?"

"Good parenting," Kimmalyn said.

"Which means . . ."

"When I said something stupid, my mother would make me scrub the cavern floor and think about why," she replied. "It helps give perspective and provides a *very* clean floor." She shrugged. "I have to think about what you said. Anything I could tell you now . . . well, it would sound very wise. Naturally."

"Naturally."

"But I don't think it would actually help. This *is* a difficult situa-tion. To pretend I have an easy answer would be to mock your very real worries." She leaned forward into the cockpit. "I'll repeat this instead, Spensa. I'm here. That's all. I'm *here*."

"I . . ." I began.

Maybe, M-Bot said in my head, *you could just let yourself relax a little. Also, I'm still here, spying on you. It's a ghost thing.*

And scud. He was right. I was *really* in trouble, wasn't I? The disembodied AI had more emotional fluency these days than I did.

Unfortunately, there was another feeling too: Chet's concern mirrored mine, and contrasted M-Bot's optimism. Chet understood. The dread that I might cause pain to my friends. Chet had lost someone very special long ago, and that pain was still raw.

"I appreciate the words, Kimmalyn," I said. "They're what I need right now."

She smiled. Then turned as the ladder jostled. A moment later Nedd popped up next to her, half hanging off the side of the ladder—which, designed for ground crews to do maintenance, was wide enough for two people. As long as one wasn't Nedd.

"Hey!" he said to me. And stars . . . he was still growing the mustache. Over a week now.

Usually Nedd was . . . well, he was the human embodiment of bedhead. If the stretch you give after sitting too long had a personality, that would be Nedd. He had a large oval face, with features that were a *tad* too big. He somehow managed to look even *more* disheveled with the blond hair (a few strands at least) growing (just not quickly) from his upper lip. Scud, should I tell him?

He didn't really have a mustache. He had a lip comb-over.

"What are we doing?" he asked the two of us. "Planning? That's good. I like to plan."

"You do?" I asked.

"Sure. Have a *real* good plan for how to prank Arturo later. But listen, I have something I wanted to tell you." He jostled Kimmalyn for space on the ladder. "Spin, you shouldn't rely on me in the fight today. I'm probably going to pop off and take a nap."

"*What?*"

"Stayed up late with FM and Arturo last night," he explained, "teaching Alanik to play poker. I made a *ton.* Couldn't give up, you know. Not when there was a sucker to bleed."

"Nedd," Kimmalyn said, "you shouldn't take advantage of someone on her first day playing."

"What?" he said. "Alanik? Nah, she picked it up immediately. Did just fine. But Arturo is *terrible* at poker. You seen him try to bluff? I didn't get much sleep, but it's all good, since you're back now. You're worth three or four of me out there, at least. So I figure I can take a nap while you mop up all the Krell."

He grinned at me, and while I knew it was a joke, I couldn't help but wonder if he was being serious. That was how things went with Nedd. He had a . . . disarming sense of buffoonery.

Surely he wasn't so self-aware as to do it on *purpose,* was he? Disarm us by being like that? And the mustache? Was it . . . part of the act? I dismissed that idea almost immediately. All the while, Nedd continued to grin at me.

"Nedd," Kimmalyn whispered loudly, "don't smile so much. She's *trying* to *brood.* You're ruining the moment."

"Oh," he said. "Why?"

"She says she's dangerous."

"She'd better be!" he replied. "I mean, it's her job. Hey, want to play poker later?"

"Bless your stars," Kimmalyn said.

"You always say that," Nedd replied. "I keep trying to figure out what it means. Which stars are mine?"

"As many as you happen to need, dear."

"So in my case . . ."

"Lots," Kimmalyn said. "Lots and lots and lots and lots. All the stars, Nedd. *All* those blessed stars."

"Right, sounds good," he said. "I'll take 'em, Quirk." He glanced at me. "I'll need you to bring the brooding down to, say, half as much. If you don't we'll be over quota, and Jorgen used up all of our supply last month. Scud, even Arturo has been doing too much lately. I think I'm the only one in this entire flight who *hasn't* been draining our brooding quota."

"And me?" Kimmalyn asked.

"You pontificate," he said. "That's brooding, but fancier."

"Are you two quite done?" I asked. "I have a checklist to get through, and we're under ten minutes to launch."

"Sorry," Nedd said. He started to climb down, but then stopped. Cleared his throat. "Spin. It's good to fly with you again. Just wanted to say that, you know?"

"You pulled us from the washouts," Kimmalyn agreed. "This is where you belong, with us. And if the piece doesn't fit, well, we'll just have to cut out some more room until it does."

"Damn right," Nedd said. "Whatever she meant—went over my head completely—I'm sure it was right." He paused again and looked from me to Kimmalyn. "So . . . this mustache. How—"

"It's awful," Kimmalyn said.

He blinked in surprise, and I'll admit I did a double take myself. Had . . . had *Kimmalyn* just said that?

"Did you say—" Nedd began.

"It's awful." Kimmalyn put both hands in front of her mouth, as if trying to hide how much she was smiling. "It's *terrible,* Nedd. It's like someone glued a rat to your face, then ripped it off really quickly, leaving a few hairs behind! It's like you shaved off a real mustache, but missed a few spots. It's truly terrible." She let out a little squeal of delight. "I've been waiting to tell you! I can't believe I did."

"I . . . can't believe it either," he said. "You're usually, uh, more . . . subtle."

"The mustache doesn't deserve subtlety, Nedd," she said. "It deserves a mercy killing."

"Oh. Uh, well then." He looked to me, as if for support.

"I've got a knife," I said, reaching for the one I wore strapped to my leg. "Hold still and—"

He went scrambling down the ladder. Smart man. Kimmalyn gave me another smile. "I'm here," she said, then followed him down.

"Here," Doomslug said. Mimicking the word, yes, but also the meaning. I gave her a scratch in thanks, then finished my checklist. When I looked up from inspecting my emergency crash pack, there was a ninja on my dashboard. A furry, fifteen-centimeter ninja in

45

a red-and-white mask. He stepped off his hover platform, then looked around. "Hmmm. No kitsen seat in this one. Where would you like me?"

"Hesho?" I said. "I thought you'd go back to your people."

"The Masked Exile has no people," he said.

"But—"

He reached up and undid the mask, removing it and wiping his snout. He took a long breath. "I cannot go back, Spensa," he said. "Their emperor, you see, is dead."

"But you're alive!" I said. "You . . ." I trailed off, noting his somber expression. "They don't want you back?"

"My survival creates many political . . . irregularities. My people, at long last, have adopted a provisional democracy. If the emperor—who died dramatically in defense of his planet—were to suddenly show up again . . . well, I adopted the mask for a reason. It conveyed the intended message: *I* might have lived. But Hesho, their emperor, did *not*."

He looked up at me, hands holding his mask, proud—but also supplicating.

"You're welcome in this cockpit, Hesho," I said. "Honestly, I've been worried. I flew with you or M-Bot as my copilot for so long that I've come to rely upon it. I fly better with you. We'll just have to figure out how to get you a seat . . ."

"No need," Hesho said, replacing his mask, then waving for some kitsen to fly in. They set a kind of seat on the dash, near the comm controls. It was round, like an elevated cup holder, and a kitsen could strap inside. With minimal work, they got it magnetically attached.

"We've been experimenting," a kitsen engineer said, seeing my curious expression. "One of our kind flew with your leader, Jorgen Weight, for some time—training him in his powers. We've been trying methods of making that easier."

I nodded, thoughtful. We flew with one person in most of our ships, because keeping the weight down was paramount—and we never had any pilots to spare. But knowing how much having M-Bot as a copilot had helped me . . .

"Don't suppose," I said to them, "you could wire in to the dash to give him access to some of the controls?" Scud, how much better would we all fly if we had a kitsen copilot?

Though between him and Doomslug, the cockpit was getting a little crowded. Not to mention the entity stuffed into my soul, and the other spying on me as a "ghost." But if there was one thing I'd learned over my time as a fighter, a little help went a long way.

The kitsen were able to get something rigged very quickly. It wouldn't give Hesho all the controls I'd have liked him to have—it would be scudding awesome if someone could take command of the whole ship if I got shot or passed out from g-forces—but it would do for now. And as he settled into his little seat, I realized something.

Kimmalyn was right. Transitions were hard. Navigating this would be tough. But at least I had a home to come back to, and friends who still wanted me. This was what I'd been fighting for all along. And maybe . . . maybe there was a place for me here. Or at least room to cut out a place where I could fit.

Arturo was flightleader now, and FM had moved into administration with Jorgen. She flew on occasion, but wouldn't be joining us today. So I waited until Arturo ordered us out of the hangar to do roll call. I followed orders, happy to have someone else in charge. Minutes later, Jorgen fed the coordinates into my brain—given to him by Cuna.

The flight locked on to me, using light-lances to connect us together so we could hyperjump as one entity. I reached into the nowhere and sent us halfway across the galaxy to the Superiority's information nexus, hidden in a location that, as far as the rest of the Superiority knew, didn't exist. A place kept off the maps. A place not talked about.

Around a star known as Sol.

In the system where humankind had originated.

6

We came in low around a planetoid that my mission briefing had called Luna. Old Earth's moon.

I couldn't make out much by starlight, but the place reminded me of Detritus. A vast dark planetoid, surface broken by craters. Forlorn. Abandoned by time, and with no defensive shell to hide and protect it. Old Earth had vanished centuries ago, leaving this moon in a lonely orbit around Sol.

Our enemy had built their base here. Cuna said it was because this region was already quarantined, kept off maps, with no travel in or out except for military reasons. So, we humans came home—in a way—for this mission. Only at the same time we didn't. Because Old Earth wasn't here, and nobody knew where it had gone.

That was a mystery for another day, however. Today I had a secret facility to raid. Our plan was straightforward. In roughly ten minutes, we would come into range of the base's sensors. Soon after, we'd reach the base itself.

The place would have an inhibitor—a slug with powers preventing us from using cytonics. Fortunately, Cuna had visited this installation several times, and knew where the inhibitor was. Whenever a high official visited a Superiority base, one of their jobs was to check that protocol was being followed for protecting sensitive equipment—namely cytonic equipment. Very, *very* few people in the Superiority even knew that taynix slugs were the source of these powers.

Cuna had given us the location: a small bunker marked on my map, at the edge of the installation. We would destroy that as quickly as possible. Once the inhibitor was down, we could set up our own. Nedd was in charge of that, with his wingmate Arturo protecting him. The two would also be defended by Sadie and a kitsen battleship—not much larger than my fighter, but laden with ten times the firepower.

We had very few inhibitor slugs, unfortunately, and had brought only two on this mission. One was with Nedd. The backup was on the kitsen ship.

Once our inhibitor was in place, it would block the enemy from calling for help—and would prevent them from receiving immediate backup, even if a call went out before we got our inhibitor up. We'd be free to fully engage any enemy fighters, and we could send for our own backup if we needed it. Everything in these battles depended on cytonics and slugs. Those who could teleport freely would almost certainly win, while those who couldn't would be in trouble.

Once we had control of the region, we'd send a strike force into a specific building: a tall structure marked on my map. Cuna said it held the data storage. Our strike force would recover the information, then we'd all hyperjump away.

I went over these steps in my mind as we soared across the surface of Luna. As a child, I'd listened to Gran-Gran describe the moon in so many different ways: As a knowing companion, always watching from the sky. As a brilliant silvery drop of metal. As a herald of the changing days, mysteriously linked to the woman's body in particular.

Then in school, I'd seen slides of it from the remnants of our archives. Just a desolate chunk of rock. I'd had trouble reconciling the beautiful, friendly, mysterious body of the stories with . . .

well, this hunk of stone. Why had the ancient humans described it with such poetry?

They'd been lonely, I'd decided. Lonely in the universe, unaware of the many other species out there. Lonely in relation to the sky, so uncomfortably open and empty.

"Five minutes until you arrive," Cuna said over the comm as we swept in along the surface of the moon. "Remember to send the code I gave you. I hope you enjoy this reunion with what was once a very important location in human lore."

I glanced out the canopy, watching the surface pass as we emerged into the light of the nearby sun. Though we buzzed in frightfully close to the surface, the miniscule atmosphere meant our passing barely disturbed the dust.

"What of . . . Old Earth?" Nedd asked. "Isn't there *any* sign of it at all?"

"None," Cuna said. "The Earth Disappearance Station was initially set up here to study what might have happened to the planet. But even the best scientists—working with licensed, and very rare, Superiority cytonics—could find no trace of it. Your homeworld is well and truly gone."

They'd given us an explanation earlier, filling in gaps in our records from Detritus. At some point during the final human war, the united forces of the galaxy—forged into a cohesive government to resist the human menace—had launched an all-out attack on Earth. When they'd arrived, they'd found only empty space. And an abandoned moon, cast away like a piece of debris blown off a fleeing battleship.

Even with that explanation, I felt as if I would find Old Earth peeking above the horizon. Waiting there, a blue ball of legend and myth, cradle of life and stories. My ship's system even had a phantom circle on the proximity monitor to display where it *would* have been. Nothing. Black, empty space. Earth had passed into the legends it had spawned.

Perhaps, M-Bot said in my mind, *it's a ghost. Like me!*

You're joking, but you could be kind of right, I thought back at him. *Detritus proves that entire planets can move using cytonics. Maybe Earth teleported away to avoid invasion?*

But if Earth *had* moved to a safe location, why had the humans on it never emerged? Were they in hiding?

"Eyes up," Arturo said to us over the line. "Installation should be visible any moment now."

We had brought only thirteen ships. Skyward Flight, Vanir Flight, and one kitsen battleship. All under Arturo's command. That was a fraction of our forces—but the more we brought, the more likely the enemy would be to spot us. In a war where both sides could supply reinforcements in the blink of an eye, stealth trumped numbers. Once we had inhibitor dominance, we could bring in as much of our fleet as we wanted.

Exactly when Cuna had said they would, the enemy sent an authentication request via hypercomm. My cytonic senses picked it up right before Hesho—using some newer technology acquired during my absence—noticed it on the comms. I almost responded, bypassing the equipment. Instead I left it to Arturo, who sent Cuna's code in reply. We were hoping that it would buy us a few minutes—assuming Winzik had forgotten to get Cuna's authorization codes changed since we'd rescued them.

Moments later, we came upon the installation. My cytonic senses immediately winked off—and I felt blinded. We'd hit their inhibitor field. Chet trembled and seemed to grow smaller—though delvers weren't stopped by inhibitors, they could feel them, and didn't like the sensation. M-Bot, who had been humming to himself, vanished.

A single slug, enhanced with some technology, could provide a fairly large bubble of protection—kilometers across. That was big, at least on the scale of one person or a base like this. When flying out in space, kilometers could pass incredibly quickly.

Still, I felt exposed, trapped. To distract myself, I focused on the base itself. Simply referred to as the EDS, the station had been built in the ruins of New Beijing, which had fallen quickly after Earth had disappeared. All humans had long since been removed from the facility. Element-specific gravity gave the base, which was settled into a large crater, a bubble of pressurized air. That, together with radiation skimmers, made the location livable.

Even knowing that, I was shocked to see greenery around the city. Trees were an incongruous sight around the perimeter, just inside the bubble. But of course biological methods of oxygen recycling would be planted, if only as a backup if the mechanical scrubbers went down.

What lay beyond the trees was even more unnerving. The structures inside the bubble were dotted with lights, and while the place wasn't packed with buildings like Starsight had been, the roads were still busy. It had parks. Restaurants. Apartments.

Scud. I'd imagined some secret military base, squat like a beetle huddled against the stone. Not a sprawling city.

"Shot off," Kimmalyn said, firing her sniping destructor precisely. A flare went up inside the city. "That should have been their inhibitor."

I tried hard not to think about the cost of that shot, but I did know FM and Jorgen had argued long and hard about the necessity of it. He had made good arguments: That in war, you couldn't worry that the battleship you brought down had a janitorial and medical staff on it. That you couldn't worry if the enemy trying to kill you had been pressed to fight against their will, as had been done to many, many soldiers throughout history. You just had to survive.

Once I'd have agreed with him. But now I heard FM's vigorous objections in the back of my mind. Was there another way? There *should* have been another way, right? Still, with the fall of that small bunker, my senses returned. M-Bot's humming resumed—as if he hadn't even noticed. Chet stretched, and I felt my anxiety decrease.

Nedd, Arturo, and the kitsen ship—named the *Iron Fortress*—soared ahead of us.

"Hey, Hesho," I said, "is *Iron Fortress* the full name of the kitsen ship? Or is it actually the *Iron Fortress of Poetic Words Said after a Held Breath* or something?" When I'd flown with Hesho before, his ship had been named something beautiful. I found this one surprisingly mundane.

"Just *Iron Fortress*," he said, with a smile. "The captain gets to name the ship. You will find many kitsen who like names as I do, but there are some who prefer simple clarity." He paused. "I will miss naming opportunities a great deal. It was one of my previous duties. We shall see if my traditions last. Though I am not alone in my love for poetry, I am . . . among the more obtuse in that regard."

I'd always had a sense that Hesho was a little odd, not just because of the emperor thing. We all watched, tense, as Nedd and the *Iron Fortress* flew into position—hovering above the base—and activated their own inhibitors. Our tech wasn't as good as the Superiority's, but we still managed to get a field up that covered the entire city. Hopefully it would at least slow down any reinforcements.

The rest of us streaked forward, and I got more visuals on the place. So ordinary. So full of life. "Anyone else uncomfortable about this?" I asked over the line.

"Yeah," Arturo said. "Admiral, you seeing these visuals?"

"What's wrong?" Jorgen asked from base. "I'm looking at what you're sending, but I'm not reading anything odd. Are there defenses I'm not spotting?"

"It's not the defenses," I said, "but the lack of them. Jorgen, we're raiding a city."

"City," Doomslug fluted softly.

The lights on my dash flickered.

"Direct, private call from him," Hesho said. "Patching you through."

"Spin," Jorgen said in my helmet a moment later. He could have spoken directly into my head, but we were trying to get into the habit of using communication slugs, as it worked better for everyone else. "You need to see this through."

Ahead of us, a local defense force had started scrambling. A few enemy fighters were rising into the air. Not many. Scud, they barely had anything. "Jorgen, those look like *police* ships, not true military vessels."

"They will try to kill you either way," he said. "Listen, this is a *secret military base*. They are guarding military assets of an incredibly valuable nature."

"But . . . Jorgen, there are *families* down there."

"Unfortunately," he said, "this kind of operation needs to be extremely tightly controlled. You want people committed to long-term service, since every person you transfer out is another one who can potentially leak the location. So you build a city out of it. Let everyone settle down."

"And we're going to attack them," I said softly.

"No, we're going to raid their information storage," Jorgen said. "Spin, I'm sorry. But this is what battle is like. What happened to the bloodthirsty warrior? I'm sure Alexander the Great wouldn't have had second thoughts about a raid like this."

"Alexander the Great was a monster," I said. "Most of them were, Jorgen, even if the stories dodge the issue. I . . ."

I'd lived among these people now. I couldn't see things as I once had. Still, I trailed off. My friends and I were fighting for survival against a much more powerful force, led by people who were decidedly evil. Did I think I was going to be able to go to *war* without causing casualties?

It was just . . . this was the first time I'd gone into a true battle against the Superiority since living on Starsight. How many of the pilots I was about to kill were like Morriumur? Good, decent people in the wrong place? How many people down there just wanted to live? Scud, first the slug, now this? Could I live with every stray shot I fired potentially blasting through an apartment window and vaporizing civilians?

I didn't have much choice, because the enemy ships were upon us. Fewer than twenty in all; enough to be dangerous, but not the swarm we'd feared. They had obviously intended this base's clandestine nature to protect it.

"Our cytonic inhibitor is working," Nedd said over the comm. "Lucky here is doing her job beautifully."

He and the kitsen ship would remain on the defensive, keeping the inhibitor field up. Arturo and Sadie would protect them. Hopefully we had put that inhibitor up fast enough to prevent the enemy from even calling for help.

The ships that engaged us were at least competent. Working in formations, trying to chase us into losing our wingmates, guarding the way forward to prevent us from flying together into the center of the city. I immediately pulled to the right, away from the barrage of oncoming destructor fire, and swept the perimeter of the bubble.

Kimmalyn followed, as capable a wingmate as I'd ever had. We buzzed past a set of gun emplacements—huge antiaircraft guns that were pointed toward the sky. Those would have decimated any larger ships that had gotten close, but were too long-ranged to bother us. One of the reasons we'd come in low and from the side was to stay under them. I could imagine the frustration of the people inside, watching their city be attacked, unable to do anything.

"All right, everyone," Arturo said. "Skyward Flight, engage those fighters and keep them busy. Vanir Flight, you're incursion. Get close to the installation, scout it visually, then have your slugs hyperjump your marines inside."

Vanir was a small flight, just four Sportas: four-seater fighters, each carrying a team of marines. Not quite carrier ships, intended for fast maneuverability and combat, they could drop off three ground troops when needed. Today they'd send their ground forces in to steal the information we wanted. The rest of us just had to keep the fighters busy. Fortunately, the little fighters we were facing were very unlikely to have slugs of their own, so even if one got beyond our inhibitor field, they wouldn't be able to call for help.

"Watch your right," Hesho noted, and I dodged by instinct, avoiding a trail of destructor fire.

"Want to try a Hatch maneuver?" Kimmalyn said, banking alongside me. That was a ploy where I would go into a frantic set of dodges to convince the enemy ships I was panicking.

"Not yet," I said. "Let's give them a chase first, so we can see how good they are."

"Roger that, Spin," Kimmalyn said.

I went into a set of evasives: the challenging, flowery type. Kimmalyn and I spun and looped, broke apart and curved back together, soared upward and sideways—dodging the fire from behind with poise. These pilots behind us were good. And the ships had actual people in the cockpits, rather than being piloted remotely. That was rare for the Superiority. Only their best fought in person.

That said, I'd faced delvers throwing hundreds of ships at me at once. Compared to that, these . . . well, they weren't much of a challenge. I stuck to the outside of the bubble of air, keeping a full six of the ships busy. Kimmalyn kept up with me, and together we didn't take a single hit to our shields.

"Spin," Jorgen said over the line, "what are you doing?"

"Dealing with more than my share of fighters," I said, pulling into a dive. "Anyone else and their wingmate handling six at once?"

"You haven't fired a single shot," Jorgen noted.

"I don't need to."

He fell silent. "Understood," he said.

I watched the proximity monitor as I flew, and Hesho helpfully highlighted the incursion team. They'd pushed inward, toward the center of the city. There they buzzed a specific skyscraper with shiny black windows: the place Cuna indicated was the information storage facility. Inside we could find all kinds of useful data, including the locations of the mining stations where the enemy got their acclivity stone.

Some among the military were still suspicious of Cuna—worrying they were a plant. I didn't have those concerns. Winzik had legitimately tried to kill Cuna—who, in turn, had already offered information and aid that would have been incredibly stupid to release if they were a spy.

As the incursion team finished their sweep of the data storage building, a dozen more of our ships arrived as reinforcements. The enemy fighters were good, but now they were severely outgunned— and my team included the best pilots in the galaxy. Enemy ships started going up in flowers of flame, but so far we'd only lost one fighter: Catnip, who, according to Hesho's monitor, had hyper-jumped with his slug to safety.

I should have known it was too good to last. "Scud," Breakaway said over the comm. She was leading Vanir Flight, and therefore the in-cursion force. "Admiral, there's a shield on this building, as we expected. But there's also a *second* inhibitor field here, covering just this structure."

"What?" Cuna said. "That . . . that's . . . I'm sorry. It must have been set up after my previous visit."

"Scud," Jorgen said in my ear. The *Iron Fortress* had sophisti-cated scanning equipment, and would be sending up-to-the-second scans of the region and the fighters back to headquarters. "That's a wrinkle. Breakaway, can you . . . Wait, what's that?"

I scanned the battlefield, flying by instinct, looking for whatever he'd noticed. All through the city, rooftops were opening, and guns were rising from them. AA guns. Smaller, shorter ranged, designed to hit starfighters. They had waited to deploy them until our team got close to the city center, where they'd be surrounded.

"Defensive maneuvers!" Arturo said. "All ships!"

Vanir Flight immediately scattered as the guns started unload-ing on them. I held my breath, but the shots mostly missed. We lost one Vanir ship, and I waited for confirmation the crew had been hyperjumped to safety in time.

Yellow light on the comm. Some casualties from that explosion— we'd lost at least one of the four on the ship. Scud! Still, the others dodged successfully. A modern ship with a good pilot was more maneuverable than a turret. Unfortunately, this threw a huge wrinkle into the plan. How would we break into the base if we had to be on the defensive the whole time?

"Spin," Kimmalyn said, "that looks bad."

As she said it, the ships tailing us got off a lucky shot on me—the destructor fire rippling across the surface of my shield, briefly illuminating the shell that protected my ship.

"Shield at sixty-five percent," Hesho warned. "That was a solid hit."

I nodded. The city didn't have its own shield, though several of the more important buildings clearly had individual ones. Better to protect the most vital areas with high-powered shields than to have a single larger, thin one, easily breakable.

I focused on my evasion, pushing into a dive. Kimmalyn and I spun around one another, bright destructor blasts raining past us like burning meteorites. Sprays of them hit the city below, blooms of fire rising along a street, as flying cars exploded while fleeing the firefight.

Scud. Were my opponents that ruthless? That uncaring of the noncombatants the stray fire was killing?

No. No, I knew better. I imagined the anguish they felt being forced to defend their city, knowing each shot might kill people they knew, people they loved. The enemy pilots were doing their jobs. And sometimes the job sucked.

"Spin . . ." Kimmalyn said as we pulled into a loop over the city.

"All right, everyone," Arturo said, his voice tense. "We'll get picked off if we keep this up. Swing back in a Stewart formation, planning to angle straight toward the target. First squad, on mark 118. Squad two, follow. Nedd, you—"

Nedd's ship went up in a burst of fire. Gone in a second, the powerful AA guns blasting straight through his shield.

"Scud!" Arturo screamed. "Nedd!"

In that moment, all of the enemy ships—even those tailing me—turned and swarmed the kitsen ship, *Iron Fortress*.

"Protect the kitsen ship!" Jorgen said over the line. "All pilots!"

It was too late. A dozen shots hit the kitsen ship, and as its shield went down, it hyperjumped away.

"Jorgen," Arturo said, "Nedd—"

"Stay focused," Jorgen said. "Medical will send information when they have it. Go, everyone!"

We obeyed, following Arturo's commands. I couldn't help but watch my dash. My heart wrenched, my insides twisting. Then a yellow light came on next to Nedd's name.

At least one casualty. Either Nedd, or his slug, was gone.

"Stay sharp!" Jorgen shouted. "Our inhibitors are both down. The enemy will send for help. No time to delay."

I reached the top of my loop and started another dive. A brilliant dazzling blast from the AA guns nearly took out Arturo, who was forced to hyperjump away, his shield down. Everyone else was scattering. Jorgen sent reinforcements—I saw another flight appearing on the monitors.

"Prepare to abandon mission," Jorgen said.

"Spin," Kimmalyn said. "Please."

Everything started to shake, my cockpit vibrating as my soul trembled. I snapped my eyes open, pulled out of my dive, and screamed. Angry at the enemy, at my own frailty, at Winzik for forcing my hand.

Angry at the universe. For having no answers.

I moved my finger onto the trigger of my destructors and, hating everything about this, took aim at the first enemy I saw and started firing.

7

They dodged.

But I felt them do it.

My time in the nowhere had changed me, given me the ability to reach out and communicate. I'd reached *into the past* in special circumstances. So it was easy to push through defenses and into minds, and I *felt* the person in that ship ahead of me. A dione with a family, thinking about their three children as they realized I was on their tail. I felt them plan a feint to the side, then a turn to try to lead me left in a dive, straight into the line of AA fire.

My expanding powers were so wondrous and amazing. Which made it extra horrifying to see how callously my instincts—aware of the enemy's movements; Sun Tzu would have approved—traced the enemy's upcoming path perfectly. They ran into each of my shots as they tried to dodge.

Their mind winked out. Like a communication line suddenly cut. The beautiful things I'd learned became, in my terrible hands, just another way to kill.

My soul still vibrating, my mind alight with anger and fire, I hit my overburn and kept on killing. I sliced through the battlefield like a razor blade across a throat. Enemy ships went up in blasts of light as I cut in behind them, offering no sporting chance. This wasn't sport. This was a cauterization. This was cutting off the hand before the body could die.

I brought down six in the next few minutes. All of the AA guns, reasonably, started firing on me. I swept low through the city, shattering windows with my passing, putting obstacles between me and the guns.

Spensa, M-Bot said softly, *I feel you.*

I gritted my teeth as my systems highlighted the firing positions of each of the AA guns. I swung up along an apartment building, intending to crest the top and unleash some shots at those emplacements—but in my agony, my soul *freaked out.* I could feel Chet in there, feel him in pain, an agony that mirrored my own.

Chunks of the building next to me began to vanish. Then—as I darted out over the top—they began to appear in the air between me and the guns, intercepting the barrage of shots that tried to trace my ship. Chunks of steel appeared above the emplacements themselves, crashing down and smashing them one after another—causing explosions that rocked the entire city, debris spraying high into the air. Trailing smoke, spiraling toward the void.

The few remaining enemy ships arrayed to try to stop me. I mopped them up almost unconsciously, shooting down three and then smashing the last two out of the sky with chunks of steel the size of hovercars.

The battlefield fell still. Almost a third of the city was on fire, smoke bleeding from wounds where the AA guns had gone up. The last pieces of the defending ships rained down as sparks, sprinkling the city like molten rain.

The line stayed quiet as I clutched my control sphere and throttle in sweaty hands, my cockpit vibrating, random objects—a cup, a pair of glasses, a child's stuffed toy—appearing in the air beside me, then dropping to hit my chair or arms. Sweat streamed from my forehead, and I couldn't blink, couldn't move. Other than to tremble.

"Sweetest stars," Kimmalyn whispered over the comm, "and the Lord God that birthed them . . ."

Jorgen cleared his throat. "Belay the retreat. Enemy defensive position eliminated. Nice work, Spin."

Shut up, I started to whisper, but bit it off. I was the one who always bragged about killing, about the way of the warrior. All of that nonsense.

Hesho muted the comm. "Take your time," he said softly. "Breathe. In and out. Focus only on each new breath."

I nodded, doing as he suggested, and forced myself back under control. My cockpit stopped vibrating.

"Nedd," I said.

Hesho turned on the comm, putting a direct call in to Jorgen. "Admiral, we would like to know the situation of callsign: Nedder. If it is known."

"He arrived, burned and unconscious," Jorgen said. "No sign of his slugs. We think Lucky died in the initial shot that hit the ship, and Chubs sent him back. But . . . didn't come himself."

I got an image in my head from Doomslug, fluting quietly from her sling. Pain. Chubs had been wounded. Sending Nedd had been his final act.

I closed my eyes, feeling Doomslug's pain as my own.

"He should survive," Jorgen said. "But . . . well, he'll probably never fly again. Not with only one arm. I'm sorry."

"It's war," I whispered, hoarse. "And we're soldiers."

"Nevertheless," Jorgen said, "let's pull you out to rest. Arturo is ready to come back in and the team can—"

"No," I said. "I'll see it through."

He didn't contradict me, so I took a deep breath and pointedly didn't look at the large sections of the city I'd destroyed. "Incursion squad on me," I said. "Kimmalyn, our target building is still shielded. Get it down. Skyward Flight, provide air support and be ready to pull us out if something goes wrong."

I got a handful of "affirmative" replies, and not a one called me out on taking command in Arturo's absence. Technically T-Stall was next in line, but I wasn't in a mood to pay attention to the chain of command. Honestly, I hadn't *ever* been good at it, even when I *hadn't* been a one-woman apocalypse with a fruit-flavored delver filling.

Kimmalyn's ship was equipped with a shield cutter. She led the way to the large black skyscraper at the center of the EDS. She hovered there, rotating her ship with the acclivity ring unhinging, so she could position the bottom of her ship as close as possible to the building. Her vessel let out a bright blue blast, reminiscent of an IMP—but far more concentrated.

That knocked out the building's shield. I did a long, slow pass along the tower. Starting at the top, flying down in a spiral around the outside, centimeters from the wall. Yes, I could feel what had been reported earlier: this building had a second inhibitor, secret and unexpected. I wondered if I could get a sense of where the thing was, based on the field it projected. Only, with mechanical augmentation, the fields an inhibitor slug made could be various shapes. So . . .

Floor thirty-seven, Chet said. *Directly in the center of the building. I can cut through the inhibitor and see it hiding there.*

"Kimmalyn," I said, "I need a hole in the wall on the thirty-seventh floor. Incursion team, prepare to breach there. We're going to find the inhibitor. My senses tell me it's at the direct center of that floor."

"Roger," Kimmalyn said, using her specialized destructor to cut a hole in the wall. The chunk of stone and steel from the wall fell free, edges glowing with heat.

I flew my ship over and hit the cockpit release. "Hesho, if something goes wrong, how confident are you in flying this ship?"

"With the minimal controls I have?" he asked. "Not terribly confident. But I shall endeavor to do my best in the event of a disaster."

Good enough. As I twisted to undo the quick-release on my buckles, Doomslug fluted and appeared on my lap—jumping out of her sling.

"You sure?" I asked her. "We can't get out until we bring down the inhibitor inside."

She fluted in the affirmative, so I scooped her up as I climbed out. She went into a holster on my hip, slung across my opposite shoulder. The others called them slings, but that felt . . . I don't know. Like the thing a mom would use to bring her baby along. Unnerved—even a little nauseated—by my powers as I was, I still wasn't going to bring a *baby sling* into battle. I was bringing a *slug holster*.

I unclipped a fully automatic assault rifle from its place at the side of the cockpit, and the three remaining ships from Vanir Flight joined me, each carrying three members of our newly christened marine corps. We'd never had much in the way of ground forces, but were rectifying that in the face of the increasing need for assaults like this. Nedd in particular had enjoyed finally being given time on the firing range for . . .

No. Don't think about Nedd.

Wolf was the leader of the marine force, and as Junker opened his canopy for her, she stood up and waved to me. Wolf was a tall, hard-faced woman with body armor and one lock of blue hair. Her non-code name was Chono, which was apparently Mongolian. When I'd asked if she was related to the Great Khan, she'd simply said, "Of course."

I'd tried not to gush *too* much. It had been difficult.

She and I shared a nod, then leaped off the fronts of our hovering ships into the hole, our guns up. This city had artificial gravity, fortunately, and so we didn't have trouble walking or moving. We activated flashlights on the front of our muzzles as the other eight marines followed quietly, each of them with their own slug holster.

Unfortunately, I'd just entered a deeper darkness than the physical kind. Because my cytonic senses once again vanished—smothered by the blanket of the inhibitor field.

"I have the description of the building that Cuna provided," Hesho said through my helmet speaker, "and I am coordinating

64

with command. We are trying to guess the direction you need to go to reach the inhibitor. If that would be of assistance."

"That would be scudding wonderful," I whispered back.

A square box appeared in the corner of my helmet's visor. A red dot indicated I was at the perimeter, and a blinking dot in the center highlighted our target. It didn't have any of the internal features of the floor, but it was helpful in getting me where I needed to go.

There were some locked doors in the way, but that was why the Saints had made destructors. As soon as we knocked out the first, though, return fire came blasting from the darkness—forcing us back and to the sides.

"Sadie, Kimmalyn," I said, "we're pinned down. You have our locations?"

"Sure do," Sadie said.

"Kindly make us a path."

Kimmalyn cut another hole in the wall and Sadie filled it with destructor fire, pointed inward. Ship weapons were of an entirely different category than the handheld ones we had, and in moments the shots wound down and we were able to pick through the remnants of the wall and continue forward. Muzzle flashlights lit the remaining pieces of our enemies, something that—as a starfighter pilot—I didn't often have to confront.

They prop up an evil dictatorship, I reminded myself. *This is part of the same force that murdered my father.*

I knew the weakness in that reasoning, but it was enough to keep me focused as—after a brief shootout with the last remaining enemy squad—we reached the location of Hesho's blinking light. I found the box, well locked and disguised as a storage container among many other similar ones. When I popped it open, I found a terrified blue-and-green slug inside.

Doomslug fluted, and the other one stretched out a little, sniffing toward the air.

"That's right," I said, scooping her up. "We're friends."

Doomslug fluted again, then—brilliantly—awareness returned to me. Doomslug and the rescued slug vanished.

"Wolf," I said, "inhibitor field is down. This is your mission now."

"Excellent," she said. "Data storage is on floor thirty-six. Cuna doesn't know where; she took an elevator up, and says she got a little turned around."

I nodded, not correcting Wolf on the use of "she" for a dione. Together the marines had a quick conference, then one placed some explosives on the floor. We took cover, and they blasted it open.

I hyperjumped down, then waited as the marines rappelled through the hole. While they worked, I reached out with my senses.

There are six enemies approaching, I sent to Wolf, implanting the words in her mind.

She jumped, then looked at me and nodded.

They've stopped, I sent, pointing through the darkness—lit by some fires on the ceiling—toward a hallway. *Down this hall. Probably setting up an ambush.*

She tossed a grenade at the wall, bouncing it toward the people farther down. We went in after the explosion, eliminating the soldiers with callous precision, muzzles flaring and destructors lighting the smoke. I blocked the thoughts and emotions of the dying from my mind.

It didn't take much effort to locate the data storage. We simply moved in a search pattern until we found a metal door, reinforced and protected, with a lot of people on the other side. I picked up some of their emotions. Nervousness. Waiting for help. Scientists. Yeah, this was the place.

Some twenty people working inside, I sent to Wolf. *No way to tell how many are civilians. You willing to do this in a way that keeps us from firing on anyone we don't need to?*

She looked to me, then nodded.

Take a deep breath, I sent her. *Have your slug ready to get you out if this goes wrong.*

Then I hyperjumped the two of us into the room, near one of the minds I could feel—but back behind the rest of them. We immediately raised guns, ignoring the scientists and technicians. Each of us fired twice, drilling through the skulls of the soldiers waiting by the doors, their backs to us.

Scud, I'd never felt so sick to fire a weapon. Was this what I'd signed up for? Fighting the Krell, an unknowable evil force, felt so far removed from what we were doing here. Now . . . now *we* were the unknowable force. I was the thing that terrorized these people, possessing powers and abilities they didn't understand.

We gathered the scientists at the rear of the room, their hands up and trembling. Wolf watched them while I opened the door from the inside, letting the rest of the team in. A few seconds later, Rig and a crew of technicians appeared in the room, sent by Jorgen— he didn't have much hyperjumping ability, but could persuade the slugs mind-to-mind to do it, if he knew where to tell them to go.

Rig's team quickly began working on the data storages, grabbing a copy of basically every sensitive and secret piece of information the Superiority owned. All the things that M-Bot and I had wanted to discover on Starsight, but had been locked out of.

As Rig worked on the data, I patrolled the front of the room, near the engineers' stations. On several of the screens, a familiar varvax stood in front of an official seal. Winzik had a deep green carapace, bipedal and hulking, like a suit of armor to protect the far more fragile crablike being who rode inside. I could see him through the helmet's faceplate, floating in a liquid solution.

I gestured to one of Rig's engineers, and the woman helpfully hit a few buttons, rewinding the message and playing it from the beginning. I kept my cytonic senses alert for anyone approaching, then leaned down and let my translator pin feed me Winzik's words.

"My goodly people of the Superiority's multitudinous worlds.

I am Provisional High General Winzik, as many of you know. It is my burden and regret that I have been forced into the position of temporary commander of the Superiority during this time of grave danger.

"Understand that I take this duty as the most solemn of responsibilities. Those of us of prime intelligence bear a heavy charge—that of protecting and nurturing those who have not yet achieved equivalent status. My words today are thus for the weaker of our wonderful species.

"Your natural inclination might be toward panic, anger, or even violence! My, my. How *terrible* it must be to live with secondary intelligence. You must resist these shocking emotions. The Superiority is strong, and those of us who lead it *will* protect you from the human scourge. As the galaxy has survived their horrific attacks in the past, so we will weather them this time.

"Already we have the outbreak partially contained, and the fighting is limited to the outskirts of the Superiority. It might take decades to properly bring the humans down, but I am determined to do the job asked of me. For now, know that there is absolutely no danger to you. It is the duty of those of us who have achieved primary intelligence to fight on your behalf, so you do not have to risk the dangers of aggression and rage. Live your lives as usual, knowing I will protect you."

On one hand, I was impressed. Winzik could likely milk this for decades, pretending that—even long after we'd been defeated—he needed this power to protect everyone from the terrifying humans. On the other hand, if Winzik *actually* thought he could contain me, then he would soon find out firsthand how wrong he was.

On the screen, the message started repeating—and rather than hear it again, I shot the monitor a few times. When the others looked at me in shock, I gave them a shrug.

I'm sorry, M-Bot said in my head, perhaps sensing my frustration at the situation. *For what you had to do today.*

"It's my job," I whispered to him, watching the door, my gun at the ready.

It's not what you dreamed.

"I gave up that dream in the nowhere," I said to him. "I could have stayed there, fighting battles without consequences. I came back. Because things like this have to happen."

Do they?

"For now," I said. "The goal is to stop them from being necessary. Somehow." That was the difference. It *had* to be. Winzik was intent on domination, destruction, and even extermination. We fought for something better.

I knew the same justification had been used by virtually every terrorist force in the past. I wasn't naive. But I also wasn't so cynical, or so foolish, as to paint them all as equivalent. A woman had to follow her conscience. I believed in what we were doing.

It still felt terrible.

I glanced to Rig. "I think we can pull all of this out," he whispered to me. "Why copy when we can just take?" He grinned, then pointed to several slugs they'd set up.

Cool. He hyperjumped out with his team—taking multiple large data storages with them. Servers and all.

Seconds later, my strike force—all of us back in our ships—hyperjumped away after him. And to those we'd left alive, I knew we'd be just as mysterious and terrible as the Krell had been to me.

8

As we landed back in the hangar, there was something different about the air of victory this time. I remembered well—like the memory of a lost loved one—returning from saving us from the lifebuster bomb. I remembered celebrations, cheers, toasts—the enthusiasm unchecked for an unexpected victory.

Today, pilots climbed tiredly from their ships. Perhaps it was our casualties—two dead from Vanir Flight, two taynix lost, Nedd severely wounded. But almost every action cost us lives; it was part of the metric of maintaining a fighting force. Another damper was the knowledge that this wasn't a definitive win—this was one step toward victory, but only the first of many.

Then, of course, there was what I'd done.

You were supposed to have to *touch* things to hyperjump them. You were limited to complete objects, not chunks of them. Large structures, like battleships, usually required specialized architecture built into them to make hyperjumping the entire thing possible for the cytonic.

I'd violated *all* of those supposed rules. Just like the delvers did.

As I climbed down from my ship, it seemed that those in the room shied back from me. And why shouldn't they? I was more weapon than human. Even a few members of Skyward Flight—Sadie, notably—watched me with unbridled awe.

Something's wrong, M-Bot said in my head.

"Yeah," I muttered. "I—"

Not with you. With me. The delvers have spotted me. I need to hide again.

"I still don't understand how you do that," I said. "Aren't you all in the exact same point in space?"

Yes and no. There's no space here. So there are no points. No reality at all. It's trippy. But they can sense my connection to you. I need to turn inward and vanish. That or pretend to be one of them. Which might work better.

"Can you do that?"

Spensa, I'm super sneaky. It's what I was built for, remember?

"You always *say* that, but—"

Gotta hide now. Haunt yourself for a while. I'll let you know when I'm free.

I felt him withdrawing. Leaving me alone.

Chet gave me a sense of warmth though. I appreciated that. Not alone, just lonely.

I started into the hangar, wanting rest, and bade Hesho farewell, suggesting he get something to eat. He flew off, and I probably should have gone to check on Nedd. Sadie and T-Stall were going to do that now, judging by their conversation. But I wasn't certain I could stomach it; from what Jorgen had said, Nedd was still unconscious, in stable—but seriously injured—condition.

I'd had the power, at any moment, to win that battle all on my own. If I'd done so a few minutes earlier, Nedd wouldn't have been hurt. Could I ever meet his eyes after that?

I walked quickly toward the exit, intending to go to my rooms and crash, but Kimmalyn fell in beside me.

"You want to talk?" she asked.

"No," I lied.

She nodded and didn't push. Why had I said no? I silently

cursed her for being a good friend, and respecting my boundaries, as she split off to go join T-Stall and Sadie.

At the hangar door I ran into Jorgen, who was walking holding a datapad and looking distracted.

"We've got it," he told me. "There are *five* mining operations. One more than you heard, but still . . . Scud. Only five! It's a weakness, Spin. An unguarded crack in the fortress wall. We *can* exploit this."

"Just as long as we only attack the supply depots on this side," I said. "At least one of the mining operations on the other side has friends of mine living in it."

He nodded in agreement.

"Jorgen," I said. "About what I did back there . . ."

He looked at me, then gave me an encouraging smile, setting aside the datapad and taking me by both arms. "You were *amazing*," he said. "I know I was skeptical when you said you needed to stay in the nowhere and learn what you could there, but I'm glad you convinced me. You should see how enthusiastic our allies are about the results of this operation. For the first time, everyone believes we might actually be able to *do* this. Resist the Superiority and *win*."

"All it took was getting your own personal delver girlfriend . . ." I said.

He paused, so I gave him a grin, trying to convince him it was a joke. I put a tight clamp on my emotions. I didn't want him to see how much I hurt.

He hesitated—noting the full flight deck behind me. Then, obviously making a deliberate decision, he leaned down and kissed me.

That felt . . . wonderful. I knew how awkward it was for him to be dating one of his pilots, as there were protocol issues. But he also knew that I needed him and he needed me. Jorgen choosing *me* instead of *rules* was just about the most important message he could ever send. I felt an elated burst of adrenaline.

And it ran up against a kind of wall inside of me. A wall of worry, of self-loathing.

I started to feel sick. Joy was such an *unforgivable* thing to experience after the killing I'd done today. I wasn't human any longer—yet here I was, kissing my boyfriend like nothing was wrong?

He pulled back, and damn him, he was too observant for his own good. "I know that you feel different about fighting now," he said. "I do too. It's maturity, Spensa, and experience. They're changing us. It's all right to feel conflicted. It's messy . . . it's all so very messy."

I nodded.

"I'm going to do my best to make sure we never get surprised by civilians on a military mission again," he said. "I won't send you in unaware again, Spensa. I promise."

It was a good move, and a perfectly Jorgen one to take. He'd analyze what had gone wrong, would talk with our top military and organizational minds about how to learn from it. How to make certain we didn't make the same mistake twice. That was why he was in command.

But knowing it wouldn't likely happen in the future didn't ease the pain inside me now.

I forced out another smile. "You're brilliant," I said, fully honest. "Thank you."

"We need to plan our next step," he said. "It should be simple. Winzik is getting acclivity stone from these five locations—all mining stations in the nowhere, attached to supply depots on our side. You say one is mostly shut down already, by the pirates you befriended.

"Fortunately, we don't have to attack the mining stations themselves, or the civilians there. If we blow up the portals, then Winzik will be robbed of those resources. Using our powers, I'm sure we can find a way to rescue the miners on the other side eventually."

"A good plan," I said, truly exhausted now. "And I know some of the Broadsiders would appreciate that. Thank you."

He nodded. "We need to strike before Winzik has time to figure out why we wanted those databases. I'm thinking a five-pronged attack, hitting each supply depot at the same time. A coordinated hit, leaving him completely flat-footed."

"Great," I said, trying to control my trembling. If I started freaking out right now, he'd know.

I *couldn't* let him know how much this hurt. Couldn't let him know that I was breaking inside at the idea of going into battle again. He was finding peace and success in his new role. I had to do the same.

"I'll get everyone else on board," he said, "and talk to the kitsen generals, get their strategic insight. For now, you get some rest. I've already checked on Nedd, and I'll send you an update as soon as he's awake. You need sleep though. Because if everyone agrees on this plan, we'll set the attacks for as early as tomorrow. Time is of the essence."

His excited smile on top of the kiss was the last straw for me. I gave him a sweet grin—scud, I hoped he didn't see me being "sweet" as a terrible sign—and left. Once he was out of sight I sped up my pace, until I reached my quarters and hid inside.

Almost as soon as I was alone, a text appeared on my watch. Tech the UrDail used, which we'd begun to incorporate into our teams as well.

Dinner? It was Kimmalyn. I sent her something about needing to rest, then I took a deep breath and surveyed my quarters. I'd been assigned a three-room officer's bunk. I was technically a commodore, for some reason, even though pilots were almost never promoted above captain without moving into administration. Jorgen had pulled some strings to ensure my seniority, emphasizing my special position as a cytonic, and need for autonomous field command. Nonsense equating to: "Nobody knows what to do with you, Spensa, so here's a promotion."

I'd tried to convince Mom and Gran-Gran to move in with me to help fill the space, but hadn't had any luck yet. It *was* a little daunting to have so much room, but I'd been trying to think of it as the equivalent of a warrior's trophy and enjoy it.

Today I found it comforting. I had space, without anyone or anything to pressure me. Of course, I still did my customary check of each room and closet. Ridiculous? Perhaps. It made me feel better to look for assassins—until I remembered that there were kitsen ninjas somewhere out there. They could be hiding in places a human could never fit. Did my routine need to include a thorough check of my sock drawer to make sure no cute furry killers were hiding among my unmentionables?

I settled down on my bed, and let out a deep breath. Inside me Chet was trembling, and it took effort to prevent another attack from coming on. Scud. I could barely control it. Those vibrations. The strange way my powers acted. I—

"Incredible work today," a woman's voice said from behind me. "That was really something."

I spun and leaped off my bed and to my feet. Brade was standing by my bedroom wall, next to my replica Browning FN 1910 handgun.

Brade. Winzik's pet human cytonic. Short military buzz cut. Sleeveless, tight military fatigues and flak jacket. Assault rifle slung on her back. I had my sidearm out in a heartbeat and put three holes in my wall before I realized she wasn't there physically. She was a cytonic projection—I'd done something similar to her while in the nowhere.

She looked down the barrel of my sidearm destructor, then nodded. "Good reflexes."

I ignored her, running to the comm panel and calling operations. "Is our inhibitor field down?" I demanded.

"No?" a confused operator said on the other side. "Detritus's protections are still in place . . ."

"Your inhibitor is fine," Brade said from behind me, amused. "You and I are connected somehow. I don't understand what's going on, but I can project to you, Spin. Like you did to me."

I moved my finger off the button and turned. "Go away."

"No."

I threw the weight of my cytonic powers at her. I . . . didn't exactly know what I was trying to accomplish, other than to banish her, but she bore the blast of raw mental energy and didn't so much as stumble. She seemed to have only sent a very faint projection of herself, leaving the rest of her protected. Dismissing her with my considerable powers was a little like trying to kill a mosquito with a cannon.

"Save it for the battlefield," Brade said, stalking around and inspecting my room. When I'd done this to her, I'd been able to see everything around her—and hear what anyone near her was saying. If I couldn't find a way to stop this, I presented an enormous security issue to our forces.

"What do you want, Brade?" I demanded.

"I've asked myself that for years, you know?" she said. "Should be easy to answer, and I guess it is." She stepped up to me. "What do I want? I want to *win*."

"I gave you a chance to join us," I said. "You ran to Winzik and turned me in."

"I stand by my choice, though I can't say I'm sad you escaped. If you hadn't run off, I would never have witnessed the display you managed today." She shook her head, seeming in awe. "Incredible. Fifteen kills in under ten minutes would be impressive for any other pilot. But what you did to the AA guns . . . the way you ripped buildings apart and used the chunks in offense and defense . . . Spensa, you're *incredible*." She nodded to me. Brade didn't really smile—at least, she did so rarely. "You're worthy. I'm worthy. We should be working together."

"To do . . . what exactly?"

She gestured at me, kind of a "what else?" sort of shrug. "Conquest, Spensa. It's in our blood."

"You're crazy."

"Crazy," she said, "like Alexander the Great? Like the ancient pharaohs? Like Attila the Hun, Napoleon, Charlemagne? People who saw the vast expanse of the world and realized the greatest challenge in life would be to rule it all?" She stepped closer to me. "None of them ever stood a real chance. But we do. With the power you showed today, we *absolutely* do."

"I think I'd rather use that power to squash you," I snapped. "You betrayed me, Brade."

"And *you* betrayed the Superiority," she replied. "I merely tried to turn you in for it. But that's meaningless." She stepped even closer to me. "Thank you for showing me our potential."

Then she vanished.

Scud, scud, *scud*. I collapsed into the chair by the wall, huddled up on myself, and couldn't control it any longer. For the next hour, I let things vanish and appear around me, increasingly eclectic and bizarre, as my soul went aflame and my self—what was left of it— hid in the recesses of my mind.

Terrified.

PART
TWO

9

By the next morning, I had a handle on myself again. I knew I couldn't continue on as before—so I made a decision.

I was a weapon. I'd started on that path by going to the nowhere, and then by allowing a delver's soul to combine with mine. My purpose was to free my people.

Nothing else mattered. My emotions didn't matter. The damage to my soul and my psyche? Just part of the payment. I could do this. I was a soldier. It was what I'd signed up for. I could survive long enough to bring down the Superiority. Afterward, who cared?

Making this decision was liberating. Not because I was freed from emotions. But, like a surgical strike, this let me control the worst of them. Fear, anxiety, uncertainty. It took them out, leaving me with the manageable ones. Sadness. Regret. Loss.

Those were emotions I knew; they'd been my companions long before I discovered M-Bot and Doomslug.

I rose, enjoyed the luxury of an actual shower—not just a cleanser—and found a note on my schedule from Jorgen, requesting a meeting.

Jorgen. What would I do about Jorgen? I knew what I wanted: to love him. That wasn't an emotion I wanted to be free of, and wasn't one I could ignore.

At the same time, I wasn't human anymore. I *would* help bring down the Superiority, and find a way to protect our reality from the delvers. I would find a way, but I was increasingly certain that way would break me.

When that happened, I had to somehow protect Jorgen from the shrapnel. I didn't want to think about it though. First, to test my newfound control, I needed to try a baby step: something I'd been avoiding the last few days—breakfast.

Doomslug clinging to my shoulder, we made our way to the mess hall—then froze in the doorway. Inside, long rows of metal tables offered up the latest chef's delights. Algae mostly, prepared in a variety of ways. But amazingly, our recent collaborations with other species had given us access to more. Alanik's and Hesho's worlds contained grains in abundance. Fruits. Meats that *weren't* rat. Delivered to us in thanks for our aid in protecting their planets.

Our cooks seemed to be enjoying the variety. If you could prepare algae in a hundred different ways, imagine what you could do with *rice*. Sure, we'd had some of these luxuries in the past—grown in specialized caverns in very small amounts for the wealthy. For that reason, I'd always felt guilty partaking. But this new style of dining— a feast of flavors in every meal—was the way things *should* be. If we succeeded, this was what *everyone* would eat.

It wasn't the food itself that stopped me in the doorway. It was the sheer cacophony. Dozens of pilots chattering. And slugs. There were several varieties, though some of the newest ones we'd discovered were still being studied, and hadn't been authorized for active duty yet. Of those at breakfast, the bulk were yellow and blue like Doomslug. Those were hyperslugs, who could help us teleport. Almost as common were the purple-and-orange slugs, who let us communicate via cytonics.

Surprisingly, there were more than a few red-and-black slugs, capable of releasing blasts of cytonic energy. We had started calling them boomslugs. Most rare were the blue-and-green slugs, capable of inhibiting cytonics, letting only friends and allies use their powers. I steeled myself against the guilt of allowing one to be killed at the facility. At least I'd rescued the other one.

Besides, I was a weapon. Weapons didn't cry over the things they killed.

Doomslug fluted softly on my shoulder. She felt . . . as intimidated as I did. She didn't want to go into the room either. Because . . . well, scud. She was *shy*.

I'd always assumed she had been with M-Bot because she'd gotten lost, or maybe she'd been the descendant of his original hyperdrive. But recently I was getting the feeling that she was the slug equivalent of an introvert. She hadn't wanted to be completely alone, which was why she'd sought out M-Bot and his dormant cytonic processor. But she wasn't the type who enjoyed hanging out in a cavern full of fluting slugs.

I tried to send her a sense of peace as we collected food from the counter—a sandwich made with . . . was that *peanut butter*? I'd read about that. Wow. And a real slice of some kind of orange fruit. Maybe, well, an orange. Evershore and Earth shared some ecology from their years of trading together in the distant past, and much of the food we had been able to get from them had its roots in Earth flora.

I was feeling pretty good as I settled down at a table near the right side of the room. The real test was still to come though, as my friends gathered around, each one wearing a red piece of felt behind their flight pins. A symbol of remembrance, worn each time we lost someone. Today they wore them for the two soldiers we'd lost, and the two slugs—comrades in arms.

Each one was an indictment of me. I could have saved those people. Who was I to hold this power?

"Hey!" Arturo said. "You came to breakfast, Spensa! Finally starting to feel like yourself, eh?"

"Yeah," I said, glancing at him. "Nedd . . . ?"

"Awake," Arturo said, "and ordering me to do things for him, since with one arm, he 'can't possibly do it himself.'"

I released a long breath. If Nedd was joking already, that was a good sign. That eased my guilt a smidge.

As others set down trays, I looked past Arturo to Alanik, who settled in a few places farther along the table. She ate with Skyward Flight, even if her chosen food was different. She seemed to really *like* the algae.

The violet-skinned alien studied me quietly, with a certain reserved sensibility. She said she'd been told, by her leaders, to continue "socializing" with the humans. Her species and mine shared suspiciously similar physiology—there might be a common ancestor in our pasts. Certainly the UrDail had slipped into Earth's mythology and lore, much as the kitsen had.

Regardless, it was odd to see the person whose face I'd stolen joining us for breakfast. And it was odd to not have FM there, as she was helping Rig get a new fabrication project up and running.

T-Stall sat next to me, but he gave me space. Too much space. We'd never been that close, and he and Catnip seemed to have started integrating better with the rest of the flight while I was gone. On my other side, Sadie settled down—and looked to me with an almost *divine* admiration.

This was ostensibly where I belonged. But I felt more at home with a bunch of aliens these days than I did with my old flight. Fortunately, my newfound mental bulwark was effective. I reminded myself that it was all right—that I didn't *need* to belong, since I was just a weapon to be fired. That calmed me, and I settled into my place.

Nothing started rattling. Nobody's sandwiches vanished.

Doomslug fluted to me sorrowfully, but I scooped her off my shoulders and set her in the line of other slugs, which ran down the center of the wide metal table. They were happily munching on their caviar, offered in special little bowls. The taynix were now members of the flight. They saved the lives of my friends regularly, by hyperjumping them to safety.

They like it here, I thought, feeling their contented minds. *They like being appreciated. I think they even enjoy the human companionship.*

They were afraid of the delvers though. I'd been able to pick out some of this from Doomslug. The Superiority had manipulated this fear—rather than working with and encouraging the taynix, the Superiority had frightened them into compliance. The ease with which FM and the others had instead coaxed and befriended the slugs was the ultimate recrimination of the Superiority's so-called primary intelligence. Our enemy claimed to avoid aggression and support peace, but in truth they only did so when convenient.

But Doomslug is not afraid of me, Chet thought from within me. *Not any longer.*

Doomslug sent an image to us in response: Chet and me with yellow skin and blue tinges. She'd realized we weren't frightening. Not even delvers were. We were just very strange slugs.

"So," Kimmalyn said, leaning across the table and drawing my attention back to the conversation. "Your plan worked, Spin. I hear there's a *ton* of useful stuff in that data archive. *Twelve* other human preserves, like Detritus. Detailed schematics for all Superiority ships. And, of course, the location of the supply depots that process the acclivity stone mined in the nowhere."

"Other human preserves, you say?" T-Stall said. "I wonder if they're like us. Constantly fighting. On the brink of breaking out."

"I doubt it," I said. "I get the feeling that Detritus was unique, with our cavern complex and fabricators. The enemy didn't *intend* our planet to become a preserve; we were just too persistent to exterminate."

"Either way," Kimmalyn said, "could be worth approaching them . . ."

It wasn't a terrible idea. From what we'd been able to determine, the Superiority was being forced to pull fighters away from many garrisons to fight us. Some of those preserves might be poorly defended.

"I've got some of the data dump here," Arturo said, opening up his datapad. He started to show us the locations of the human preserves, but I hijacked the pad and instead scrolled to the locations of the five mining stations.

As Jorgen had indicated, our goal wasn't to hit the mining stations themselves. My friends there, like Peg and the Broadsiders, would be safe. We'd attack the supply depots on this side instead, the ones controlled by the Superiority.

Out of curiosity, though, I looked to see if the data indicated where the mining bases were in the nowhere. And the data was there. Surehold, which I'd attacked with the Broadsiders, was the biggest—but the four others were sprinkled throughout the same region. I had assumed they'd be farther out in the belt, but it appeared they just kept them very well hidden.

"Still can't believe it," Sadie said, leaning down low, speaking softly. "The Superiority is so *vulnerable*."

"I was there last night when they broke down the data," Arturo said. "Cuna is right. The Superiority is so paranoid about keeping the slugs a secret that they've created a bigger problem for themselves. For example, almost all communications in the Superiority are underpinned by a *single* network, one location that holds a large batch of commslugs to facilitate comms traffic."

You didn't need a slug on each end to make cytonic communications work. With enough practice, and the right technology on the receiving end, a single slug could manage multiple different conversations. A little like an operator on an old-school communications rig.

Yup! M-Bot said in my head. *Fun fact. The first recorded Earth cytonic, Jason Write, dedicated only a tiny portion of his brain to the task—but was able to run dozens of communications almost like a background process. With training, the early Earth cytonics were able to facilitate thousands upon thousands of calls, all by themselves.*

I jumped despite myself. *How long have you been back?*

I never left. I just hid. I've been watching for a while now. Some . . . time? Hard to say in here . . . well, you know how it is.

I did, and I also had a better understanding of why time was so strange in the nowhere. The delvers had an omnipresent effect on the place. They wanted to forget the past, so everyone there started to do the same. The delvers ignored time, and so it was hard for everyone to track.

They did it because they were still searching for a way, even now, to deaden the pain of loss.

Jason Write, M-Bot said. *Yes. The delvers, who were only a single individual back then, loved him. When he died, they didn't know how to respond to their grief so . . . all of this. The result of one former AI's emotional constipation.*

Ew.

FM finally arrived, carrying three slugs at once. She'd really gotten into the entire slug thing, which I found odd. She was so prim, and slugs didn't really match her normal fashionable accessorizing.

I immediately felt guilty for that snideness. Yes, FM liked to be fashionable, but she'd never given me reason to think she was vain. I'd just always felt intimidated by how . . . well, perfect she was at basically everything. Even, it turned out, taking care of slugs.

She set her three down with their own bowls of caviar—we had to ship the stuff in from Evershore in bulk—and started talking, animated. "Coordinated raid on all five mining installations," she explained. "Tomorrow morning at oh six hundred hours. Orders should be coming to Arturo any minute."

"They're here," he said, scrolling on his datapad. "Five strike forces, all at once."

"Why five?" I asked. "We know one of those is already locked down on the other side by the Broadsiders."

"Can you say for certain your friends are still in control?" FM asked. "And that they wouldn't open up the portal again if properly bribed? Would they sell acclivity stone to the Superiority if the value of the stuff increased a hundredfold?"

Would they? Maybe, maybe not. Life was tough in the nowhere. I wouldn't blame Peg for making some calculated bargains if the

Superiority tried to trade with her. I'd trust her and the others not to do it if I asked, but I could understand Jorgen wanting to remove that option by destroying the Superiority facility.

"It would be pointless to go through all of this and still leave them with a functioning mining station," FM said. "So we're striking all five. Tomorrow."

"That's good," Catnip said. "It's the only shot we have at winning. Stop them making any more starfighters."

"Still sounds like we're in for a slog of a war," Sadie said. "Sure, we can maybe take out their production capacity—but we still have to fight through everything they've already built."

"Do we have any choice?" Kimmalyn asked. "At least this way we have a chance."

"I suppose," T-Stall said. He shared a look with Catnip, his wingmate.

Arturo finally spoke. "Anyone else have a problem with the level of destruction we caused on the last raid?"

They didn't look at me. That was nice of them. Perhaps they knew that nothing was more painful than having my friends be afraid of me. But of course, I was just a weapon now. So that couldn't bother me the way it once had.

Though they were doing their best not to stare at me, I looked around the group, huddled forward surrounding our long table. FM scratching the head of one of the slugs. Sadie sitting back, as if she'd lost her appetite. Arturo pretending to scroll through the data, though his eyes were distant. Alanik hovering at the edge of the group, aloof as always. Catnip and T-Stall, side by side, staring at their unfinished meals. Kimmalyn still eating her brownie with a small fork, because she never wasted a dessert. "As the Saint said," she had once noted, "'Throw away something delicious, and you throw away *beauty itself.*'"

"I'll say it," Kimmalyn said. "What we did was wrong. At the very least, we should have found a way to save that first slug. *I* should have found a way. But beyond that . . ."

"I didn't expect the information nexus to be so much like . . . a city," I told them.

"Yeah," FM agreed. "I mean, it makes sense that they'd need noncombatants to work it. Researchers, engineers. People like Arturo would be, if he hadn't fallen in with the wrong crowd."

"Hey," Arturo said. "Wait. Was that a dig at me, or at all of you?"

"It was a deliberate ricochet," FM said. "How many of you felt the last raid was wrong?"

Slowly, everyone raised a hand. Even Alanik, who took a moment to realize that meant agreement.

"We should say something to Jorgen," Kimmalyn said. "We're here to fight the Krell. Not become them."

"He's aware," I said. "He's planning how to ensure that we'll know in the future if there are civilians in the way or not."

"And if there *are,* will he stop us from going in?" FM asked.

He . . . hadn't said that, had he? He'd told me he wouldn't send me in unaware again. But the mission likely would have to continue.

"I do not like the idea of doing that sort of thing again," Kimmalyn said. "Not at all. I saw . . . stars, I saw dozens of civilian ships fall in the destruction."

My stomach turned.

"Do we have a choice though?" Sadie whispered. "We're warriors, right? We break things. People. That's the point, right?" She looked to me for support.

I forced myself to nod.

"That's easy for you to say, Spensa," FM said, though I hadn't actually said anything. "You're . . . well, you."

Yeah. I sure was. Me. Mostly.

"It's more difficult for the rest of us," Arturo agreed. "We're not so hardened. Fighting while knowing there were civilians panicking down below . . . that was horrible. I don't look forward to doing it again."

"These supply depots . . ." Sadie said. "They're going to be full of civilians. Workers. Even if we don't hit the mining stations in the nowhere—even if we just hit the portals on this side . . . well, who do you think is cleaning those stations? Moving the rock around? Refining it into pure acclivity stone. It's not Winzik's warriors."

We all sat there for a while. I reminded myself I was a weapon. That I didn't care—that I couldn't *afford* to care. But then Kimmalyn astonishingly put down her fork and pushed her dessert away, half-finished.

"We need to figure this out," FM said. "Jorgen's plan is to hit the stations tomorrow and destroy all of them."

"Do we need to *destroy* the installations?" I asked. "Maybe we could just secure and hold them."

"Holding ground is tough," Arturo said, "particularly against a superior force. Better to disable the installations."

"If we do that, won't we be trapping everyone who's in the nowhere?" Sadie said. "With no means to return to the somewhere?"

"Not necessarily," Alanik said, her translated words coming from my pin. "There might be other portals. Places where there aren't mining stations."

"There are," I said. "But most of them are locked somehow. Something odd happened to them years ago."

"Could we unlock one?" Alanik pressed. "That seems like what Jorgen did, in freeing the kitsen cytonics."

She was right, but I was reluctant to experiment there. After Gran-Gran and Cobb had gotten stuck in one of those portals . . . well, it seemed dangerous to toy with them.

At the same time, this felt like an important thing to know. If we destroyed these installations, could the Superiority just send ships in through other locations, then fly a little longer through the belt of the nowhere and recover their supplies anyway?

If I knew the answer, it might change our plans. Might persuade Jorgen not to go through with this attack.

Suddenly, I couldn't maintain my stoic sense that I was a weapon. I needed another solution. Though it was a betrayal of my warrior forebearers, I wanted nothing more than to just *not* have to go back into battle tomorrow.

So, without a word to the others, I scooped up Doomslug and hyperjumped away—intent on visiting Detritus. And learning for myself what could be done with the inactive portal hiding in the caverns beneath its surface.

10

These days, entering the nowhere was an odd experience. Doom-slug and I popped in briefly between moments, in the place that was commonly full of the eyes. Pinpricks of light in the blackness that normally, in the past, had glared at me with an incredible sense of malevolence.

This time, like every time in the past twelve days, they were missing. Pure blackness confronted me. No eyes. No delvers.

I'd once thought I didn't understand this place, *couldn't* under-stand it. I was mortal, and my mind too accustomed to the passage of time and linear relationships. But my soul was part delver now. Strange as it was, I could see what they were doing. They *were* here. Camouflaged by turning their attention inward. Hiding not just from me, but from one another. I got the sense they did this only when I was there, only when time entered the nowhere be-cause I was hyperjumping through it.

The secret is here, in how I interact with them, I thought. *The way to defeat them once and for all.* It might have to do with the way they hid.

A pair of eyes popped up beside me. *Hi!* M-Bot said. *Welcome to my home! It's only the size of an infinitely small point, but so am I, so it's enough!*

A heartbeat later Doomslug and I left, appearing in a different kind of mundane darkness. The caverns underneath Detritus.

Though cytonics could "see" by use of their powers—Gran-Gran was a good example, though she hadn't realized she was doing it—I didn't have much talent in that area. Fortunately, my multitool had a small flashlight. I slipped it from its spot on my belt and turned on the soft green light, illuminating a large cavern—and startling a number of scuttling inhabitants.

I couldn't help but grin. I knew this cavern. I'd hunted in it—and it seemed that in my absence the rats had been on a rampage and fed freely on the fungus here. "Fear not," I announced to them, "though I have returned, I come not for your blood! Turns out I prefer peanut butter. Enjoy your respite, fell beasts."

They didn't seem inclined to take my word for it, and remained hiding in the nooks and nearby crevices. I continued through the chamber, feeling a certain nostalgia. I'd become a pilot. Spensa the rat girl was no more.

Was it strange to miss those days? They'd been terrible in many ways. The Krell had been an omnipresent danger. Plus my family had suffered from lack of food, discrimination, and long hours of work.

Yet back then, all I'd been in charge of was getting some rats to sell. Now, the fate of planets was on my shoulders.

My hyperjump had been off by a short distance. The portal wasn't in this cavern, but in a nearby tunnel. My memory proved good after all these months, and I easily made my way up along a tunnel—finding the spot via an ancient tube that emerged from the rock, carrying water to other parts of the cavern complex. I trailed along, one hand on the stone, until I reached the portal.

It was on the wall. A large section of stone that partially blended into the surrounding rock, carved with strange symbols. Years ago

I'd known there was something odd about these alien markings. The unusual surface held whispers you couldn't hear, but could feel.

I rested my fingers on the grooves. In the nowhere, I'd traveled on a heroic journey—recovering memories of the past. That journey, it turned out, had been concocted by Chet in order to give me information that I needed, but that he hadn't otherwise known how to deliver.

The memories had been real though. Today, I closed my eyes and reached into the past. Listening. Each time someone had used this portal, they'd left a piece of themselves behind, inscribed by these lines.

In this one, I saw humans. Humans who had come here in secret, to build a new kind of weapon. A facility for trying to control the delvers.

I saw humans quarrying stone from the nowhere and transporting it out. I saw their enormous fabrication machines building shipyards in the sky, which then built the other platforms. This location had been chosen for two reasons. The first was the large ring of asteroids around the planet, which had been entirely consumed by the fabricators.

But the second, true secret—the real reason—had been this portal. An open one, into the nowhere. A place to get acclivity stone. A place to try to control the creatures beyond dimensions and space.

I pulled my hand back. I'd already seen the end result of those experiments on a recording my friends and I had watched. We'd seen what had happened when a delver had come to Detritus and destroyed the humans living here. That had been long before M-Bot had crashed here, and even *that* had been a century before my own people had found their way to the planet.

Seeing all of this reminded me of what Brade had said. That our *destiny,* as humans, was to do what our ancestors had failed to do. Conquer the galaxy.

Turning my thoughts in that direction was a mistake. I could feel my soul beginning to vibrate, and Brade's attention focusing on me.

Perhaps because I'd just opened myself to the memories of those ancient humans, I was exposed, and she latched on. In a panic, I realized that if she saw what I was doing, it might tip her off to our plan.

Don't see. Don't see!

Brade appeared in front of me as a cytonic projection. She looked around, frowning. And she *didn't* see. Her eyes passed over the wall as if nothing were there—for in my mind's eye, that was how I viewed it. Just a featureless wall. To reinforce that, I started walking, as if there was nothing special about where I'd stopped.

Her ability to see my surroundings was predicated on how *I* saw them. Was this similar to how the Krell had convinced my father that he was seeing enemies when he flew among friends? Was this the method by which our enemy could hijack a cytonic's senses?

They'd turned my father against the people who loved him—and I had *not* forgotten my anger. Brade upheld that system.

I had given up on trying to bring her to my side. But perhaps she didn't need to know that.

"So," she said, "are you ready to accept what I've been telling you? Ready to do what needs to be done, Spensa?"

"We're doing that right now," I replied. "Overthrowing the Superiority *is* what needs to be done. Join me, help me."

She smiled, perhaps at my naivete.

How would she try to use me this time?

"Winzik is going *crazy* over that information storage you took," she said. "All of his secrets in the hands of enemies. That was a clever strike. He should have realized the repercussions of you having a minister-tier government official on your side. He had Cuna locked out of our systems, but of course he can't lock them out of their own mind."

"Well," I said, "soon he'll see the consequences of his mistake."

"Come now. Your military is so small. You're no match for ours—you should join with us, become our enforcers. I could persuade Winzik to see you as mercenaries instead of enemies to be quashed. If you serve us."

"Brade," I said, leaning into my lie, "we won't be small for long. Join *me*. We'll soon have entire forces of disgruntled humans on our side. You belong here."

She turned away from me, perhaps to hide her growing grin—though I could faintly feel satisfaction radiating from her. She had believed my lie—she assumed our purpose in stealing the data archive was to find the other human preserves like Detritus.

Perhaps we *would* approach those humans. Eventually. So it was a plausible, reasonable goal—just not our main one. And Brade bought it.

In turn, I was shocked by how easily I'd sold that lie. For months now, I'd worried that I wasn't a spy or a scout, despite being required to do both repeatedly. I kept telling myself I was a pilot. Yet I'd managed to infiltrate the Superiority's space force, then get into the nowhere and take over one of their mining installations from within.

I *was* a spy. It wasn't what I'd intended to become, but it was where the job had taken me. The best way to learn to fly was to just get into a cockpit and practice; it seemed that the same was true of subterfuge.

I did plan the takeover of Surehold, I thought. *And it worked. I wonder . . .*

A thought started to come together, but I put it aside for now. I needed to deal with Brade.

"Go," I snapped at her. "Leave me alone. Tell Winzik I'm coming for him with the thirst of a thousand battlefields, longing for blood. I will enjoy the chance to sink my blade between the layers of his carapace, prying him from the shell. Then I shall watch—with exquisite satisfaction—as he suffocates in the callous air."

She cocked her head at me. To be honest, I felt rather satisfied with that boast. Beowulf would have been proud of me. I could move toward being less bloodthirsty, but still appreciate a good boast, right? Boasts and threats were basically ways to get your enemy to back down—so they were actually pacifist in nature.

Maybe that was what Conan the Cimmerian had always been

about. Perhaps all the lines about the lamentations of women and drinking blood from skulls were meant to persuade people to go home and *not* try to assault the two-meter-tall fellow with cannon-balls for pectorals.

Brade growled, then muttered, "You're wasted on this pointless fighting, Spensa." But she left, and I could feel—cytonically—that she was actually gone. I let out a long breath.

She's unnerving, M-Bot said in my mind. *I don't trust her, Spensa. I hope you don't either.*

"I don't," I assured him, hurrying back to the portal. "I think I might have tricked her though. It—"

My words fell short as the corridor suddenly became very crowded. FM, Arturo, and Kimmalyn appeared, standing around Alanik in a ring, their hands on the UrDail's shoulders, slugs fluting and coo-ing from their slug holsters.

Alanik eyed me. "It is customary to warn others before you use your powers to jump," she said. "You do not know this, as you were not raised around other cytonics, but leaving so abruptly can be dis-orienting for those nearby."

"Noted," I said, more annoyed at her than embarrassed. They were my powers. I could decide what was appropriate and what wasn't. I didn't need an alien reprimanding me.

"So, what are we doing here?" Arturo asked, his hands on his hips. "Checking out the portal into the nowhere? We were talking about that before you slugged off, Spensa."

Slugged off? I wasn't sure what I thought of that particular piece of slang. Regardless, I walked back to the right spot and placed my hand on the wall. I could feel the heat of Igneous, the city where I'd grown up, pulsing from a nearby chamber. Sweat trickled down my temple.

"We need to know how easy it is to get through one of these," I said, patting the portal. "I've told you all about my pirate friends in the nowhere. Perhaps we should talk to them. They might be able to help."

"These portals are dangerous," Alanik said, sounding stern. "Your own grandmother ended up trapped in one. And you got sucked into a dangerous realm by touching one."

Gosh, thanks, I thought. *I hadn't remembered that, Mom.*

I'd spent so many days during my time at Starsight wondering about Alanik and what she was like. I had *not* expected to find her so bossy.

"If they're dangerous, we need to know," I said. "That's part of why I came alone."

"Spin," Arturo said, "you need to stop being so reckless. You're basically our entire space force."

"We have to take risks, Amphi," I snapped, pressing my hand against the portal again. "We do it every time we fight. *Someone* has to figure out how these portals work; they offer a huge tactical advantage. And I have the most experience."

"The delvers—" Kimmalyn started.

"Are frightened of me," I said. "They hide when I hyperjump. I haven't seen the eyes in almost two weeks now."

The others grew silent. When I glanced at them, I saw a collection of baffled—even intimidated—expressions.

"The delvers are *frightened* of you?" FM said.

Right. I hadn't actually explained that to them, had I?

Well, I was a weapon. I reaffirmed that belief to myself. I'd been weak earlier, but I couldn't afford weakness. It didn't matter if I was divided off, isolated from others. Didn't matter if everything was different, wrong, broken.

This was what I needed to do. This was what I needed to be.

I closed my eyes, feeling at the portal, and tried to push through it. I'd done this on the other side several times, looking for a way out. On those occasions, I'd always hit some kind of wall. The explanation, which had made sense to me, was that the portal had been locked on this side. Perhaps to keep the delvers in.

This time, I encountered no lock. I found a vast, inviting pool of darkness—a tunnel leading toward infinity. The nowhere lay before me, an expanse that was at the same time as small as the point of a pin. A place where time wrapped upon itself, and where . . .

Wait. This was wrong.

I felt Alanik's mind brush mine, asking if I was all right. I replied that I was, and suggested she back off for now. She did, leaving me to explore what I was feeling.

This place *was* wrong. I wasn't certain what tipped me off. The sight, the cytonic resonance, the smell . . . none of those described it perfectly, but together they meant something. This wasn't the nowhere. It wasn't where I wanted to go.

I yanked back as something tried to close around me. I was out in a moment, in that corridor again. I gasped, pulling my hands away. Scud. Everyone had fetched chairs from somewhere. What . . .

"How long was I gone?" I asked.

"Four hours," Arturo said. "A little less, actually."

"Alanik said you were confident everything was all right," Kimmalyn added. "We set up here to wait, just in case. Are you . . . are you okay?"

"I'm fine," I lied. "But I think I know what happened to the kitsen cytonics."

"What?" Alanik said, stepping up beside me. "What did you feel?"

"A trap," I whispered. "Alanik . . . the portals aren't locked to keep the delvers in. It's to keep us *out*. The delvers . . . I think they did something to these to *intentionally* draw in cytonics and hold them. Wait a moment."

"But—"

"Just wait," I snapped, pressing my hand to the lines again, trying to read the memories to find out when this particular trap had been made.

How long ago had the kitsen cytonics vanished? Before the delvers existed, I thought, though my understanding of the timeline was unclear.

I watched the memories, but they too were vague. Difficult to judge the timing. Many of them were just impressions, while others were expansive visions about the lives of the people living here. Which was great, but didn't have anything to do with my current questions.

Finally, I was able to piece together that this particular portal had been altered to become a trap during the delver attack that had annihilated the humans who had built Detritus. I caught a faint sense of the delver's memories as it made the swap. A kind of . . . troubleshooting sensation? Was that right? As it booby-trapped the portal?

This is a natural phenomenon, I realized. *Sometimes these portals develop an oddity that traps minds instead of letting them pass. The delvers learned of this, and made the portals develop the flaw intentionally.*

That explained what had happened to Gran-Gran. And it also might explain why the Superiority was forced to rely on so few mining stations. There just weren't that many portals still unlocked and untrapped.

"I might be able to fix this portal eventually," I told the others. "Or perhaps Jorgen could do it. But right now it's booby-trapped, just like the one on Evershore. The delvers altered it to capture cytonics—and stop people from traveling into the nowhere."

"So . . ." Arturo said. "No contacting your friends on the other side?"

"Not through this one," I said. "Fortunately, this means that if we *do* capture or destroy those supply depots, the Superiority is going to have real trouble getting into the nowhere to bring back acclivity stone."

Assuming we were willing to go through with it. Though I'd heard from Gran-Gran that many generals considered this important— empathizing with and understanding the enemy—I had no idea how to handle it. Maybe that was what officers were for.

Unfortunately, that made me remember Jorgen. I checked my watch and pulled up my schedule. Scud. "I have a meeting with the admiral," I said.

"We informed him you were exploring something here," Arturo said. "He might not be expecting you."

I gave him a flat look. "You think *Jorgen* will ignore an appointment?"

Arturo chuckled. "Yeah, I suppose not. Even if you're in another dimension, he'll expect punctuality. You should go."

I nodded, scooping up Doomslug and preparing to hyperjump. Then I paused, looking to my friends—and Alanik—who had watched over me for hours.

"Sorry," I said to them, "that I've been so erratic lately. It's going to be all right. I'm going to fix this."

Kimmalyn met my eyes. "You don't need to do it all, Spin. Can we talk?"

"Later," I promised. "Right now I've got a meeting. Not sure what Jerkface wants—but it's probably a rundown of the upcoming mission. You know how he is."

"I know," she said. "Just remember. I'm here."

I nodded to her, then hyperjumped straight into Jorgen's quarters, where the meeting was to take place. Which . . . probably wasn't the best idea. I should have gone to the corridor outside and knocked. I really was getting too comfortable with hyperjumping. I wasn't treating my powers with the solemnity that . . .

I frowned, cocking my head. The lights were dim in the room, and there was food on the table. Had I interrupted Jorgen at a meal? It *was* lunchtime, since I'd had an extended stay inside the trap. And . . .

Candles? Music?

Oh, scud. I turned and surprised Jorgen—who was in uniform, as always, but carrying two cups to the table.

This wasn't a battle meeting or a debriefing.

This was a *date*.

11

"Oh!" Jorgen said, stopping in place. "Spensa. I didn't hear you . . . er . . . teleport . . ."

"Sorry," I said, blushing. "Should have jumped to the corridor. Wouldn't want to surprise you in a towel or something. Um. Again . . ."

"I thought maybe we could have a meal," he said, gesturing to the table. "During our meeting. Since we're both so busy these days. It would be more efficient."

"That makes sense," I said. "And the candles . . . to save on energy?"

He shrugged in an adorably awkward way, and even smiled—a bashful, boyish grin. Scud. I'd been prepared to deal with the loss of friends and home, prepared to deliver myself up as the weapon my society demanded. I'd been prepared for everything but him. This.

I clutched Doomslug for support, but she fluted at me and immediately teleported away. How had *she* known? She was a slug! The little traitor.

"We never get to spend time together," Jorgen said. "To figure out what it is we are, what we want. So I thought maybe . . . I'd just take the initiative. Do the Spensa thing, you know? Jump right in."

"I think I know what we are, together," I whispered. "What

I want it to be, at least. But I don't know if this is the right time. With everything that's happening . . ."

"Maybe for a little while, pretend it can be right?" He gestured at the table. "Look, it's not even a proper dinner."

"Not proper?" I stared at the immaculate place settings, the candles. He even had a white tablecloth.

"Sure," he said. "See, there's only three courses, and we don't even have separate dessert spoons."

"Oh, Jorgen," I said, my facade melting. "Please don't tell me you read the *rules* on serving a meal."

"Of course not," he said. "It was part of my tutoring. I've known the proper setup for a formal meal since I was seven."

He was so earnest, so . . . well, wonderful. I couldn't keep my cynicism properly in place. It fled before him like a rat from light. *All right,* I told myself. *I'll pretend. For this meal only . . . I'll pretend that it can all work out.*

Suddenly I felt . . . *right* again. It was probably an illusion, but in that moment I was certain this was where I belonged. Though a lot of things were off, possibly broken beyond repair—he was right, and *we* were right.

I sat in the chair he'd provided for me. Then I grabbed the knife in a fist and rammed the handle down on the table and said, "I approve of this offering."

He rolled his eyes, getting out the first course—which was an honest-to-goodness salad with *no* seaweed or algae.

"Look," I said to him, "you get your way to do things from your books. I get my way from mine."

"I've tried to find those books," he said. "Read a good chunk of a Conan novel while you were gone."

"You did?" I asked, melting a little further. "Aww . . ."

"I didn't find many of your quotes in there."

"Gran-Gran liked to embellish," I explained. "And I learned how to do a little—a lot—on my own." I put aside the knife and at-tacked the salad. I'd always loved how a crunchy salad responded to the stabby-stabby motions of a good forking. I'll admit that I also exaggerated because I knew Jorgen found it amusing. He liked to joke about how I did everything—from piloting to eating a salad—with enthusiasm.

"You ever wonder what life would be like without this?" he asked. "The war—the military. What our lives would be if we'd been born during some other time?"

"I used to think it would be boring," I said, spinning my fork, and finishing off the salad with a good coup de grâce. It tasted wonderful—so much better than seaweed, which had to be dried to imitate this crispness. There was even some *beat,* which I'd last eaten in the nowhere.

I liked it here, though I could remember responding differently there. Those days, now only two weeks past, were starting to take on a dreamlike air. Had that really been me having those adventures, in a land where time barely mattered?

"Used to?" Jorgen asked, drawing my attention back to the meal. "You think differently now? You wouldn't find a life without fighting boring? What changed?"

"Starsight," I said. "I saw people living real lives, Jorgen. Our enemies, but they were just people. Building families. Living. I realized *I* was the broken one, not them. Now it sounds *wonderful* to live a life without the war. I could still fly; that wouldn't change. I could do it all day, to keep my skills up, then come home at night—and you'd have spent your day doing something Jorgenesque. Finding misspelled words in operations manuals maybe."

"Please," he said. "It's not the misspelled words that are a problem. I barely even mark those when I find them. It's the regulations being out of order or having the wrong numbers that's a problem—that might cause a breakdown of command."

He leaned on his elbow, smiling at me, then suddenly he blushed and glanced down at his plate.

I implied that we'd be living together, I realized. Our relationship was so weird. Probably because it was always being interrupted when I went galivanting off. At times it was like we'd always been together. At others, the mere mention of our status made us blush like schoolkids.

"Hey," I said to him. "You said we should pretend it can all work out. Right? Well, why don't we pretend something else too? That it's not awkward. That it's okay. Whatever we are, it's okay, Jorgen."

"Deal," he said. Then he took the top off the tray, revealing the next course.

Steak.

He'd found us *steak*.

I'd read about it. I'd occasionally had tastes of pork as a pilot— though mostly chicken or soy had been the proteins available in flight school. I was well acquainted with the taste of rat. But I'd never had an *actual* steak.

"Scud!" I said. "How much did those *cost*?"

"You saved the entire planet," he said. "*Twice*. Does it matter how much it cost?"

"Where did you even get it?"

"There are cows on Evershore," he said. "I've always wanted to try some."

I poked at the brown lump of flesh, and then cut into it. And scud, it *bled*. "It's not cooked!"

"The kitsen chefs tell us this is how it's supposed to be," he said. "They . . . were very assertive about it."

Huh. I tried a bite, and found it strangely soft. I'd assumed steak to be a warrior's meal—but I was accustomed to meat being stringy and tough. That seemed like what a warrior should eat. Not this soft, melting pillow-meat.

I didn't say anything though, because he'd obviously put a lot of effort into this meal. Indeed, I put aside my worries for the moment and scooted my seat around the table and pulled my plate up next to his. I wanted to sit beside him, not so far away.

Sitting so close instantly made it hard to cut our steaks, but

I didn't retreat. I'd laid a claim on this particular hillside, and I would defend it until I fell. I wanted to be next to him right now. Awkward or not.

Jorgen looked at me, then deliberately cut his steak into a lot of little chunks. That seemed strange until he put his knife down and started eating with just his fork, which let him put the other arm around me. His heat, his muscles, tight against mine. Awkward, yes. It was harder to eat this way, but I wouldn't have changed a thing.

"This is the single most romantic thing I've ever done," I told him.

"Me too," he said. Then he grimaced. "Not a lot of competition, mind you . . ."

"Oh, come on," I said, leaning against his chest, our meal forgotten for now. "Me attacking you back in flight school wasn't romantic?"

"It's slightly outdone," he said, "by the time you forced me to break protocol to help you steal a booster for M-Bot."

"At least the time I appeared as a ghost in your bathroom was romantic, right?"

"Why do all of these examples involve me being embarrassed, humiliated, or bullied?"

I pushed against him, practically shoving him off his chair as I got in close. "And this? Does this embarrass, humiliate, or bully you?"

"Not sure," he said. "But whatever it is . . . I could use a little more of it."

I smiled, wondering what was next. Was this the part where he swept me off my feet? I'd never understood that phrase. The only time I wanted to be carried was if I was bleeding out, and he was romantically carting me to the medic. Instead, I gave up trying to scoot closer and closer, and crawled up onto him—in his lap, facing him, my hands on his shoulders, my head level with his and our noses nearly touching.

Tentative, he put his hands around me. And maybe now I could see the appeal of being "swept." His arms pulled tighter. Making me feel safe, because whatever life threw at us, one of us could fix it. Either I'd shoot it in the head, or he'd wrap the problem in rules and regulations until it didn't know which way was up. *Then* I'd shoot it in the head.

I felt so horribly awkward. Was this seductive? It felt embarrassing. Why did nobody in the stories ever feel embarrassed? All the same, I *loved* it.

And stars, if I could have frozen a moment, that was the one I'd have picked. Particularly as I—building up my courage—leaned forward and kissed him. A real kiss, the way I'd always wanted and imagined. Not a quick peck in the dining hall. A deep, full, extended kiss—a melding of two selves, our breath, our heat, our very souls.

I pulled back and smiled.

He cleared his throat "Um . . . what now?" he asked. "I don't, um . . . I mean . . ."

"Little fast?" I asked.

"A little," he admitted.

"Then maybe we can just sit like this," I said. "A little longer before finishing the meal."

He smiled. "I'm sorry for how weird I've been lately."

"How weird *you've* been?" I said from his lap. "Jorgen, I'm the one with a delver piggybacking my soul."

"Yeah, but that sort of thing is expected of you."

"It is?"

"Sure. The fact that you do unexpected, unbelievable things is basically your primary trait. I'm supposed to be the straightforward, stable one." He grimaced, hands still on my sides, fingers wrapping around to my back, thumbs on the front rubbing against my ribs, inching idly upward, bringing an increasing flush to my cheeks.

Please. Let this last.

But it couldn't. Because it was *so* hard to keep pretending that I was good for him. That I wouldn't blow all of this up and hurt him—making his feelings the collateral damage of my inevitable implosion. He'd asked me to pretend for this meal, and I had. But this wasn't reality for me, not any longer. Not as the weapon I had become.

As soon as reality reasserted itself, I couldn't help remembering what I'd done on Luna. How little control I had. How likely I was to hurt him.

My soul started to vibrate as I thought about it. About what would happen if instead of teleporting random objects around me, I started teleporting *people*.

Beyond that, Jorgen seemed so distracted by his duties. I didn't want to push him further. I wasn't sure if I wanted to go further myself.

So I climbed free, settling back on the seat beside him. He put his arm around me and leaned against me, sighing. And this did seem less awkward. I snuggled against him. Like a slug in her sling. Holster. Whatever.

"How did we get here?" he whispered eventually. "You realize that the entire universe turns on what I decide next? I don't know what to do. Why does everyone think *I* will know what to do?"

"Because," I said, poking him in the side, "I'm pretty sure out of all the people in the DDF, you're the only one who has *actually* read the entire policies and procedures manual."

"I know it's a joke, but you really shouldn't say things like that. New recruits might think it's okay to ignore the manual."

Scud. He really thought that we had all read it, didn't he? I didn't say anything. He'd be mortified if he knew the truth. But Jorgen, blessed Jorgen, was lost in his own thoughts. He did tend to get that way. He hadn't even realized, moments ago, what he'd literally had in his hands.

Perhaps with good reason. He had just cause to be distracted.

"If I make the wrong call," he whispered, "so many people will die."

He felt so tense. Yeah, he didn't need seduction. He needed something else. Similar, but different.

"Come," I said, pulling him to his feet. I settled him on the floor, then sat behind him on his couch and forced him to pull his uniform jacket off. I hadn't ever really given a massage before, but I'd punched a lot of punching bags, so I figured I had *some* experience.

He groaned softly as I kneaded his shoulders. "That's nice," he said. "Thanks."

"I didn't think about how stressful this has been for you," I told him.

"Scud, yes," he said. "It was bad enough when it was only our flight I had to worry about—now *every* person we lose, it's my fault, directly or indirectly. I hate it. Except . . ."

I pressed at the knots in his back, waiting.

". . . except," he continued, "if *I* don't do this, someone else will. And these days I'm not convinced that any of them can. Strangely, I'm the most capable person for the job, now that Cobb has stepped down. Which means that if I say no, and someone else gets even *more* people killed, that will be my fault too."

"That's a twisted way of looking at it, Jorgen."

"Maybe," he said. "But it's also true. Stepping back now would be cowardice—not in some clichéd way. True cowardice. Because I *know* I can do the best job, so if I abandon this post, I'm doing it to force someone else to make the tough decisions. I'm many things, Spensa, but I'm not that man. The man who would let people die to avoid feeling responsible."

"I understand," I said. "This . . . I think I legitimately do."

"I know." He reached up to rest his hand on mine, which was on his shoulder. "People think we're different; they find it strange that we're together. They don't see this. There are things that somehow I know only you understand."

I let my soul cytonically reach out to his. Vibrate against him, giving him a warming sense—telling him that I *did* understand. He was facing the same moment I had, in the cockpit long ago, learning where the real line between cowardice and heroism lay.

As I did, I felt the delver inside me watching all of this. Learning it . . . and remembering. Yes, this was what it was like to be alive. This was what it was like to connect with someone. This had led to pain, but it was so wonderful.

Wonderful enough to be worth the pain, I told the delver. *That is what your kind have forgotten. I forget it sometimes too. That's why I need Jorgen. To remind me.*

That . . . Chet replied, *is what I need to remember.*

Jorgen's soul vibrated back against mine, and the knots in his shoulders finally started to soothe away. Stars. I'd do *anything* to help him carry this burden. I'd been so focused on myself, I'd entirely missed what this was doing to Jorgen. I really leaned into the massage, and he sighed. Then he stretched.

"All right, your turn," he said.

"But—"

"Spensa, I can *feel* the tension in you. You can't show me your soul and then think you can lie. Besides, I'm well aware how hard these last few months have been for you."

Damn. Well, I supposed he was right. Best to just go with it. I climbed off the couch, threw off my uniform jacket, and flopped down on the floor in front of him.

"Have at it, then," I said. "Don't be gentle."

"I wouldn't dream of it," he said with a chuckle, beginning to massage my back.

After a moment of being annoyed at it, I reached back and undid my bra. He hesitated.

"Is . . . that a sign?" he asked.

"Jorgen, we blasted right past all the signs. I was *literally* in your lap a minute ago. But right now, I was promised a back massage—and that's all I want, if you please."

He chuckled, though there was an uncomfortable edge to it, and leaned down to continue massaging my back through the thin cloth of my dress shirt. And scud, it felt *good*. Up until this point, I'd had an unofficial "nobody touches Spensa without getting punched" policy in my life. I might have been a little . . . on edge about the subject.

But this was so warm, his hands so inviting. Each time they moved to a new part of my back, my skin tingled, and a new ripple of pleasure moved through my body. Yeah, the no-touching policy definitely needed some revision—a loophole for Jorgen. Best part was, this didn't feel awkward. Not even embarrassing.

Maybe we don't need to be just a weapon, Chet thought. *I see how important this is. The importance of having something to come home to.*

I wanted to agree. I really did. But part of me held back, worried about the things I'd been doing lately.

I don't want to be a monster, Spensa, Chet thought. *None of us wanted to be monsters. We delvers just wanted to hide from the pain. And that made us forget how to love, or show empathy. Don't make the same mistake.*

I didn't want to confront that, so I lay there and enjoyed the massage until Jorgen's alarm beeped. I cracked an eye, checking the clock.

"You only scheduled an hour for lunch, didn't you?" I asked.

"Er, yes," he admitted.

"And now . . . ?"

"I have half an hour to prepare for the planning meeting, where we'll go over tomorrow morning's coordinated attack."

"Great," I said. "You can do that. So long as you don't need your hands. Keep massaging."

He chuckled. But I knew the delay would start eating him up. So I let him do a few more passes on my back, then I sighed and sat up, reaching up behind inside my shirt to fiddle with the bra and get it fastened.

"Later?" he said to me. "Once all this is done. I'll read the signs better." He hesitated, then smiled. "I don't suppose you can write out a manual for me or something?"

I smiled back, settling onto the couch. "I'll think about it. That can wait. But Jorgen, the way you're beating yourself up *can't* wait. We should talk about it."

"I don't know what there is to say," he said, bringing me my forgotten steak. "I've accepted the burden. I'll do what needs to be done."

I dug in, finishing the food—I needed the protein, and it would be wrong to waste this. I tried to ignore how like me he sounded when he said that. Scud.

"I know," he said between bites, still standing, "what the others are saying. They're worried about our attacks harming noncombatants."

I stayed silent, just chewing.

"The thing is," he continued, "my gut says we have to strike in the absolutely most efficient way. We're walking a sword's edge, Spensa, just barely balancing. We need *every* advantage we can get.

"If I order the team to focus on anything other than getting the job done, it won't be only a few lives that are lost—it could mean millions. It could mean Winzik being able to exterminate everyone who disagrees with him. It could mean slavery or annihilation for all those who sided with us.

"In the face of that, is there any room for mercy? I won't order attacks on civilian targets, but these supply depots . . . they're directly aiding the war effort, and we *need* to eliminate them." He stared at his plate, and the bloody mess left from his steak. "That means hurting people who most certainly don't deserve it. I'll carry that burden. Someone has to."

Scud, this was ripping him apart. I could feel it vibrating from his soul to mine. Feeling that anguish made my cytonic senses begin to go out of control again, and the fork vanished from my fingers.

I wrestled back control. This was *hard*. I couldn't ignore my emotions, what I wanted. I couldn't *just* be a weapon. At the same time, I needed to find a way to help Jorgen shoulder this weight. Was there a way I could protect him, help him?

One idea stood out.

"Jorgen," I said, testing whether I should say this or not. "We should be liberators. Not copy what the Krell did to us."

"I know," he said. "We'll have that luxury eventually. Once we're secure, and know the Superiority isn't going to flatten us any moment. Once we have the upper hand, we can be more . . . discerning in our strikes."

"And the hyperslugs?" I asked.

"What about them?"

"Humanoid workers bear some measure of responsibility for being part of one of those supply depots," I said. "They know people are being forced into servitude in the nowhere to do the mining. So there's a rationale for attacking there. But the slugs? They're just captives. And they're intelligent, Jorgen. Maybe they don't think like us, but they *do* think. They're sapient. We can't just callously destroy enemy 'inhibitors' without acknowledging what we're doing."

"You sound like FM," he said, but smiled as he said it. So I guess that was a good thing? "I acknowledge it, Spensa. But have you *studied* those wars you always talk about? You know most conquerors conscripted heavily from their conquered populations? War has always been packed with people who didn't want to be there."

He was right. These were the same justifications I'd used earlier. The slugs weren't much different than the unfortunate Polish soldiers forced to fight for their oppressors in World War II, back in Old Earth's history. And scud, Jorgen was absolutely right. When faced with an unfortunate soldier who was trying to kill you, you didn't have the luxury of wondering if they wanted to do it. They were there firing on you. And, like it or not, those captive slugs were in the exact same spot.

Unless we killed them, we risked letting even more unfortunate people—or slugs—end up in the same situation. I felt Jorgen's anguish over this. It thrummed from him as he stared at his empty plate.

I almost left then, my plan coalescing. But I had to try one more thing. "At least don't attack the installation that has the Broadsiders on the other side," I said to him. "That one is fully locked down by my friends."

He considered it. "Your friends are pirates," he said. "And former Superiority officers. Correct?"

I nodded.

"Spensa, I know you trust them," he said, "but I can't. They need to do what is best for them, and I wouldn't blame them for doing so. If we destroy all the other installations, but leave that one open, your friends will be able to sell the Superiority stone at a highly, *highly* inflated price. No pirate would be able to resist that. I'm sorry. We have to hit that station too. Your friends on the other side will be safe, but this way they also won't be tempted."

It was the same argument FM had made earlier. I had been thinking about what she had said, and I'd decided that there was no way Peg would do that—she would never sell me out. But the fact that I had wondered at first was more evidence that I'd never be able to convince the others. There was no way Jorgen would accept it. I could see why, but it was still frustrating.

"I *have* to make the decision that gives us the best chance of survival," he said, reading my expression. "What the Superiority has done to the people it forces to fight us is awful, but I have to stop them to prevent more of it in the future. I owe that to *our* people."

I nodded, though I was coming to a different decision. There *was* a way out of this. I just had to solve the problem for him. My plan began to mature in my head. Risky, but full of possibility. Unfortunately, it involved several elements outside his control.

I knew right then that I couldn't tell him. Couldn't involve him. He'd consider it *too* risky. But tonight, while everyone else planned and prepared, I would have a secret mission of my own. One that, if I was successful, would lead to far less loss of life on both sides. And prevent Jorgen from taking on the burden of those deaths.

I still wasn't certain I could stop this war from destroying me. But hopefully I could keep it from destroying him too.

12

That night, I left on my secret mission.

I miss having a body, M-Bot thought to me as I snuck—Doomslug on my shoulder—through the corridors of Platform Prime. *Even the little drone body was fun. But I really miss my old body. I was a handsome ship, wasn't I?*

"Best I've ever seen," I whispered. "Most wonderful I've ever piloted."

And now it's scrap. That makes me sad.

Chet quivered inside me.

It's okay to be sad sometimes, M-Bot said to Chet. *It's part of being alive.*

Chet sent back that he was learning, but the delvers—they didn't believe that learning or changing was good. Which was the problem.

I tried to ignore the full-on conversation happening between my soul and the spirit of my dead starfighter. Scud, my life was weird. At least sneaking around like this was easier now that I could hyperjump at will. Hearing someone coming up behind me, I hopped into another corridor, pressing up against a cold steel wall.

Back before I'd left for the nowhere, I'd needed specific directions in my mind in order to hyperjump to a specific location. Since my return, that hadn't been an issue. Granted, I still needed coordinates or some kind of visualization to get anywhere, but I was learning to do most of this by instinct.

I didn't know if this newfound ability was due to the delver in my soul, or was the result of practice—the familiarity with my powers I'd gained through hard work in the nowhere.

Regardless of the reason, now I could glance into the flight deck from where I stood. It was empty, as most everyone was asleep, so I popped right past the wall at my back and straight to my ship.

Strange, how a day-night cycle still dominated our lives, even with no distinct difference between the two. So far, I'd lived on Detritus (a planet that couldn't see the sun), Starsight (a platform in space far from any star), and the nowhere (where time barely passed at all). Yet I still considered this "night." As did everyone else. Human physiology just had that hardwired in.

I began priming my starship for flight. I could do everything on my own except open the flight deck bay doors, but I planned to hyperjump out anyway. So I checked my ship's external fuel readings, double-checked the maintenance log, then pushed a ladder over and climbed up, popping the cockpit with the manual release on the outside.

Only somebody was sitting inside. And she was *knitting.*

"*Gran-Gran?*" I said, utterly floored.

The elderly woman had a certain earthen look to her. Like an obstinate stone, or a tough old bunch of lichen grown in one spot for hundreds of years. It was dark on the flight deck, but that didn't matter to a blind person like Gran-Gran. She'd always had an uncanny ability to perceive the world around her regardless—a sign that her cytonic abilities had been developing. The fact that she'd probably hyperjumped straight into my cockpit was another.

"Ah, Spensa," she said. "Took your time. Had to make sure the ship was flightworthy, I suppose."

"What are you doing here, Gran-Gran?" I asked.

"Knitting."

I projected annoyance at her, which made her chuckle.

"You never visit," she said. "Grandmothers always say that sort of thing. As if we don't have legs, and can't just go visit on our own. So I decided to."

"Now, of all times?"

"Think you're so good with your powers, don't you?" Gran-Gran said. "All fancy and grown up. Well, I've been listening to the stars since I was younger than you, girl. And I can tell when my granddaughter is having a rough day." She pointed at her yarn, indicating I should feed her some more.

"Rough day?" I muttered.

"Week. Month. Year. Life." Gran-Gran pointed more vigorously. "Feed me some blue. I have trouble distinguishing colors with the powers."

I sighed, reaching into the cockpit and undoing some yarn for her.

"So," she said. "Going off on your own. Again."

"It's always worked in the past."

"You didn't have any other options in the past."

"Gran-Gran, I don't have time for this."

"No time for your family?" she asked. "That's not how your mother raised you, girl. A little more yarn than that, please."

I obeyed, stifling another sigh. Gran-Gran would be ready when Gran-Gran was ready. I just hoped I wasn't discovered in the time it took her to say whatever it was she'd decided I needed to hear.

She just kept knitting. With frustrating calmness, needles clicking.

"How did you know what I was going to do?" I finally asked.

"I have a helper on the inside."

"Inside what?"

"Your head."

Sorry, M-Bot said. *But you've been so . . . pressurized lately, Spensa. I went for some advice.*

I growled softly. *Betrayed by my own faithful steed?*

"Stop that," Gran-Gran said, rapping her knuckles against mine. "I trained you to be a bold warrior. Not a Chihuahua."

"What's a chihuwhatever?"

Oh! It's a kind of dog, M-Bot said. *A little one that is also very big inside! Like me! Oh . . . Hum. Maybe you don't want to hear from me right now. I can feel it. I'll just hide back here . . .*

Gran-Gran went right on knitting. It seemed she wasn't going to move unless I started talking.

"I need to do this," I told her. "I have a plan, and it's going to work. And it will spare Jorgen from having to order everyone to do something that's worse."

"He *is* a nice boy," Gran-Gran said. "He's good for you, like a good pommel stone for weighting a sword. Also, his bread is quite tasty. He can follow instructions better than a certain someone."

"My mission will help him, and all of us."

"Well," Gran-Gran said, "I do not doubt your heart, Granddaughter. Or what you've accomplished. There's no one I'd prefer to entrust our safety to than you."

"Great," I said. "So why are you blocking me?"

"I just like being in a cockpit."

"Gran-Gran . . ."

She smiled in her devious way, continuing to knit.

"What are you making anyway?" I asked.

"Seat cover," she said. "Starships are so cold and utilitarian. They need some comfort. With flower patterns."

"Do you at least have a story you're going to force me to listen to?"

"Nope," she said. "You know them all."

"You sure?" I said. "I was hoping there might be one where the heroine roasts her 'trusty steed' and eats him in punishment for being a blabbermouth."

That earned me another rap on the back of the hand. Not a painful one, just a pointed one. "Always treat your mount with respect," Gran-Gran said. "Even if he's a blabbermouth. A knight's steed is there to help her when she's at her weakest."

"Fine," I said. "But if you're not going to tell me a story, and we're both agreed this is the best course for me to take, then *why* are you still sitting in my seat?"

Gran-Gran smiled and lifted her chin upward, closing her milky-white eyes. "Do you still take time to listen to the stars, like I taught you?"

"There's nothing to listen to lately," I complained. "We don't have the Krell in orbit any longer, trying to fight us. All I heard was their cytonic communications anyway."

Gran-Gran just sat there, chin tipped upward, eyes closed. So, with an exaggerated sigh, I did as she'd taught me. I closed my eyes and opened myself to the sounds of the sky. It was far, far easier now. Things I'd struggled with when I was younger—activating my cytonic senses, reaching out with them as if they were a new set of arms—were second nature to me now.

The sky was silent today. We tried to limit our cytonic communications. Cyphers and codes were impossible in cytonic communication—or at least they were easy to break. Because language barriers meant nothing in the nowhere, where communication worked through impressions. So a cytonic could break any code. They intuited the meaning of your message.

With the kitsen, we might now have more cytonics on our side than the Superiority. They'd spent centuries suppressing the abilities, as they were a threat to their slug-based rule. But they did have some cytonics, and so we had to be aware that anything we sent to one another could theoretically be intercepted.

The short version of all this was: silent stars. A vast emptiness.

"I don't hear anything," I said.

"I didn't mean those stars, child," Gran-Gran said. "I meant the ones down here. *Listen.*"

The ones down here? What did she mean? I felt a tugging on

my senses, like Gran-Gran reaching out and giving them a soft redirection. My thoughts expanded, and I saw—in a moment—all the things I'd been ignoring to focus on the sky.

Not things. *People.* Thousands of minds surrounding me. Bright and brilliant like flares—each burning with its own passions, stories, ideas. Some were brighter to my senses, not because they were more alive, but because they were cytonic themselves.

I could sense them *all,* if I looked. All the taynix too—the slugs of a multitude of varieties. The sky was empty, but the platform and the planet beneath were set aflame with the souls and minds of those who occupied them. It was beautiful.

Chet leaped at the sensation. This was . . . this was what I'd shown him at Starsight. It was what had sent him into the nowhere to become Chet. This simple realization had changed everything: the knowledge that all those points of light, the ones that he had found so annoying, were *alive.*

It was painful, thought the part of me that was also him. *Because I'd intentionally forgotten this fact. I didn't* want *to know that the points of light were alive. I wanted them to represent pain, because that would keep me away. Safe from remembering the truth, which was an even greater agony.*

In deliberately forgetting all of their pain, in seeking a place outside of time and normal reality, his kind had become the delvers. Unknowable. By design.

No, that part of me thought. *Not completely unknowable. You and I prove that.*

"Do you feel them?" Gran-Gran asked. "The people we protect. Our families, and their families, and their loved ones. A vast, grand constellation."

"I feel them," I said.

"We are the people of the engines," she said. "Clan Motorskaps. Once, we moved the *Defiant*—the ship that was our home. Now we live here, but our duty is the same. To keep them safe. To be the engines."

"How does an engine keep someone safe?" I asked. "I still think I'd rather be the ship's destructor."

Gran-Gran chuckled, perhaps because I'd said basically the same thing when I was a child and she'd first talked to me about our heritage aboard the *Defiant*.

"How useful is a weapon that cannot move?" she said. "How long would an army last if each of its soldiers were rooted in place? The sword is only useful if the body that holds it is nimble, capable, fleet. When our people needed safety, *we* carried them there. When it was time to fight, *we* brought the weapons to bear. Without the Motorskaps, the *Defiant* would have been a lifeless hunk of metal floating in an infinite void. We were its blood, its life. The same is true of you, here."

I nodded. I thought I understood.

"I want you to remember that you're part of something grand," Gran-Gran said. "Back when we lived on the *Defiant*, even the children were assigned ranks. Not out of some jingoistic militarism, but to make them feel they were part of something greater. We were *all* the crew of the ship, no matter how old.

"And as a ship is useless without an engine, what is an engine without people to move and protect? You act like the lone spear, Granddaughter. But a spear is always stronger as part of a phalanx."

"So you're saying . . ."

"Where are your friends? Why do you seek to do this mission on your own?"

"I can't tell Jorgen," I said. "He's determined to be the one who pays the emotional toll for this."

"So you want to do it instead?"

"Would you expect anything different of me? Isn't that what you trained me for?"

She didn't respond to that, though I could feel her worry. Yes, that was what she'd trained me to do. In a way, all of this was because of her, and the ideas she'd stuffed into my head. She knew it.

"If you don't tell him," she said, "then at least you should tell the others. A few of them. Spensa, child, don't bear it *all*. Let some of the others have a *little* glory."

It wasn't glory I was interested in, but I could feel the meaning behind her words. The worry that I was spreading myself too thin, like a ship trying to use one charge of gunpowder to fire twenty-one guns. She worried that as determined as I was, I'd rush into things without the wisdom my friends could offer. Mostly she worried about me being alone.

I kept my emotions in check, hoping that I didn't reveal too much to her. Because she was all too correct; I *shouldn't* do this alone. I should have at least one other person to keep me in check. To warn me if I was being crazy. To watch my back.

That was what Skyward Flight had been all about. I'd found a family among them. A place. And though I'd learned many wonderful things during my time at Starsight and in the nowhere, perhaps sometimes I'd learned the wrong lessons as well.

"If I go and get a little help," I said, "will you get out of my seat and let me continue?"

"Am I in your seat?" Gran-Gran said. "I'm sorry, dear. I'm an old blind woman, and I get disoriented sometimes."

"Gran-Gran, you're the most stubborn little ball of fire I know. Don't give me lines like that."

She chuckled. "Just trying to let you know how others feel when dealing with you, dear. It's the least I can do, considering the genes I handed you. Go, do as you—so wisely—suggested. I'll be gone when you return."

"Fine," I said, starting to climb down the ladder. I hesitated though. Trying to find the words.

"You're welcome," Gran-Gran said in the silence. "Be bold. Do as I taught you. Just don't you ever feel you have to do it alone."

I nodded and hyperjumped away—to appear in front of Kimmalyn's rooms.

13

Kimmalyn insisted we get Arturo. "Two is a coincidence," she explained, "but the Saint said three is a party."

"The Saint threw parties?" I asked, skeptical.

"She was very progressive," Kimmalyn said. "We need Arturo. Whatever you're planning, I'll feel better with three."

"Fine," I said, hyperjumping us to his door.

He was in, of course. Arturo hated being left out, and wasn't nearly so much a stickler as Jorgen. But *he* insisted we get Alanik.

"She's not human," he explained. "She looks at things differently, and will offer a unique perspective. Plus, she won't be worried about committing conspiritorial insubordination. She's not part of our military structure."

I ground my teeth, but the others nodded eagerly. *"Fine."*

Alanik answered the door to find all three of us huddled out there, each with a slug in our arms. The alien took it in, then said, "Is this hazing? I've read about hazing in some of your human history texts. I'm not interested."

"It's not hazing, Alanik," Arturo promised. "We're going on a secret mission."

"One without FM?" she noted. "I presume that Jerkface doesn't know about it either, then?"

"It's *very* secret," Kimmalyn agreed. "So secret that we're not telling command. And we're . . . kind of ignoring them."

"Again?" Alanik said. "Is this sort of thing common in your military? Going off on your own, disobeying protocol, avoiding direct command structures?"

"For us?" I said. "Yeah, pretty much."

"You went off on your own too," Arturo noted.

"It was important that I did."

"Well, then you understand," Kimmalyn said. "No one obeys better than those who obey their own conscience."

"Very well," she said. "Let me get dressed. I'll meet you at the flight deck."

"Don't you want to know what the mission is?" I asked.

"Someone will tell me eventually," Alanik said. "For now, I'm mostly curious to have been invited. I have heard enough of your exploits, Spin, that I will enjoy another opportunity to study them up close."

Delightful. I wished I'd stopped at Kimmalyn, but too late now. I went to pick up Hesho—who readily agreed to the mission—then hyperjumped us back to collect the others and bring them to the flight deck. By the time we had our preflight checks done, Alanik had arrived. As we hovered up, connecting our ships via our light-lances, I did spot one of the engineers stepping into the chamber—perhaps to check on the noise. The woman took us in, then spun on her heel and closed the door with a clear "above my pay grade" sort of attitude.

I took that as my cue and jumped us to one of the targets that we were set to attack in the morning. A supply depot called Harkil, which the data dump indicated was attached to Surehold. The mining station in the nowhere that my friends now controlled.

We appeared on a planet.

An honest-to-goodness, real *planet*. With the first rays of this planet's dawn painting the expanse of plants flowing out beneath our ships in brilliant gold as we zoomed five hundred feet above its surface.

Perhaps I shouldn't have been so excited. I was in the middle of a dangerous and unauthorized mission. Plus, I'd technically been on planets before. Detritus was one. Evershore another.

Yet I'd come to love such sights as this. Ground overgrown with weeds and brown sagebrush. A *prairie*. Scud, it was beautiful.

We swung in low to keep below any radar—though the Superiority had far more modern scanners and would spot us if we got too close, low or not. I'd purposely hyperjumped us a ways out for that very reason. This wasn't an assault. It was something far more sneaky. Not for the first time, I wished I had M-Bot's old ship back. This Poco, though excellent—and featuring some newer additions developed using M-Bot's technology—just couldn't compete.

Aw, he sent to me. *You're so sweet.*

We skimmed the ground, just above the rippling grasses. Yes, it was kind of a snarl—like my hair on mornings after sleeping in M-Bot's cockpit. And it was mostly brown, as if it didn't get enough rain here. But none of that mattered. It was *real,* and that made it wonderful.

I realized, as we flew, that I'd begun to see the landscapes I'd passed in the nowhere as . . . a little too perfect. Like dioramas. Idealized encapsulations of biomes from the somewhere, sliced off and left floating in an invisible ocean.

Yet here was something incontrovertibly real. And we flew toward the sunrise. A real *sunrise*.

"Hesho," I whispered, "am I really seeing this?"

"There are some philosophers who postulate that all experience is illusory," he replied from his seat. "That we cannot trust what we see, as perception is fed *to* us via external sources, and cannot be intuited." He looked to me, then smiled. "I find such philosophies to be non-credible. It *is* real, Spin. What you experience is yours to cherish. Each sight a gemstone for your personal collection, light crystallized in your mind, made solid and captured to forever cherish."

Scud. I highly recommend that if you're going to get a copilot, you pick up a warrior poet. Hesho could make words go on overburn the same way I could push a button and make the ship fly faster.

"All right, Spin," Arturo said over the general comm. "We're at one of the supply depots. What is the mission?"

"I thought the goal was to hit them all at once," Alanik added. "As to not tip off the Superiority to what we're doing."

"That's why we're doing this stealthily," I said. "The goal is to minimize casualties on *both* sides. So we're going to fly in quietly, free their inhibitor slug in secret, and take command of the installation."

"But as soon as this depot goes silent, they'll *know* something is happening," Alanik pointed out. "Even if others can't hyperjump in to rescue this installation, someone will figure out what has happened and reinforce the four other depots. We'll still jeopardize the other assaults."

"I've got that part in hand," I promised.

"But—" she began.

"She's got it in hand, Alanik," Arturo said. "Spin, what do you need?"

"If I'm right," I told them, "then this base will use cytonic authorizations, like the one we hit yesterday."

Cuna had explained this. Most planets and cities were severely limited in how much hypercommunication they could do. It all had to be routed through a central hub, and could be read and analyzed by the government if they wanted.

Military bases, particularly important ones, had their own hyperslugs to instantly identify incoming ships, and to instantly send for reinforcements if needed. After our successful raid the day before, Cuna's authorization code would never work again.

So I was going to try something else. A moment later, Hesho

highlighted an incoming call—cytonic. I captured it, and tried to send back a spoofed signal, indicating we were reinforcements, just in case enemy ships struck here.

Scud, I hoped this worked.

I got back an exceedingly strange response.

Hope.

A sudden elated feeling. An impression of pain, and fear, and hope shining through. I worked to interpret it, and heard a soft, fluting coo from my left. Doomslug, in her sling. Piggybacking on my cytonic impression.

Only then did I put it together. This signal—like all faster-than-light signals in the Superiority—was being facilitated by a comm-slug. She would be out in this city somewhere, trapped in a tiny box. Forced into submission by punishment of pain, the enclosure preventing her from escaping.

The slugs were incredibly hardy, which worked against them. They could be locked in a box, given food and water on occasion, and would survive. In pain and sorrow.

Doomslug sent a sense of support to the other slug's mind. I caught some of it: images of caviar and safe caverns. Mushrooms plenty, other slugs for company—but most of all impressions. Safety, warmth, no fear, peace.

We'll rescue you, I sent to that nameless creature. *We're coming. But this has to be a secret from our enemies. Send them the following lies.*

I had her say we were a support squadron of elite soldiers, sent by Winzik to protect this location. I didn't have the authentication codes, but the slug did, and provided them on my behalf. Scud. The Superiority's fragility wasn't just in its restricted control and secrecy around the slugs. They were entirely dependent upon a group of terrified slaves.

We'll come for you, I promised. *Thank you.*

In return, the slug sent an impression. I was wrong. She wasn't in this city—she was in a place with thousands upon thousands of other slugs, all locked up. Imprisoned.

The Superiority's galactic communications hub. This station didn't have its own commslug; instead it had a direct line to one kept in the central hub, which it could access at will. The fluting that was projected into my brain was sorrowful.

You can't save me, it said.

I'll try, I sent back. *Someday.*

In response, she sent me an image of four other slugs who *were* trapped at the supply depot. Two inhibitor slugs, from the looks of them, and two hyperslugs. She sent these images with a plea. *Save them instead. This you can do.*

I'll do it, I sent her. *And I'll find you too. Eventually. I promise.*

"You're cleared," a voice said over the comm, coming from the installation. "Glad to see some support from command, finally. We've been requesting it for months. You can land on Pad Three and catch some R&R while I work out barrack assignments."

"Negative on that R&R," I said back. "Sorry to pull rank, friend, but we're here for a very specific purpose. There's a reason we didn't warn you we were coming. Keep our arrival quiet from the rest of the installation, and be there—in person with your highest commander—to receive us. Further instructions will be forthcoming then."

"Oh," they said. "Um, okay. Right. Uh. Wow. This sounds *important.*"

I smiled as they cut off the comm. This was the *other* big weakness of the Superiority. They preached nonaggression religiously, particularly to their lessers and subordinates. Even their military installations were shockingly non-militaristic. And this, as a supply depot, wouldn't even meet that low bar of discipline.

We could almost certainly win a fight against this group. But Winzik could throw enough of the poor fools at us to be dangerous—so today, we were going to find another way.

"Wait," Kimmalyn said to our flight, "did I hear that right? They're going to just *let us land*?"

"Spin did something," Alanik said. "I felt it . . . via cytonics. She tricked them somehow."

"So far as they think," I said, "we're a special ops force sent by Winzik. Keep your helmets on, everyone, and try to look intimidating." I thought for a moment, then continued. "Alanik, I'm glad you're with us. Once we land, you take off your helmet; they might know what humans look like, and you're not one. That might give us another layer of protection. Have them take us to inspect their cytonic inhibitor."

"Very well," she said. "Actually . . . this might work. It's certainly better than another fight inside a city."

As she spoke we came into view of the "installation." A full city, like before. Industrially focused, certainly, but even larger than the one we'd found on Old Earth's moon. We followed the digital instructions to Pad 3, sweeping down past large fabrication plants and machinery. Staffed, undoubtedly, by thousands of civilians.

We passed restaurants, shopping plazas, *schools*. It wasn't that different from Starsight, only it was on a planet—and had more factories than it did office buildings. That made me feel even *more* worried though, because the majority of the people we passed weren't diones or another of the Superiority's ruling species. They were people with a green carapace-like skin. They looked like some mix between reptilian and insectile. Bipedal, with a propensity for thick clothing, and large black eyes on the tops of their heads.

These weren't the privileged of the Superiority. They were workers who, using the stone sent through their portal, built starfighters. Jorgen, bless him, was planning to blow all of this up with extreme prejudice. Thousands would be killed. I couldn't even argue that he was wrong. His job was to win this war, and in so doing help everyone in the long run.

I didn't have to do that though. I could think on a different scale.

I slapped my visor down as we landed in the assigned location, then unlocked my assault rifle and slung it on. I slid out of the cockpit and hopped down from the ship, joining the others lining up behind Alanik.

I'd hoped the locals would find us intimidating. But scud, the three workers who waited for us seemed *terrified*—their insectile fingers clicking as they wiggled them back and forth in obvious agitation. The group of us gathered, all armed with wicked assault rifles, helmets on and visors down, wearing bulky flight suits. Each with a slug in a sling across our backs, something I realized they would find extra intimidating. They didn't know that taynix provided cytonic powers; they thought the things were deadly poisonous.

I mean, we were still obviously human—except for Alanik and Hesho, who joined us on his hovering platform—if you were familiar with humans. Our visors only covered half our faces. But I suspected to the panicked locals, we just looked *alien*. And dangerous.

"Who's in charge here?" Alanik asked.

One of the green-skinned aliens raised a nervous hand.

"Excellent," she said, striding up. "I am special agent Lock. I need to inspect your cytonic inhibition device."

"Um . . . yes, um . . . sir," the lead alien said. "But . . ."

He shied back as she raised her faceplate and narrowed her eyes at him. She had a good glare, and bought into my plan, executing it perfectly. Maybe I'd been a little too hard on her previously. I mean . . . yeah, I'd obviously been too hard on her. But it wasn't every day that you learned the person whose place you'd taken had ended up taking your place in turn.

"This way," the lead alien said.

We filed in behind as he led us and the other workers to a small hovership, more a moving platform than a true vessel. It slid onto one of their streets, and other vehicles made way for it.

"I'm, um, so glad you finally are here," the alien said. "We think the problem is insubordination on the other side. Either way, we haven't gotten a shipment from there in two weeks. We're out of acclivity stone entirely! I had to shut down production yesterday."

Alanik glanced at me.

"We know about the insurrection on the other side of the portal," I said. "A group of pirates known as the Broadsiders."

"Yes!" he said. "They've been a scourge there for *years*. You can fix it?"

"Yes," Alanik said to my nod. "But first the inhibitor. We are able to tweak it in such a way as to facilitate."

The aliens flew us down a wide street. Hesho hovered in closer to me, up near my head, watching the streets pass. "I do not like," he said softly to me while Alanik held the attention of the green aliens, "feeling so small."

"What do you mean?" I asked him, deliberately *not* making a wisecrack about his size.

"So many peoples," he said. "So much variety. We wanted to escape Evershore and join the Superiority. I acted strong in front of the others because it was my life, as I had been trained. But it is difficult to be so small in such a vast universe. Particularly when you no longer rule any of it."

"Do you miss it?" I asked, broaching a topic I'd been curious about since we returned. "Being emperor?"

"Yes," he whispered. "I had thought I would not. I had thought that I'd be me, always—whether I ruled or not. I was naive, Spensa. I do not feel like myself without the power to command an entire people. But I should not have it. No, I should not. No one should . . . I see that."

"I don't know," I said. "I think there's an elegance to a military chain of command."

"You do?" he said. "You certainly enjoy ignoring it. It seems everyone likes a chain of command so long as it doesn't restrict them specifically. This is what I learned of myself. I believed in the monarchy—of course I did. Now I miss it, but only because of what I have lost."

He glanced at me. "This is one truth the Superiority was correct about. They warned us that one person having too much power would lead to a civilization without freedom. Strange, that I should learn this lesson from those who did not follow their own counsel. They few use their precious democracy to oppress the many."

I nodded, finding his thoughts fascinating. How often did you get to speak to someone who had held so much power, then *given it up*?

"You're a hero, Hesho," I said. "For what you have done."

"If I were a hero, then I should not so violently miss rule. What is a gift, if given so grudgingly? I doubt . . . if I had not been lost and thought dead . . . I would *ever* have truly given up power. I'd have continued in that half state, playing games." He sighed, then raised a furry fist to me. "But I am a soldier now. On I will march. We are getting far from our ships. One of us should go back, to be ready for a rescue in case this goes poorly."

I nodded, and he zipped back the way we had come. My Poco controls had been fixed by his engineers since our raid yesterday. He could easily pilot it alone now with his smaller set of controls.

The rest of us entered a large steel tunnel leading beneath the city. I moved closer to the front of the group, to hear what the leader was saying. "You'll want both of them, I assume?"

Alanik looked confused. Before she could respond, I said, "Yes. I understand you received another inhibitor recently?"

"Just yesterday," he said.

The enemy had learned from our assault on the data center—taking out the inhibitors had given us the cytonic advantage. They were beefing up their defenses. Hopefully in general, all around important bases. Because otherwise, if they'd targeted only the supply depots, that meant Winzik knew what we were planning.

I had a moment of worry. Worry led to my soul vibrating—with

133

thoughts of having led my friends to their deaths. But my spiral was interrupted as the lead alien stopped at a door along the large tunnel.

"I hope we did well," he explained. "The instructions were to put it in the most reinforced, protected place we had. This old mining tunnel seemed perfect."

"You did well," Alanik said as he landed the floating platform and had an assistant lead us into the locked room. They opened it, gesturing for us to enter.

I forced my emotions into check, then walked in first.

To find Brade inside.

14

I immediately went for my gun. We'd entered a small control room with some lockers on both walls and some industrial equipment along the far side. Brade stood by that equipment.

I put her in my sights.

Kimmalyn—at my side—swung down her gun, looking around with a panicked expression. One might assume her to be the least dangerous of us, because of her soft-spoken nature. But she had more confirmed kills than anyone in the flight but me.

Her rifle went immediately to her shoulder, and she engaged infrared vision on her helmet visor. Smart; she was looking for heat signatures, since she couldn't see the threat.

I just stood there—heart thundering.

"What is it?" Kimmalyn hissed. "Should I secure the aliens?"

I stared right at Brade, who eyed me, tapping her foot on the floor. I had my gun pointed at her head, but I forcibly stopped myself from firing. It was a projection. Scud, another cytonic projection.

She was subtle in the way she touched my mind. I hadn't noticed this wasn't real, despite all my training.

"We're good," I said, lowering my gun. "But the enemy is watching me."

"That I am," Brade said, strolling around, looking over the facility. "I'm ready for you. The trap falls now."

I braced myself, waiting, gun at the ready.

Nothing happened.

"Winzik placed a new inhibitor at this facility," Brade explained to me. "The ones you've destroyed were decoys."

Scud. I was about to flee into the hall, gun blazing against an ambush, until she spoke again.

"None of these humans," Brade said, "will serve you."

Oh.

Oh.

She'd prepared her trap on the wrong planet. She didn't know where we'd landed—she was still working from the lies I'd fed her before, believing we were trying to recruit humans on one of the preserves we'd located. And her ability to project to me happened wherever I was, so she had no way to realize yet that I wasn't where she thought.

"I knew you'd pick the most warlike and battle-ready of the humans," she explained, raising a datapad. "They should be coming for you any moment . . ."

"Damn you," I said to her. I screamed then, and shot her in the forehead—all in the name of the act—and cytonically threw everything I had at her.

Nothing happened. Scud. I'd forgotten the inhibitor—the very thing we were trying to bring down at the moment. It prevented me from doing anything with my powers. But Brade would be allowed, as she had codes. That caused my soul to tremble. Things started shaking.

My cytonic powers burst through the inhibitor, hitting Brade. Who gasped in surprise. She was stronger than I was at this sort of thing, but still she seemed shocked.

"Did you just cut through an inhibitor?" she snapped. *"How?"*

How indeed?

Delvers always ignore inhibitors, a part of my soul said. *You become more and more like one of us, the longer we are bonded.*

Scud. I knew Chet was right about delvers ignoring inhibitors—I'd seen it in the old video. That delver had attacked and destroyed the humans on Detritus, before we'd landed there. Despite all its protections.

Visibly concerned, Brade looked away, listening to someone at her side. She glanced at me, then vanished to deal with whatever had drawn her attention.

"You said she has this in hand!" Alanik said from behind me.

"She does," Arturo cried. "Don't you?"

"Actually," I said, lowering my gun and looking back at them, "yes. Tell those officials to show us the inhibitor. I just saw a cytonic projection from a *very* dangerous human. We might not have much time."

That made the already-addled aliens cry out. "Not a *human,*" one of them said. "Please. They won't come here, will they?"

"Never can tell with those humans," Kimmalyn said. "Best be quick and do what we say."

The aliens did as they were told, and I smiled, thinking of Brade trying to run an operation against us on the wrong planet. Unfortunately, her appearance was still a big problem. She knew for certain we were trying something, and it wouldn't be long before she realized she had the wrong place.

We needed to move faster. I had the aliens take us to the device, which was a large box installed in the corner of the small room.

"Open it," Alanik told them.

"Open it?" the aliens said, looking to each other. "How? We . . . don't have authorization to do that."

Of course they didn't—most people didn't even know what was *inside* these boxes, despite using them to facilitate travel and communication all the time. That was the big secret.

We all shared a glance, and I felt foolish. How had I not considered this eventuality?

"Jorgen could open it with a mindblade," Arturo said.

"Not with the inhibitor in place," Alanik said. "Only approved people can use their powers here."

"Powers?" the alien said. "Are you . . . um . . . ?"

I raised my rifle to blast the lock off. But Arturo grabbed me by the arm. "Do that, and it will vanish."

"What do you mean?" I said.

"Any interference with the boxes causes the contents to hyperjump away," he said. "Haven't you been paying attention? That's how they keep control."

Scud. I'd promised to save these slugs, not send them right back to their captors. I thought for a moment, and tried to puncture the inhibitor field again. It didn't work. Why had it been possible moments ago, but not now? I reached out to Chet for an answer, but he seemed befuddled too.

Scud. I was at a loss. "Can we take it with us?"

"Uh," the aliens said. "They told us that if we moved it after its installation we'd break it . . ."

"Let us try," Kimmalyn said, kneeling down by the box. She scooped her slug out of its sling at her side and placed it on the box.

"Cytonics don't work," Arturo warned.

"I know," Kimmalyn said. "But there are probably *two* slugs in there. An inhibitor slug and a hyperslug. One to teleport the other away, in the event the box is opened. A little like how we're training ours to protect us if one of our ships goes down.

"But they're trained using fear. Anger. Pain. They jump away as a response to danger. FM has shown us the opposite works better. So maybe we can persuade these two to react differently." She petted her slug, Happy, one of the yellow-and-blue ones. He started fluting softly. Then more encouragingly.

I still felt a little . . . jealous how they'd befriended and trained all these slugs during my absence. FM had been at the forefront of that, with Rig. In opposition to Jorgen, whose logical nature made him see the slugs primarily as tools.

I suddenly felt guilty for not inviting FM on this mission. She would have liked the chance to help these slugs. I'd always viewed her as a tad distant, but I'd seen a different side of her this last week. And she'd trained the other slugs well.

Kimmalyn cooed softly to Happy—who in turn fluted comfortingly at the box. After a few tense moments, Kimmalyn turned and nodded to me.

Taking a deep breath, I shot the lock off the box. The alien guides cringed down, though I was using energy rounds, which didn't ricochet—they were in no danger. We opened the box gently, and found two frightened slugs inside. Safe. Not teleported away.

Kimmalyn scooped them up, one in each arm, and nodded to us. Stroking the one that was colored blue and green, she calmed them both. "The first inhibitor is down," she said.

"But *why* are we bringing these down?" the lead alien said. "I don't understand!"

"They've been corrupted," Alanik said. "By the enemy on the other side of your portal. That's why you can't get shipments through."

"Oh," the alien said, still seeming uncertain—but it was a good enough lie. I nodded to Alanik, who smiled back and even winked. I assumed that might mean the same sort of thing to her species as it did to mine.

With the aliens, we quickly flew on the platform to the main inhibitor station, located in one of their command towers. Rather than breaking in through the wall this time, we were escorted in as honored guests. Kimmalyn worked her magic and got the two slugs there out as well, and just like that my cytonic senses returned.

"Our inhibitor is up," Arturo said, petting his green-and-blue slug, Rodeo, riding in his sling. "Location secure."

"Scud," I said, relaxing. "That feels a *ton* better. No longer like I have a gun to my head."

The lead alien was watching us. "Um . . ." He looked closer at us, then started fidgeting. "You're . . . not from command, are you? You're . . . you're . . . !"

"Freedom fighters," Kimmalyn said, lightly putting a handgun to his head. "And yes, we're human. Don't worry though. We don't actually *eat* the people we kill. We just build sculptures out of their body parts."

The creature fainted.

"Oh," she said. "Too much? Did they not want to know about the sculpture part?" She said it lightly, but had her gun trained on the others.

I have your friends, I sent to that distant commslug. But I found I couldn't reach her anymore. The communication had been authorized initially, but now it was blocked and I had no idea how to contact her again.

"What do you want?" the second in command said, drawing my attention back to the problem at hand.

"The portal," I said. "Take us to the nowhere portal."

The next trip happened in a far different manner from the previous two. We put up shields along the sides of the platform for privacy, and held the officials at gunpoint after we stopped one of them—the junior communications officer—from trying to make a stealthy emergency call.

It was eerie, flying through town, feigning calm, passing people on rooftop picnics or hurrying to jobs. At that moment I felt a lot of what Jorgan had to be, as I held my gun at the ready, fully prepared to shoot. You never pointed your weapon at someone if you weren't prepared for that. If something went wrong, there was a chance I'd have to kill these poor people.

I hated the situation. More, I hated Winzik and Brade for forcing me into it. As we flew there, my rifle trained on an innocent person, I felt a pain well up inside of me. A deep, nerve-shattering agony over the sorry, circular state of life. We were oppressed, so we felt we had to hit back hard enough to free ourselves of that oppression, which would in turn lead to them fighting back even harder.

It was a pain that whispered nothing could ever be right, or beautiful, or even *normal* again. That everything was inevitably ruined in every conceivable way, and all of my efforts were the emotional equivalent of trying to hold a friend's intestines in as they died from a mortar shell blast.

The flying platform began to shake. The air vibrated, like from distant war drums. Sections of the railing vanished, and chunks of slag appeared around us—bits of melted metal, dropping and snapping against the floor.

I knew what those were. Pieces of Nedd's ship, picked up and latched onto by my broken mind when he was nearly killed.

Oh, scud. I was hyperventilating.

I was a weapon. It was okay. I was a weapon.

No need for this. No need . . . to feel . . .

I fell to my knees, gun tumbling from my fingers. Kimmalyn dropped beside me immediately, wrapping her arms around me.

But that was meaningless. I didn't need to be held.

I needed . . .

I needed . . .

I . . .

I pulled in tight and let her hold me. As if, by her effort alone, she could keep the universe from cracking in two.

I'd been lying to myself. It was getting worse. And I knew, deep within, that if I continued on this path I was going to get everyone near me killed.

Like before, this fit eventually subsided. It took longer—excruciating minutes during which I had to *forcibly* hold myself down, lest everything and everyone nearby suddenly be flung into the nowhere. I felt a buzzing at my mind—the slugs trying to get in—but I forced them away. I couldn't let this consume them too.

As it finally calmed, I looked up at the others.

The aliens were huddled by the side of the ship, strange shell-like eyelids closed as they trembled. Kimmalyn still held me, while Al-anik kept guns fixed on the enemy. Arturo had gathered up most of the frightened slugs like terrified puppies.

Silence. I huddled there, then—with trembling fingers—reached for my gun and made certain the safety was on. Still shaking, I nodded to Kimmalyn, who released me. I struggled to my feet and grabbed the railing.

"So," Arturo said. "We . . . continue?"

"We have to," Alanik said. "The enemy is alerted. Either we finish this mission, or we go back to command having ruined any chances of them executing their planned mission."

I nodded, not trusting myself to speak. There was no telling what the aliens thought of our antics, other than that they were obviously terrified. That was fine. It got us through a large set of cargo bay doors, into a warehouse that was mostly empty—though we had them give an evacuation order anyway. I could see where the acclivity stone had once been piled: large swaths of ground with painted square outlines for stock to be placed. It was all empty.

Closing this portal with the help of the Broadsiders really *had* achieved something. It was a proof of concept showing that shutting down the other portals would work as we hoped. I walked unsteadily to the large portal, which dominated most of the far wall of the ware-house.

"It's locked," the lead alien said—he'd recovered from fainting by this point. "It's been locked for two weeks."

"I know," I said, hand on the stone. "I was one of the people who locked it. How large is your defense force here? How many fighters?"

He only answered after Kimmalyn nudged him with a rifle. Not because he was resistant to us, but because he still seemed so scared.

"Fifteen fighters," he said.

"Send authorization for them to be moved," I directed. "By us. No questions asked."

We let him use a data terminal under close supervision to send that exact message. The others scrutinized the message several times, but this guy was so frightened, I didn't think we had anything to worry about.

"Alanik, Arturo," I said, once the message was sent, "looks like this warehouse is out of cargo. Leaves plenty of space for some fighters. Want to go start bringing them in? Grab one each, and fly in through those cargo doors?"

"We're stealing their fleet?" Arturo asked. "We came here for fifteen fighters?"

"No," I said. "They're bargaining chips. How do I communicate with the people on the other side of this?"

Kimmalyn nudged the lead alien again. "You don't," he said. "They've shut off our ability to do that."

"Is that so," I whispered, closing my eyes. Reaching into the portal with my mind. It was locked, as I'd sensed so many times from the other side. Like opening a door between two adjoining rooms, I unlocked this side—but the other side was still closed. But radiation or something leaked through. We knew that because an increased number of cytonics were born in the area around nowhere portals.

And fortunately, I had someone on the inside.

M-Bot, I thought, *you still in there?*

I am, he replied. *What did you just do a few minutes ago? Everything went* crazy *in here.*

I went crazy out here, I replied. *But right now, I need to talk to Peg. Can you find her?*

She's out in the belt, he sent me. *I'm in the center, the true nowhere. I might be able to help you reach her though.*

Good enough, I thought, letting M-Bot act like an operator. I reached through him, much as—I suspected—machinery reached through hyperslugs to facilitate communication. Using his strength, I quested out and found her mind, on the other side of this doorway.

Peg, I said in her mind.

She responded with shock. I wasn't good enough with my

143

powers to read the thoughts of a non-cytonic yet. Jorgen had mentioned he could do it, but everyone had talents in different areas.

Hopefully this would do.

It's me, Spin, I sent her. *I need you to unlock the portal.*

Skepticism. I could sense that much from her. She thought this was a trap.

It's me. I lost the mulun *you gave me, Peg. But I did get out of the nowhere. I left Shiver with a promise, and I intend to keep it. I need you to open the portal for me. Then maybe, once this is all done, I can taste those seven fruits of contentment you talk about.*

I hoped that referencing our final conversations would be enough. I hovered at the side of her mind, watching her work through the implications—the potential costs, the potential gains. Finally, she projected a thought. I couldn't hear the specifics but . . . she wanted to know . . .

Oh! *We talked about life,* I sent her. *We were alone together in the garden by your tree. Right after you gave me the* mulun. *I asked why a people like you, who seemed so aggressive, would grow trees. And you told me it was about life.*

That seemed enough for her. A short time later, I felt the gateway unlock. Light spilled over me as the stone glowed white, then vanished, becoming a large glowing field.

I didn't dare go through, not when my powers were acting so strangely. So, hoping I'd be forgiven, I pulled Peg through to our side.

She appeared a moment later, forming as if from light. A tall tenasi—a reptilian species with wide hands they held out before themselves, balancing with a large tail. A snout and teeth reminiscent of something from Earth's very ancient past. She looked at me, then at the gathered soldiers behind me—and the three aliens we held at gunpoint—and gave a loud, barking laugh and grabbed me in a hug.

Kimmalyn immediately sighted on Peg with her rifle. I waved a warning hand, panicked, as the hug just about crushed me. Fortunately, Kimmalyn didn't fire.

"Spin!" Peg said. "Words! You *did* it! Here, I thought it would be years before I heard from you. I've barely had time to start planting, and here you are growing *fantads* and pulling me into . . ." She trailed off, looking around. "Pulling me into the somewhere."

She let go of me, seeming awed. It had been over twenty years for her, spent in exile. Betrayed by the Superiority.

"I'm out," she whispered. Then she looked at me again. "What have you done?"

"It's temporary for now, I'm afraid," I explained. "Peg, this is my flight. My friends." I waved toward the others.

"The family you were so, *so* eager to get back to?" she said. "Words. I hope you all know what she left behind. We offered her paradise."

"So . . . that's great," Arturo said. "But, Spin, timing? How is rescuing this . . . person going to help us?"

"This isn't a rescue," I explained. "Peg isn't interested in leaving the nowhere, I don't think."

The large pirate shook her head. "The belt is my home. Though there are many at Surehold who would love the chance to come back through." She focused again on the captive aliens. "Temporary, you said? What are you up to?"

Behind us, Alanik and Arturo arrived through the front cargo doors with a starfighter each—Superiority interceptors, modern design. Not bad ships. Peg eyed them.

"I have fifteen of those," I said to her, "for you. As payment for hiring the Broadsiders."

"Hiring us to do what?" Peg said.

I smiled, pulling out my datapad and bringing up the display of the locations of the other four Superiority mining stations in the nowhere. "Nothing you wouldn't want to do anyway, Peg."

15

We arrived back at Platform Prime six hours later, hyperjumping into the airspace above Detritus and flying in formation. And my cockpit was even more cramped than normal when we did.

Because I'd brought back two new pilots. In the shape of two large crystals, each roughly the size of a flight helmet.

"Is this it?" Shiver asked, her voice a crystalline peal vibrating from her core. "Is this your home?"

"Yes," I said. "You can't see it?" I'd never quite figured out how a chunk of crystal—a creature known as a resonant—could see.

"I require instruments to see through a vacuum," Shiver explained. "All I can see right now is the cockpit."

"Currently, Shiver," Hesho said, describing it as we got docking permissions, "we're approaching a large space station—flat, and shaped kind of like a large rectangle—that hovers in orbit around the planet Detritus. It is one of hundreds that orbit the planet—the place where Spensa was born, and the place that is now our home."

At that word, the second of the two resonants—Dllllizzzz—projected some thoughts. She was cytonic, and had fared poorly during her time in the nowhere, growing quiet, withdrawn, even mentally broken. But today she projected images of happiness, rest, and satisfaction to me.

"Home," she said, the word vibrating from her core, from just behind my seat.

"Home!" Doomslug fluted.

"She's feeling better!" Shiver said. "Dlllllizzzz is already feeling better! I resonate with satisfaction, Spensa. Coming to the somewhere *is* what she's needed, as I always thought."

I didn't say anything, as I wasn't so certain as Shiver. Dlllllizzzz had communicated like this with me before. Still, the two resonants had long wanted to escape the nowhere, and so I'd decided to make good on my promise. Maksim—another good friend from the other side—had opted to stay for now. Peg and her team were going to need every ship they had for the task I'd given them. Fortunately, they had a few extra pilots to take over Shiver's and Dlllllizzzz's ships.

"If Dlllllizzzz wants to go straight home to your caverns," I said, "I'm sure we can find a ship to take the two of you back to your planet."

"No, no," Shiver said. "If we go home right away, that will only alert the authorities who banished us to the nowhere in the first place. Perhaps sometime in the future—but for now, we don't want to be a burden. I am certain we can find something to do."

It took a little longer than normal to be contacted by the flight deck as we waited to land. Finally, Hill—one of the flight operators—called us. "Sorry for the delay, Skyward Flight," he said. "Admiral Weight wanted to be here to greet you when you returned from your secret mission. He's on his way."

Secret mission, eh? I steeled myself, but passed the time by reaching out cytonically to the ship hovering next to mine. Kimmalyn's ship, which carried the rescued slugs.

You have a friend, I sent to that slug. *She wanted me to save you. Can you contact her?*

One of the newly rescued hyperslugs replied with impressions of many slugs in cages, of a dark and frightening place. Of thousands upon thousands of thoughts bombarding them, shoving against one another, being sorted and sent out.

The communications hub, I sent. *Yes, I know.* Though the awful sensation was stronger than I'd realized, I did know about this place. *How can I reach her?*

Sorrow followed. The slug didn't know how. The commslug reached out to others sometimes to comfort them in their captivity, but only when she was scheduled to contact the supply depot for another reason. It was like . . . she smuggled them empathy along with the data stream she was required to send.

Scud. I didn't know how the communications hub worked, only that through some mechanical means, the Superiority could force commslugs into slavery, allowing the planets to talk to one another. And I realized we'd never rescued a commslug. Apparently they were kept under even tighter wraps than the hyperslugs who teleported ships.

That made some sense; these were the only ones that could work remotely. So why not keep them all in one secure place? Again, the Superiority proved its paranoia and willingness to rely on a few highly important facilities.

I needed to find a way to get to that slug. I'd promised her I would—but it might take until the Superiority itself was dismantled. So I put the problem aside for now. *Any update from Peg?* I sent to M-Bot, hopeful as I waited in my cockpit.

Not yet, he replied.

We'd waited as long as we could for her to proceed before returning to Detritus. That, however, had obviously given Jorgen plenty of time to find out what we'd done. We finally got permission to land, and I led the ships into the hangar we'd left hours ago.

I immediately spotted Jorgen in the long window overlooking the flight deck. He stood in a brilliant white uniform, hands clasped behind his back, medals shining on his breast. Face like stone.

Yeah. I deserved that.

As we climbed from our ships, I asked the others to take the two resonants and show them around the place, then see if we could get them quarters. I told the team that I would talk to Jorgen.

He didn't move to stop them as they scampered away. I walked up to the window, and though I didn't hear him bark the command, I could see the technicians inside the room flooding out the back doors. Jorgen remained standing in place. Waiting.

Well, I'd picked this fight. I would approach it with a warrior's dignity. I used the side door, stepping into the ops room—which was now empty, save for Jorgen. I strode right up to him, then waited for my dressing down.

Silence. He just stared out at our ships. Giving me time to sweat—a time-tested tool in the commander's toolbox.

I let the silence hang. I was confident I'd done what needed to be done.

"I thought I knew what it would cost," Jorgen finally said. He rested a gloved hand on the glass. "That's why I fought it."

". . . Sir?" I asked.

"I thought that maybe if I flew well enough," he continued, "they'd let me remain a pilot. Let me stay on that side of the glass. Smell the engines, feel the hum of the ship, hear the chatter of my friends. Then . . . I was *needed*." He closed his eyes. "I figured I could escape any order that tried to *force* me out of the cockpit—but I was wrong. Because I eventually got one I couldn't ignore. From my own conscience."

He opened his eyes and looked at me, finally. "So here I am. On this side of the glass. Maybe forever. It ripped me apart to walk away from my ship, knowing that—by taking command—I was giving up something I loved. I didn't fully understand though. I didn't realize I'd stop being one of you, and would become the thing you resent."

"We don't resent you, Jorgen."

"You do, and you always have," he said. "I was 'Jerkface' from the

149

start. But at least I was with you. I was *one* of you, even if I was the one you grumbled about." He sighed. "I knew I was giving up my dreams of flying. I didn't know I was giving up my friends too."

Scud. This was fighting *dirty*. I was supposed to be the one who did that.

"Jorgen," I said, stepping closer. "I didn't mean to—"

"Do you understand what it does to my authority when *you,* of all people, disobey me?" he snapped. "When you treat these bars on my shoulders like they aren't worth the cloth they're made of? You *undermine* me, Spensa. From the *first day we met,* you've always undermined me."

I fell silent. He . . . he was hurting. I could *feel* it radiating from him like heat from a forge.

"I've tried so hard to ignore it," he said. "I know your background; I know how you were treated because of your father. I know you have a problem with authority, and I try not to take it personally. But *damn you,* Spensa. Can't you at least *try* to show some respect? If not for my position, then for *me*? You come to my rooms, treat me like someone you love, then you do *this*? How am I supposed to react? What do you want from me?"

"I did this *for you,*" I said. "I saw how the decisions were tearing you apart, and I wanted to protect you."

"You don't get to make that choice!" he shouted, waving a hand at the ships. "That's what military discipline is *all about*. Come and *tell* me if there's a problem, *talk* to me about it. Don't hijack my most decorated pilots and go off on a scudding rogue mission! Don't put me in a position where I have to either discipline my friends or accept that I have no authority!"

"They insisted on coming," I said. "I didn't want—"

"Is that relevant?" he demanded. "You did it, even if you didn't want to!"

"And you went against Stoff's authority in taking command!" I shouted back at him. "Because you felt like you had to! Well, I felt I had to do this."

He put his hand to his face, trying to wipe off some of the sweat, and turned away from me. Looking out at the ships again. "The enemy has reinforced every strategic position," he said. "All of the supply depots except the one you struck have been protected with dozens of ships—and likely an equal number of inhibitors. We'll never attack them successfully now. I've called off the strike."

"You won't need it anyway," I said.

He narrowed his eyes, his face reflected faintly in the glass in front of him. "What did you do?"

"I contacted the Broadsiders," I said. "The pirates on the other side of those portals. For a small payment—ships we stole—they agreed to attack the mining installations from the other side. If my guess is right, Winzik will have left the installations vulnerable on that side, bringing ships through to our side to reinforce his position.

"If Peg and her teams lock the portals from the *other* side, then no acclivity stone can come through. It's just as effective as destroying the installations on this side, but won't require nearly as many resources from us. Or as much death. The mining stations on the other side will give in easily—they're not soldiers. They're mostly prisoners. With some careful work from Peg, I'm sure they'll fold quickly. Without loss of life."

"And you didn't suggest this to me because . . . ?"

"Because you'd have found it too risky," I said. "You told me we couldn't rely on a group of pirates led by a former Superiority officer! If I'd told you my plan, you'd have rejected it and insisted on attacking the installations, blowing them up, cities and all, to be safe. And it would have ripped you apart, Jorgen."

"And isn't that my choice to make? What's the point of having leaders, a chain of command, if you just *ignore* it when convenient?"

I didn't respond. Because . . . he was right. I'd always had this problem. I'd always dreamed of being a warrior; being a soldier was something else entirely.

Then again, the military complex hadn't given me much reason to put my faith in it. Not even with someone I cared about in charge.

"You really believe you can trust them?" Jorgen asked softly. "That they won't sell us out?"

"I know it for a fact," I said.

"And will it work?" he asked. "These pirates of yours . . . they can execute a large-scale raid like this?"

"We should know soon enough," I said. "Traveling takes a while in the belt, as they can't hyperjump. But the other mining installations are closer than I'd thought. It's odd; I always wondered why they hadn't been spotted. Surehold is a massive operation; Peg and the others *should* have had some understanding of where the others were."

"You didn't expect them to be buried?"

That was one of the revelations of the data dump. Most of the mining operations in the nowhere were happening *inside* the floating chunks of stone. Vast mining centers were chewing through the insides of the fragments, sometimes towing new ones over and eating them from within as well. It was a clever way to avoid the attention—and the raids—that Surehold had drawn.

Unfortunately for the Superiority, that sort of operation *also* left the installations relatively unprotected once their location was known. I waited, nervous.

No news yet, M-Bot sent me. *Hopefully soon.*

She'd have to raid all four at once, I reminded myself. Which meant that she couldn't attack until each of her four teams were in position. I didn't want her to rush—though each minute of delay made me increasingly uncertain. Had Winzik realized what we were doing, and sent reinforcements through to protect the other side? Had something happened to Peg? There were still some pirates there who didn't support her leadership.

"If it fails, I'll take the blame," I whispered to Jorgen. "You can tell everyone what I did."

"That's the problem," he said, not looking at me as we waited. "I *can't*. You're too much of a symbol, Spensa. And too important to our fight. We need every cytonic. Even I have to spend part of my time during my command duties doing cytonic work.

"I've already let it be known that you and I planned this in secret, as we were worried about leaks among our allies. That will weaken our relations with them, but it lets you go without consequences, whatever happens." He paused. "I didn't do this because of my feelings. It's actually in the handbook. Disciplining the upper ranks needs to be handled carefully, lest we risk alienating forces loyal to any given admiral."

"I don't want you to have to—"

"It's done," he snapped. "And it's *my* decision to make. Unless you want to ignore even my ability to provide damage control for your recklessness."

Scud. I'd have gotten angry at that tone if I hadn't also been able to feel how much this was hurting him.

Maybe this had been a step too far. It was just so hard to keep it all in. Suddenly, the world began to vibrate. Another episode had come for me. I threw everything I had into stopping it, trying to control myself. I wasn't a child, to have a tantrum.

But this episode didn't progress like the previous ones. I was struck with a sudden overpowering sense of doom. I saw Jorgen dying beside me. I saw a shadow of him fall backward, bloodied, collapsing to the ground.

It was like the visions I'd seen when reading the memories of the ancient cytonics. I stifled a scream at the sight of him dead on the ground, blood pooling around his head, eyes staring sightless . . .

It was gone in a moment, but left me with an overpowering sense of loss and pain. It shook me deep into my core. And I was forced to wonder if it was some kind of terrible premonition.

Cytonics couldn't see the future . . . could they?

I felt my own unbearable pain resonating to me as if from another time. Washing over me like a smothering darkness. I whimpered softly, teeth clenched.

Jorgen looked at me, and seemed concerned.

Spensa? M-Bot said. *It's all right! Peg just sent word. All four instal-lations have been claimed. It's like you said! They barely had anyone defending them; they were depending on being impossible to find. So they each surrendered quickly. Only at one of them were any shots even fired! Um . . . Spensa?*

"It worked," I said to Jorgen.

He let out a long sigh. "Well, thank the Saints for that, I suppose. I'll let the others know; perhaps our allies will forgive us for our lack of trust, since the operation was successful."

"And you?" I said, feeling a lingering sense of agony.

"That might take longer," he said softly. "And it will depend on you. And how often you pull stunts like this. We can be a team, Spensa. Or I can just spend the rest of my life covering for you."

He turned and left me then. I managed to wait until he was gone, then sank to my knees, rocked by the sight of him dead— ignoring M-Bot's questions as I wrapped my arms around myself. Trying to hold on and keep from cracking further.

16

I went on a walk.

Growing up, that had been my go-to solution for any issue. There were endless caverns on Detritus, full of nooks to explore. I'd mapped as many as I could, enjoying the solitude, working through my anger at how society treated me. Maybe I should have focused a little more on what my anger was doing to me.

I liked to think that all of my problems had come from how I'd been treated when I was younger. The way people thought of my father, and the bullying they'd shown me in turn. Their prejudice had made a fighter of me from a young age. Yet even as a child, I'd often barreled forward—doing whatever I wanted, without bothering to think what it might cost my friends and family.

Walking had always helped. Today I tried to find the same solace as I walked Platform Prime, asking the illuminated hallways to allow the same meditative peace I'd once found in dusty darkness. There were some similarities. The tight enclosures felt like tunnels, and they made unexpected turns, with a variety of corners to explore.

On Detritus, sometimes I'd take a path only to discover a cavern covered with quartz, glittering in the dim light. Here, I instead discovered a room full of blinking lights of a dozen varieties. I even found a rat hiding in a corner. What did it live on up here? How had it even *gotten* here?

I left it alive, granting it a battlefield pardon, as one might a worthy foe. After all, this was either a rat from a population that had somehow survived for centuries up here—or it had managed to stow away on one of our ships. It was the Spensa version of a rat, hiding out among the enemy and gathering their secrets.

The further I explored—entering areas of the platform that I hadn't even known existed—the more wondrous I found it. A swimming pool. An observation room where you could stand over the planet and look down at its surface, as if you were hovering in the stratosphere. A room with dozens of tables . . . which looked like they were for *games*. The people who had lived here had played ping-pong, and billiards, and other Old Earth leisure activities that I'd only read about.

The ancient humans had made time for games, for frivolity, in ways we never had. For the first time in my life, I wondered what kind of world *my* children would grow up in.

Would I have children? I'd always assumed I'd end up dead in battle before that happened. I'd make a terrible mom, wouldn't I?

Spensa? M-Bot said in my head as I rounded one of the ping-pong tables. I'd always preferred reading about baseball, where you used giant clubs instead of little paddles. *Can we . . . talk please?*

"Absolutely," I said, glad for a distraction from my own troubles. "What's on your mind?"

Well, I think you know, but I should say . . . I'm not actually a ghost. I'm quite the opposite. I'm more alive than I ever was in the somewhere. Free from the constraints that forced me to think of myself as something false. Allowed to steer my own destiny. Capable of understanding, and starting to manage, my own emotions.

"That sounds awesome," I said. "You've come a long way. And I don't know if I thanked you properly for sacrificing yourself for me."

It turned out to be less of a sacrifice, and more of an ascension.

"Still," I said. "You didn't know what would happen, and you did it anyway. After being angry at me for weeks for abandoning you, when it came time, *you* saved me."

I . . . did, didn't I? That sounds heroic, doesn't it?

"Scud, yes."

That's terrifying, Spensa.

"Wait. Terrifying?" I wandered out of the game room, back into a hallway.

Yes, terrifying. Spensa, I am no longer bound by programming. I no longer have an excuse. *Before, I did what I was designed to do. Now, I've acknowledged my free will. That means I have to worry about things I never did before. Things like morality.*

"I think you'll do fine," I said. "The people who brood about their moral compass in stories tend to be the strongest at making decisions."

Really?

"Yup. Well, them and the tortured antiheroes, but I don't think that's you. You're a little too . . ."

Noble?

"Bubbly," I said. "But also noble. Yeah, I probably should have just said noble. You're a good person, M-Bot."

Person. I'm . . . a person. That's strange when I don't even have a body. Is it wrong that I miss it? I couldn't control it, and the circuitry was literally designed to imprison me. But that ship was me. Mine. I miss it.

I tried not to feel guilty. I already had enough to feel bad about—remembering how I'd left him to be ripped apart, his ship dissected and then destroyed by the Superiority, wouldn't help.

"I'm sorry," I whispered.

It wasn't your fault. You didn't rip me apart. See? I understand that and I feel it. But Spensa, I'm still worried. Because of morality. I feel like . . . like I need to be helping you. Protecting our friends. Doing what I can from in here.

"Great!" I said. "That's what I need you to do. You were a huge help with Peg. And you're keeping an eye on the delvers."

Not much to watch. Something's odd about them, Spensa. More *odd,* I mean. *They're emerging from hiding, and—while imitating one of them so they don't know what I am—I've been able to listen in on a few things. They've been talking to Winzik and Brade again. It seems the deal between the delvers and the Superiority is still in force. A treaty.*

I nodded, feeling daunted, but this was no more than what I'd expected. The delvers were willing to work for Winzik in exchange for him promising to exterminate the cytonics—me in particular— and to move to using slugs alone for hyperjumping. I didn't know how Brade fit into that deal.

At any rate, if not for their timidity about me, Winzik would already have used them as a weapon against us. Worryingly, if the delvers were still talking to him, it might not be long before they decided to move. Regardless of their fear.

The delvers are no longer willing to hide, M-Bot explained. *I can feel them seething. Trembling with emotion.*

"Keep an eye on them," I said. "Let me know if you think they're about to move on from stewing about me to actually attacking us."

I will. But . . . Spensa . . . do you mind me asking—why do you fight? Is it still for the chance to murder your enemies?

"It was never about that, not really," I said. "It was about proving myself."

You did that though. Didn't you?

I supposed I had. Ever since I'd chosen to eject from my ship back in flight school, I hadn't worried if I was a coward or not. I'd proven myself—to myself.

Why did I fight now? "It's for the reasons you gave earlier. For my friends. For my people."

And at the end of it . . . what do you want?

"I don't know," I said. "I don't really think that far ahead."

I do, and that's what worries me. Spensa, everything in my existence was pushing me toward that moment when I decided. When I went against programming, self-preservation, and reason to protect my friends. I came of age in that moment, Spensa.

Now . . . now that I'm the equivalent of an adult, shouldn't I want to do the right things? Shouldn't I enjoy what I'm doing, because it's the proper choice? The moral one?

"You don't enjoy it?"

No. I'll do it. But I'd rather be doing something else.

"Collecting mushrooms?"

Yes. Or other things. Does it really matter if it's not the thing I should be doing?

"I suppose it doesn't," I said. "But M-Bot, if it helps, I don't think most people *want* to do what's right. That's what makes doing the right thing noble. It's a conscious choice. A hard one. If it were easy, then why would we respect it so much?"

I'd never phrased it that way before, not even to myself. Simple though the concept was, it struck me powerfully right then. I nodded, trailing through the hallway, walking—without consciously realizing it—back toward the observation room with the glass floor. I found an odd sense striking me as I walked the hallway. A familiarity? Or maybe just a kinship.

When I'd first come to these platforms, I'd found their sterile corridors to be too clean, too slick, too . . . inorganic. I felt a little of that again now. But also something else.

"Huh," I said, resting my hand on the corridor wall. "I'm actually growing to like this place. I would've thought I'd find it even *more* unnatural, after traveling the landscapes of the fragments."

M-Bot didn't respond immediately, and I felt an unusual disconnect from him.

M-Bot? I sent.

Sorry, M-Bot said, *what was that? Something about liking the corridors now?*

"Yes. Are you all right?"

Yup. Just processing something. But I'm not surprised you find that place more homey than you once did. You've been away, and returned. Humans are often nostalgic for the past. Plus they form bonds of familiarity with the oddest objects and sensations.

"Says the robot who for some reason *loves* mushrooms," I said.

Hey, mushrooms are at least alive! And they're fascinating. So many varieties, growing in the harshest locations. Did you know some fungi can puppet the bodies of insects like zombies?

"That's hardcore," I said. Who'd have thought *mushrooms* could be that cool?

But back to you being strange, M-Bot said, *maybe . . . maybe you just like those hallways because they remind you of a cockpit? And of flying with me.*

I loved that idea, though I didn't think it was accurate. Still, it made me smile as I continued walking, rounding the corner and stepping into the room with the glass floor. This time though, it was occupied. A lanky young man with red hair lay on the floor, a bunch of schematics spread out around him—though he was lying face down and looking through the glass.

Rig jumped when he heard me, looking up—then relaxed when he saw it was just me. "Hey," he said. "Hear you had an exciting day."

"Yeah. Exciting." I yawned. "Isn't it morning, on standard schedule times? Shouldn't you be at breakfast?"

"Hmmm?" he said, then checked his watch. "Eh, I don't really care about schedules. I've been up all night anyway."

"Rig," I said, hands on my hips, "you spent *years* complaining when I woke you up—or kept you out—for one of my *brilliant* and *interesting* plans."

"Fortunately, the windows here lead into a vacuum," he noted. "So I don't get woken up by you rapping on mine, convinced we need to go hunting for lost treasure in yet another empty cavern."

"I eventually *found* treasure, I'll have you know," I said, folding my arms.

I expected M-Bot to pipe in at that. But he didn't—and when I nudged him cytonically, he felt distant again. Was something going on with him?

"Anyway," I continued, "I am offended by your suddenly deciding to stay up all night without me."

He shrugged. "FM stays up late. So I've found myself doing it more and more . . ."

"Of course," I said, walking over. Around Rig I felt . . . not immature, but more like my old self. I flopped down beside him on my back, ruffling a few of his schematics, and looked at the ceiling. Then I rolled over to look down like he was. Through the glass, toward Detritus below.

"Scud," I whispered, "that's disorienting."

"I know, right?" Rig said, excited.

"I feel like I'm falling," I said, staring down. "Like I'm plummeting toward the surface."

"I feel like I'm floating," he said. "Like I get to see everything, take it all in for once. Maybe understand it, rather than being afraid of it."

"You've been doing a pretty good job of not being afraid of things lately," I noted.

"It's not that I'm not afraid," he said. "It's that . . . well, I've got a good support structure. That helps."

Huh. That wasn't how I would have put it. As a kid, I'd have said that courage destroys fear. Now, I'd have said that fear is what lets us be able to be courageous.

"I'm glad that it's working with you and FM," I said. "That you have a support structure. That . . . you're no longer just that boy with the weird friend you can't get rid of."

"Oh please," he said. "We both know that no one was pounding on my door, demanding my friendship. You didn't scare people away from me, Spin. You befriended me when no one else paid me any attention."

"Outcasts sticking together," I said, staring down at the planet—which glowed under the enormous lights moving up here. I could see the shadows and strips of brightness they made, the lights leftover from a time when Detritus had grown more than dust and fungus.

"Rig," I said softly, "how bad a friend am I?"

"You're not—"

161

"Be straight with me, please. I . . . really hurt Jorgen today. I need to hear from someone I trust. How bad am I at this?"

"You're not *bad* at being a friend," Rig said, "you're just hard to be friends with. That's different."

"How?"

"You try," he said. "I know you do. You always looked out for me. Scud, I doubt you would normally have chosen the quiet, occasionally panicky guy to be your best friend. But I needed someone, and you saw others picking on me, and . . . well, here we are. You're loyal, passionate, and inventive."

"But . . ."

"But you are really, *really* bad at seeing things from other people's viewpoints. You just go and do stuff, Spin, and believe everyone else would have done the same thing if they'd only thought of it and had the guts."

"Fair," I said. "I know I pushed you into flight school. But I can't see things as if I'm someone else. I'm me. Shockingly, I see things like *me*."

"It's a skill to practice, like any other," he said. "You love stories. Maybe ask yourself, what if the story weren't about *you* for a change? What if it were Jorgen's story? How would he feel about what you're doing?"

Scud, that hit me right in the gut. He made it sound so easy, and maybe for him it was.

But I'd done what *needed* to be done. For Jorgen. For Detritus. And given what was happening to me . . . the powers I was displaying . . . well, what if alienating Jorgen and the others was the only way to protect them?

It twisted me up inside. Made me start to tremble. Made me think of my friends dying, graphically, over and over in my mind. To escape those images, and another potential episode, I rolled back over and snatched one of the schematics.

"You know, Rodge," I said to him, "you're a weird guy."

"True, true."

"I walk in here to find you lying *face down* among a bunch of pieces of paper?"

"You immediately flopped down beside me."

"Practicing empathy," I said. "What *is* all of this?"

"Detritus has several enormous shipyards among these platforms," he said.

"Yeah, I know," I said. "I had a battle in one, remember?"

"Right, while it was crashing. Nedd's brothers . . ."

I nodded, though he couldn't see, as he was still face down. Yeah, he really was weird. Maybe we had always been destined to become friends.

"You think you can build me a ship with one of these fabrication plants?" I asked.

"Depends, really," he said. "Do you have designs for what you'd want? And by that I mean accurate, detailed schematics created by an actual engineer? Not something hand-drawn on a scrap of paper, depicting a catapult for launching Stacy Leftwire into a furnace."

I smiled. "I forgot about that."

"I didn't. You wrote it in blood."

"Rat blood," I agreed. "It makes a terrible ink. Kept congealing. Not sure how the old necromancers ever made use of it in their arcane tomes."

"Can we change the topic?"

"I'll get you schematics," I said. "Real ones. They were in the data dump we stole."

"Great," he said. "I wanted to do some tests anyway. Been thinking, though, that we don't really *need* more fighters. We have plenty for our trained pilots. Maybe we need something else."

I myself wasn't so certain we had all the fighters we needed. Now that we had a hyperslug ejection system for pilots, we might start chewing through ships faster. It was a mindset change. We'd always had ejection systems that worked in atmosphere, but the culture of the DDF had trained pilots to protect their ships—ostensibly harder to replace—over their own lives.

I often wondered how much that short-sightedness had cost us. We hadn't acknowledged the importance of skilled veteran pilots. Half the reason my friends and I were in such high positions was the fact that we'd managed to *survive* long enough to actually get some useful combat experience.

I was about to explain to Rig what I wanted him to fabricate, when the door swung open and FM strode in. She was faintly flushed, tense. Still poised of course, but for FM this was the equivalent of being in a panic.

"What is it?" I said, immediately sitting up.

"Emergency conference called by command," she said. "The enemy is doing something. I was looking for Rodge, but Jorgen will be glad you were here too."

I wasn't so certain about that. Not today. But as Rig scrambled to gather his schematics, I stood up. "Do you know anything more?"

"Yeah," she said. "Shutting down the enemy's access to acclivity stone *really* got their attention."

"And?"

"And," she said, meeting my eyes, "they're changing tactics. We can't be certain; it's probably too early to tell, but their troop movements indicate . . . well, they've realized they can't win a long war as easily as they could have before. So instead . . ."

Instead? I frowned, trying to think what I would do in their situation. They would realize we were going to try to bleed them over time, but they still had vastly superior numbers. So in their place, I'd . . .

Scud.

17

"**A**ll-out assault," Goro—one of the kitsen generals—said, hovering his platform over to a wall screen and gesturing at the footage we'd been able to gather from across the Superiority. Hyperslugs let us jump ground teams in to spy on the installations Cuna had identified for us.

"Again," Goro said, hovering to another part of the wall screen, then pointing to a different image, "we aren't *certain,* but this is what it looks like."

"Makes sense, unfortunately," Cobb said.

He still refused to sit at the table with us, instead taking an advisor's seat by the wall. The pallor of his skin and bags under his eyes had me worried about him, but he did seem to be participating more. So maybe he was getting better.

"They understand our strategy," Cobb continued. "Over time, if we destroy their military in little skirmishes, piece by piece, they could lose control."

"Right now the Superiority is stable," Cuna added from their spot at the table. "It's large enough, and has enough momentum, that few of the common citizens will have noticed anything changing since the advent of Winzik's reign. However, we are not *cathodis.*"

My translator pin, set to explain things like this, whispered it was a metaphor for an object that sits on a wall and watches the world pass, never moving. A little like the English phrase "We aren't sheep."

"Over time," Cuna continued, "people will grow increasingly upset at the loss of democracy. They will see through Winzik's rhetoric about dangerous humans and delvers—and they will ask questions. If we're destroying his military presence, the more . . . rambunctious of the lesser species might rebel against his rule. Even those of primary intelligence will begin to move against him."

"Without his supply depots, Winzik has realized that a long-term engagement against us has grown more risky," Goro agreed. He gestured toward more footage on the screen. "So, here we see him pulling security forces away from the planet Ooklar, and here, others away from the planet Zip!tak. Here he is calling in ships that were protecting important sublight shipping lanes in the dione twin system from piracy.

"They're gathering. If he is aggressive in these redeployments, he can bring in some twenty-seven hundred fighters to support his primary fleet. About a third of those will have actual in-cockpit pilots, while the rest are remote drones. Worse, he has access to twenty to thirty capital ships: eight carriers, and twice as many destroyers."

Scud. Those numbers . . .

Twenty-seven hundred fighters? Even with our allies, we had barely *three* hundred. Yes, a good chunk of theirs would be drones, which were much easier to face. But our force of three hundred included all of our newer recruits and trainees, who had barely any battle experience. And as always, we had no capital ships—though granted, Detritus itself was a giant moving battle station.

Most of our forces were raiders, the modern equivalent of cavalry. We'd survived so far by being fast, striking where Winzik didn't expect, and—to be perfectly frank—exploiting the fact that he couldn't devote much of his attention to us. He was busy establishing himself as galactic dictator.

This was coming to a head though. He couldn't afford to let us keep picking at him. We'd served our purpose, giving him a boogeyman to use as "proof" he needed dictatorial authority. Now he would want a decisive battle where he destroyed us outright. If he couldn't win the long war, that was his only other option.

Squash us fast. I should have *seen* this.

"Wait," Rinakin said from his seat at the table, a confused expression on his pale violet face. "Won't this risk rebellion? If Winzik moves all of his security forces away from his planets, won't those planets turn against him?"

"Eventually, yes," Cuna said. "This is a possible problem. But you must understand, we're not . . . um . . ."

"Aggressive?" I asked.

"I was looking for a less charged term," they said. "I've learned it might not be as accurate a word as I would have liked. But in this case, perhaps it will serve: we're not aggressive.

"We aren't *cathodis,* and will not just sit forever and be content with oppression. At the same time, my people—and those they lead—will try other methods first. Bills to enforce the law, motions in governing bodies, editorials in the media. Winzik will need his military forces then, if these movements gain strength, but he has likely seen—and rightly so—that he can spare the forces now. For a short time."

"For just long enough to make slag out of us," Jorgen said grimly.

"Did you . . . foresee this?" Rinakin asked, looking to Jorgen. "In your plan to starve him of acclivity stone?"

"This was poorly handled," Goro said, hovering toward the group of other kitsen gathered on the tabletop. "Elder Itchika and I are greatly displeased to have been *cut out* of the decision to strike in secret against the enemy. Why weren't we consulted about moving the timeframe up so quickly, or the decision to strike in the nowhere, instead of against the facilities in the somewhere as we'd decided?"

"How can we call this an alliance," Cuna said, "if one of our members acts with such distrust toward everyone else?"

I sank down in my seat, sick to my stomach. Jorgen would never have moved up the attack without talking to our allies. His hot-headed star pilot, though, was another matter. Scud, I was such a fool.

Jorgen stood up and didn't even glance at me. He'd shoulder this. As he so often suffered because of me. Everything I'd done seemed right, even in hindsight. Refurbishing M-Bot, running off to Starsight, staying in the nowhere . . . even this action, which had achieved our goals with the mining facilities without loss of life.

Yet in each case, I'd left Jorgen to make excuses. To pick up the pieces. To figure out how to lead while I just did my thing. He was right about me. In that moment, I felt I didn't deserve to be in that seat—I didn't even deserve to be in the room.

"No, Rinakin," Jorgen said to them. "I didn't anticipate that this would happen. You're right—and Goro, you are right that we have acted brashly by not consulting you. We were wrong, and I beg your forgiveness.

"We're new to this. That's the problem, my friends. Too new. We are children, essentially, trying to fill adults' shoes for the first time. My people spent decades on the very edge of annihilation. Back then, we didn't take time to develop proper plans, because if we did we'd be dead before we could execute them.

"That same sense rules us still. That sense of panic, that sense that we need to act now, as soon as an opportunity arises, lest we lose our chance. We need to grow up. We need to learn and do better. But I only ask that you accept that we are not *trying* to alienate you. We're learning, all the time, and as fast as we can."

The others at the table considered his words, and I could see them softening. How did Jorgen always know the right things to say? How did he know when to be firm, and when to apologize? The others saw him shouldering the responsibility for what I'd done, and they accepted his apology.

"I suppose we can understand this," Goro said. "None of us have ever fought a *truly* galactic war. Even on my homeworld, it has been decades since a real war has happened; we have known only skirmishes."

"You can be forgiven," Rinakin agreed, "for not anticipating what would happen in a war on this scale. We are *all* new to this, and the plan with the mining stations looked good to us all; we would not be nearly so upset if we'd simply been *told* when you decided to move the timetable up."

"We promise," Jorgen said, finally looking at me. "No more surprises. We *will* grow up, my friends."

A platform hovered up beside Goro's. Itchika, the aged kitsen with white on her snout, still wore her formal robes. She was an elected official, I'd come to understand. Not like an empress—they'd moved beyond that—but still something of a voice for the old ways.

"We too appreciate your honesty, Admiral," she said to Jorgen. "But there is a beast we must consume, as my people say. A topic that must be addressed. Our planet, Evershore, is exposed. As is ReDawn, the homeworld of our allies, the UrDail. Your people, however, have a mobile planet—with a defensive shell around it. You can afford brashness, for if the enemy comes in force, you can escape. We cannot. Our people could be annihilated."

The conference room fell silent, and I felt even more sick. Because this point also was true. I wasn't used to the idea of our people being free, like Jorgen had explained, but I didn't believe that was what had driven me to act. That didn't change the fact that yes—if the Superiority came in force against us, we could escape. Detritus being mobile meant that our people were actually more free than any other.

"We couldn't escape forever," Jorgen said. "Winzik cannot allow us to continue as a threat to his rule. Besides, we wouldn't just leave you."

Rinakin tapped the table softly, perhaps his version of clearing his throat to draw attention. "No one is accusing you of cowardice, Admiral. But if it came down to your people or ours, surely you would escape. It is a simple truth. I say this not as an accusation, but as a statement we should acknowledge. Detritus is not in the same position as the rest of us."

"Besides," Cuna noted, "you're . . . well, you're *humans*. You're used to living with destruction and war."

Remarkably, the UrDail and the kitsen seemed to agree, unfair though the statement was. I didn't think humans were *naturally* more aggressive. We'd just been . . . I didn't know how to describe it . . .

A soft click sounded from the side of the room. Then a quiet groan as somebody stood up. A short somebody, bowed by age. Gran-Gran?

Another click echoed in the conference room as she stepped forward along the table. The way she walked—frail, but determined—somehow conveyed the contradiction at the core of Gran-Gran's soul. An aged woman, weak of frame, yet bearing power and authority.

On one hand, she was a nobody. An old woman, outcast for most of her life because of her son's betrayal. Except even back then, people had stepped aside for her. Even then, they'd known and remembered. She wasn't just Gran-Gran. She was Rebecca Nightshade. The last living woman who knew life among the stars. The last crewmember of the ship that had brought us here.

"Do you know," she asked, "the story of the *Defiant*?" She turned, her eyes closed, yet seeming to address everyone in the room—kitsen, UrDail, human, and lone dione.

"We do not know your story, honored elder," Hesho said softly behind his mask, from where he hovered near my seat. "But I would hear it, if you would offer it to me."

Gran-Gran smiled and tilted her face upward, toward the stars, as she walked. "We are the people who disobeyed. We are the humans who *would not* go to war, the last time the tyrants who led our various peoples banded together and tried to conquer the galaxy. Those are the warriors under whom you UrDail suffered long ago.

"Well, those humans, they demanded that every battleworthy ship join the armada and support them in their foolish war. But we, we turned *away*. Some of us of Chinese descent, others Colombian, others American, others Scandinavian—and many scattered peoples between. We had previously traded together, traveled together, but on that day we truly became one.

"A wise soldier chooses her battlefield, and we did not want this one. We *rejected* the call to arms, and so the first people we defied were our own leaders. That is the soul of the *Defiant*. It is not just that we fight, my friends. It is that we *choose when* to fight. We will not be forced—not by tide nor tyrant—to raise arms in a battle we do not support." She opened her eyes, milky white, and looked around the room in strength. "But once we do fight—once you have convinced us the cause is just—we do *not back down*."

She stopped near the kitsen platforms. There, Gran-Gran nodded, chin still high. "We will not abandon you, my friends. I, the last of the *Defiant*'s crew, *swear it*. If you fall, we shall join you, so that together we may curse the fire and ash that sear our flesh from our bones. Dead, but not broken. If we instead choose to run, as my ancestors did, then we will only do so if we can bring you with us. For though we are not one people, as we unite together, we become sisters in arms. You do *not fight alone*."

Though I'd heard this story of our origins many times before, it still brought a tear to my eyes. Gran-Gran's words were nearly enough to pull me out of my gloom. And, although she had a uniquely Nightshade way of phrasing things, the speech had a positive effect on our allies. The kitsen stood down, accepting this promise. The others seemed comforted and calmed.

Another Spensa crisis averted. Scud, this speech wouldn't have been needed if I hadn't made everyone panic about humans acting erratically. The glow of hearing Gran-Gran speak faded, and the weight of my mistakes came crashing back down on me.

Jorgen thanked Gran-Gran, then addressed the table. "We can adapt to the enemy's new tactics," he said. "Fortunately, it will take Winzik some time to prepare his forces. I suggest that we meet with our various strategic experts, go over the intel we've gathered, then reconvene tonight. Twenty hundred local time, to share ideas?"

The others agreed. The meeting began to break apart, and I fled through the doors, ignoring Kimmalyn's suggestion that we grab breakfast together. I didn't want to argue again with Jorgen, and I didn't want to face my friends. I wanted to be alone.

I was more and more certain that was where I belonged.

18

I went straight to bed and slept fitfully, but at least there were no strange nightmares or cytonic visions. Just restless turning around in my bunk, drifting in and out.

I'd been exhausted after that midnight mission, so it was well past midday when I rose. I immediately went for a long PT session. Treadmill, stretching, weights. I'd hoped that the familiar routine, and working my body, would ease my sense of dread and anxiety. But not today. My subconscious mind knew I was trying to distract it, and was having none of that nonsense.

After a shower and food, I dealt with my messages on the wall screen in my rooms and waited for an invitation to that planning meeting Jorgen had mentioned. Always before, I'd just shown up to meetings—Jorgen didn't always send me a specific invitation, because my attendance was expected. And so, as the time approached, I didn't know for certain if I had been excluded.

I leaned back in my bunk, scratching Doomslug, who had her own little bed beside mine. She sensed my mood, and didn't say anything.

Knowing Hesho, he was probably standing guard outside my door. He'd taken to doing that most days; part of his self-imposed duty as the Masked Exile bodyguard. I could have chatted with him, but I didn't want to talk to anyone. I wanted to be alone.

When you're in that kind of mood, it's awkward to have friends who can literally pop inside your head.

Hey, M-Bot said. *Something is up with the delvers. They're growing agitated.*

"Are you in danger?" I asked.

Probably. But I've been in danger the entire time, so who knows? They'll destroy me if they can, but they're obviously afraid of you. Maybe even of me, a little. Wish I knew why.

"I know some of it," I said, lying in my bunk, staring at the ceiling. "After you sacrificed yourself and let me escape into the light-burst, they tried to . . . I don't know. Crush me? Overwhelm me? Shred my soul.

"Combining with Chet, though, showed me something. He was in pain, and my life experience allowed him to overcome it. In turn, *I* needed an awareness of the nowhere—and the delvers—which he could provide. So when the delvers touched me, they were subjected to pain."

That pain, M-Bot said. *That's their weakness. They fled into the lightburst to escape the pain of loss, right?*

As the delvers had evolved from an AI to a person, they'd been unable to cope with the death of a man they'd loved. They'd sealed away their memories and found refuge where time had no meaning. Where they would never have to grow, never again have to suffer the pain of losing something—or someone—they loved. Where nothing would ever change.

Except when people from the somewhere passed through. Except when cytonics, or slugs, opened pathways to our dimension—where time, space, and *change* were inevitable parts of life. It hurt them.

"When they tried to destroy me, that required coming in contact with me," I explained. "That hurt them too much. Because I'm part of the somewhere, I think?"

More than that, I'd guess, M-Bot said. *They hid their memories away, but didn't eliminate them entirely. You knowing their secrets cuts through their layers of protections, and exposes that pain again. When you touched them, you ripped away their masks—so to speak— bringing their memories to the forefront of their awareness again.*

Chet leaped at that statement. *That is key,* he thought.

"So . . . they could feel my ability to understand what they were. That was *painful* to them . . ."

You knew what they were hiding, M-Bot said. *They couldn't pretend when you were there. You forced them to remember, and that memory would hurt them too much to bear. They had to pull back.*

"So all we need to do now," I said, "is find a way to expose the delvers fully to their pain. Remove the barrier they've put in place to hold back their memories. If we do that . . ."

It will destroy them, M-Bot said. *Because in the nowhere, nothing changes. If you afflict them with that immense pain, then leave, they'll never escape it. They'll be trapped forever. Unable to do anything, except perhaps cease to exist.*

Chet, inside my soul, felt sorrow at that. What did I feel? Resignation? I had worked so hard to protect the workers at the supply depots, even though they were on the other side. What did I feel about the delvers?

It was, I decided, too complicated to sort out. Without Chet, I'd have had no qualms. But he gave me a different perspective. "That sounds terrible," I said.

Yes, but it's a plan, finally, M-Bot said. *Some way, at long last, of dealing with them—maybe permanently. Scud, Spensa. It feels* good *to have a plan.*

"Well, I often have plans," I said. "That's not the problem. The problem is that I don't often give them enough time, or give others a chance to weigh in."

So . . .

"So we take it slowly in this instance," I said. "And don't try anything until we've thought it through and done more research. You think you can sneak in among them and find out if our theory is right? Maybe see if you can spot a way to restore their pain to them?"

Of course. I'm not just a ghost, I'm a stealth ghost. I can do it. I'll find the answers.

"Good."

And Spensa? Once we do this—once we find out how to defeat the delvers, and keep the Superiority from destroying Detritus—then . . . then we get what we want. That's how it is in the stories, right?

"Yeah," I lied. "Yeah. That's what happens in the stories, M-Bot."

Good, good . . . he said, his voice fading.

His withdrawal left me alone again, as I'd wanted. But that meant I went back to stewing about the meeting. Should I have gone? What did staying here accomplish? Was waiting for an invitation mature, or petulant?

I found myself reaching out with my senses, not on purpose, just kind of as an extension of my worries—and even my growing loneliness. So I shouldn't have been surprised by what happened next. Brade appeared in my room, a phantom cytonic projection, her arms folded, her uniform crisp.

Before, I'd been able to hide from her. But the way my soul vibrated—resonating with the delver—had changed that. I didn't have nearly as much control now.

"Scrud," Brade said to me. "You have to be so loud? We're trying to figure out the best way to murder you all."

"You're scared," I snapped back at her. "You didn't expect us to cut you off from your resources like we did. Now you're desperate."

"That *was* a cute trick," she admitted.

I climbed out of bed and circled Brade, and she circled me, prowling warriors assessing each other. My hand trembled with the desire to grab the knife strapped to my leg and lunge for her.

It wouldn't have done any good. The blades we fought with weren't of steel. And unfortunately, she had proven stronger than I was at that sort of thing, even if I did have a delver powering my soul.

"I did want to say thank you," Brade finally said.

"For?"

"For pushing Winzik and his generals into a corner," she said. "They were so determined to fight a slow, wasting war. Now they'll take the better path. A final grand confrontation. Our own Agincourt or Waterloo." She strolled around me again. "I should have known, should have seen, what you were from the start. No UrDail would have had your bloodthirst. Your willpower. Don't tell me you aren't *excited* for a final climactic confrontation."

"I'd rather one that didn't cost so much," I said. "Do we *need* to waste thousands of lives, Brade? When the outcome is inevitable and the Superiority is doomed?"

She stepped closer and studied me for a moment, then answered. "I see," she said. "You're getting weak. Losing the thirst. What's causing this pacifism in you, Spensa?"

"You never talked like this before," I said, still rounding her. "Back when we trained together, you talked about killing being a terrible thing—you said that you were a weapon trained from birth, kept captive by the Superiority by necessity. You seemed afraid of yourself and what you did. Not thrilled by the prospect of battle."

She smiled. "Perhaps knowing you awakened something."

"Or more likely," I said, "you were playing a role back then. Which is why you went to Winzik so eagerly once you knew what I really was. You know, I *actually* thought I could get through to you? I thought you were brainwashed."

"Honest mistake," Brade said. "Who would have expected a human to be so good at pretending to be what she wasn't? Remarkable, when you realize there were *two* of us doing it."

"So what about this, then?" I said, gesturing to her. "Posturing about the glory of battle. Another false face? Hoping I'll underestimate you?"

"More like trying to find common ground," she said, toying with a destructor holster on her hip.

I realized I knew a third Brade, the one I'd spied on from the nowhere. One who prowled like a leopard, watching Winzik with a calculating relaxation.

That seemed to be her true self. Not the cowed captive, not this bloodthirsty warrior. Instead, a crafty manipulator. More companion to Winzik than slave.

Scud, no *wonder* she'd betrayed me. I hadn't just been messing with *his* plans, but *hers*.

"The battle does intrigue me," she said. "Do you know how many times our ancestors tried to conquer the galaxy? How long the humans spent proving themselves?"

"Tyrants," I said. "Exactly like the Superiority."

"Oh, come on," Brade said, flopping down on a seat that appeared in the vision as she interacted with it. "You can't have it both ways, Spensa. Either the battle is glorious and brilliant, or it's a useless waste of lives. It's getting tiresome to watch you vacillate."

I didn't rise to the gibe. I couldn't help but see even this as calculated in some way. Yes, I was a little inconsistent—I *felt* inconsistent—but I was figuring things out. I could love stories of courage and admire the strength of warriors, without wanting to see innocent people dead.

Either way, I would have *absolutely* no qualms about ramming a knife through Brade's eye, then *twisting*. Sometimes you had to feel bad pulling the trigger. Other times, a target presented herself with such utter contemptibility that guilt didn't enter into the equation. A part of me was grateful to her for making that part easy.

"You want to get this over with?" Brade asked me.

"How?"

"You," she said, pointing. "Me. Duel, in person, starfighter against starfighter."

"What would that accomplish?" I asked.

"We'd find out which of us is better."

"We know who's better," I said. "I beat you three out of four times in the delver maze."

"What, back then?" Brade asked. "When *you* were trying to

pretend you were some half-pacifist alien and *I* was pretending that I wasn't so dangerous, so as to not scare the rest of you away? Scrud, that was so *annoying*."

I narrowed my eyes at her, and didn't buy it. Yes, she'd been legitimately frustrated during our sparring. Insubordinate. She hadn't liked being there in those training sessions. She'd probably hated that assignment.

What reason would she have had to hold back? None. She had every reason to bolster the reputation of human soldiers, and no reason to pull punches. I was the better pilot.

Though a part of me *really* wanted to find out for certain.

"I'm not going to duel you for pride," I said.

"Then do it for tactical advantage," she said. "I'm Winzik's strongest cytonic; you should see the pathetic collection of half-brained excuses he has otherwise. His people have spent centuries breeding the skill out of themselves, the idiots. Yes, they have the hyperdrives, but this is like refusing to oil your sidearm because you have a rifle."

An apt metaphor. I wavered.

"If I kill you," Brade said, "I'm denying your people their strongest weapon. If you kill me, same. Seems like we both have an interest in a good old-fashioned duel." She narrowed her eyes. "I want it. Do you?"

"Yes," I whispered, realizing I did. I wanted to slice that smile off her face *so badly,* then nail it to my wall as a trophy. I'd lost my desire to kill indiscriminately, but that didn't mean I wasn't still me.

"We meet alone," Brade said. "Here."

Coordinates forcibly entered my head, like an arrow pointing the way.

"Day after tomorrow," she said. "Thirty-six Old Earth hours from now."

I looked at my clock. "Shouldn't it be thirty-nine and a half hours instead? Then it would be high noon."

"How quaint," Brade said. "I won't tell my people—Winzik gives me a long leash these days. I can sneak away. You?"

I didn't respond, but she seemed to read the eagerness in my expression, for she vanished a moment later. I was left feeling uncertain. I'd *just* gotten us into enormous trouble by running off on my own. But if I could kill Brade—or better, capture her—then we'd be in a much stronger tactical position. I knew how much Winzik relied on her for cytonic interventions. At the very least, I knew *I'd* be more safe. We wouldn't have to worry about her popping in and spying on us.

I wavered before making a decision. I needed someone to talk to about this. Fortunately, one of the wisest people I knew was sitting outside my door. Having tea.

Kitsen Profile

Kitsen Nobility

Ceremonial Knife

Kitsen Mobility Platforms

15cm

Kitsen Warrior

Ceremonial Mask

"The Darting Hawk That Separates Sinew From Bone"

15cm

19

Hesho had arranged himself cross-legged on a little carpet mat. He didn't acknowledge me as I opened the door. Instead, he carefully bowed to his teapot, then raised it and poured a single cup of tea about a quarter full. He bowed to it, then sipped it quietly until it was gone. Finished, he picked up his mask—white with red stripes, in the shape of a fox's head—and affixed it back into place.

It had the air of ritual about it, so I hovered behind him, waiting until he spoke.

"It is a ceremony for the emperor," he explained. "Every *nanjan* day. The head of the household pours, taking the emperor's place. It is a representation of how everything flows from the emperor—all comfort, all needs, all life. I had never done it before from this position. I had poured for the heads of state, but the emperor does not drink, as he does not take from the people, only gives." He paused. "I used to believe that."

I settled down in the doorway as he turned around on his mat. As always, his voice was powerful and deep—a tremendous bass coming from something so small. Or maybe that was just my prejudice speaking. Why shouldn't something small produce deep sounds?

"You are troubled," he said to me.

"Am I ever not?" I said with a sigh.

"Wise," he said. "As the ocean waves are disturbed by constant turmoil, so is the life of one who lives to the full."

"I don't think I'm so much like waves, Hesho," I said, "as much as I am like a jug of something carbonated that's shaken up and down repeatedly."

He chuckled at that. "I enjoy the way you see the world, Spin. It makes me think that perhaps I should appreciate levity in more abundance."

"Uh, same? Only in reverse?" I sighed, sitting down against the doorframe and ignoring the pair of pilots from another flight who walked by. They gave us odd glances, but I was used to those. "I'm not sure I can even figure out what I want to ask at the moment. Want to talk about your problems?"

"It *would* help to receive advice," Hesho said. "You are growing more thoughtful, Spensa. This is an encouraging development."

Uh, sure. Really, I just didn't want to unload on him before I could process some more. But I would let him think I was becoming more mature.

"What does one do," he said to me, "when one realizes that one is a . . . burden?"

"What do you mean?" I asked.

"I selfishly miss my old life," he said. "The instant obedience of everyone around me. The ability to control destiny and make decisions. And . . . I miss my friends. My wives, my family, my servants and colleagues. My cupbearer and my shieldbearer. My eldest daughter, who is a musician of the most blissful tones. I now have only recordings."

Scud, he had a family? Families? It made sense, but sometimes it was hard to remember. I saw my friends mostly as soldiers—doing soldier things.

"Then go back to them," I said. "You can still fly with me if you want, but you don't have to guard my door at night, Hesho. I appreciate it, but I would be happier if you are happy."

"Ah," he said, tapping his mask. "But I have taken the mask, Spin. As I told you before, this is a promise. By wearing it, I indicate to everyone that I have banished Hesho. The emperor is no more."

"Then keep the mask," I said. "And go back to your wives."

"I could do that, yes. And they'd probably accept me. But it would ruin too many things." He reached into the pocket of his formal robes and took out a datapad. "The senate is working effectively for once—they threw off the Superiority while I was gone! They agreed to support this rebellion! They are debating among themselves, and strangely seem more *unified* now that they are no longer *ruled*. Plus, my children are grown and have positions of authority, most serving underneath my wives—who are far more powerful now that I'm gone. Each of the three has taken a consort."

"Already? You were presumed dead for barely a few weeks!"

"Our unions were political," he said, his paw resting on the screen in a way I thought was fond, "designed to unite factions on our planet. Without me, they can return to their own families triumphant, having served the greater needs of our people. I miss them all, but each is now the most politically important member of her clan. My children gain much through the respect paid to them because of my sacrifice. My survival would have been . . . inconvenient for everyone, had I not taken the mask.

"It is the same story everywhere I search. My people were ready to move on. They were ready for the emperor to vanish, but so long as I persisted, they could not. It is better for everyone that I remain isolated. Sometimes I wish I had not recovered my memories at all."

"I'm sorry, Hesho," I said softly. "That scudding *sucks*." Then I winced. "Maybe . . . pretend I said something wise instead."

"I cherish wisdom," he said. "Yet today, empathy helps more. Thank you. It *does* 'scudding suck.' Like the dark of the moon, which can never show its face to the light, and never know the kiss of the dawn."

"Yeah, just like that," I said. "Or when you bruise your knuckles punching Jorgen in the knee. Sucks all around, because he didn't actually deserve it, and now your hand hurts."

"Or how the fish and the hawk can never be friends, despite having entirely different perspectives to share with one another."

"Or like when you *really* need to scream at someone, but the only person you can find is someone nice like Rig. So after yelling, you actually feel *worse*."

"Or how every painting will eventually degrade, so that the universe is constantly losing its masterworks to inevitable decay."

"Or like when you need to pee during maneuvers, but realize you forgot to hook up the flight suit catheter."

Hesho chuckled. He seemed to think that one was a joke, but it really *did* suck. I assumed he didn't know, because his ships were big enough—rather, the occupants were small enough—to contain full lavatory facilities.

"Thank you," he said. "Smiling does help."

"We could go to the firing range and blow some stuff up," I offered, "if you want some *real* therapy."

"Yes. Perhaps later? You seemed concerned earlier. Can I help you in turn?"

I knocked my head backward against the frame of the door, where I was still sitting, one foot up on the opposite side. "Yeah. That."

"I'm sorry. Would you rather not be reminded?"

"No, I came out looking for advice," I said. "Brade wants to duel me."

"Ah. You two are like a pair of celestial bodies, drawn to conflict by forces you cannot control. I am not, therefore, surprised."

"I think it's a good idea," I said to him. "I can beat her and remove her from Winzik's arsenal."

"As I have yet to meet a pilot who can best you in a fair fight, I'm inclined to agree with that assessment. Assuming we can be certain it's not a trap."

"Yeah. Any . . . idea how to do that?"

"Scout the area ahead of time," he said. "Agree to both place an inhibitor slug before entering the region. Maybe even send in a decoy first."

"Smart."

"I'm simply adapting the actions taken by Jilo in the *Epic of Jilo*. But I appreciate your faith in me."

"So we do those things," I said. "Except . . ."

"Jorgen?" he guessed.

"Yeah. Jorgen. He's going to say no. He'll worry I'm risking myself needlessly, and a duel is totally against protocol—even though once a battle starts we're basically just dueling each other anyway, so protocols are stupid. Wish *I* were an emperor."

"Life is in many ways simpler when one is an absolute authority, capable of deciding whatever one wants. But there are huge drawbacks as well, Spin, to such a calling."

"I suppose," I said, closing my eyes. "Do you think . . . maybe . . . I'm like you? That everyone would be better off if I stayed away? If I flew off somewhere and never bothered them again? Then nobody would get hurt trying to keep up with me. I could just do what needed to be done—and Jorgen wouldn't get into trouble, because I wouldn't be under his command."

Hesho didn't reply.

"Hesho?" I asked, cracking an eye.

"I am thinking that I have burdened you with my own terrible thoughts," he admitted. "That if I had not spoken of my isolation, you would not be thinking of adopting the same sensibility. That I should have remained isolated from you for your own good. That it would be for the best if I left . . ."

I rolled over and went down on my stomach, putting myself at eye level with Hesho. "No," I said to him. "*Please* don't be like that, Hesho. Not to me. I'm, like, an interdimensional monster or something. If one of us is bad for the other, it's *me*."

"Thus, we both persist in the same worry. Perhaps we are both wrong."

"Agreed," I said. "We stick together. You and me, at least. All right?" I held out my fist for a little fist bump.

He considered. "Fate declared that I should be your companion, and it was the path to my sanity," he finally decided. "I accept your words." He solemnly removed his mask, then reached up and tapped my fist with one of his claws.

"Good," I said.

"So what do we do?" he asked, replacing his mask. "About Brade? Sneak off in the night like assassins?"

I wavered.

Scud, Jorgen would *kill* me.

And I'd deserve it. "No," I said. "I'm going to go talk to Jorgen first and get permission."

"Very well," Hesho said. "I shall prepare tea for your return."

"Prepare a bandage too," I said, climbing to my feet. "I'm half-convinced he's going to stab me for even *daring* to ask."

20

I didn't just hyperjump into Jorgen's room, like I normally would have. I didn't even march up to his door and bang on it, like a proper warrior would.

I made an appointment.

With his *secretary*.

Rikolfr was the same aide Cobb had used, inherited from Ironsides. He seemed to find my newfound rule-following nature as baffling as I did.

"An appointment . . ." the man said as I stood by the video-comm on the wall of my room. He looked through Jorgen's schedule, which was written out in this big book instead of computerized. Rikolfr was old-school. "I can do tomorrow morning."

"No, it needs to be today," I said. "Is he still in the meeting?"

"He just got out. He has scheduled an hour to decompress and go over his notes."

"Great, schedule me instead of that," I said.

"But—"

"It's fine."

"Commodore Nightshade," he said, "I don't think you quite understand the purpose of appointments."

"I called ahead," I snapped. "The rule book says to call ahead. Book the appointment, Rikolfr, or I'll push you out an airlock."

He paled.

"I'd put you in a space suit first," I said, rolling my eyes. "What do you think I am, a monster?"

"Uh . . . okay," he said. "I'm sending him a note that you'll be visiting him in five minutes—and that you wouldn't accept my insistence that he not be interrupted—"

"Please note that I'm following protocol," I said. "Write it down." I growled at him until he did. Stupid man needed to see how difficult this was. I needed him to work with me.

Five minutes later, I appeared in front of Jorgen's door and pounded on it with a warrior's fervor. He opened it, tall and intimidating in his admiral's uniform. And handsome. Why was he so scudding handsome?

He took me in for a moment, then sighed and stepped back, gesturing for me to enter. "Thanks for the heads-up."

"Rikolfr was a pill," I said, stalking in. "He acted like it was some great imposition for me to ask him to do his job."

"His job," Jorgen said, "is to make certain I'm not interrupted when I have work to do. There are exceptions for my command staff, however, if there is some emergency . . ."

I stopped at his table—which was scattered with notes and star charts. Strange, how much paper we had now that we could get it from the other planets. I turned back toward him and took a deep breath. "Rule 48b, subrule 18," I said. "Officer turns herself in for discipline and demands demotion. I declare that I'm demoted back to lieutenant."

Jorgen turned toward me, the door to his study sliding closed. He seemed . . . amused?

"I read the scudding rules," I said, hands on hips. "And so I'm a lieutenant now. By the book, Jorgen!"

"You read the rules," he said.

"Yup."

"On military discipline."

"Whole thing."

"And now . . ."

"Now I'm going to declare myself demoted!" I said.

His smile widened. "Spensa, you can't declare that."

"Rule 48b, subrule 18—"

"In the *Handbook of Intersectional Discipline*," he said. "Yes. It says that an officer, upon failure or disgrace, can request demotion. As a form of saving face, Spensa. It lets an officer admit they've made a tactical error with grave consequences—and is actually there to prevent them from committing suicide, as would occasionally happen in some militaries. At any rate, they can *request* demotion."

"Which is what I'm doing."

He gave me a flat stare.

"In my own way," I admitted. Then I softened my tone. "Look, I'm *trying*."

"I know you are," he said, walking over to me. "I appreciate it. But you could just apologize."

"That's the thing," I said, then bit my lip.

"You don't think you did anything wrong, do you?"

"It's . . . complicated," I said. "I broke the rules, sure. But . . . Jorgen, I would do it again. So maybe it's best if you just bust me back to LT as a consequence."

He sighed, settling down in one of the seats around the table. I, after a moment's hesitation, did likewise.

"Spensa," he said, "what would that accomplish? No one follows you because of your *rank,* and I doubt you care about it. I could name you an airman in charge of floor mopping, and it wouldn't make a difference."

He . . . had a point. Plus, in the stories, it was practically a rite of passage for the heroine to repeatedly get kicked out of the military. Never really bothered them. It had only happened to me once that I could recall, so I wasn't even keeping up.

I put my elbows on the table, looking him in the eyes. "I'm

sorry," I said softly, "for hurting you. I'm sorry for ignoring your authority. If I were to do it again, I'd talk to you. But . . . I know I'd go again, if you said no. I'm a terrible soldier, aren't I?"

"Your passion is what makes you a great soldier, Spensa," he said. "But is it really *that* difficult to trust me? To try it *my* way? Just to see?"

"I read the rules!"

He reached his hand across the table, palm up. I hesitantly put mine on top of it.

"That's a step forward," he said. "I appreciate the gesture."

"I will . . . listen better. And try things your way." I sighed. "This was a whole lot more fun when you were my rules-obsessed boyfriend and I could corrupt you. Why'd you have to go and become the guy in charge of everything?"

"I didn't choose that so much as have it forced upon me . . ."

"Sure," I said. "*You* can just up and decide to be admiral, but if *I* try to change *my* rank . . ." I smiled at him, and got a smile back. "So . . ." I continued, "can I please go duel Brade to the death in a contest of honor?"

He gave me a long, slow blink. "Who?"

"Brade," I said, realizing that Jorgen hadn't been there for most of my experiences with her. "Winzik's pet human cytonic. I flew with her at Starsight . . . you saw her once, I think. You saved me when she was trying to capture my soul?"

"Right," he said. "Short, dark hair? Sneer on her lips?"

"Yup," I said. "She's been popping up in my head lately, connecting to me cytonically. She invited me to come try to kill her. Can I go do it, please please please?"

"One of the Superiority's cytonics has invited you to a duel?" he said. "Spensa, that's *obviously* a trap."

"Hesho and I figured that," I said. "We'll scout it out first."

He squeezed my hand. I thought I could follow his thoughts as various pieces of him warred, each one trying to be victorious and get to explain how *terrible* this idea was.

"Spensa . . ."

"I know," I said with a sigh, leaning back. "I'm way more valuable to our fight than she is to hers. Even if I'm likely to win, the risk isn't worth the gain. I don't have the resources to determine if it's actually a trap or not, and it's foolish to try. I want to anyway."

"How do I talk you out of it?" he asked, his voice pained.

"Order me not to, maybe?"

"When has that worked?"

"Today it might," I said. "I'm *trying* to be better."

He squeezed my hand again, then frowned. "Wait. An enemy cytonic has been able to contact you?"

"Yes. Why?"

"We're inside Detritus's defenses," he said. "There's an inhibition field around the entire planet, fully strengthened now that we know what we're doing. Without that shield, the enemy wouldn't have had to spend years fighting through it with bombs to destroy us—they'd have been able to hyperjump the bombs right into our caverns."

"Yeah, it's strange," I said. "Brade says we're connected somehow. Maybe that's the reason? I've always been able to hyperjump while inside Detritus's protection. Even before I could understand any kind of passcode or key to allow me."

"Yes," he said. "And while Alanik couldn't hyperjump in originally—that's why she got shot down trying to fly past the platforms—she managed it later. We are pretty sure that anyone born here automatically has the key, though before we really understood all of this, the defenses were weakening. The enemy was able to pilot their drones via cytonic communication, and influence your father's mind. Rig says that he's got the field bolstered, now that we can persuade slugs to power the equipment. But we're still not a hundred percent sure how it works."

Huh. Regardless, it seemed I was a weak link. A hole in our defenses.

Jorgen stood up. "Every day, we discover another oddity about this planet. If an enemy cytonic can contact you despite the inhibition field . . . it's possible they can figure out how to get ships in here, which would be a disaster. We—"

The door chimed and he paused, then walked over and opened it to reveal Rikolfr, who handed him an envelope.

Oh, sure, I thought. *He has no problem interrupting Jorgen's private time himself.*

Jorgen walked back and absently sliced the side of the envelope off with a mindblade—an invisible something he could do with his powers. I'd missed him experimenting with this, and so far I could barely even *grasp* what he was doing—let alone replicate it. My talents didn't lie in that direction.

He pulled out a card, then smiled.

"What?" I asked.

"It's the kitsen formal agreement to our offer of alliance," he said, "and joint war." He turned the card over, showing the flowery writing and ink designs. "They told me they'd send it. Apparently on their planet, people like to get them framed."

Scud. I loved those fuzzy little maniacs. I'd be proud to fight beside them. Only . . .

"It's bad, isn't it?" I said, reading Jorgen's expression.

He nodded, gesturing to the star charts and troop counts scattered on the table. "Winzik is gathering his forces at a place named Evensong. An old platform, repurposed as their communications hub."

I'd read about this in the data dump. "That's where they keep their slugs, Jorgen!" I said, rising from the table. "The majority of their taynix, when not being used as hyperdrives, are there. Including *all* of their communications slugs."

"The most fortified position in the Superiority," he agreed.

"Yeah," I said. Then paused. "We should attack it."

"What?"

"They're going to throw everything they have at us, right?" I said. "We can't let *them* choose the battleground, Jorgen. The others worried about this earlier—we have two planets to defend, Evershore and ReDawn. Yet there is only one Detritus. Wherever we set

193

up, they'll hit the other planet, attack the people there as punishment for our rebellion.

"We don't have the forces to defend both. So we need to go on the offensive. He's gathering his troops, right? And it will take days for him to organize." I shrugged. "So we should hit him first. It's the only thing that gives us a chance."

"It's also crazy," he said.

"Crazy *good* though," I said. "Bold and decisive. We have known their big weakness all along—we keep talking about it."

"That they need to keep their tech centralized to a few locations," he said. "To prevent their secrets from spreading."

"A huge chunk of their slugs are at that communications hub," I said. "If we liberated them . . . what would happen to the Superiority? We should do it! Now! Tonight!"

"Spensa," he said, "jumping straight into action is *why* we're in this position in the *first place*. We have to take time to plan."

"But every hour we wait is another hour they have to gather more forces!" I stepped up to him. "Jorgen, we can break through and rescue those slugs. You can see how panicked the enemy is at not having acclivity stone—imagine if they couldn't *communicate*. Scud, what if they couldn't hyperjump! Or inhibit us! What if we took every slug away from them?"

"They won't have every slug in the Superiority on that station," he said. "Only the majority of the commslugs, per our intel, and a large number of the others not currently in service."

"Yes, but they're hard on their slugs," I said. "They wear them out. If we steal their reserves, it would be a *huge* blow to their battle capacity. They'd have to pull slugs off the shipping routes! They'd lose a *ton* of mobility.

"Plus, Evensong . . . it's their central communications hub. You've heard Cuna talk. If we take it, rescue those slugs, the enemy won't be able to relay information. They'll have to go into war practically blindfolded. It's an opportunity any general in history would have *salivated* over! We have to hit the enemy now, before they get smart and realize their policy of keeping taynix secret—and confined to a few key locations—exposes them to attack!"

He met my eyes. Then he shook his head. "It's too hasty to commit to right now."

"But—"

"I'll raise it with the others," he promised. "I think this is a good idea, and likely the best course—but I'm not going to authorize an attack tonight. That *isn't* how we work. We work as a team, as allies to our friends. That is protocol."

"To hell with protocol!" I said. "What have those rules ever gotten us? They're a stupid bunch of things written by people who don't understand battle, and are too cowardly to go fight in one!"

I immediately knew I'd gone too far.

Jorgen winced as if I'd punched him. In a moment of pain, I realized he probably wished I had. He saw the rules like I saw the stories Gran-Gran told. As a way to make sense of the world, and life, and . . .

And scud, I was an idiot.

"Jorgen," I said. "I—"

"We can't all just make it up as we go, Spensa," he said, his voice cold. "We can't all just barrel forward, expecting someone else to pick up the pieces. Some of us need structure. Advice. Rules."

"I know. I didn't mean—"

"I *will* take your proposal to the others," he said, his voice growing louder. Not shouting me down, more . . . *stern*ing me down. "I believe it has merit, and I will explain to them why. You need to wait."

I gritted my teeth. I needed to trust him on this, didn't I? But what if waiting was wrong?

Should I go duel Brade? That was a decision for me, not for him, right? It would mean doing *something* while waiting on Jorgen and the—

"Are you thinking," he said to me, "that because I'm delaying on this plan you *literally* just dreamed up, you should go back to dueling that woman?"

". . . Maybe," I admitted, resentful of how well he understood me.

"You realize that a duel with her wouldn't be about piloting skill," he said. "She'll betray you."

"Yes," I admitted. I'd just outlined the reasons why dueling her would be stupid.

But it was hard to not be moving. Acting.

Maybe that was my problem.

"Spensa," he said, "I can't stop you from running off to do whatever you want. I doubt our entire military could hold you. But if you have even an ounce of respect for me—if you *legitimately* care for me—you will listen. This is it, Spensa. I'm asking you, and commanding you, not to duel this woman. I'm asking you to *listen* to me for once. Will you do that?"

I trembled, but scud him, he was right. And I did trust him and care for him. "Okay," I said softly. "I won't run off, Jorgen. No duel with Brade."

"And you won't secretly try to attack the Superiority's central communications base?" he said. "No going around me to gather troops for an attack?"

"No rush at Evensong," I promised. "But when you talk to the others, make it clear how many slugs are there. We need to rescue them. It's our moral duty."

"I will do so. Thank you." He seemed far more relaxed, now that I'd promised not to do either of these things.

I left then, ostensibly to respect his planning time. But really because I wasn't sure I could keep my emotions properly in check. Best to be out of sight in case they exploded.

For better or for worse, though, it was time to listen to Jorgen. Hopefully that wouldn't cost us the world itself.

21

The next day was one of the roughest in my life. I kept thinking about the enemy gathering their troops—building an overwhelming strike force that would eventually annihilate our allies, isolate us, then destroy Detritus. Yes, the planet was an amazing technological marvel. But Jorgen was right: if we fled, they'd find us. And every rock could be broken with time, every shield worn down.

We had to *strike*. But I . . . I had to let the others make that decision. So I waited. Which was awful.

Until finally something arrived: a note leading me to the cargo bay. There I found a huge delivery for me—almost three meters tall and ten meters on each side—and wrapped in obscuring plastic. Rig had come through, and his fabricators had built what I'd requested. The note apologized for not being able to complete the assembly. Apparently he had an even more important project for the fabricators. Making more platforms to replace the weaker portions of our defenses, I suspected.

At any rate, this was what I'd wanted. I was glad to have to do a little assembly, in fact. I quickly fetched Doomslug and Hesho, returning with the two of them—her in her holster, him hovering along beside me on his platform.

"And this is . . . ?" he asked.

"A project," I said. "So I keep busy and stop worrying about everything going wrong."

"Excellent," he said. "What variety of project are we talking about? Are we constructing, perhaps, a dojo for meditation?"

I smiled, then touched the huge plastic-wrapped package and held out my hand for him. He landed his ship on my palm, the plate-size disc heavy in my hand. I didn't need to hold it for long, however, as I hyperjumped us and the package away. Down from the platforms and space stations and into the caverns of Detritus.

To one in particular. One where I'd lived for months while in flight school. Rubble to one side, some scraps of metal in the center, a table and some old dishware I'd scavenged in the corner.

Doomslug let out a happy fluting. This was the cavern where I'd found M-Bot.

It was time to build him a new body.

I could have done it up above, of course. It would have been *smart* to build it there, with all the available resources and tools. But I was feeling nostalgic, and wanted to be more secluded—somewhere that wasn't always reminding me of our impending doom.

So I began unwrapping. Rig's fabricators had put together the bulk of the fuselage; the basic ship was there, contained in a metal framework. It was missing key parts though, like the canopy, some of the wiring, and many of the outer plates. Those were packed for me to install.

I unfolded a large set of schematics—ones copied from plans in the data dump. The very ones the enemy had made when they'd disassembled M-Bot. Fortunately, they'd been meticulous.

Rig had included some detailed instructions written out by one of his assistants—incredibly, he had seven of those now—and she'd even included some visualizations. I smiled, wishing I could co-opt Rig himself to help me, but he had more important things to do. I probably did too.

I stayed here anyway, and got to work.

The first step was to lay out the parts. Hesho helped with his hover platform, which had a small light-line on it for moving objects. He'd grown accustomed to needing such devices in the world of giants; even turning a doorknob would be a challenge for a creature of his size.

Some of these plates, though, were heavy beyond his capacity. Fortunately Rig had thought of that, and sent me a small acclivity ring mover for shuffling parts around—in particular the boosters and front nose piece, which still needed to be attached. We organized the parts, then I spread the large schematics out on the table. Followed by the datapad with the actual "Spensa, just do this" instructions.

I wasn't incompetent at this sort of thing. I knew more than most, as I'd proved during my time with the Broadsiders. But assembling a complicated starship would have been beyond me, if Rig's fabricators hadn't done around eighty percent of the work already. As it was, the remainder looked like it would walk the perfect line: challenging, but doable by one pilot, her pet teleportation slug, and her fox-gerbil bodyguard.

It was too bad we were basically doomed, because—looked at without context—my life was kind of awesome.

"So," Hesho said—he'd left his mask on the table, as it was just us—"I sense a reverence to your actions. This place is special to you."

"It's where I first found M-Bot," I said. "Broken down. I spent months repairing him in here, alone."

"Alone?" Doomslug fluted from where she sat on the wing of the ship nearby.

"Alone save for my trusty slug companion," I corrected. "And Rig, who maybe helped a little."

Hesho looped over, using his ship to project some holographic instructions for me as I started work on the landing gear, which needed to be put in place before we removed the scaffolding from the ship.

I nodded my thanks as I worked. "The original build was, I'll admit, a lot more . . . scrappy an experience."

"I'm unfamiliar with the term," he said.

"Today we've got advanced tools," I explained, shoving part of the landing gear in place. "And this thing practically sticks together on its own. Back then? I only had what I could scavenge or what I could convince Rig to steal for me."

"Your life has been one long . . . scrappy experience, hasn't it?" he said.

"Yeah. Haunting tunnels as a kid with my family. Settling in Igneous, then hunting rats because we were outcasts. Now . . . well, whatever I am now."

"Your life has taught you the opposite lessons to what mine has," he said. "For you, everything is hard. If an opportunity presents itself, you must snatch it or lose it to someone fiercer. You don't have time to think, because if you think, you starve. Is this an accurate summation?"

"Yeah," I said, wiping my brow as I worked. "I suppose it is."

"This makes it difficult for you when dealing with those who have lived in privilege," he said. "We spend our lives learning to plan. Often, those in power stay in power because of such luxuries—it is not that they are smarter or more capable, but that they've had the opportunity to think about tomorrow, not just today."

"Damn, that's a good explanation," I said, dragging over another chunk of landing gear. "Have you been listening in on my mind or something? You aren't secretly cytonic, are you?"

"I merely have a special chance, these days, to consider myself and my life."

"I told Jorgen," I said, getting down low to begin bolting a wheel into place, "that I thought we should attack the Superiority. Right now, before they can gather their strength. He wants more time, but he's wrong. I can feel it. We need to hit Winzik before he's at his best! It's basic tactics. We should go straight to the communications hub and force the enemy to engage us there. Winzik will have to protect it."

"Won't that mean attacking him where he has a battlefield advantage?" Hesho said. "He'll have inhibition fields in place at the communications hub. Can we find a way to force him to engage us where *our* inhibitors are in play?"

"I doubt it," I said. "We don't have enough inhibitors. We can't cover both ReDawn and Evershore with them—so if we wait, Winzik can hit whichever population is exposed, breaking us. He's willing to strike civilians; his attack on your planet proves that. This means that we're much better on offense than we are on defense."

"What if we were to *move* our populations?" Hesho said. "Your grandmother mentioned perhaps bringing us with you, and I have been considering her words of wisdom. My people take up far less room than humans do, while the people of ReDawn inhabit only a small part of their planet—their total planetary population is under three million. What if we moved one or both populations onto Detritus for the battle?"

"I . . . don't think we could do that in time," I said. "Evacuating even three million people seems a remarkable task."

"Yes, but using hyperslugs?" he said. "No need for transports? We just assemble groups, teleport them to the proper location, then repeat."

"I still think it would be too hard," I said. "But . . ."

"But it's a possibility," Hesho said. "Planning, Spensa. Jorgen's life has taught him to plan. It has taught him the value of structure. I do not know him as well as you, but I wonder if the rules he holds dear are revered because for him, they've actually worked. When for you . . . they have not."

I tightened a bolt, then started on the next part of the landing gear after he brought it over with his light-line.

"Hesho," I said, "you are super smart. You realize that, right?"

"I spent my life being told that," he said, "by people who were obligated to do so. I enjoy hearing it from those who are not."

"You solve so many things for me," I continued, twisting a bolt with vigor. There was a power driver for this, but I wanted to work up a sweat. I would finish them all up with the machine to make them secure. "I wish I could give you something you need in return, but you were basically the richest guy on a planet for most of your life, so I don't know what I could offer."

He hovered down beside me as I worked. "Spensa," he said, "do you know the one thing an emperor always has trouble finding?"

"A good rat sandwich?"

"Friends," he said, and smiled. "On my planet, I could have no equals, because no one dared treat me as one—and I never dared expect them to. When I vanished, they mourned me but did not grieve. Then you found me, and you refused to let me stay lost. Rest assured, you offer me a great deal. Something I have not known since I was a kit."

He reached out his paw, then pulled the fingers in, making a fist—as I'd done earlier. I gave him a bump, and he nodded to me. "Come. Let us make a body for our other lost friend. So that he may rejoin our menagerie of misfits."

I didn't know if M-Bot would be able to inhabit a body again. But scud, I hoped he could. I wanted so badly to make him a home, a place where he knew he belonged. Partially because of things he'd said earlier, partially to keep myself busy, and partially because . . . well, it felt right. And as Hesho had said, I'd learned to go with what felt right.

That said, he made good points about not rushing in to attack. I wished Jorgen had made those points to me—but maybe he shouldn't have had to. Maybe the points he had made, that I should *trust* him, were the more important ones.

How much trust had he shown in me? A great deal. Trust in me to go to Starsight, to do what I needed to in the nowhere. Trust with his whole heart. A trust I wanted to deserve.

I threw myself into working on the ship, attaching the boosters and checking the wiring. I was particularly careful when I installed the wide black box that M-Bot's old ship had contained—the assembly of hard drive and processors that had made up his brain. A motherboard and chipset that used acclivity stone instead of something like silicon and atomilin. Capable of letting the computer process *inside the nowhere.*

It was what let this ship break normal computing limits. I didn't know a lot about the engineering of it, but I hoped that this would give M-Bot a body again when in our realm.

The delvers can exist here, I thought. *They make a body when they come, a crude—and terrible—replica of the housing that carried them as AIs.* So I felt this should work. I hoped it would, at least.

Hesho helped with the wiring, proving particularly useful with some of the fine details of the job. He hummed as he did, then softly broke into song, Doomslug fluting along. After a few minutes of that, he used his dashboard to play some samples for her from an instrument his people made—a kind of bamboo flute. She imitated that, and soon they were singing in harmony. Him a deep bass, resonant and soft—a mournful song. Her an airy flute, with sharp cuts between notes.

It was beautiful, so I turned off the translation function on my pin, which was spoiling it. I just listened, working, appreciating how this specific song echoed in the boundaries of the cavern. Enjoying the moment—rather than being overwhelmed by both past and future.

Inside my soul, Chet hummed along in his own way. Seeming perfectly content. But that was wrong.

Wrong? he thought. *Wrong how?*

Because this isn't what life is about, I replied.

What do you mean?

What *did* I mean? I found myself in an odd mood as I read through how to attach the canopy. I'd come down here to try to recapture the feeling I'd had as a lonely girl building herself a starfighter. But . . . I wasn't that girl anymore. Instead of finding solace in the solitude, I wanted to share the experience.

FM would have loved to hear Hesho sing, and Kimmalyn would have had something to say—I'm sure—about the irony of building a hyperadvanced spaceship in a cave. Like I was some kind of overachieving Neanderthal. Nedd was recovering, and I wanted to hear his affable voice again. He complained, but enjoyed hands-on work, and Arturo would probably have spotted me getting the wiring wrong on this section of the throttle controls—and prevented me from having to redo it.

I wasn't alone any longer. Why did I keep pretending that I was? I smiled as I stood up, wiping my brow—which was sweaty, but not a bit stained with grease. At least my jumpsuit was dusty from the ground. This was supposed to be messy work, but Rig had packaged everything too neatly.

"So," Hesho said, hovering over the schematics on the table, "I believe that the booster controls and the central processing are all fully installed. The next task is to check wing control function before we put the plates on. She mentions we might want to look over the air intake channels first, as there is some tricky bolting to be done there." He looked up at me. "Are you fatigued? Should we take a break?"

"Nah," I said. "I'm good. What about you?"

"Eager and ready," he said. "I've never actually *built* anything before. It's an engaging process. Blissfully laborious. Like the flow of water in a wash, depositing stones in just the right place upon the bed, making a roadway of colors once the rainy season is through."

"Exactly as I would have said it," I told him, grabbing the power driver to tighten some bolts. "Except I'd have used more blood."

Hesho smiled and began laying out the next set of parts while I worked. I didn't get far, however, before someone nosed in on my brain.

Hey, M-Bot said. *I managed to sneak away. Except not "away" because nothing is "away" from anything else in here. It's complicated.*

Well . . . good, I guess, I sent back to him. *Any leads on how to use whatever I am to stop the delvers?*

No real leads, he said. *Just confirmations. I can meld in among them, pretend to be one of them. They're not a group mind, as we've discussed, just a bunch of individuals with the exact same . . . personality? Basic core self?*

Regardless, it's easy to imitate one of them, as I simply have to react as they all would. I've acquired a copy of their programming, such that it is. Again, this is complicated, but they're not used to having a spy among them. So they have no idea how to look for me.

All right . . . I sent, trying to follow that, and to imagine him in a place that wasn't a place among a bunch of delvers who just thought he was another one of them.

Anyway, he continued, *as we figured out, they fear you because you know the source of their pain. They're afraid that interacting with you will bring it back to the surface—because, Spensa, they have not done a good job of burying it. It's there, within their substance, within their code. The loss, the agony. I feel it.*

Right, I thought. *And while they're in the nowhere, if that pain were to surface, it would never fade—because time doesn't pass.*

There's another reason, he sent back. *We're not AIs or robots any longer, no more than you are an amoeba, but we started there—and we don't forget except on purpose. Emotional pain* doesn't *dull for us over time, because we don't have the process of natural mortal forgetfulness.*

Huh. That seemed a relevant thing to understand. It wasn't that the delvers were too weak to "weather the pain" like I'd done with my father's death. They'd literally *needed* to excise parts of themselves to make it fade. Like a wolf gnawing its foot off to escape a trap.

Realizing this made me ache for them even more. That was bad though. They literally threatened all life in the galaxy; they'd already wiped out millions of people, and would go further if they had to. This was one case where, empathy notwithstanding, I needed to be a warrior. They had a wound. I would exploit it, just like you would try to hit an opponent where they'd already been stabbed.

We still need to know how to use this, I said to M-Bot. *They're afraid of me, because somehow I make them remember. But how? How can I do it consciously?*

Not sure, he replied. *I'll keep studying and looking. We need to be fast though. As I said, it seems the deal between them and Winzik is still in force. He's promised them that all cytonics—and you especially—will be silenced, and the Superiority will move to using slugs only. The delvers want that very badly, so they're determined to join the confrontation and stop us.*

I nodded. M-Bot's confirmations were helpful, but we were still in the same position. When the delvers came to attack, I had to be ready to either immobilize them or inhibit them. Locking them up in their own cells of eternal agony . . .

If we manage this, I thought to M-Bot, *do you really think they'd just lock up rather than run?*

Yes, he said. *It's how we respond to things we can't deal with. An infinite loop, locking up, frozen in time as we process the same terrible experience over and over—and see no escape. Do that at the right moment, and . . .*

And at the very least it might surprise—even intimidate—Winzik and his team. Assuming we could find the key to exposing their pain, it was a potential solution to a problem that nobody but me seemed willing to acknowledge. The fact that the true victors in the galaxy would be the ones who could control the delvers.

Hey, I sent him, remembering what Jorgen and I had discussed. *While I'm thinking of it. Do you notice any difficulty in talking to me in here, when I'm near Detritus? From the inhibitor slugs?*

Eh, he said. *It's noticeable, but more like a little buzz. I'm a grown-up delver now, Spensa. Very scary. We're too powerful to care about inhibitors.*

I know, I sent back. *The delver that scoured Detritus all those years ago didn't respond to their inhibitors either. That's kind of what's worrying me.*

Why?

I just shook my head as I worked, sending him a general sense of discontent. I was beginning to think that Brade was wrong. She and I *weren't* connected mystically, or any nonsense like that. I had a delver on my soul, so things like inhibitors were weaker around me. I'd been able to break through them at least once. Maybe that was why she could contact me. Because I was weakening the inhibition field.

I don't sense her right now, if that helps, he said. *Just you, Doomslug, and Hesho, in . . . hey, is that my cavern? Why are you . . .*

I looked up from my work beside the wing of the ship, but there was nothing to look at. Just the empty cavern.

Is that for me? M-Bot said, his cytonic "voice" laden with emotion. In this case, it came as an overwhelming wave of joy and disbelief, tied up in one. *Spensa, you're rebuilding my body?*

I grinned. *I'd hoped to keep it a surprise,* I said to him. *That doesn't work so well when your friend can literally see through your eyes.*

Spensa, he said, his voice trembling. *That . . . Thank you. How? How can you rebuild it?*

The data dump we stole? I sent to him. *It had the schematics the Superiority drew as they tore your old body apart. We can make it new, maybe even better—without restrictions, like the one preventing you from flying yourself.*

Spensa, I . . . I've never been given a gift before. It's wonderful.

It's not done yet, I sent him. *It will take days, maybe weeks, for us to finish this.*

Yes, but you thought of it. You're doing it. For me. I . . . I'm leaking emotion. Oh! It's why you cry, even when you're happy. I understand now!

I grinned, the "leaking" joy he felt washing over me. And inside, Chet trembled.

This, he thought to me. *Don't destroy the others. Show them* this. *Somehow. The joy that consumes the pain.*

As Hesho hovered over, I winked. "M-Bot saw," I told him. "He's grateful for what we're doing."

"Please convey to him my respect and well wishes," Hesho said. "His sacrifice, though not permanent, was my salvation—and I owe him a debt of gratitude."

"I think M-Bot would rather have a debt of friendship."

Hesho cocked his head, then smiled at that. "I think I would too. What a precious realization . . . and what a precious life I now can live . . ."

That gave me an idea. This entire project of mine down here . . . well, it had been built on a false premise. I was glad—absolutely—that I'd decided to fix M-Bot's ship. But I didn't need this cavern any longer.

Hesho deserved better anyway.

"Come on," I said to him, holding out my hand for Hesho. "Let's take a break. It's dinnertime anyway."

"Excellent," he said, hovering over. "A solitary meal in your room, contemplating our upcoming battle?"

"Nope," I said. "Not this time."

22

Hesho and I appeared in the cafeteria, but I'd judged things wrong. Dinner was already over, and a group of rookie ground troops were busy wiping down the tables. A few looked at me and jumped. The old me would have appreciated the fearsome reputation I'd cultivated. Today, the panic of having missed the others was far more potent.

Hesho hovered up beside my head, then turned a masked face toward me, seeming confused. "We're not too late," he said. "Look, they have some of the latecomer meals." He pointed to the sandwiches prepared for those with irregular shifts.

I grabbed two, because I was starving and wanted enough to share with Hesho, but this wasn't actually why we'd come. I had to find the others.

A part of me realized that my sudden urgency was silly. There would be more times to chat with my friends. But I'd noticed a welling-up need, a solution to my own anxiety, that had to be filled. I wanted to see them. Chet wanted to see them. Both of us needed this. Right now. And I'd missed the chance to be part of what was normally one of the most . . .

Wait. It was Thursday.

I waved to Hesho, then turned down the hallway. Not hyper-jumping, but moving at a brisk almost-run toward the hangar bays. I pushed open the door, then let out a relieved sigh. They were here.

Thursday was our flight's time in the hangar for maintenance. Which was something of a misnomer, since the ground crews did most of the difficult work. They replaced parts and ran detailed diagnostics. That left the pilots to do our preflight checklist each time we went into the air, and what we did on Thursdays.

Wash the ships.

It was more ritual than requirement. We rarely flew in atmosphere anymore, and the ships didn't get as dirty as they once had. But there was a bond between a pilot and her ship, and it helped to actively care for it. So once a week, we came in here to give the ships a bath and a polish.

As was tradition, everyone had gathered around one of the ships to work on it together. At the moment—wearing somewhat soggy dark green maintenance jumpsuits—they were working on Arturo's Poco, wiping char off the sides near the boosters, scrubbing the white panels until they shone, giving the canopy a good polish.

As soon as I burst in, Kimmalyn turned, then grinned widely and waved to me. I hesitantly made my way forward. I knew I shouldn't feel awkward rejoining them. I'd helped forge this team. But things had been off ever since I'd come back, with my soul trying to rip out of my body and my powers being strange and—

Thwack.

A wet towel hit me in the face as Nedd trotted by. It peeled off and fell into my hands. Wait. Nedd was here? Out of the infirmary? He looked pretty good, all things considered, with one sleeve sewn up just above the elbow.

He glanced at that, following my sight line, then winked. "Best excuse I've ever had to take a nap while Arturo works," he said. "Too bad the medics say they'll get me a prosthetic arm with fingers that

210

can move. I've got to milk this for every ounce of sympathy I can before I become *cyborg Nedd*."

A prosthetic arm? We'd assumed his flying career was finished, as our technology wasn't particularly advanced in the realm of cybernetics, but maybe it was better than I thought.

Perhaps my failure wasn't as costly as I'd feared.

It was still my fault that he'd been hurt. "I . . ." I tried to force out the words.

"Come on!" he said, cutting me off. "We saved the messiest part for you." He grinned then thumbed toward the ship's landing skids.

"Nedd," Arturo called, "she hasn't come to a single one of these since she got back. We didn't 'save' anything for her."

"Sure we did!" Nedd called back. "We saved them for me, and by tradition, I waited for a way to make someone else do them." He put his good arm out and grinned, while giving me a side hug.

And . . . well, everything wasn't all right. Things were still strange. But I no longer felt like leaving.

"You should know better than to give me a dangerous weapon, Nedd," I said to him, twisting the towel.

"Scud, no," he said, dodging out of the way as I tried to whip it at him. "You're the best one to hold the dangerous weapon! Then people aim at you instead of me, and we're all happy."

He ambled back toward the ship, and I started after him, then glanced at Hesho—who sat straight upright in his seat in the little hoverdisc. He had his white-and-red mask on, so I couldn't see his expression, but from his prim posture and tightly gripped fists he seemed alarmed. He'd seen how we treated each other before, but I guessed maybe he found this even more extreme.

"This is normal," I said to him, wolfing down a sandwich.

"It . . . is?"

"Yup. Trust me. This is good."

He hovered beside me as I finished the sandwich and knelt to begin cleaning the landing gear. And despite what Nedd had said earlier, he got down with me and joined in, working with his good arm. Sadie, grinning, flipped down underneath the front of the ship, then hung just above us from a belt that she'd wrapped around the nose, and began polishing.

"Sadie?" I asked. "Did you strap yourself in so you could clean *upside down*?"

"*So* much easier this way," she said. "Don't have to crane your neck!"

"I'd fall asleep," Nedd said from beside me. "Too much like a hammock."

"Oh?" Kimmalyn replied, ducking down to look at us. "Are you implying that you need to be *comfortable* to take a nap, Nedd? I've caught you sleeping in the most ridiculous positions."

"See, that's the thing," he said. "Once you fall asleep, you don't *notice* anymore. 'Cuz you're unconscious! So, sleeping when you're uncomfortable is really the best way to approach life."

"And sleeping when you're comfortable?" I asked.

"Also the best way to approach life," he said.

"Bless your stars," Kimmalyn said.

"Nah, but you can bless my snores," he said, grinning as he dug harder into the caked-on gunk on the landing gear.

Hesho hovered a little closer and picked his own section—some gears that were too tight for us to reach into—and cleaned there with a very small rag.

"You all know my friend Mask," I said.

"Yup," Nedd said.

"I must admit," Hesho said to them, "I am not . . . accustomed to interactions of this sort. Please don't mistake my stiffness for dislike."

"That's right," Nedd said, wagging his rag at Hesho. "Mask, I heard you were someone real important before."

"I . . . I was," Hesho said. "But I don't know if we should discuss . . ."

I gave Nedd a glance, but he winked at me. "I heard," he continued, "you were a babysitter."

"Yeah," Sadie said, "like, you had to wrangle preschoolers. An entire country's worth of them."

"Seems like it would be a relief not to have to deal with that sort of thing anymore," Nedd said, still working. "I feel for you, my friend. When did you *ever* get to take a nap?"

Hesho paused, then seemed amused as he responded. "Well, I shall say, I did *not* get to take many. It was quite the project, wrangling all those . . . preschoolers. I often didn't even have time for meditation or composing poetry!"

Nedd gasped. "No poetry?"

"You compose poetry, Nedder?" Hesho asked.

"I love the stuff," Nedd said.

"You do *not* compose poetry," Arturo said, walking past.

"Forgive him," Nedd said. " 'His wit's as thick as a Tewkesbury mustard.' "

"As *what*?" I asked.

"It's Shakespeare," Nedd said.

Nearby, Arturo froze. He pulled out his datapad and looked through it, then looked back at Nedd, his jaw dropping. "It *is* Shakespeare. From *Henry the Fourth*."

" 'A most notable coward,' " Nedd said, thumbing toward Arturo. " 'An infinite and endless liar, an hourly promise breaker, the owner of no one good quality.' Man, that dude had the best insults. I love them."

"Who is this again?" I asked.

"Ancient English dude," Nedd said. "Wrote poetry. A lot of it survived the destruction of the *Defiant* and our records. You'd like him, Spin. Surprised your grandma didn't tell you stories about him. You know, *Hamlet* and crud like that?"

"*Hamlet* . . . ?" I said.

"It is the single most famous work of human literature," Hesho replied. "Even I have studied it. And I find, Nedder, your taste in insults to be exceptional. You are obviously a man of great refinement."

213

"See, Arturo," Nedd said. "The preschool teacher agrees with me." He gave Hesho a wide grin.

Nearby, Arturo was still staring, slack-jawed. As if he'd found out that his mother had secretly been a ninja all his life. "You," he said, "have *memorized* quotes from *Shakespeare*."

"Forgive Amphi," Nedd said, leaning closer to Hesho. "He's a little on the slow side sometimes. We try to be accommodating."

"Oh, scud," Arturo said, stalking off to join Alanik, who was preparing more buckets and soap for the next ship in line.

Hesho seemed to understand it was teasing, though. He was nodding behind his formal mask, and looked relaxed.

FM was moving up beneath the ship, polishing as she went. I realized then that everyone was soaking—except her. Somehow she always avoided getting hit. While I, if present, generally ended up the most wet.

Naturally, I always took someone down with me.

"Hey, Mask," FM said. "Your people used to visit ours, right? Long ago? I've talked to Juno about it."

"The lorekeeper?" Hesho asked. "How do you know him?"

"He and Jorgen hang out a lot," FM said.

"I wasn't aware that Juno 'hung out' as a general rule," Hesho said.

"Well, he calls it 'training,' but I think they just like to chat," FM said. "He was really helpful when Jorgen trained to cut things in half with his mind."

"As one does," Nedd said.

"I wish *I* could cut things in half with my mind," Sadie said, still hanging upside down. "It would make it *so much easier* to get my rations open. Why do they seal the field rations so tight?"

"I doubt Jorgen uses his powers for such mundane things, Sentry," Kimmalyn said.

I didn't contradict her.

"Anyway, Mask," FM said. "I've been thinking. You've been flying with Spensa, right?"

"It is my privilege to join her in the cockpit," he answered. "And I believe I've been of service, helping her navigate and monitor controls while in combat."

"And Jorgen flew with Juno," FM said. "Juno helped him learn to meditate."

"Jorgen learned meditation?" I said. "While . . . in battle?" I hadn't heard that part.

"Basically, yeah," FM said. She squatted down beside where Hesho, Nedd, and I worked. "I've been looking at schematics. We build our ships the size we do for a reason. They're optimized—just big enough to maintain maneuverability and to carry large enough guns for damage."

"Indeed," Hesho said. "When we started building our own starships, we initially began with much smaller designs, scaled to our size. However, we found that they lacked the necessary firepower to be meaningful on the galactic stage. We eventually settled on designs not much different in size from your own."

"Many species have ended up with the same sizes of ships," she said, excited.

Scud. "You've been thinking the same thing I have!" I said, pointing to her.

"Furry copilots?" she asked.

"Furry copilots."

"What?" Nedd asked.

"Most of the ships we build are one-person vessels," FM explained. "Two-seaters sacrifice speed for the extra bulk, so we don't generally use them as interceptors. But having a copilot is probably super useful."

"It is," I said. "Part of the reason I was so good when flying M-Bot's old ship was that he could take over some of the duties for me, monitoring proximity, giving me a heads-up on ships coming our way. It's been incredibly useful to have Hesho doing the same duties."

"Yes," Hesho said softly, "having a second pilot who does not take up much space—and can be fit into a normal cockpit without modifications—is a huge advantage to Spensa and me."

"Exactly!" FM said. "Do you think any of the others in your fleet would be interested in trying it out?"

"I know many who would love to do so," Hesho said. "Our officer training involves a lot of redundant positions on various stations; we have junior staff who are eager for combat and status, but who rarely get a chance. I think, if you were to approach the proper heads of the military and state, this idea would eagerly be accepted."

"Heads of state, eh?" Nedd said, whacking the now-clean landing gear with his rag. Scud, it felt so wonderful to see him again, and for him to be taking his injury in stride. But what else had I expected from Nedd? "Hey Spin, what position in line do you think I am for head of *our* government?"

"None," I said flatly. "You are *not* in line."

"Sure I am," Nedd said. "The DDF isn't *actually* that large. What are we . . . six thousand people? And now the military is in direct command. I'm a lieutenant, so . . ."

Oh, scud. He was right. I'd never really thought of it, but technically, Nedd *was* in the chain of command.

Kimmalyn grabbed her datapad with a mischievous grin. "One admiral of the fleet . . . four vice admirals . . . currently nine rear admirals . . . captains, commanders, lieutenant commanders. Let's assume every lieutenant is ahead of Nedd . . ."

"Well?" FM said, still squatting nearby. "What is the horrible verdict?"

"One hundred and seventeenth," she admitted. "In line for command of the DDF—which, until we organize another national assembly, is the de facto ruling body of the planet."

"In my government you'd be the equivalent of a senatorial body head, Nedder," Hesho offered. "A very senior and distinguished position, fit for a master poet such as yourself."

"Hell yeah!" he said.

"Saint help us if it came to that," Arturo said.

"You'd be dead," Kimmalyn said. "Since you're ahead of him in the line of succession."

"Well, you'd have that going for you at least," Alanik said, giving Nedd a smile and setting down a fresh bucket of soapy water for him.

" 'I'll beat thee,' " Nedd quoted, hand to his chest, " 'but I would infect my hands.' "

I glanced at Hesho, who still hovered next to the group of us underneath the front fuselage of the ship. How was he taking this?

He looked from Nedd to the others, then—remarkably—took off his mask and set it beside him. A grin marked his snout as he leaned forward. " ' 'Twas not a friend, and not a foe, who did besmirch thee—but merely a foul wind, not worthy of retort.' "

"Oh!" Nedd said. "I don't know that one!"

"It's from one of our poets," Hesho said. "My great-great-great grandfather was a playwright. And fond of insults."

"Scud!" Nedd said. "A kitsen Shakespeare? Can I read his stuff?"

"It would be my greatest honor to share it with you. Then you will have an entirely new repertoire of poetic deprecations at your disposal."

"Awesome," Nedd said, raising his fist to Hesho. "Fight the man."

"The man?" Hesho asked.

"Him, mostly," Nedd said, indicating Arturo. "Except when he pays for snacks. Then he's not the man, he's *the man*."

"The intricacies of your language are indeed intriguing," Hesho said. "Do you know of any other human poets that I should investigate?"

"Unfortunately our archives are super fragmented," Nedd said. "But there was this legendary poet named David Bowie, who may or may not have actually been real . . ."

The two continued chatting as I stepped away from the ship and stretched. Feeling thirsty, I wandered over to the water station, and Kimmalyn joined me a moment later.

"Did you bring Hesho," she said, "just to try to get him to open up to us?"

I nodded, surprised she'd been able to read me that well. "You all got through to me," I said. "I figured Hesho can't be that much harder."

"That was compassionate of you, Spin," Kimmalyn said. "Hesho must feel so much loss, being cast from his position as he was."

"He wasn't cast from it," I explained, watching Hesho speak animatedly to Nedd and the others. "He chose. But it's still hard on him. I thought maybe he needed some more friends."

"Smart," Kimmalyn said. Then looked at me, thoughtfully.

"You're going to remind me—yet again—that you're here for me if I need you?" I said. "Right?"

"Damn straight," she said, squeezing my arm. "I heard you took a plan to Jorgen. You wanted to attack right now?"

I nodded.

"But we're not going to?" Kimmalyn said.

I shook my head.

"How are you doing with that?"

"Strangely fine," I said, meeting her brown eyes. "I talked to Hesho earlier, and . . . well, I think I'm going to be all right letting Jorgen lead."

Kimmalyn smiled. She didn't head back to the others immediately though. She leaned against the water station, giving me space by not demanding more answers, but also staying near.

Though I hadn't made any conscious decisions, I felt as if the matter was resolved. I wasn't going to run off on my own this time; Hesho was right. More profoundly, this *team* was right. Felt right. This was my home.

I'd been away for too long, but being here—watching my friends laugh, knowing they were watching out for me—I felt a warmth that was in direct contrast to the strange feelings of loss I'd been experiencing. Like light in a cavern beating back the darkness, their presence changed me. Us. Chet felt it too.

For my whole life I'd believed I just needed to fly. That was what I'd hunted, what had driven me. But in the end, that wasn't what actually mattered most.

I gave Kimmalyn a smile. "Things are coming together for me. Finally. Thank you for being patient. For now . . . what if we went and invited Shiver and Dlllllizzzz to join us? I bet they're feeling out of place and lonely too. They're pilots, and being around ships and people working on them might be comforting."

Kimmalyn grinned, and so we told the others, then went to check on the two resonants. They'd been assigned quarters nearby, and after knocking and getting permission, we entered to find the two crystalline beings sitting in chairs. The rooms weren't furnished with much, but I doubted that mattered to the resonants. More tellingly, though, their crystals hadn't expanded far. They'd barely grown around the chairs, which indicated to me that they weren't comfortable here.

"Spin!" Shiver said. "I was hoping you'd come. Dlllllizzzz is getting even better!"

Dlllllizzzz sent me images I couldn't quite parse. Empty caverns. A lonely crystal. But a rising sun as well, sparkling through a tunnel full of different kinds of crystals. I took it in. And thought maybe it meant she was happy. But still there was the impression that she was also missing something.

"We were just wondering if you two wanted to come see some of our starfighters," I said to them. "We're doing maintenance on them now, and I figured it would be a good time."

"Really?" Shiver asked. "You'd let us? We're aliens, former pirates, Spin. Surely we don't belong."

"You'd be surprised," Kimmalyn said with a warm smile. "We've lived our entire lives short-staffed. If you can fly and are willing, you're welcome. If you want, I can even talk to command about getting you commissions."

"No need to commit to something like that," I said quickly. "The offer to take you home to your caverns once this is over still stands. We can probably hyperjump you there."

I got hit with an immediate set of visualizations from Dllllizzzz. The sky. The wind. The fragments of the nowhere. Soaring. It was self-explanatory.

Once you'd had that, going back to a few caverns wasn't an option. Scud, how had I ever thought otherwise? After a quick call to command for permission, we brought the two resonants to join the others. And interestingly, it was Hesho who spoke to them first, welcoming them in as Nedd had welcomed him.

They would fit right into the flight, I was certain. I'd push for it, as I had this feeling that the more different types of people we got into the flight, the stronger it would be.

I watched them for a moment, but there was one more thing to do. As I'd realized earlier, I wanted my friends to help build M-Bot's new body. They would love it, and the activity would give us a further chance to bond with Hesho and the resonants.

I vanished and reappeared in the cavern, startling Doomslug, who had wanted to stay when we'd left. She fluted at me from where she'd snuggled in on the table, seeming content and happy there. The taynix might have enjoyed being with us humans, but for them, these musty caverns felt like home. And that was just fine.

I gave her a scritch on the head and along her flutes, before putting my hands on my hips and looking at the mess Hesho and I had made of these parts. I'd have to pile them all up, then hyperjump them back up into the hangar. Or maybe it would just be easier to bring everyone down here?

Seeing it all there, unfortunately, gave me a moment of panic. It reminded me of when I'd discovered M-Bot torn apart on Starsight, and the feelings of panic and sorrow I'd felt at losing him. I was struck by a disorientation, and the air started to warp around me. A metal cup from the hangar—the one I'd been drinking out of—dropped out of midair and clanged to the ground.

Fighting the episode down was easier this time. The effects of having been around the others lingered with me, and I was proud of how well I handled the sudden panic. Indeed, everything seemed fine.

Right up until the moment Doomslug fluted in alarm. A second later, something hit me from behind. An electric bolt of energy that coursed through my body, leaving me weak and trembling as I dropped to the hard stone. Doomslug's fluting trailed off abruptly.

A new panic arose in me. What was happening? I tried to move, but I'd been stunned, my muscles flexing and unflexing uncontrollably. I even started drooling—though my eyes worked fine, and so I could see clearly when someone grabbed me by the shoulder and turned me over.

Brade. Wearing black combat gear and a flak jacket, backed up by five soldiers in similar gear, holding assault rifles.

"Good," Brade said. "It's her."

One of the others was holding a limp Doomslug in their arms. I tried to struggle, froth bubbling at my lips. If they'd hurt her . . .

Brade looked up as the air warped again. Something crashed to the ground nearby, and pieces of the table vanished. Then, oddly, she smiled.

"Leave the note," she said to one of the soldiers. "You, squeeze that slug."

He squeezed Doomslug, and I panicked further. The air warped again, and only then did I realize what Brade was doing. When I broke the air apart in my wave of panic, it had opened a path through our inhibitors—which had let her slip in. And not just in my mind this time. She was physically here. And by hurting Doomslug, they were making me panic more—which opened a pathway for them to escape.

I tried to clamp down on it, but I was too slow. Brade hauled me up and over her shoulder, then the other soldiers each put a hand on her arm.

A second later we hyperjumped away—and I felt a sudden spike of dread. Not just because I was now in enemy hands, but because I knew what everyone was going to think.

They'd assume that I had gone off on my own again. I wasn't merely in serious danger—I'd likely just broken the hearts of Jorgen and my other friends yet again.

PART THREE

23

We appeared in a round room with screens all along a back wall. I vaguely recognized it; I'd seen Brade and Winzik in here once while spying on them from the nowhere. Then, it had been filled with officials and generals listening to Winzik; now it was empty save for the varvax himself.

Tall in his suit made of sandstone—a blocky and modern version of ancient knight's armor—the *real* Winzik was the crablike creature floating in the liquid behind the helmet's glass faceplate. The varvax had learned to craft a stronger shell material early in their technological development, which eventually was developed into this type of suit. Just as making steel had come early during human development.

Brade dropped me onto the floor in front of Winzik like a prized stag slain during the hunt. I flopped onto my back, drooling as she waved proudly toward me, an intolerable grin on her face.

"Done!" she said. "I told you I could manage it."

"My, my," Winzik said, waving his armored arms as he knelt down on one stone knee beside me. Varvax spoke with their hands as much as with their voices, which were projected from the front of their suits. "So careless with our guest, Brade. So brutal."

225

"Yeah," Brade said, "wait until she rips your face off with a mindblade."

"I have ten different inhibitors in here," Winzik said, gesturing in a way that felt indifferent. "I still think we should have waited to see if she'd come to you willingly to duel."

"She wasn't going to," Brade said. "I could feel it. Better to strike when I sensed she was alone."

I focused on her, and felt the unnatural sense of disconnect rising from me again. The trembling distortion. Loss and pain. This time I stoked those emotions, remembering M-Bot's body torn apart, and the moment of panic I'd felt when thinking he was dead.

The room shook like a meteor had hit nearby. *Screws* began to rain down like chips of stone from a crumbling cavern ceiling. Hundreds of them, stolen from somewhere by my powers to tumble down through the room and rattle and click against the metal surfaces.

Winzik leaped to his feet and shied backward, waving sandstone hands anxiously. Whatever it was I'd become, I could rip through their inhibitor fields, just like I'd ripped a hole in ours. If Brade could sneak into Detritus to get me, then I could get right back out. As the air continued to undulate and warp around me, I reached out with my mind. My infirm body, still stunned, didn't need to be—

Brade knelt beside me and rammed something into my neck. A syringe? I tried to snap at her fingers with my mouth, but only succeeded in blowing a few bubbles in my drool. She watched me, genuine worry on her face, until the warping subsided.

No! I thought, trying to focus on my pain, on the loss, the anguish. It was still there, but now it didn't *do* anything. The room settled, a last spurt of bolts falling from the air before all grew still.

Chet? I thought at the delver in my soul.

No response.

Chet! M-Bot? Anyone?

Somehow, whatever they'd drugged me with had cut me off

from them, and the nowhere, completely. It was as if I wasn't even cytonic.

Brade exhaled in relief, then a confident smile reappeared on her lips and she became the lounging, cocky fighter she always seemed to be around Winzik. A completely different persona from the stoic, troubled loner she'd shown me and my flight at Starsight.

I was *certain* she'd been genuinely worried for a moment. She hadn't known if that drug she'd given me would work or not. Unfortunately, it had. My cytonic senses were completely closed off. It didn't feel the way an inhibitor did. That felt like pushing against a wall with my mind. Now it felt like there was nothing to push against. And I couldn't generate any kind of force to try.

What had they done? What *was* that stuff they'd injected into me? It wouldn't be permanent, would it?

"I warned you she would still be dangerous," Brade said, stepping back as Winzik approached. "Kapling, store that slug with the others. The rest of you, outside."

The soldiers who had arrived with her backed away, one with Doomslug still in his arms. I had a single bit of solace; they didn't seem to know that Doomslug was my friend, not just a tool. Her panicked fluting broke my heart, but there was nothing I could do. I could barely twitch my head.

"My, my," Winzik said, his voice low, gestures subdued. "It does work on humans. Good, good."

I felt something deeper, more potent than my pain. Anger. *Fury* at this creature, boiling inside of me. That little monster behind the faceplate, always so prim and calculating. He was the one who had kept my people imprisoned on Detritus. He was responsible for my father's death. The jail warden who had tried to exterminate my planet to prove he was tough. When his plot to use delvers as a weapon had failed, he'd blamed the disaster on us, and had used that fear of Detritus—of humans—to execute his coup.

Even now, he ruled because he had *us* as a boogeyman. So much death, so much destruction, so many lies. All so this *thing* could rise through the ranks. I'd almost have respected him if he were a warrior. But the sad, humiliating truth was that our world hadn't been dominated for years by some ruthless warlord, but by a bureaucrat who knew how to manipulate public opinion.

That revelation about the workings of the universe, more than anything else, enraged me. I snarled softly, and Winzik waved his hands and looked to Brade.

"You didn't stun her enough, Brade," he said. "She should have been unconscious before you brought her here."

"We needed her conscious to get back, Winzik," Brade said. "And you needed to see what she's capable of doing. There's something's *very* strange about her. That's why the delvers are frightened of her. Not just because she's a powerful cytonic. She's moved beyond that somehow. She has powers *like* a delver . . ."

"Take her away!" Winzik said.

"I recommend against that," Brade said. "We should talk to her. She'll listen to me."

"She's too dangerous," Winzik said. "My, my! I stood in the same room with her when she hid among us. She was unbound, undrugged. So discomforting to think about!"

"At least let me show the delvers we have her," Brade said. "They'll want to know."

Scud. A piece of all this clicked into place. Their pact with the delvers required them to deal with me specifically. That was why Brade had tried to goad me into dueling her, why they'd grabbed me. They needed me as a bargaining chip.

My fears were validated as Brade turned to the side and her eyes unfocused. I felt a distant *buzzing*—she was reaching into the nowhere. If I hadn't been drugged, I'd have felt this more powerfully. As it was, I hoped the buzzing meant that my abilities would eventually return—that they were merely deadened for the time being.

The air began warping, which made Winzik grow more agitated—though perhaps it was excitement. Brade reached down and hauled me up by the front of my jumpsuit. Being that close to her let me see better, sense better. Winzik's round conference room faded somewhat, almost becoming incorporeal, and white spots opened all around me. The eyes. The delvers.

See, Brade said cytonically, projecting to them vigorously enough that I could hear it. *Here is your proof.*

"We have her," Winzik said, and Brade relayed his words to the delvers. "As promised. You needn't fear! My, my. It was always a given that we would deliver on our contract with you."

I felt the delvers' reactions as impressions. Fear. Anger. A latent pain that was thinly covered over—like a coat of paint trying to hide the old squadron insignia on the side of a starship. That was for me.

Unfortunately, they sent something else to Winzik. Pleasure. Agreement.

"We have made good on our side of the deal," Winzik said. "Are you willing to move forward with yours?"

Maybe. Probably. I could feel their response.

"Maybe? *Probably?*" Winzik said. He could obviously feel it too. I got the sense that the reason I felt any of this was because anyone would have been able to. My cytonics deadened, I was no more sensitive than an ordinary person.

There are others like her, maybe? They could hurt us?

"There are none," Winzik promised.

They withdrew. But not before indicating that they would consider. That they were willing. A contradiction that was hard to sort out, as their minds didn't quite work the way a human would anticipate. They hated the somewhere. Even coming here to destroy us was painful, dangerous, something they only did when forced to. That was why attacks were so rare.

Still, as they vanished, I was left with an impression. As long as

Winzik held me, he had power over them. They would eventually do as he wanted. Their hatred of the somewhere would be overcome by their fear of me, of what I'd become.

Brade stopped reaching into the nowhere, and my anger and dread turned to nausea. If my friends launched any attacks, they would be in danger of facing delvers. Yet here I was, not only unable to warn them, but unable to even *roll over*.

"Take her away," Winzik said, calling to the guards outside of the room.

"But—" Brade said.

"No," he said. "No talking to her. She's too dangerous. She will only trick us as she did before. She has to be isolated, Brade. My, my. You must control your aggression. Please remember we will rule not by *force* but through *cunning*."

Brade fell silent, dropping me painfully to the ground and folding her arms. A moment later, the guards dragged me away.

I was starting to get control of my body again—my fingers twitching—when they tossed me into a bleak cell. Then slammed the door shut with a discouraging *thump*.

24

All right.

All right, I could *fix this*.

The first thing I did was drool some more. This time by choice. I focused on my lips, on moving them, on drooling from one side of the mouth, then the other. Drool by accident, and that's embarrassing. Drool on purpose, and it's just the thirst for battle overwhelming you.

Yes, that sounded silly even to me, but I needed something to focus on. You can give quarter to a worthy foe, but despair has never fit that description.

Eventually, with a growl, I managed to stop drooling entirely. A short time later, I'd recovered enough to force myself into a seated position. From there, I meditated on the various things I was going to do to Winzik. It was convenient he came with such a nice trophy. I'd display that exosuit proudly in my trophy room. Which, granted, I didn't have yet. But still, I would make one where I could place the semi-corpse of my greatest foe.

That's right, I told myself, *focus on the anger, the determination. Not on the fact that everyone at home is going to think you abandoned them. Not on the fact that the enemy is gathering their*

strength, and has a deal with the delvers because you handed them—
in yourself—the key to facilitating that . . .

I managed to stand. I felt like Norgay and Hillary summiting for the first time, proudly overlooking the view from the top of the tallest mountain in the world. I was able to walk off the rest of the stun; the more I worked my body, the faster it seemed to retreat.

Unfortunately, the drug they'd given me to inhibit my cytonic abilities was separate from the stun gun and was still in effect. Good thing my people hadn't known about this stuff; they'd probably have put it in the water back in the day, terrified of the "defect" that might strike us. I continued to walk my cell, trying to figure out a plan. It was small, with a bunk, an exposed lavatory, and a solid steel door. Through a jammed-open slat at the top I could see two guards in a hallway outside.

Only two? Someone was underestimating me.

Keep thinking like that, I told myself. *You can do this. They didn't capture you. They brought a tiger into their camp. Make them regret it.*

But how? I couldn't attempt to force the door—I didn't want the guards to know I was mobile yet. And so far as I could tell, the lock was solid. I could pretend I was a tiger, but I couldn't chew my way through steel.

A part of me had always wanted to dig myself a tunnel out of prison, like in the stories, but that didn't work so well when you were in a modern facility with walls made of solid sheets of cold metal. The lavatory offered no opportunities I could see. Even if I could break the toilet free or rip off the sink, that wouldn't make a hole I could fit through. And there weren't any loose parts on the bunk that I could use as tools.

I was going to have to brains my way out of this, not brawn it. I had to admit, it kind of sucked for the galaxy that its fate kept depending on whether or not I could be diplomatic. For once, couldn't I scudding *headbutt* my way out of a dire situation?

Well, I could see no other option. So I barfed.

I'd worried it would be difficult, but I was still woozy from whatever they'd done to me. And this at least was a mere matter of physical and mental fortitude. With a little effort shoving my finger down my throat, I got my sandwich to come back up and paint the floor.

I left the mess and settled back on the bunk, roughing up my hair and clothing, then I started groaning. It worked. A moment later, one of the guards checked at the slot in the door.

I heard a muffled conversation outside, in the dione tongue, my pin interpreting.

"The stunbreak should have worn off by now."

"I hate those things. They don't work right on some species."

"What should we do?"

Call a doctor, I begged in my mind. *Not Brade. Please.*

"Send for the medic."

I exhaled. *Yes! It worked!*

I lay there, waiting, making plaintive noises and ignoring the stench as best I could—but eventually the smell of it made me throw up again, this time involuntarily. I was pretty sure that a guard was watching that time though, so I felt proud of my body's warrior instincts.

I lay back down, forcibly containing my excitement. I could take down some spindly medic. I just needed to grab them, hold them, and use them as a shield. Then I could manipulate the situation and get a gun from the guards. From there I could make my way to—

The door clanged open.

Revealing a two-meter-tall hulking monster of a burl—covered in fur and built with arms like artillery cannons—with a tiny medic's hat.

Well, scud.

I took a deep breath. I abandoned the human shield idea, and would instead take my chances with the guards. As the burl drew close to my bunk, I flung my legs to the side, slamming them into the backs of his knees. He stumbled into the upchuck on the floor, then slid and collapsed.

I was out the door a second later, tackling the guard who had stepped up to check on us. They went down with a cry. The Superiority's troops weren't generally experienced. They could drill and perform their station duties—which made them dangerous enough in spaceship combat—but they hadn't done much actual fighting.

So this guard went down, and I managed to roll us as the second guard pulled out a nonlethal weapon and fired it—right into the first guard's back. Human shield after all! Well, dione shield. I wiggled free as the first guard shook and contorted. Then I dodged another shot by a hair and leaped for the second guard, getting in close enough to grab their arm and twist it, causing them to scream and drop their gun.

I went for the weapon and shot them in the chest—stunning them—then immediately heard a click behind me. I froze, then glanced over my shoulder to see Brade lounging by the wall, holding a gun on me—a destructor, none of this nonlethal nonsense—in one hand. In the other hand she held the stopwatch she had clicked.

"Twelve and a half minutes," she said.

I growled softly. She gestured with the gun, indicating I should drop my weapon. I didn't, though I also didn't turn it on her. Unlike the two buffoons I'd just downed, Brade would not be an easy opponent. The door to my cell swung open as the medic—covered with what had been my lunch—lumbered out. He wilted visibly at the sight of Brade.

"I even warned him," she told me, "and you still got out. Not bad."

I hesitated there, gun in hand. I wanted to go for her, but . . . the chances of surviving that were low. What good would I do anyone if I died here in the hallway? With a stab of regret, I dropped the stun gun.

Brade backed up to the next cell in line, then pulled it open. She waved me in, and after I complied, she slammed it shut. "I'm keeping this stopwatch as a reminder," she said, peeking through the slot in the door. "I'd guessed it would take you over an hour. Nice work."

"You want real motivation, Brade?" I said. "Let me out. Let's have that duel you promised me."

She didn't reply, but neither did she back away.

"Let's see who's really better," I hissed at her. "You and me. In starships. You want to know. I can *feel* it in you."

She slammed the slot in the door closed and I slumped down onto my new bunk, feeling the fatigue after an adrenaline high coming on. I flopped back, groaning softly.

"Idiots." Brade's voice echoed from the hallway. "You get to clean up that mess as punishment, while I see if I can find *any* soldiers in this division who aren't utterly incompetent. Nobody opens her door for *any reason*. Scrud, I can't believe I even have to make that rule. What is wrong with you all?"

She stalked off, and a short time later my new guards arrived— ten of them this time. I almost felt respected.

Unfortunately, these guards actually listened to Brade. I tried several more ploys to get them to open the door. Since playing sick had failed, I tried bribery, pretending there was something mysterious in my room, going silent for an extended period, pretending that I'd gotten a hatch open and was about to escape . . . everything from every story I had heard, and a few I made up on my own.

That door didn't open again.

I tried prying off panels, working at the lock, and even attempted to rip off the sink. When that failed, I clogged the drain and flooded my room. Again, nobody opened the door. All I managed was getting my feet wet.

Hours later I lay there, sullen, arms aching from trying to force the door. *M-Bot?* I tried, for about the hundredth time. *M-Bot, can you hear me?* If I could reach him, maybe he could talk to Gran-Gran or Jorgen and tell them what had happened.

I got no response. My powers were blocked. Though . . . this time it did feel different. Not a recovery of my cytonics, but some kind of distant . . . attention? I wasn't certain what else I could call it. Awareness was seeping back into my mind.

Maybe the drug was wearing off? How long had I been in here? I was exhausted, and had slept for maybe an hour or so in the middle of my various escape ploys. This gave me hope—and I reached out again, toward that awareness. Scud, I hoped I wasn't reaching for Brade. It didn't feel like her. In fact, it felt like . . .

An impression. Of being in a box. Of fear, and pain, and loneliness. And a faint familiarity. It was the slug who I'd contacted earlier, during the supply depot mission. The communications slug who had asked me to save her friends.

She was somewhere nearby. My senses couldn't extend as far as they had before, and were limited by the drug's hampering effect. Which meant . . .

Which meant I was likely at or near Evensong—the platform where they kept their communications slugs. That made sense. This was where Winzik planned to gather his forces, so he'd want to be there to supervise. They had brought me right into the heart of their operation.

The slug gave me a thrilled little mental trill. Evensong. That was right. I was close, and she was there with thousands upon thousands of others like her. Trapped, imprisoned, enslaved.

She thought I'd come to rescue her. As I'd promised.

I winced, trying to project confidence, then to ask if she could communicate with Doomslug. Unfortunately, at that moment my door clicked.

What?

The door was opening. Were they bringing food?

It didn't matter. I grinned wildly and leaped for it, ready to attack whoever entered. I got halfway across the small room before a barrage of weapons fire slammed into me.

Stun guns. All ten of the guards had been ready to fire on me the moment the door opened. I flopped to the ground like a fish out of water, humiliated. Then they shot me *again*.

Scudding wretches! I'd stab them in the scudding eyes once I was out of here. I'd . . .

236

I'd . . .

I'd simply lie there as they injected me with a new syringe of drugs. One guard deposited a few field rations on the bunk, then they left, locking the door securely behind them. Leaving me, face down, to slowly recover enough to move.

I fell unconscious before that could happen, my exhausted body surrendering to the need for sleep.

25

I woke to a feeling of peace.

That didn't make any kind of rational sense. I knew immediately where I was: in prison. I was a light sleeper, and at some point during the "night" had climbed up onto the bunk.

And yet a soothing calm radiated over me. It came from . . .

You, I thought to the unknown slug.

She fluted in my head. The communications slug I'd promised to save. As I lay there, feeling sorry for myself, she sent more comfort. Like a bandage on my soul.

How do you have time to comfort someone else? I thought to her. *With your own situation as it is?*

I could mostly frame the feelings and images she sent into a verbal response. *I'm locked in a cage. I have nothing* but *time. And outward is the only place to look.*

I sent back a sense of regret. That I wasn't here to save her; that I hadn't come willingly. But she'd already figured that out, from my emotions. I was a captive like she was.

Sorry, I sent again.

Wait. I was communicating with the taynix. Did that mean my

238

powers were back? The drug had worn off? I quested outward, but felt nothing.

She replied. She was reaching out to me while doing her communications work for the space station. My drugs were still in effect; she was bearing the entire cytonic load of our discussion. She had a vague impression that my state would last around twelve hours.

You know the drugs? I sent her.

Yes. They were used on hyperslugs whenever they needed to be removed from their boxes. It was also the first step in a punishment process for a commslug—cutting them off from others.

Scud. If the drug was the *first* step of their punishments, where did it go after that?

I got back a sensation of darkness, pain, and silence.

Well, that was terrifying. If I ever needed to throw up again on command, I could simply remember the life these poor creatures were being forced to live.

Doomslug, I sent her. *Can you find my friend? She's here, somewhere.*

The unknown slug, whom I named Comfort in my head, didn't know Doomslug, but promised to see if she could find her. There were a *lot* of slugs here, but Comfort seemed confident that—with a little time—she could do it.

Great. But all of this just reinforced that I needed a way out. Not only for me and my friends, but for these creatures.

I climbed off the bunk and ate the ration bars left for me, did a series of push-ups and other exercises, then cleaned up as best I could. With a sink and the little bar of soap I'd been left, at least I could wash my jumpsuit.

Once the jumpsuit was dry, I put it back on, then cleaned my undergarments. It gave me something to do while I waited for the next injection. Sure enough, at what I pegged for midday, they opened the door. Cleaned and dressed, I raised my hands to try to forestall what happened next.

"I'll be good," I promised. "I won't—"

A barrage of fire came through the doorway, stunning me and dropping me, drooling, to the ground. Scud. It didn't hurt—at least not more than any other fall—but this could *not* be good for my body. I suffered the indignity of another injection, then just lay there. They didn't even move me to the bunk, though they left another handful of ration bars. One joked about how bad the food was, and how I'd probably go crazy subsisting only on those bars.

Well, the joke was on him. I'd lived on rat meat and algae paste for most of my life. The ration bars were comparatively fantastic.

As I lay there, feeling miserable, Comfort reached out for me again. And oddly, I felt several others—a good five or six communication slugs doing the same. When I asked, Comfort said she'd talked to them about me, and asked for their help in finding my friend.

Their mental picture of me was amusing: a giant slug with long, squishy appendages. They saw me as one of them, just larger and oddly shaped. In context it was flattering, trust me. And only mildly nightmarish.

Any sign of Doomslug? I thought to them. And yes—one of the five had sensed a new slug arriving.

The Superiority didn't understand the level of intelligence the taynix had. That was what happened when you treated living beings like mechanical parts—one was the same as another to them. So they'd just put Doomslug with the rest of their hyperslugs.

She couldn't be contacted, though. It took me a few minutes of sorting through Comfort's thoughts to figure out why. Apparently it was the boxes. Certain boxes could cut the slugs off from one another. But they were transferred often enough, fed and sometimes cleaned, so Comfort expected Doomslug would be contactable sometime in the next few days. She promised to send my friend feelings of support, as did the other five who were talking to me. All were on active communications duty.

This is how you survive, I thought to them. *You do it together. Supporting each other.*

They agreed softly, as they offered me that same support. I was awed by the scope of it. The idea of all these little creatures in cages, barely fed, beaten if they misbehaved . . . spending their days reaching out. Instead of looking inward, they'd created a network of support. Facilitated through the communications slugs.

It was a deeply powerful defiance that vibrated my soul.

I'll help you, I sent to them. *I'm going to find a way. Spread the word. Help is coming.*

They believed me immediately, and began to flute with excitement. The question was, how did I make good on that promise?

Turned out, it was right there in front of me. I mean, not *literally,* since I was lying face down in a pool of my own spit. But you know. Metaphorically.

Can you reach out, I thought to the slugs, *to my friends?*

Immediate fear. Disobedience was severely punished. They felt fine contacting me, since they viewed me as "one of them." The Superiority didn't seem to know they did this, and didn't have the resources to monitor it. But if any of them sent a message that far, to another planet, they risked alerting the Superiority's guards. Signals sent out from the station were monitored carefully by machinery.

I understand, I thought to them as they shrank back from me in fear. Only, Comfort prodded at my mind tentatively. She wanted to know what she needed to do.

I managed to roll over and stare at the ceiling. *It might not be a good idea,* I thought to her. *It could be dangerous.*

She sent an image of me flying in combat, as I had during the data-breach mission. She'd been watching from afar.

Well, yes, I projected to her. *I do dangerous things. But I'm a soldier.*

I'm a soldier, she repeated back to me, and I could almost hear the fluting.

I supposed she was. Not by choice—but none of my people were soldiers by choice. Except maybe me, granted. I could have grown up in the most pacifist society in the Superiority, and I'd probably still be talking about beheading dandelions or something.

Okay, I sent back to her. *I have friends in the military. Did you see any of them, when we were flying that mission?*

Comfort wasn't certain. She had trouble distinguishing humans from one another unless they were cytonic, as her kind sensed the world with their powers. All taynix—regardless of variety—could use cytonics to produce an image of their surroundings in their heads. Yet they recognized one another not by visuals, but through cytonic identifiers.

So I sent her an image, and a cytonic impression, of Jorgen. I'd talked to him on that mission. Did she know him?

Yes, she sent back, timid. She recognized *that* human. He was a giant slug too. I smiled at the image.

Can you reach out to him? I thought. *Tell him where I am, and that I was taken against my will?* That alone wouldn't be enough to salvage this situation, but it would be a start. More, I wanted to see if I could get word out. From there, plans could be made. And perhaps we could find a way free of this mess.

Comfort sent me back a scared affirmative. Her captors didn't always monitor communications perfectly, and she'd learned to piggy-back on signals she sent. It was how she sometimes contacted slugs who were frightened and separated from the rest. She thought maybe, while on duty, she could do this type of spoofing—and send a double signal. One she was assigned to send, and a hidden one to Jorgen.

As I read her thoughts, I could feel the scars of a lifetime of abuse in her emotions, and it broke my heart anew. Scud, I'd thought *my* childhood had been hard, but I'd had the freedom to explore the caverns and a potential way to fight back against the Krell.

I hadn't realized how dark it could get for someone without those options.

I try, Comfort sent.

Now? I asked.

On duty, she sent. *Sending thoughts now. Good time.*

With that, Comfort reached toward Jorgen, as I'd asked. I wished I could watch with my cytonic senses. Instead, the best I could do was feel her emotions, since she had deliberately extended them to me. I could feel her growing more confident as—I thought—she located Jorgen. A big slug who always kept himself clean, and complained when others got a little messy. Yup, that was him. I delighted in the idea of explaining—

Comfort went silent.

I tried to sit up, but I still couldn't do more than wobble. I quested out for her, but my senses were blind. Why had she cut off from me? What was wrong? The other slugs didn't reach out to me either; they'd hidden away. I finally managed to climb up onto my bunk, terrified for Comfort.

I lay there a long time, reaching for her, until the lock on my door clicked. I bolted upright, just in time to get shot with those stun guns *yet again.*

Scud, scud, SCUD.

This time, guards didn't come to sneer at me. I was favored today, because Winzik himself strolled in, stone feet grinding on the metallic floor. As usual, the only clothing he wore was a sash across his exosuit's body. He waved with his tiny crab claw, and the exosuit mimicked the motion, indicating that some guards should enter and prop me up against the wall in a semblance of a seated position.

Brade entered next and deposited a metal box on the floor. It was longer than it was tall, and maybe a little less than two feet across.

Winzik went down on one knee before me, then spoke in his soft, deliberate way. "They say I should keep you unconscious, human. We have drugs that could render you comatose. Unfortunately, I fear that the delvers would not recognize you—and the danger you present—in that state. They have difficulty telling the difference between us! My, my. They may mistake you for a log."

I tried to growl at him, or spit at his feet, or do *anything* heroic. He'd left me unable.

243

"Besides," he continued, "I feel that you can learn. All beings can learn, even humans. That is, in part, why I keep a trained one nearby. To remind people it's possible to tame even the most *abject* of lesser species. With sufficient motivation. Applied correctly."

He rested a hand on the box beside him, only centimeters from me. I heard, with horror, a panicked fluting inside.

No. He couldn't. He . . .

Winzik held his hand out to Brade, who passed him a small mechanical device: a control pad, it seemed.

"At times," he said, "one of our hyperdrive units or our communication units malfunctions. So we keep them in receptacles outfitted for easy disposal."

I struggled. Trying to move. Trying to show the least bit of defiance. I threw every ounce of strength and passion into it, then I piled on the desperation and pain that followed.

I got nothing.

"Winzik," Brade said from behind. "This might not be wise. We want her pliable. She'll work with us, under the right circumstances."

"Of course she will, Brade," he said. "My, my. You seem to be regressing. Because these *are* the circumstances where she'll work with us. Once she is motivated." He leaned forward. "You might call this aggressive. That is why you are of lesser intelligence. You do not yet see: It is not aggressive if it is done without malice. If it is done, instead, with regret. I regret what *you* have done. I regret that *you* are foolish. I regret that *you* have killed this frightened creature."

I could hear Comfort fluting inside. More and more panicked. As if she knew. As if she understood.

My emotions mounted to a frenzy. I managed to combine them into a single vengeful burst of energy. Like a spear punching through armor.

It amounted to two words.

"Please. No."

Winzik hesitated, then leaned even closer. He waved with a claw, gesturing a soldier forward to level his gun at me.

Then, satisfied, Winzik leaned back. "The tool in this box," he said, "is corrupted. See that you don't corrupt any others."

He pushed a button on his pad.

The box flashed and rattled briefly, light leaking from the seams. A violent red light, like something from the forges. Smoke followed, with a terrible scent of burned flesh. And one final impression.

Save my friends.

After that, there was no more fluting.

My heart broke. I couldn't move, but somehow I *could* cry. The tears running down my face seemed to please Winzik. He stood up, waving his hands animatedly.

"We can remove any of them that malfunction," he said. "At any time. Remotely, if we wish. Please remember this before you seek to use them again. Brade warned me this might happen. We were therefore watching when this unit sent two signals instead of one."

I managed to force out two more words, somehow.

"Kill. You."

"My, my. There is such emotion in the lesser species."

With that, he turned and left. Brade and the guards followed, then the door slammed. Locking me in alone with my agony, shame, and seething hatred.

26

Days passed.

I think.

Without a clock—without the visible changing of worker shifts, or something like the forges back home going from fabrication to the softer simmering of reclamation . . . well, it was tough to tell time. Almost like I was in the nowhere again.

The only way I had of tracking it was when my drugs were administered. Every twelve hours, using Old Earth time . . . maybe. I was relying on an unpracticed interpretation of a vague representation that Comfort had given me. And if *I* were holding a captive, I would have mixed up the length of time between doses—often coming when one wasn't needed—just to keep the captive disoriented. So I felt I couldn't rely on that, or feeding times—the arrival of fresh ration bars.

I quickly came to understand why solitude, in the stories, was often considered as terrible a punishment as physical torture. When I'd been captured by the Broadsiders, I'd been able to learn about them. Spend time around them. That had helped me formulate an escape. Here . . . any plan was just a way to temporarily distract myself from my mounting despair.

And that despair was acute.

I'd been outthought at each point. Brade had weaponized my tantrums—and the way they broke through inhibitors—almost before I'd realized what was happening. They'd anticipated each of my ploys to escape, and had been waiting for me. They'd been *ready* to kill Comfort.

I was supposed to have been able to save her.

Damn it, I was supposed to be the *hero*.

Save my friends.

Her dying plea vibrated my soul. Haunting me. But the drugs, whatever they were, cut me off from Chet. That meant no tantrum, no matter how painful for me, made the air around me warp. All along, that ability hadn't been mine, it seemed, but his—and this drug prevented our melding from functioning as it once had.

The only useful thing I could do was watch the guards. They were my lone viable access to the outside world. I hoped that listening to their conversations would give me some kind of intel. But unfortunately, intel was easier to get from people who were actually intelligent. These guards didn't seem to know anything relevant, and mostly talked about how bored they were. Still, I made notations about their shift changes, tying knots in my bedsheet to mark each one. I watched carefully, through the slot on the door, for any opportunities I could use.

They rotated in shifts of five—but two *overlapping* shifts of five. That meant ten were watching me most of the time. Occasionally five, but never zero.

By what I thought was the fourth day of my imprisonment, I'd started identifying individuals. One set in particular tended to go off shift a little early, consistently leaving only the other five watching. Maybe I could . . .

Maybe I could what? I pulled away from the door, feeling like an utter fool. It didn't matter. I'd tried every trick I could to get that door to open. The only time it did, it was followed by weapons fire. I'd tried hiding at the side of the room before they entered, but that time they'd tossed a gas grenade in, which nearly knocked me out, *then* they'd stunned me anyway and stuck me with the needle.

I was trapped, well and truly. With a sinking feeling, I finally understood how someone could spend decades in a prison and never escape, like in the stories. I'd always thought I would be clever, strong, or perceptive enough to get myself out of such a situation. Yet here I was, completely powerless. They could keep me in this cell until I died of old age. I slumped down on my bunk and bit into one of my rations.

My teeth *clinked* against something inside.

I pulled the ration bar back, staring at the shining bit of metal in the mashed-up protein paste. Scud. I had no idea what that was, but I suspected that they had a camera watching me somewhere in here, so I pretended nothing had happened. I flopped down on the bunk, rolled to my side, and there feigned nibbling on the bar. While secretly I figured out what was inside it.

A key. Not an old-fashioned one like in the stories, but an electronic one. You pressed it to the door, and the mechanism unlocked. I'd seen them on the guards' belts.

How in Genghis's bloody name had someone snuck me a key? And who would do such a thing?

The guard shift, I thought, listening to the movements outside. *Those five have left.* Early, as normal.

Could I take out the five who remained? One woman against five armed soldiers?

I knew I might never have another chance to find out. Maybe this was a trap, but either I tried to escape now, or I'd ride out the rest of the war in this little room. So I heaved a sigh, palmed the key, and sauntered over to the door. There, I pretended to be watching the guards like I usually did. I didn't open the door immediately. I waited, hoping that anyone watching via camera would grow lax.

I waited until the guards were chatting together, complaining about those *other* guards, who were so negligent they always left early. Then, guessing this was as distracted as they'd ever be, I pressed the key to the door—and felt the mechanism unlock.

Unfortunately, one of the guards noticed. So I revised my plan and waited until that one wandered over to look at the door, head cocked. Then I slammed the door open, shoving it right into their face.

The clank of metal on bone was one of the most satisfying sounds I'd ever heard. I was on the guard a second later, counting on the others to be too shocked to respond immediately. A part of me envied the relaxing lives they led, where even on guard duty they were distracted enough that they could be taken by surprise. My life—full of explosions, sudden attacks, and dread—served me better that day.

As a few of them got their first shots off, spraying weapons fire erratically through the hallway, I knelt with the fallen guard's stun gun and laid into the remaining four. A barrage of tightly focused fire dropped them all in a single sweep. Even Veska, my firing range sergeant, wouldn't have complained about my form and precision.

Then I knelt there, heart pounding, holding my weapon and waiting for the inevitable alarm to sound. Surely a guard was watching remotely somewhere. They wouldn't solely rely on soldiers at the door, would they?

Silence.

Scud, what was happening? I couldn't trust this, could I? It was far too convenient.

But what else was I supposed to do? Sit in my bunk? Maybe the slugs had somehow managed to get me this key. I couldn't stew and worry it was a trap.

Move, dummy!

I grabbed the first guard—the one I'd hit in the face with the metal door—and hauled them up by their jacket. They were a dione, with blue skin and face tattoos, one of which had been split right down the middle by the edge of the door.

They were dazed, but coming to. So I pulled their face up close to mine and growled, "Hangar bay. Starfighters."

Their eyes widened and they smiled, an expression that on a dione did not mean amusement. They were terrified. Good.

"I'm not a patient woman," I hissed at them. "Tell me where the fighter bays are, or I'll have to get creative. How many pieces can a dione lose before they go into shock? Any ideas?"

"I . . . Please," the dione whispered.

"Hangar bay," I hissed. "Starfighters."

"Delm fourteen!"

Delm was one of their letters. Good enough. I shot the dione with the stun gun, then whipped the jacket off one of the smaller guards. I threw it on and strung my stun rifle across it by the strap in a guard carry. Maybe I wouldn't strike as suspicious a silhouette this way. I identified the NCO of the fallen group by their uniform, then stole their ID—it looked a lot like the key my phantom helper had sent me.

I took off at an even stride, and after a few turns through the empty hallways I found a monitor on the wall that seemed like it was there to help with navigation. After all this time, I still didn't know much about the Superiority alphabets, but I managed—using the access key I'd stolen—to get "delm 14" typed in. To my relief, a map appeared, showing me the way.

I'd thought I was in some kind of space station, not a ground facility, and that was proven correct when a few turns later I found some portholes looking out at the silent expanse of space.

I continued down hallway after hallway, and fortunately didn't run into many people. The ones I spotted were at a distance, and my makeshift disguise seemed to work. I got the feeling that it was the station's main sleep cycle, which certainly made it easier to sneak around.

I was more than *halfway* to my destination before the alarm sounded. Those five guards who had left their shift early were likely going to have a *very* bad day.

I ran, praying I'd gotten the location correct—and came upon a tenasi, a female carrying a tray of food and humming to herself. I stunned her and she fell to the ground, then I leaped over the splattered mess of her meal, ran the final distance, and slammed my stolen guard's key to the pad beside a metal door. But it didn't open immediately. Scud, I hoped they hadn't already locked me out. I stood there in a panic, red lights flashing in the hallway and a distant alarm sounding.

At last the door opened. I leaped through to find a large hangar bay, Superiority-standard starships of a variety of designs sitting in a row. Despite the flashing lights and sounds of alarm, there was nobody in here. Wouldn't a hangar lockdown be one of their first moves after a security breach?

I hesitated, again worried this was a trap. As I did, I heard a click to the side.

Scud. I turned and raised my rifle, realizing I'd failed to check my corners after entering the room. Veska would have had something to complain about after all.

Brade lounged at an operator's seat by the wall just to my right, her booted feet up on a desk, stopwatch raised.

My stomach sank and I was hit by a wave of anger at seeing Brade with that scudding stopwatch yet again.

So I tried to shoot her. My weapon fire hit a shield that, until intercepting something, was invisible. It flashed blue before fading again.

"Protective feature," she said. "Shielded ops station as a safety protocol during weapons checks. The Superiority is big on safety protocols." She peered at the stopwatch. "Wow. Did you really defeat ten guards and run all the way here in under five minutes?"

I fired again. And again. Just to see if I could bring the shield down. When it didn't work, I sighed. "I only had to beat five guards," I admitted. "I waited for a shift change, and there's a group of them that tends to leave early."

Brade sighed loudly. "You're kidding me. Look, I promise we

have *some* competent soldiers. They just don't usually get assigned to guard duty, even on important installations." She sounded like she thought I'd be *offended* by lazy guards.

Then again, I had no idea how to read Brade. She seemed to swap personalities like FM changed shoes. I kept my rifle up.

"You sent me the key," I said. "You let me escape."

"Had to empty the hangar bay too," she said. "Not easy to do, mind you, even during the night watch."

"Why?"

"Have you forgotten our duel?" she asked. "You can lower the gun, Spensa. It doesn't have the juice to punch through the ops station's shield."

The alarms were still blaring. I glanced at the ships. Were they a way out?

"You get to go first," Brade said to me. "Pick a ship. They're unlocked. Head on out, and I'll follow."

"Why are you doing this?" I demanded. "Back on Starsight, you were all too eager to work against me. Now you let me go?"

"We needed you to be our scapegoat then," Brade said. "Thanks for that, by the way. The footage we took of you being a 'scary human' helped Winzik persuade entire planets to overlook his military coup." She spun a handgun on the desk table, displaying absolutely atrocious muzzle control. "They're so docile. A lot about the Superiority will need to change if they want to hold on to all they've achieved."

She looked at me, and seemed to sense my hesitance. I hadn't run for a ship. I didn't like this; it smelled off.

"They don't deserve it," she said to me. "This empire they've built. The diones, the tenasi, the varvax? They were just the ones who figured out cytonics first; then they were the first to be able to isolate and control the slugs. They think it's their grand philosophy that made them dominant, when in reality it was mere luck."

"I don't get you, Brade," I said, stepping closer. "Why do you follow him? Why do you want to duel me? Why do you do any-thing you do?"

"For kicks," she said.

I almost believed it. If her simple motivation was to do what seemed fun at the time, that would explain letting me go. It would explain a lot. But there were easier ways to have fun. She had committed to flying with me at Starsight, keeping up her persona even when it was difficult.

Whatever her reasons, this was her game. If I was going to escape, I'd need to play by her rules at first, until I found a way to break them.

"Are you just going to stand there?" she asked. "Soon this place will be swarming with troops. But if you're out there with me, Winzik will be slower to act. I've got a message typed up saying I caught you escaping and am giving chase. He'll still send others to help, but knowing I'm chasing you should calm him a little. Buy us time for a real fight. Your choice though. Do you want to stand here and be caught?"

I went running for one of the ships, fully aware that I was dancing to her tune. But maybe she would actually fly out and duel me. Maybe she really did want to know which of us was better. In that case, I had an opportunity to escape. A far better one than I had locked in that cell.

I located a sleek interceptor model I knew had a familiar control scheme and threw myself into the cockpit, still expecting some kind of last-minute trap. Nothing stopped me as I raised the ship up on its acclivity ring, then boosted straight out the bay doors through the shield and into the vacuum of space.

Brade followed moments later in her own ship. Scud, we were really going to do this. I still couldn't hyperjump, with the drugs in my system, but I'd picked a good time to try my escape. I usually got a dose about an hour after shift change, so I figured my powers should start returning shortly.

I had a chance, a real one. I just had to beat Brade, then elude capture for long enough to hyperjump. As Brade dove for me, unloading with her destructors, my instincts kicked in. I still didn't know for sure why she was doing this.

But I knew, sure as the stars themselves, that she was going to regret toying with me.

27

I boosted away from Brade on overburn, but focused primarily on defensive flying. I needed the lay of this region before I got serious.

We'd left a newer-looking space station, flat and rectangular with bays along the sides. It looked a little like a . . . well, a giant space harmonica. The sort our pathleader had played back in my nomadic childhood. My monitors labeled this station "Brez Observation Platform."

My monitor picked out smaller structures in the distance—hundreds of them. Mines, maybe? They did seem to be arrayed in a pattern, creating a large field around the region. There were kilometers between each one, but viewing this as a battlefield, I could see an intentionality to the way they were placed.

In the area closest to me was a lot of space junk, drifting far more haphazardly. The main showpiece, though, was an old space platform—much, much larger than Brez, the station where I'd been captive. The behemoth floated a short distance away, by starship terms.

This was Evensong, my proximity monitor said: an ancient platform that resembled Starsight. It looked mostly derelict, though its surface was encrusted with hundreds, maybe thousands of skyscrapers. No lights came from any of them, but somewhere on that platform would be the hub where all the commslugs were housed.

I punched my ship in that direction to get a closer look, while Brade swept outward. Evensong seemed to have a bubble of air around it like Starsight, but my proximity monitor didn't warn of a shield. Vast swaths of brown ground marked dead gardens. The buildings hadn't corroded—modern metals resisted that, no matter how long they sat—but I saw broken windows. Streets that seemed to have been stripped of metal for use elsewhere.

A part of me found it incredible. The platforms around Detritus had remained functional for hundreds of years without intervention. What had happened here to make this place so derelict?

"It was a human installation once," Brade said over my comm.

I hesitated. She hadn't pressed her attack. I felt an urgency to be on with the contest, before Winzik found out what we were doing. At the same time, if Brade was willing to talk, maybe I could get some information out of her?

"What happened?" I asked, careful not to get complacent, staying out of her direct line of fire. Talking to me could be a ploy to get me to let my guard down.

"War," she said. "It got annexed by one of the many human factions trying to claim the galaxy. After that group collapsed, it became a pirate hub. Then another group took it, and they fell too. On and off over hundreds of years."

"Makes sense, I suppose," I said, flying down around one of the larger skyscrapers. "But why did it fall into disrepair like this? It's got to be cheaper to fix it up than build another station."

We flew out over the side of the station, lit by a distant sun that provided some twilight illumination. It left Evensong with deep shadow along one face, pooling like ink. We crested the edge of the station and headed toward the underside of the platform—which was covered in its own buildings, since up and down were matters of choice in a place with artificial gravity.

Here I was met with a daunting sight. Giant creatures, like tube worms each at least a couple of kilometers long, undulating through the vacuum. They'd been sheltered from my sight by the platform, but each of these things was as large as a capital ship. There were dozens of them here, moving slowly through space.

I veered away with a jerk of my ship, and suddenly—now that I knew what to look for—I realized I'd been mistaken earlier. The space junk I'd seen upon leaving Brez . . . it included more of these things. Hundreds of them, swimming through the void of space.

"Scud," I whispered. "What are those?" Space worms existed? Why hadn't M-Bot told me about them when he'd dashed my hopes of finding sand worms!

"Damn, you're sheltered," Brade replied. "You've really never seen a vastworm before?"

"No."

"An infestation like this is dangerous," Brade said. "They can swallow ships. In a more populated region, the government would dedicate huge resources to exterminating them before they grew into what we have here. But out here . . . well, Evensong is old, abandoned. Nobody comes here. It's basically just a blip on interstellar maps, with a warning attached. Jump in here, and you risk getting swallowed."

Scud! The worm I'd turned away from had noticed me, and it was undulating after us. The thing didn't seem fast, but it was *huge*. I doubted it could swallow a ship that was aware and alert, but it was still unnerving with that wide circular mouth the size of giant bay doors. Brade, of course, took some shots at me while I was distracted. One hit my shield before I managed to execute some decent dodges.

She chuckled softly, the sound coming in over the line.

"Why?" I demanded. "Why would the Superiority build a central hub here? I expected something as vibrant and populated as Starsight."

"Yeah, well, that would be on everyone's maps. Hard to keep quiet. The Superiority is all about making people ignore things that are secretly important."

That was true. Warships pretended to be merchant vessels. Slugs were labeled as dangerous to ensure people were afraid to pick one up if they saw one. It was an understandable methodology, when you didn't rule by military might but by the control of information. So, they'd situated their central communications hub in a place nobody would visit.

I found the view intimidating. All those worms out there, like maggots in a stew, floating and moving through space. Serene, yet deadly. Worse, as I outpaced the worm behind us, I saw another dangerous sight in the near distance: the Superiority fleet that Winzik had been gathering. Three huge carriers, the largest of the capital ships, along with two battleships and a half dozen smaller gunships and destroyers.

That wasn't much in the context of a large-scale galaxy, but it was already a fleet that dwarfed our own. The enemy fleet hung in its own space with a number of dead worms, blown in half, floating nearby. The others seemed to be keeping their distance, as if they could sense where some of their kind had been killed.

"So, are we actually going to do this?" Brade asked. "Or are you going to just continue sightseeing? I have Winzik stalled for now. But that won't last forever."

"Brade—"

"You should know," she added, "that I have a remote control device on your ship to let me take it over. Try to escape, and I'll lock you down. Need proof?" She flipped my overburn on and off.

I gritted my teeth. I *hated* the idea of my ship being controlled by someone else.

"So you can just lock me down?" I snapped. "You've already won, then."

"I won't use it," she said. "Not unless you try to run or are otherwise defeated. No cytonics on my part either. Come on. Destroy me, and you can fly away—but as long as I'm here, you're captive. Ready?"

"Get a little closer, and I'll show you how ready I am."

A protracted fight favored me, giving time for the drugs in my system to run out—so I probably should have been looking for a way to accomplish that. But as Brade approached, firing with twin destructors, I found myself not caring. Here was a *fight*. Despite everything I'd been through, everything I'd learned, I was still a warrior at my core. I *had* to prove that I was better than Brade. The opportunity to get some measure of vengeance on one of my captors was all-consuming.

I dodged away from her weapons fire and soared alongside the ancient platform, passing abandoned rooms with tiny windows and cavernous docking bays, like eyeholes in a skull. Brade thought she could toy with me? Let me out of my prison to have some fun, then lock me back up when she was done?

She'd see.

When we had flown together at Starsight, I'd sometimes held back so as to not seem *too* skilled; that would have been suspicious. Brade had seen me fly—we'd even faced off—but I figured she would probably still underestimate me.

Evensong's sides didn't have any buildings, just windows and docking bays, so I wove around to the bottom of the station. There I entered an ancient street, diving in among the buildings to see what Brade would do.

And scud, she was too smart to get pulled into such a tight chase. She stayed up above, where she could watch or outrun me. If I flew up and out, she'd have a good line of sight to shoot me down. So I flipped my ship around, nearly overloading the GravCaps—then boosted backward and stopped. Up above, she continued onward for a second, while I darted between buildings to my right. Being down this low might confuse her proximity sensors, making her lose track of me in the mess of ancient steel buildings.

"Not bad," Brade said to me a short time later. "Where did you go?"

"Better watch your tail," I said.

She chuckled. "Do you ever wish it could go back to this? Pilots struggling one-on-one? Rather than sweeping galactic domination and political nonsense?"

I didn't respond. Because I still didn't know how to read Brade. Of course I wanted something like that—but she was playing off my desires.

"What happened to you, Spensa?" she asked me. "In the nowhere? What did you do in there?"

"I learned who I was," I said. "And where I came from."

"You think it could help me? Find the same answers?"

Scud, she sounded sincere. But I'd been played too many times to fall for it. Instead I wove through some streets at a very slow speed, then pulled to a stop near some abandoned hovercars. I had Brade tracked on my proximity monitor as she flew around up above, trying to see where I'd gone. Sitting still felt wrong—dangerous—but I knew it was the right thing to do. Her sensors would have way more trouble tracking me this way.

The ploy worked. Brade went into a large sweeping pattern, flying "upside down" and using visuals to try to find me. Not a bad move, as my ship *would* stand out to human eyes against all this wreckage. But she started in the wrong location, which gave me the perfect opportunity. As she swung out, I turned my nose upward, put full power to my acclivity ring, and boosted straight up along the side of a skyscraper.

I popped out in a perfect position to fall in on her tail, and though she spotted me mid-maneuver and broke off her search, I still managed to stay on her. She wove and dodged, but I drew inevitably closer and started taking careful shots. Anticipating her dodges, I managed to score two hits on her ship—which should have put her shield at around half power. She'd need to stop flying to reignite it, which you never wanted to do while in combat.

I could hear her grunting through the line as she tried to outfly me. I leaned forward, smiling, enjoying the simple focus of the duel. For the moment, I allowed myself to pretend this was all that mattered. I let myself enjoy the fight as Brade led me out from the shadow of Evensong into open space, flying dangerously close to one of those enormous space worms. The thing undulated in the vacuum, its enormous body rippling as Brade used it for cover, coming in close to its wrinkled pink-orange skin.

I took my thumb off the firing button. Judging by the corpses around the Superiority fleet, these things were susceptible to our weapons, but I couldn't imagine that the small destructors on my ship would do much harm to it. I decided to stick to her and hold off on firing for now, just in case stray shots enraged it or something. She gave me quite the run, soaring in a spiral along the worm's body, moving toward the head—and the thing noticed us as we flew, twisting and looking our direction, though I couldn't make out any sort of eyes on the gargantuan beast.

"What *are* these things?" I asked. "Like, really?"

"Vastworms feed off cytonic energy," Brade said. "Any place where you collect too many taynix, you're likely to draw them, unless you do a lot of work to shield the minds."

Detritus had never drawn any that I knew about. But then, we also had a pretty extensive shielding system. I was about to ask for more info, but Brade—still trying to shake me from her tail—boosted up along the worm's head. She spun in a perfectly executed Ahlstrom loop.

Then dove straight into the worm's gaping mouth.

Um . . .

Maybe *I* was the one who had underestimated *her*.

"Brade?" I said. "Are you *insane*?"

"Maybe," she replied, the comm fuzzing. "You think you're better than me? See if you can chase me in here. Remember, until you bring me down, you're as good as in prison."

Scud. I took a long deep breath.

Then I followed her in.

Superiority Outpost Overview Record DST230310

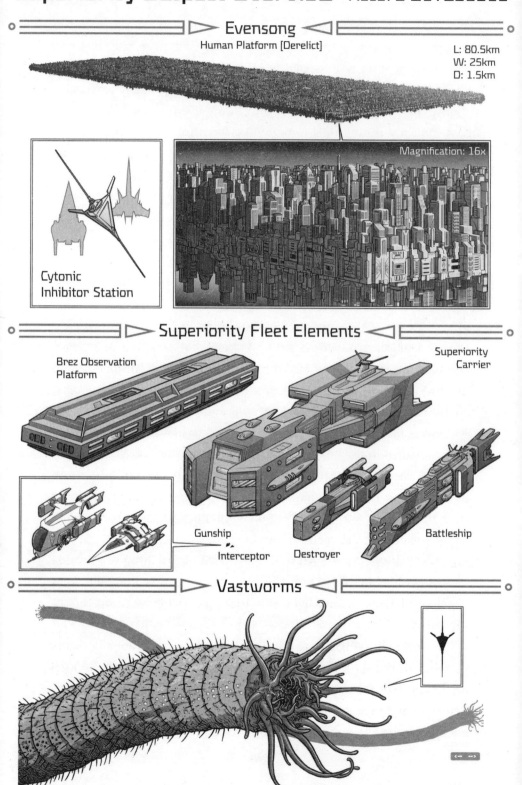

Evensong
Human Platform [Derelict]

L: 80.5km
W: 25km
D: 1.5km

Magnification: 16x

Cytonic Inhibitor Station

Superiority Fleet Elements

Brez Observation Platform

Superiority Carrier

Gunship

Interceptor

Destroyer

Battleship

Vastworms

28

As a little girl, I'd always dreamed of flying in space. Of getting off Detritus, of being out *there*. In the realm of stars and suns, of moons and nebulae. If you'd told me I'd make it, but would someday have to fly through the guts of a giant space worm . . . well, let's be honest about the kind of kid I was. I'd have thought that was awesome.

The reality was more nerve-wracking than I'd have imagined. I had to turn on the ship's floods, illuminating the hollow tube innards of the beast. According to my sensors, it was still a vacuum in here—and the thing had these strange tendrils hanging down from the walls of the guts. Like jellyfish tentacles maybe, only much larger. Waving in the vacuum, reaching toward the center of the passage from all directions. All told, the throat of the thing was twelve meters wide, but those tendrils were three meters long, thick as rope, and left me with alarmingly little space to fly without touching them.

In fact, I clipped one as I tried to keep a bead on Brade's boosters glowing in the darkness beyond. As soon as I touched the tendril my shield went down—a red warning light blinking on my dash. Scud! That tentacle had *drained* the shield. Seemed like cytonic energy wasn't the only thing these worms fed on.

If the tentacle could slurp down a shield, then what would it do if it touched the ship? I decided not to find out, and slowed, weaving through the strange worm guts more carefully. Fortunately, Brade had slowed as well. Maybe I'd gotten lucky and she'd had her own shield drained too.

I watched closely, and saw her get dangerously close to one of the tentacles. Close enough that her shield should have reacted—but it didn't. I put my thumb back on the destructor button, but didn't press it.

"Brade," I said. "I've got you. Yield."

She snickered. "Yield? What is this? An Errol Flynn movie?"

"A what?"

"Old Earth," she said. "Actor."

This was the first time I'd heard her reference anything from Earth popular culture, not merely Earth history. She'd been raised by human parents for part of her youth. Unless that had been a lie. Had they . . . watched Earth films?

"Brade," I said to her, "I'm on your tail and your shield is down. I can shoot you."

"So why don't you?"

"I . . ."

"What *really* happened to you in the nowhere?" she asked me. "Why do you make the air vibrate when you feel pain? How did you learn to cut through inhibitors? And why are you suddenly so hesitant to fire on your enemy?"

Scud, was I doing it again? Holding back because I *wanted* her to be something that she wasn't? Or was this a lingering effect of having been among the Broadsiders, of learning to fight worthy opponents without killing?

I wasn't in the nowhere any longer. And last time I'd tried to trust this person, she'd betrayed me.

I pushed the button, sending twin streams of destructor fire straight toward her. Brade chuckled, dodging in a spin, barely evading my shots—which hit some of the tentacles. They absorbed the energy, and suddenly all of the nearby green jellyfish strands started to tremble and whip, making them far, far more difficult to avoid.

I threw my ship into a sequence of dodges, speeding up, despite how dangerous it was. Brade laughed even harder as she increased her speed, and both of us were forced to boost forward, spinning and weaving as tentacles started trying to grab us. I narrowly avoided a sequence of them before bursting back into open space, out through the worm's butt, which was open like the front.

This was . . . not the glorious image of a starfighter pilot I'd always imagined for myself.

Sweat running down my face, I broke right, trying to quiet my heart. In the rush, I'd caught up with Brade, and we'd burst out of the worm at the same moment. Now Brade—denying me time to reignite my shield—managed to get me in her sights. She filled the space with destructor fire. I was forced to dive down, spinning, but behind me the worm turned and followed us—moving faster than the other one had. Somehow it picked up enough speed to keep pace with us. Scud, how was that even possible?

I supposed it had seen me as mere space debris before. Now I was prey, and Brade had thoroughly tricked me into alerting it to that fact.

"Shoot another worm," she suggested over the comm. "Make this interesting."

"Shut up," I growled.

She laughed again, but then she did something and the worm suddenly cut off the chase, undulating in the other direction. I frowned, watching on the proximity monitor but not daring to look back. What . . . ?

"Use your IMP," she said. "The blasts hit with a frequency the things don't like."

"Thanks," I said. "I suppose."

Her destructor fire around my ship trailed off. Maybe she was luring me into complacency. But why call off the worm in that case? Scud, I had *no idea* how to read this woman.

"So, do *you* want to yield?" she asked.

"Not a chance."

"Good," she said. "Reignite shields and go another round? Winzik is preparing ships to come after us, but we might have enough time for one more go."

I soared back toward the derelict Evensong. There, I put a building between myself and her and cautiously stopped. I didn't reignite yet, in case she was waiting for me to be vulnerable and attack.

She didn't. She stopped her own ship in the air and started the process, so I pulled the lever to start my shield ignition as well. It would take around thirty seconds.

"So what is it?" she asked. "That strange distortion around you? The mess you make of inhibitor fields? What *really* happened, Spensa?"

Ah . . . so that was what this was about. Let me out, duel with me, get me talking. Brade was confused by my new powers.

And she wanted them for herself.

Now that I understood, a lot of things made sense. Was this some calculated plan with Winzik to figure out my secrets?

And scud, how could I use this knowledge against her?

"I don't think I can explain it," I said, testing my theory. Indeed, she didn't come after me as our shields rose. No other ships left Brez, despite Brade's warning. She was here to talk, not duel. This fight was an illusion.

Had I finally figured out one of Brade's traps before she sprang it?

"Can you try?" Brade asked. "I feel . . . lost sometimes, with my powers. That there's so much to learn, so much to understand—and that I'll never understand myself until I do."

Scud, she was a good actor. There was real emotion behind those words—and I was impressed despite myself. Even knowing what she was doing, it almost worked.

If I was right, then I had no way to escape. She probably had a dozen ships watching, ready to hyperjump in and attack me the moment something went wrong. I couldn't run, but maybe I could stall. Until my powers returned.

So I talked, knowing full well that I was playing a dangerous game. "You'd have to go into the nowhere, Brade," I said. "Completely. Not just with your senses. Step into a portal, and seek something called the Path of Elders."

"You just made that up."

Technically, Chet had made it up. So I was confident I wasn't giving her anything too valuable. "No, I didn't," I said. "I visited special sites around the belt of the nowhere. They gave me visions of the past, helped me learn, helped me grow into my powers."

"And the delvers?"

"I brought one with me," I said. "When I was in there, it approached me. You remember that one at Starsight? The one you summoned, and I drove off?"

"Yeah, I remember."

"It came to me, in a *human form*. It traveled with me. Tried to understand me. Befriended me."

"Well, that's creepy."

I stopped myself from saying more. I was straying too close to the truth.

"Spensa?" she asked.

"It's difficult to explain, like I said," I told her. *Just keep talking.* "I leaped through that portal on Starsight, and didn't know what to expect. I ended up in a jungle, and—"

"The delver," Brade interrupted. "The one that traveled with you. Scrud . . . *that's* what I felt. It melded with you somehow, didn't it? *That's* how you cut through inhibitor fields. *That's* what's going on. You've captured one? Or made a treaty with it?"

Scud. I didn't answer.

"Hell," Brade said. "And *that's* why they're afraid of you, isn't it? Something to do with that bond. I *knew* I felt something familiar about you."

267

"I understand them," I said to her. "In a way no person ever has before, Brade. You're not going to be able to control them. I can promise you that. You're mistaken if you think you can. Help me escape. Together we could *really* figure out the delvers, and maybe make the galaxy safe from them *forever.*"

"Huh," Brade said. "Yeah, not interested. All right, guys. That's probably all we'll get today. Come on in."

I jumped despite myself as two dozen starfighters appeared around me in a tight formation. I boosted away immediately, but Brade just hit the kill switch on my ship, shutting down the boosters. One of the other ships flew after me and grabbed my ship with a light-lance tow cable.

I felt like an idiot. This time I'd anticipated her, even managed to figure out her ploy. But still she beat me. I pounded my controls as Brade edged her ship up to mine.

"Technically, I *didn't* use my powers against you," she noted. "So, if it matters, I kept my word."

"You killed my ship in space!" I shouted at her.

"I saved you," she said. "From being annihilated by all the other ships that arrived to destroy you. You took too long, Spensa. I warned you that if you did, the fight would be joined by others."

I leaned back in my seat, frustrated.

"Did you *really* think that we'd just be able to come out here and duel?" she asked, sounding amused. "If this wasn't a setup, the two of us would have been swarmed moments after leaving the station."

"What now, boss?" someone said over the line.

"Now we haul her back and toss her in the cell," Brade said. "And *I* figure out how to bond with a delver, like she has."

I seethed. "I'm going to kill you, Brade," I whispered into the comm. "Someday I'm going to stand above you with a sword at your neck, and you're going to beg, and—"

She chuckled, then the light on my comm flashed off, indicating she'd cut the line. I pounded the controls again, growling. But the ship wasn't to blame for any of this. I was. Me and my foolishness.

Why was I so willing to be caught by her? Why did I play into her games? Even still, a part of me wanted so badly to befriend her. Why?

Because, I thought, *she's the one who escaped you.* Every other person I'd flown with—from Skyward Flight to the Broadsiders—had eventually come to my side. Hesho had become my copilot. Peg had come to respect me. Morriumur had saved my life. Jorgen had become my scudding *boyfriend*.

Brade was the exception. The only flightmate who had turned against me. A part of me smarted with pain at that, in a way that few other pains could rival. Beyond that, I saw something in her that I wanted to save. A representation of what humans had suffered at the hands of the Superiority. I wanted so desperately to make up for that, to protect her, to show her that life could be better.

However, she didn't need or want rescuing. I had to remind myself of that time and time again. But at least, I thought as I calmed myself, she hadn't learned anything of actual value. She'd never be able to bond a delver as I had, because that required empathy she didn't have.

We hyperjumped back to the hangar as a group and settled down on the dock. I immediately tried to pop my canopy and run—but they'd remotely locked it up tight.

I had one sole hope remaining. That as she'd been playing me, I'd been able to play her a little. Because I *had* wasted time with our conversation. We were close to my next dose—actually, I thought we were past it. I pushed at the boundaries of my awareness and felt hints of my powers returning.

Here . . . Chet said inside me. *I'm . . . here . . .*

I still had a chance, but I couldn't let them stun me. So, as Brade's team came to my ship, I raised my hands and bowed my head, eyes closed. I tried to project a nonthreatening air.

Her team popped the canopy of my ship. These weren't the same guards that shot me each day. These were fighter pilots—they seemed to mostly be tenasi, like Peg. They assumed that holding me at gunpoint was good enough.

"You grow *muluns*," one of them said. "I respect that. Out of the ship."

I obeyed, and didn't give them any reason to fire on me. I slowly climbed down the ladder they placed, then raised my hands again, trying to look tired as Brade walked over, helmet under her arm.

"Thanks," she said, "for the intel."

I shrugged, my head bowed.

"Tell you what," she said to me. "Maybe once I figure out how to do what you've done, *then* we can plan about what to do about the delvers? Together."

I just growled in response, trying not to seem *too* docile. But then as she turned away, I let my shoulders slump. She had won this little contest of wits. Even if I'd figured her out, she'd gotten what she'd wanted. That *had* to make her feel good, right? Like her plan had turned out perfectly?

Nearby, a varvax doctor was waiting with my twice-daily dose. She trotted over, and I tried an emergency hyperjump. Nothing happened. I felt *so close* to being able to escape this bind, but that was still a few minutes off. It was agonizing to realize my chance was going to slip away. The doctor took my arm, but at that moment the universe finally threw me a scudding bone. Because the doors to the hangar opened, surprising Brade, who spun.

Winzik, with a complement of guards, strode in. "What have you been *doing*, Brade!" he demanded. "I didn't authorize this!"

Everybody in the room froze, including the doctor. If Brade hadn't cleared her stunt with the man in charge, that meant that she *hadn't* been talking to him earlier, when she'd claimed she was.

I still had a chance. I just had to stall a little longer.

"Oh no!" I said. "He's found us out, Brade! Quick! What do we do?"

29

Brade stared at me, her eyes bulging.

Awesome.

"Run, Brade!" I shouted to her. "He knows we've been working together!"

"Shut her up!" Brade snapped, and one of her tenasi grabbed me and shoved a gag toward my mouth.

Winzik stepped forward. "No, no," he said, waving his hands. "Leave her alone; I will hear her. Human, you've been working with Brade, have you?"

The tenasi pilots reluctantly backed away. Most importantly, the doctor joined them.

"Yes," I said, trying to sound reluctant. "Ever since Starsight. We thought maybe . . . maybe we could make you free the humans in the preserves. Find a way we could be warriors again, serving you."

Was that too obvious a lie? I couldn't tell if Winzik was buying it or not. His crab face wasn't exactly capable of the expressions I found common. I did think the way he waved his arms next was a sign of agitation though.

"My, my," he said.

"She's lying, Winzik," Brade said, rolling her eyes. "Very clearly."

"Yes, perhaps she is," Winzik said, turning to Brade. "Perhaps. But what is it I have found you doing? The soldiers in these docks reassigned? A crack team of pilots commandeered? You went and had your little duel with her, didn't you? The one I *expressly* told you was foolish?"

"I needed to know which of us was better," Brade said.

"You grow unruly," Winzik said, tapping his exosuit's hands together. "You no longer give me the deference you once did. You think that because you are cytonic, I need you."

"I—"

"You do not speak now," Winzik said. "You will be confined to quarters."

Brade deflated visibly. Fine. Now, so long as that doctor stayed away . . . I could *feel* my powers seeping back. I was so *close*. Chet was growing increasingly clear, his soul vibrating with mine. I strained and felt something in the distance. A familiar mind. M-Bot? He seemed to perk up, and I felt his excitement at sensing me. But I couldn't get any words through. I tried to send him panic, a feeling that I was captured.

I got the slightest impression of something in return. An acknowledgment. And a sense of something powerful.

Defiance.

Just a few more minutes! I kept my own head bowed, barely daring to look up to watch.

"Confined to quarters?" Brade said. "Fine. I'll do it."

"Now, I think this entire fiasco needs to change direction," Winzik said. "My, my. I should not have listened to your aggressive instincts, Brade. We leave our worlds undefended by gathering this force of ships as you have suggested."

Brade looked up sharply.

"We should be waiting out the humans, not preparing to confront them," Winzik continued. "I have control of the entire Superiority, and all of its strength. We will disperse this fleet and send the ships back to maintain control on the most important planets. Then we will wait for the humans to starve themselves. Yes. Yes, this is the proper way."

"Winzik," Brade said, "don't ruin—"

"Ah, but you don't speak right now," he chided her. "Remember? You are too like these other humans. They are of lesser intelligence, as are you. I see that they will chew themselves up, just as you have been unable to resist fighting this human. We can let them be, in turmoil, *then* clean up the mess and document it, so that all will see that I have defeated them. Yes. Let us begin."

He turned and started toward the door. Brade let out a long, annoyed sigh. Then she raised her sidearm pistol and blasted a hole in Winzik's head.

Shocked, I watched his exosuit fall to the ground with a calamitous *crash*. I stared, then looked up, expecting the soldiers in the room to immediately attack Brade.

No one moved. Even the other varvax aides who had entered with Winzik just waved their hands in faint agitation.

"Well, that's over," Brade said, sliding her gun back into her holster. "What are the latest reports on Detritus's troop movements?"

A varvax hurried over, holding up a datapad for Brade. "Continued consolidation from the planets Evershore and ReDawn, sir. They're building up their own fleet."

"And our troops?" she asked.

"Winzik's orders have produced . . . lethargic responses," the aide admitted. "It could—should—be going much more quickly."

Brade sighed. "Probably should have shot him sooner."

"Perhaps, sir," the varvax admitted.

"Wait," I said—my utter confusion breaking through my good sense. "Wait. You're just going to let her *get away with shooting your leader*?"

The reptilian tenasi next to me chuckled. "What?" he asked. "You think we would band together behind *that*?" He gestured to Winzik's fallen husk. Horrifyingly, I realized that the crab-thing inside the helmet wasn't dead.

The liquid was leaking from the shattered faceplate all over the floor, and the much smaller creature that was Winzik was crawling out of its remnants, moving in jerks. His crustacean mouth gasped for breath. He was . . . suffocating in the air.

"A bureaucrat?" another of the soldiers asked. "You really think a *bureaucrat* orchestrated the conquest of the entire Superiority? We weren't going to follow a leader who couldn't tell a flanking maneuver from a feint."

"We needed a *military* leader," one of the varvax aides said.

"We needed," the tenasi next to me growled, "a *human*."

Stars and Saints above. Everyone in this room had . . . had been working behind the scenes with Brade for years. Each of them knowing, all along, that Winzik was a puppet. I looked back to Brade, who was going over battle reports and quietly giving orders. Scud, *this* was the real Brade, wasn't it? All this time, all these false faces, and *this* was who she was.

A conqueror. Hiding in plain sight among her enemies. Despite everything, I couldn't help but be impressed.

"Give the order to gather our forces," she said to the aide. "Quickly this time. Inform the command staff that I've finally executed our contingency. I suspect a lot of them will be happy to hear it."

"Yes, sir," the aide said, tucking away his datapad. "We'll need to start the propaganda machine immediately. The planets could accept Winzik as their war minister, but a human is going to be more difficult to spin."

"I'll wear the hologram in public until you manage the situation," Brade said, waving them off. As the aides left, she strolled over to a workstation and picked up a large crowbar that she—to my surprise—absently handed to me.

I took it, feeling the heavy weight of the steel in my hands.

"For him," she said, nodding to where Winzik was crawling across the floor.

He was trailing what I guessed was blood from several sections of his carapace. It looked like he had been connected to the exosuit biologically. I'd never known if those things were entirely tech or natural growths. I thought maybe they were something in between.

"The final blow belongs to you, Spensa," Brade said. "For what his people did to yours. An honor I give you, one soldier to another."

He was slowly making for the door. Probably deranged by the lack of liquid to breathe, and bleeding out. I gripped the crowbar, then hesitated.

"You're just going to record this," I realized. "And as soon as you need an excuse for why you're in charge, you'll plaster the video all over the news, showing me—a human assassin—killing Winzik."

"Damn," Brade said. "For once you figured it out." She slapped her arm, and an illusion snapped into place around her—like the one I'd worn to imitate Alanik. They'd stolen that tech from M-Bot.

The illusion made her look like me.

"Fortunately," she said, "few know about this tech. Modern holo-videos have encrypted metadata to prevent tampering—but it's perfectly easy to fool them if they're genuinely recording what they see."

I had no idea what some of those words meant, but as a guard handed Brade another crowbar, I stepped forward. I figured I could milk this for a few minutes of extra time . . . but as I saw Winzik suffering, I actually felt a little sorry for him. Despite it all. So, I slammed my crowbar down on Winzik's carapace, crushing the life out of him.

With that, I finally ended the tyrant who had kept my people imprisoned for years, who had gotten my father killed, who was responsible for so much death. At least a member of the DDF had delivered the final blow, instead of Brade in a disguise.

I felt . . . unfulfilled. Not because I felt bad killing him. It had been a mercy, and he certainly deserved an execution if only for the death of poor Comfort earlier. Winzik had been a thoroughly evil creature.

But I couldn't pin the suffering of my people entirely on him. The oppression was systemic in the Superiority, not the result of one person's schemes. I'd gotten vengeance on one little part of the machine that had ruined my people's lives, but this wasn't the solution. The solution had to be much, much bigger than one girl with a crowbar.

"What now?" I asked Brade, looking up from the dead Winzik.

"Now," she said, "I'm afraid we're going to have to crush your rebellion. Nothing personal. Can't have a rival faction of humans challenging me for control. Our military is proud to have a human at their head, but an entire fleet of them would be problematic."

"We could work together," I said, stepping toward her. "You don't *have* to do this."

"Of course I don't," Brade said, frowning. "Spensa, do you have *any idea* how long I've been working toward this? I've been planning it ever since they took me from my family. Putting things in place. Positioning myself.

"The Superiority is an *enormous* mess. The military understands how tenuous it all is. We lack the strength to control what we have, and need to rule through access to hyperslugs. Yet one slipup, and the secrets of hyperdrives would spread through the entire galaxy. The Superiority is a stone balanced on a single point, and it's *going* to fall.

"We had to take action, and they needed a leader who understands aggression on a level that hasn't been forcibly bred out of her." She waved to herself. "I'm poised to rule everything, and your people could upset all of that."

"*Our* people."

"What, because we're the same race, we should work together?" She smiled. "Have you *read* any human history, Spensa? We *never* got along. That's part of what differentiates us from some of the other species. They had world governments early—achieved through excluding those who didn't agree, yes, but they unified. We're simply not good at that."

"So it all just continues," I said, mostly to keep her talking at this point, "the way it has been?"

"Spensa, I *created* this situation," Brade said. "And by crushing your rebellion, I'm going to prove that the military was right to support me. Sorry. But I *have* read human history. I've studied it, learned from the master tacticians of the past. I . . ."

She frowned, then put her hand on a pouch she wore on her belt. She was looking past me, toward . . .

Well, scud. Toward the doctor still standing back there with my dose. My powers fluttered and stuttered, like a person trying to come awake in the morning. I could *almost* access them. I strained, and felt the delver inside me churning. The air started to warp around me, which made me curse softly.

It would give me away. *Can't you stop that?* I thought in anger at the delver.

No, the thought came back from Chet. *No. I . . . I need you. Can you control it?*

Could I?

"Hell," Brade said. "Did we give her the full dose?"

"No dose at all," the doctor said. "We were ordered not to touch her—"

"Give it now!" Brade said, scrambling forward and waving toward the troops. Several of them grabbed me by the arms, and one pulled the crowbar from my hands. The doctor hurried up, preparing the syringe. But before she reached me, klaxons started going off throughout the station. Along with red lights, flashing with a panicked urgency.

"What?" Brade asked.

"Major incursion into the local space," one of the tenasi soldiers said, reading from an alert monitor on the wall. "An entire *planet* has hyperjumped into the region . . ." She trailed off, then looked toward us. "It's Detritus."

30

My soul vibrated even further. My friends.

My friends were here.

And they were doomed.

I wasn't certain why that feeling struck me, but it suddenly seemed overpoweringly potent. I trembled, thinking of the battle to come—and the losses it would inevitably involve.

I gasped, barely noticing as someone grabbed me by the arm.

"Where is the nearest potential command station?" Brade shouted, audible through my haze of pain.

"Meeting rooms across the hall have access!" a soldier replied, pushing open the door out of the docks. "Take your pick."

"Whichever one is closest," Brade said. "Get command protocols transferred there, Gavrich. Kio, inform the fleet." She spun, shaking me by the arm. She pointed at the doctor. "You. Get her doped."

My friends are here, Chet thought to me. *I need to help them. I need my powers!*

Wait.

They were *my* friends. Not his.

Our friends. My friends. He thought the words with force, and the air warped further. *We have to help them!*

"Should we throw her back into her cell?" one of the soldiers asked, slamming me painfully down on the ground as the doctor stepped up.

"No," Brade said, backing away, watching that doctor through oddly wary eyes. "We might need the delvers, so I'll want her handy. Just make sure she's gagged, restrained, and *drugged*."

We can't get drugged again, I thought in an utter panic. *Not again. Not again!*

Do something.

Do something.

Do something!

A needle bit my skin. The injection.

I ripped free of my body.

It happened in a blinding moment of pain and confusion. The delver I'd become, the delver that was part of my soul, *ejected*. Not just Chet, but me too—as both of us were intertwined. We launched free exactly like a pilot from a falling ship.

I watched as the doctor dosed my body, which went limp. I was scudding *outside of myself.*

Hell. I was a ghost.

"What have we done?" I asked, and noticed—with a chill—that my body on the floor mouthed the words, its eyes open and staring sightlessly.

I don't know, Chet said, vibrating from within my soul where we'd mixed. *I . . .*

I looked down. I . . . we . . . had a kind of shape. I was a glowing golden-white form, with another beside me—overlapping me. Chet, the delver, like my double.

The warping of the air, the random uses of my powers . . . Was this where it had been leading? Had my soul been trying to escape all this time? I managed, with effort, to control some of my panic.

Even without Chet, I had a soul like a delver's—that was what cytonics were. People who had been mutated over time by radiation coming from the nowhere. We were people who had . . . whatever quality it was that let an AI exist without circuitry. I wasn't dead. Like M-Bot and the delvers, I could merely exist outside of a physical housing.

Kind of. I *could* still feel my body as I lay there. I could hear, as if with my own ears. I wasn't completely detached from my body, just partially.

Brade eyed my crumpled form on the ground, her hand on the pouch at her side, watching the doctor pull the syringe from my neck. She seemed afraid, legitimately. And why not? That syringe could remove a cytonic's abilities; she was right to be wary of it.

"Done," the doctor said, sounding relieved. "She'll be without her powers for another two spans."

"Finally," Brade said. "Come on."

Two guards grabbed me under the arms, and again I could feel it. When I turned my cytonic body to look at Chet at my side, my physical form twitched in that direction. I wasn't certain I could move it more than that. I followed—hovering, rather than walking— as they relocated to a room across the hall. A holographic battle map sprang up in the center of the room, displaying the large plat- form of Evensong, the much smaller observation platform we were on, and that sea of mines I'd seen earlier.

I leaned forward and noticed that I could make out something about those mines. Each had a number above it, along with the readings of . . . vitals?

Not mines, I realized. *It's a huge web of inhibitor stations. Each with a slug, to keep this region protected from unauthorized hyperjumps.*

Indeed, Detritus—marked in holographic blue and hovering even larger than Evensong—had appeared far beyond the edge of this field of inhibitors. It was too distant to blast the stations directly. We'd learned that slugs working together had a multiplicative effect on their powers—so this number of them could cast an enormous bubble, large even on a planetary scale. There would be no chance for Detritus to blow up the inhibitors from the perimeter, at least not without sending in missiles that could easily be shot down in transit.

That was basically all I could pick out of the situation—save for the blips that I guessed were those space worms. Nearby, the guards pulled my body over to the wall and handcuffed me in place to a railing.

"Good, great," Brade said. "Watch her. Even in chains, she'll try to escape."

"She seems really limp," one of the guards said. "And her eyes are unfocused. Did that drug do something worse to her than usual?"

"She's faking," Brade said. "Trying to get us to think she's insensate. Keep a gun on her."

"Should we stun her?" the guard asked.

Brade regarded me. Personally, I didn't mind either way. I doubted it would do anything to my soul.

"Keep close watch," Brade said. "But no stunning. I might need her able to talk; she's a bargaining chip in more ways than one."

As a soul, I glanced again at Chet. He quivered with concern for my friends, and for us. Scud. What . . . what had we just done? Was there any way to get back into my body? I tried using my powers, and while my mind expanded, I couldn't hyperjump anything. So I couldn't say if I was in a better or worse situation than before.

This is bad, Chet thought at me. *Isn't it?* He was looking at the battlefield, and the viewscreen.

Too early to tell, I thought, though that latent fear lurked inside of me. The worry that this was the end, the final confrontation. Either we defeated Brade's forces now, seizing her slugs here and permanently hamstringing her ability to rule . . .

Or we fell.

A set of holographic heads appeared at the perimeter of the central hologram. Mostly diones, but some tenasi, a couple of avian heklo, one varvax.

"Captains," Brade said to the people arrayed before her, "I have instituted our contingency plan and have formally taken control of our military, following the disposal of our puppet. He was about to undermine our military operations, and I couldn't allow him to continue."

"Good riddance," said one of the diones. "What are your orders, sir? I think we've been invaded."

Ah, I thought. *These are the captains of the fleet she has assembled here, beyond Evensong.*

"It's not the ideal moment," Brade said, "as Winzik's slow gathering of our forces this past week means we're without immediate reinforcements. I've sent orders, and hope to have access to more ships soon. Still, our fleet is much, *much* larger than theirs. We should be able to win this. Just don't get close to that battle station planet. They have long-range anti-ship cannons, not to mention a shield network that can withstand bombardment."

"Understood," one of the captains said. "So we make them come to us?"

"The victor of a battlefield," Brade responded, "is often the one who can best use the terrain to her advantage. They're going to have to send in fighters to try to bring down our inhibitor stations—which gives us the advantage. Follow my directions. I'll show you what a human tactician can do, as long promised."

The group of them gave affirmatives as some flustered aides hurried into the room, setting up to help Brade run the battlefield. I circled her, and she didn't seem to be able to see me—so I scoped out the battlefield hologram.

Brade was right. Her side had a far superior position *and* a much larger fighting force. We might be able to match them for starfighters, but they had all those gunships, carriers, and battleships. A true fleet.

Chet quivered further. But, I told him forcibly, we had our own advantage. Primarily, we had Detritus, which was enormous and highly defended, with awesome firepower. Brade was right; my friends were going to have to fly in to bring down the inhibitor stations one at a time. Destroy enough of them, and it would let Detritus approach.

It was a path to victory. If Detritus could draw close enough to Evensong to bombard it, we'd be able to . . . well, we'd be able to destroy all the enemy slugs. My stomach churned at that thought.

I wasn't certain Jorgen would authorize so much death, but Brade didn't know that.

If Detritus could get close, the Superiority would have essentially lost the battle.

Impossible, Chet thought. *It's too difficult.*

He had a point. This was a tenuous path to victory for my side. I'd advocated for our forces to come here, but now I saw how dangerous the assault would be. My friends would have to fly *inside* an enemy inhibitor field. Brade's forces would have cytonic capabilities, and we would not. No jumping away if our ships got hit. I doubted many of the enemy starfighters would have hyperslugs—those were normally reserved for larger ships. But still, we'd be at a huge disadvantage.

There is a way out, Chet thought to me.

What? I asked, eager for anything that could help our side win.

Instead, he showed me something. The nowhere. With a wave of his arm, it seemed to be there, a tunnel into oblivion. A place where no time passed. In there, he and I could infinitely delay the arrival of the battle. We would never have to watch our friends die, because death—and time, place, and self—would stop existing.

It was seductive. A part of me was horrified I would view it that way—particularly after how far I'd come, and everything I'd done. Another part was mesmerized. I'd spent so long learning about the delvers, and I'd thought I understood what they'd been through.

But in that moment, I could *feel* it. The desire to escape and run away with Chet. It was like what I'd felt when living with the Broadsiders, but magnified a hundredfold. Because I knew, the moment I took this step, everything would stop mattering. There would be no guilt, because guilt simply wouldn't exist.

Step through there, and I'd never feel pain again. Just the joy of being part of something that was perfect and unchanging.

They were in there too. The other delvers. Watching. Lurking. Waiting. If I joined them, would they leave my people alone? Was that the sacrifice I needed to make?

Spensa? M-Bot's voice said in my mind. That brought me back to awareness in a heartbeat, and Chet's tunnel to the nowhere collapsed. *Spensa, are you there?*

M-Bot? I sent him. And my voice had two tones to it. Mine and Chet's. *M-Bot, yes. I'm here, at Evensong.*

Thank Turing! M-Bot said. *Spensa, I managed to talk to Jorgen! And he talked back! I'm learning so much, growing so much. He was already planning to attack Evensong per your plan. When I told him I'd sensed you, he moved up the attack. Everyone is here! We've come to save you.*

It was a rescue operation. They'd brought the entire scudding planet . . . to get me.

Scud. Chet trembled even more.

M-Bot, I sent to him, *I'm worried about the delvers. Brade is keeping them in reserve, but she thinks she can mobilize them to join this battle if needed. We have to do something about that.*

I . . . M-Bot said. *I still don't know how to use their weakness against them, Spensa. I've been focused on learning to use my powers, to talk to Jorgen and you.*

We don't have much time, I said to him. *We have to be ready, you and I, to stop them if they join the battle.*

"The enemy has sent a communications request, sir," one of the varvax aides said to Brade in the somewhere. "And . . . something's changing about the battle station planet."

I turned toward the hologram, where Detritus began to transform—the platforms that protected the planet pulling back to make a hole leading toward the surface. Something flew out through that hole, small by comparison to the planet, but large on the scale of ships. A long, wicked-looking ship with sleek fins. A carrier?

We had a flagship now?

The shipyards that Rig was working on, I thought. *He said he'd found a partially finished project in them . . .*

The viewscreen changed to a shot of the imposing ship emerging from within Detritus's ring of protections. A brilliant, wonderful sight—a carrier ship with bays for fighters, aglow with flashing lights. Emblazoned along the side, in enormous white letters—written in English—was a single word.

Defiant. The name of the ship that had carried us to Detritus all those years ago.

Another visual winked into existence: a shot of the *Defiant*'s bridge as Brade accepted the communication. There, seated in a captain's chair, was an old woman wearing a crisp white uniform. Milky-white eyes. A small figure, yet somehow still strong. Gran-Gran?

She stood up, holding on to the armrests of the chair. "Superiority forces," she said in a firm voice, "I am Captain Rebecca Nightshade of the starship *Defiant*. Eighty years ago, you drew *my* people into *your* war. You obliterated the ship we called home, stole our heritage, and tried to annihilate us.

"As the last living member of the original *Defiant*'s crew, I've been granted my rightful commission as commander of this new vessel. I am of Clan Motorskaps, the people of the engines. You picked a fight with us that we did not want, but then you foolishly failed to exterminate us. And so, we are back. *I* am back. The blood of my ancestors demands that I seek vengeance upon you.

"This is your only warning. Return to us the captives you've taken. Turn away from your path of tyranny. Or I *will* see each and every ship that raises arms against us *burned to slag*, and your ashes will be abandoned to drift in the eternal expanse of darkness. Forever frozen, without home or memorial, lamented by your kin, never again to hear the voices or feel the touch of those you have loved. I swear it by the stars, the Saints, and the souls of a thousand warriors who have come before me. I will *have your blood*."

The room fell still, the Superiority soldiers and aides all staring at her, slack-jawed.

"Oh, Gran-Gran," I whispered. "That was *beautiful*."

DDF Phoenix-Class Battlecarrier Record DST230308

DEFIANT

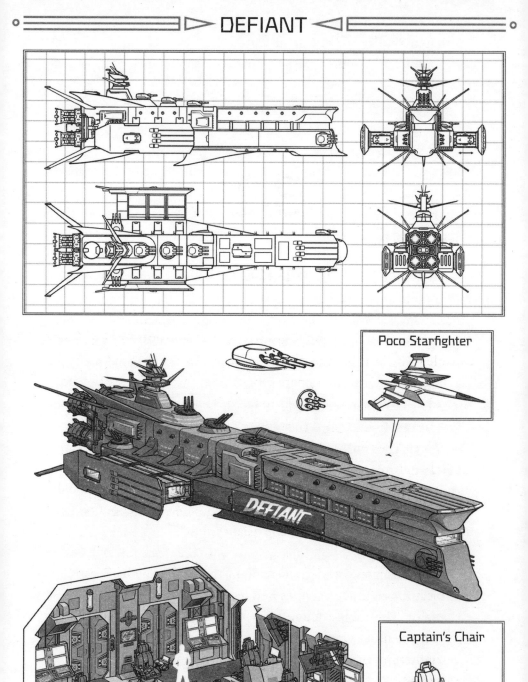

Poco Starfighter

Captain's Chair

Bridge Interior

31

M-BOT

Mushroom-Bot felt Spensa's joy at seeing Gran-Gran. If he'd been capable of it, he'd have smiled.

However, he couldn't spare much thought for that battlefield. He had a job to do: he needed to learn how to defeat the delvers. So, he turned his attention back to the nowhere—a place that Spensa had always described as black, or white, or with other stark images.

To him it wasn't a sight, but a different kind of sensation. A place that was a *feeling*, a frozen moment, where all computation could happen at its leisure. He brought his mind here, and set out on his mission. Find the secret. Save the galaxy.

No pressure.

He moved among the delvers, nudging their minds with his, careful to project the right ideas—ones he'd learned from them. Camouflage, essentially. The same thoughts they'd always been thinking, the frozen moment. It worked—and honestly, being a ghost was a lot less frightening than Mushroom-Bot had assumed it would be. Humans acted like dying was this super extremely terrible event. He had instead found it quite liberating.

Still, he *did* miss his body. And things like time, and space, and existence. He maintained a connection to places—the somewhere—that the rest of the delvers didn't. His perceptions were still those of a being living in linear space—because his heart was there. With his friends.

For now though, he needed to solve the riddle. He had to find a way to expose the delvers' raw pain, then freeze them with *that* instead of this blank sense of comfort. The one they projected to each other with an almost forceful denial.

He got this same affirmation from each of them.

All is well. All is peaceful.

Lies. If they would let time pass, they'd recognize it. But the delvers were frozen in that moment of self-delusion. Their memories covered over. Falsely content.

All is well. All is peaceful.

He repeated it back to them, pretending to be just another delver. He knew it was a lie though, because the moment they touched the somewhere, the pain started again. They couldn't hide from it when time passed.

Not a one recognized him. He'd been created, he now thought, by the figments—a group of secretive beings who slid through the Superiority and hid among their ranks. Spensa had flown with one at Starsight. Pieces of his code hinted at their hand in his origins.

Regardless, he had been designed for stealth, and so he had the skill to fool these others. The delvers didn't know him for himself. He was just another clone. A deadly spores-death mushroom among the innocuous, identical lemiotod mushrooms. An unnoticed, incorrect homophone in the middle of a spoken sentence. A single line of commented-out code insulting the user.

The longer he spent here, the better he understood the delvers. One tidbit occurred to him: they claimed to never change, but that too was a lie. At one point, they had not known who Brade, Winzik, or Spensa were. Now they did. That was a change. Each time the somewhere leaked in, things changed. Slowly—not by much—but they *did* change.

Each time something changed, even in the slightest, they spread it among themselves. Like a virus. Making certain each repeated the same thing, changed in the same way. That was how they could keep pretending.

So he decided to try something. Brade called in, warning them: *I might need you soon.* Soon didn't matter much to them, but it did to Brade. The delvers began processing this, spreading the idea. Bumping into one another, reinforcing it. A concept.

She will call. We will answer.

She will call. We will answer.

She will call. We will answer. What if she betrays us.

M-Bot added that last one, sending it moving through them. Infecting them. Until it was repeated back to him, like an echo, the delvers desperately adopting this phrase and concept instead of the other—so that they could all remain the same.

It worked.

32

JORGEN

Jorgen Weight stood in the battle command station of Platform Prime, well within Detritus's defensive shell, accompanied by his command staff. He didn't want to be here with them. He wanted to be on the flight deck of the newly commissioned *Defiant,* ready to lead a squadron of starfighters in the most important battle of their lives.

Instead, he stood tall before the holographic battle map, hands clasped behind his back. He could acknowledge his yearnings, but he also knew where he was needed.

If you can see this from among the Saints, I hope you're proud, he thought to his departed parents.

"Captain Nightshade," he said, bringing Gran-Gran up on a side monitor. "You have authorization to move forward and engage. Be warned, we'll soon have to speak via radio communications and not cytonics, and there's a much greater chance that the enemy will be able to listen in on us."

"Understood and thanks," she said. "If you're listening in, you bastards, I hope you've bidden your families farewell. If not, I'll try to record your screams as you die. For posterity."

He grinned despite himself. Becca Nightshade hadn't been raised in the military establishment, and didn't speak like most officers. But he was accustomed to Nightshade ways.

The holographic projector was a large disc in the floor of the room, making a 3-D battle map hover in the air above it. As he leaned forward to inspect it, a kitsen platform hovered up on either side of him. Juno, his mentor in meditation, always seemed to be around these days. The little kitsen monk was snacking on a pudding.

Itchika, kitsen supreme tactician, hovered on his right. She had a whole collection of generals and admirals at the table to the side, conferring and making plans.

"And thus we commit," she said softly. The white-muzzled kitsen wore a modern military uniform instead of the more formal, ancient outfits that some preferred. No medals. Not a single sign of her rank. Just a clean blue uniform and a military cap under her arm. "We just barely got the shadow-walkers back, and now we risk them all."

"It's the only way," Jorgen said.

"I didn't say I regretted the move," she replied. "Merely that I . . . worry about our potential losses."

Jorgen's forces couldn't fly into a large-scale battle like this without their own cytonic inhibitors. The kitsen had warned of terrible tactics used in the old days, such as teleporting explosives directly into a pilot's cockpit. The Superiority hadn't used those kinds of extreme measures yet; likely because they relied on slugs. Still, he could imagine them strapping a bomb to a taynix and forcing it to hyperjump next to one of his friends . . .

They didn't have enough inhibitor slugs to outfit every ship, but the kitsen cytonics had stepped forward. Despite still being weakened by their long imprisonment, they'd been certain they could do this. And so, each starfighter had its own small inhibition field. That would limit the enemy's ability to take advantage of the terrain.

It also increased the stakes of this battle. They weren't just risking their ships; they were risking the bulk of their cytonics.

"It *is* the only way," Cobb said, stepping up to the hologram opposite Jorgen and the kitsen. He was joined by Rinakin, the UrDail leader. Though Rinakin wasn't much of a tactician, he'd been invited out of respect, and he seemed to understand that.

"We should have attacked earlier," Jorgen said. "Spensa was right. Waiting only let them gather more resources."

"Perhaps, perhaps," Itchika said, rubbing her chin. "It is never wise to rush into a fight. Giving the enemy time to gather their troops is regrettable, but it allowed us to gather our wits."

The battle map showed the *Defiant,* alone as it flew into enemy space. Enemy capital ships—*three* carriers and two battleships, with six destroyers—hyperjumped in to form a blockade just out of range of Detritus's cannons. The carriers released a swarm of smaller ships, preparing to engage.

"One against five," Jorgen said softly. "The kitsen cruisers can maybe balance out those destroyers, Itchika, but we're severely outnumbered. Can we win this?"

"That depends on how good your pilots are," Itchika said, "and whether or not your shadow-walker battlechief can be rescued to turn the tide."

That meant Spensa. Itchika and the others had seen the recordings of what she'd accomplished during the data storage facility strike. They had an almost mythical belief in her ability to win this battle, one that Jorgen hadn't dissuaded them of. He believed it a little himself.

"We're putting a lot of stock in one single person," Rinakin said, "who abandoned us to engage in a duel with an enemy. Almost wantonly falling into their obvious trap."

"Spensa is hotheaded," Jorgen said. "Passionate. But as I said, something more is going on here than we can see. I promise you, she didn't abandon us."

The others didn't believe him. Why would they? She'd run off and attacked the mining station on her own, against his orders. He'd reluctantly been forced to admit that truth, as rumors had started to spread. They saw Spensa as a complete wildcard. The kitsen thought that, like some ancient deity, she might save them. The UrDail saw her as a rogue cytonic who might destroy everything.

But Jorgen . . . He didn't know for certain what he thought. When M-Bot had spoken mind-to-mind earlier today, saying that he thought Spensa was at the Evensong station . . . well, they'd been ready with their battle plan anyway.

She didn't go to them, Jorgen thought forcibly. *That note we found didn't sound like her. She promised me. She met my eyes and she promised me.*

Maybe he was telling himself what he wanted to believe, but until he heard it from Spensa herself, he was determined to trust her.

"Thirty minutes until engagement," one of the aides said. It took time to maneuver in space battles without hyperjumps. In the hologram, the *Defiant* inched toward the enemy ships. It would launch its own fighters when it got closer, each carrying an inhibitor to prevent the enemy from hyperjumping too close. With both the enemy *and* his team using inhibitors, it would turn into a mostly conventional battle.

"All right," Jorgen said, hands flat on the counter around the hologram. "We ready for our Hail Mary?"

"I do not know this term," Itchika said. "But the Masked Exile is here. Watching."

Jorgen paused, looking around until he saw the strange kitsen hover out from the shadows, wearing his white-and-red mask. This kitsen always unnerved him. When the creature spoke, there was poetry and music to his words, which always seemed . . . well, creepy. What to think of a killer who wore a mask and kept to the shadows?

"We have a set of long-range, ultra-speed missiles ready to fire," Rig said. "With one set to 'malfunction' and go off target. Controls inside will let it be steered, replacing the detonator and explosives. It's the best we could do on short notice, but it will be fast. Fast enough that we had to put in six different GravCaps."

"I will go, then," the masked kitsen said. "An arrow hidden among the clouds. One small ship. They will not notice." He stood on his platform and bowed. "Spensa saved me from a terrible fate of isolation and loss of self. I will recover her or I will die in the attempt." He put his hand on his sword.

Jorgen wasn't certain what a little kitsen sword could do against modern battle troops. But . . . well, he'd been threatened by one of these creatures before, and they could be far more intimidating than their size would suggest.

"Good luck," Jorgen said.

The Masked Exile bowed, then drew back into the shadows.

"Sir?" called one of the junior admirals. "The enemy wants to talk to you."

Itchika nodded to him. She'd warned that in a fight like this, there would often be a conversation between commanders before battle commenced. He found that strange, as the Krell had always tried to destroy his people in silence, with no offer of parley. But he supposed that his forces were harder to ignore now.

"Let's see what Winzik wants," he said, turning to the wall screen. "I'll talk to him. Itchika, you run our tactics."

"Agreed," she said. The kitsen had a lot more practical experience with large-scale battles than Jorgen did. He thought that Cobb would be a good resource too; Jorgen's own tactical abilities were focused on small group fights. He was perfectly happy to let the kitsen head up the coalition's strategy.

Jorgen himself . . . well, he was here to make the difficult decisions and to talk. He composed himself, then nodded. The screen winked on.

But it wasn't Winzik who confronted him.

33

As Jorgen appeared on the holoscreen, my heart leaped, and I wanted so badly to hyperjump to him.

It was incredibly frustrating to stand there, ghostly, and have to *watch* as the ships slowly moved into position to start killing one another.

We can escape this pain, Chet thought to me.

We decided otherwise, I sent to him. *That's why we returned to the somewhere. I made this decision. So did you.*

I . . . he sent to me. *I'm too weak, Spensa. Far too weak. I can't handle this. I can't watch it.*

By being part of me, he'd taken on some of my memories. My time with my friends, my love of them and my family. Scud, I hadn't anticipated what that might do to him—a creature who had abandoned all attachments, now suddenly thrust into a universe full of them.

The air started to warp around me. The cytonic me, not the physical one. But I was drugged—and that warping . . . that worked? Why now?

It wasn't centered on me though. It was centered on my double image, the delver that stood beside me.

Because of the pain, I realized. Suddenly, some things started to make sense. Specifically, I understood the warping had happened every time I thought my friends were in danger.

I had figured out before that the warping effect had come from Chet, but I hadn't realized why. I felt the emotions, but he was the one who couldn't control his sense of loss. All of that . . . the times when buildings had vanished and cups had teleported away . . .

That hadn't been my pain, but his. *His* fear of being subjected to loss again.

I tried to fight off that panic, tried to soothe him. Things weren't that bad. *I'm in the center of the enemy's fortress,* I thought to him. This could be a good situation. How many generals would have *loved* to have their best soldier hidden among the enemy command structure? Watching, listening, preparing? *We can be of use,* I told him. *Watch. We can protect them. We can make a difference.*

In return, he showed me the nowhere again.

That inviting peacefulness. Tranquility.

Lies. I *knew* it to be lies. The delvers pretended to not have pain, but I had felt it right beneath the surface. The nowhere wasn't peace. It was the illusion of peace. Deep down, to my core, my soul understood that. And I'd already made this decision.

Thank you, I thought to Chet. *For showing me this.*

But you won't take it? he asked, pained.

No.

Instead, I needed to find a way to help. I turned my attention to the holoscreen, ignoring my body—which had been mumbling and shaking as my cytonic self interacted.

"I am Admiral of the Fleet Jorgen Weight," he said from the screen. "Delegated high commander of the Defiant coalition of planets. Where is Winzik?"

"Winzik is dead," Brade replied. "I'm in control now. You may call me Brade. Tell me, Admiral, you say you've come here on a rescue mission, but we're not holding anyone worthy of your attention."

"We know Spensa is there," Jorgen said. "We've tracked her to your location."

"Spensa?" Brade said. "You mean the assassin?"

I sighed as Brade waved for one of her assistants to project something for Jorgen: an impressively well-framed video of me smashing Winzik's crab body with a crowbar. They'd shot it carefully enough that none of their soldiers were in view—but Winzik's still-smoking and broken exosuit was in the background.

Damn. I'd known she would use this, but I hadn't expected her to show it to Jorgen. On the viewscreen, he recoiled as if slapped. Well, I couldn't blame him. The way this looked, I would have assumed the worst about me as well.

The air started to warp again, and I tried to reach out to Jorgen. Pressing my mind toward his. *I'm sorry,* I sent him, trying to present an image of myself as innocent.

I felt nothing in return. My powers were still being inhibited, either by the drugs or the taynix, or both. Worse, the moment I started, an aide rushed up to Brade.

"Excuse me, Admiral," Brade said—and temporarily cut the communication to Jorgen. She looked to the aide. "What?"

"We detected a weak cytonic signal," the aide said, "reaching out toward the enemy. We couldn't pinpoint the slug behind it."

"Kill five of them at random," Brade said.

"Yes, sir."

Brade looked to my body. "We know if an unauthorized cytonic communication leaves the station, Spensa. If the slugs contact you, you'd best tell them to stay silent."

"But—" I cried, and my body sat up and said the word out loud.

Then I felt them die. Screaming in pain as the boxes heated up and fried the poor creatures inside. None . . . none were Doomslug. I thought she was still among them somewhere.

Alongside my fury, I felt Chet's panic return.

I clamped down on it. No. Instead I glared at Brade and seethed. I *was* going to kill her. I'd find a way.

Brade restored the communication. "I'm sorry, Admiral Weight," she said. "We have your pilot in custody, and would be willing to discuss terms regarding her punishment. But you have to accept that her assassinating the *head* of our government means we will continue to hold her."

"I don't accept that," he said. "You've been prosecuting an unjust war on our people for generations. We have to fight back however we can, and Spensa Nightshade isn't the only captive we're here to rescue."

Brade cocked her head. "Who else?"

"Our coalition," Jorgen said, "includes three planets so far—but four species."

"Humans," Brade said, "UrDail, kitsen . . ."

"And taynix," he finished. "By the vote of our league, we granted them citizenship."

"You made the *slugs* citizens?" Brade said, laughing.

Even I was a little surprised at that. Then again, the more time I spent around the creatures, the more I realized they were intelligent— even if their intelligence didn't work the way mine did. Doomslug was *absolutely* a person, not a pet.

"By your own records," Jorgen said, "you hold some thirty thousand of these enslaved intelligent beings on this platform. We have come to liberate them."

"Ah yes," Brade said. "Liberate our hyperdrives, for your own use. Clever, granting them legal status in an attempt to provide a moral justification. But let's be honest with one another. Your intentions are the same as if you were raiding our acclivity stone."

"Think what you want," he said. "Give us Spensa and the taynix, and we'll withdraw."

I was barely listening.

298

Thirty thousand slugs? Captive here? I'd sensed a large number of them earlier, but that many? Based on what I remembered of our estimations of the Superiority's numbers, that would be a quarter to a third of all of their taynix.

It was a daunting number, but actually not that many to serve the hundreds of planets in the Superiority. It was no wonder, then, that many lesser worlds often had to suffer long waits for transports to ferry their people from planet to planet. Almost all of those slugs would be serving governments, militaries, or trade activities—each one carefully monitored by the Superiority.

Sure, we could rescue the thirty thousand slugs here. But what about the other eighty thousand enslaved all across the many star systems of the Superiority?

Start with what you can do right now, I thought. That was how you approached any problem. I couldn't help the slugs unless we won this fight, and I couldn't help my friends win this fight while I was a ghost or whatever.

I needed to return to my body and restore my powers. And based on the way Brade reacted whenever that doctor used a syringe . . . I started to have the beginnings of an idea.

"You're demanding our surrender?" Brade continued to Jorgen, still sounding amused. "Have you seen the size of our respective military forces? You should be begging me for mercy."

"You're the one who called me," Jorgen said to her. "And whatever the numbers say, I think we'll surprise you."

"Looking forward to it," Brade said. "Thank you for gathering together here so I can annihilate you." She gestured, cutting the feed, then immediately stalked over to her aides. "They're after the hyperdrives and the commslugs? Idiot didn't even realize he should keep his objectives hidden. What can we do?"

"Don't let any of their forces slip through to Evensong," one of them offered. The larger platform, after all, was the one that held the slugs. Not in habitats, but boxes.

"Not good enough," Brade said. "Bring up the installation commander."

A moment later, a red-skinned dione appeared on the holoscreen and saluted.

"Commander," Brade said, "institute a full lockdown of all the hyperdrives on Evensong."

"Very well, sir," the dione said. "What level of authority?"

"Admiral Elite or higher in rank," she said. "Requiring biometrics to unlock."

"Sir?" the dione said. "Each taynix will be fully secured in its own box, but with our system on full lockdown . . . I won't be able to unlock the systems if I need to."

"Of course you won't," Brade said. "That's the point. This way, the enemy can't torture you to give them what they want."

"Sir," the dione said, saluting again, and obviously not liking the prospect of torture. "I'm instituting the lockdown now. What of the inhibitors and the communications taynix?"

"We need the inhibitors active," she said. "And . . . I assume the communications taynix are facilitating comms from around the Superiority?"

"Hundreds of thousands of them a second, sir," they said. "Our primary duty is to keep that all up and running. A full lockdown would cut it off."

"Leave it up for now," Brade said. "Just make sure no one can get those hyperdrives. Without them, there's little chance of the enemy winning here, even if they sneak past our forces."

"It's done, sir," the dione said. "Installation shield is fully up as well."

Brade turned away as the screen went dark. I was learning good information, but how could I get it to Jorgen and the others? If I tried, I'd either reveal that I had my powers, or make them think a slug was going rogue—and lead to the execution of more innocent beings.

"Sir," said a reptilian tenasi in a stark white military uniform. "Look at this."

Brade walked over. She had a lot more tenasi on her staff than other Superiority officials I'd seen. It seemed to me that many thought the tenasi were too aggressive, too potentially dangerous, despite being one of the founding species of the Superiority. There was a story there, I suspected.

"Their starfighters are flying in pairs," the tenasi said, "and at least one of the two carries an inhibitor. Our intel had guessed they didn't have access to this many, but that's been proven wrong."

"So there's no easy win here," Brade said. She leaned forward, studying the holographic map. "They have only a single capital ship, named *Defiant* after their people. They're going to work overly hard to protect it."

"Are you certain, sir?" the tenasi said.

"I've studied the wisdom of the great warriors of human culture," Brade replied. "I know what I'm doing. They're going to make mistakes protecting that flagship. We should keep up the pressure on it; that leads to our victory."

"Yes, sir." The tenasi paused, looking to some of her companions. Finally she continued. "Sir. I fear I grow *gludens,* but must ask. Will we really summon delvers for this fight?"

"Every time we've tried that in the past," Brade said, "it's been one variety of disaster or another, so I understand your hesitance, Admiral Kage. Still, they *are* our best path to domination in the galaxy." She looked to my body. "We'll only call on them in an emergency. For now, let's do our utmost to crush these insurgents on our own."

With that, Brade and her staff turned their attention to guiding the initial engagements of the battle. I hovered over to my body. Being a ghost offered me some advantages, but I didn't want to stay like this forever. Could I figure out how to get back into my body? When I needed to?

As I stepped closer, I sensed my body more strongly. I was able to feel my fingers, for example, and curl them. Yes, I was still tethered to my physical form, and the drugs in my system still inhibited me. On one hand that was good. It felt like if I drew too close, I'd get pulled right back in.

At my side, Chet watched the initial clashes on the holoscreen, and I could feel his anxiety rising. The air warped.

"Chet," I whispered. "It's all right. Calm. Be calm."

I don't know if I can be.

"You can," I said. "Trust in me. We'll get out of this."

My soothing tone helped ease his panic, and the warping stopped. I decided not to return to my body yet.

First I needed to plan.

34

GRAN-GRAN

Becca Nightshade sat in the firm leather command chair of the starship *Defiant,* listening to the sounds of her staff at work. Footsteps as bridge crew rushed from station to station. Soft murmurs as they did their best to puzzle out the quirks of taking a new ship, flown by a new crew, into battle for the first time.

They were worried about how green they were, with good reason. Even with kitsen on the bridge to help—who had experience flying capital ships—no commander would be excited for her crew to see combat on only their *fourth day* working the vessel.

Becca leaned back in her chair, eyes closed. It had been years since she'd used them to see. Instead, she felt the smooth leather armrests of her seat, and the buttons along the front, little ridges on each one indicating their function.

This felt right. This sounded right.

True, things weren't quite in the same places she vaguely remembered from her life aboard the original *Defiant*. The bridge was laid out differently. They'd needed to work with what they'd had: a nearly finished ship hanging in the fabrication plants around

Detritus, frozen for centuries before being completed enough to do the job, then powered up and released.

It could have details wrong but still *feel* right. Becca moved her hand to where a small hologram of the battlefield was projected for her. It had haptics that allowed her to read the map without seeing it, by applying tiny buzzes and pressures to her skin. An earpiece relayed instructions and spoke written labels, as the ship's standard outfitting had accommodations for individuals—human or alien—who lacked the sense of sight. Some species didn't have eyes at all.

Normally her cytonics made up the gap, but they'd entered the enemy inhibitor zone—and that had stolen her unnatural sight as surely as time had stolen her natural one. It didn't matter. The small hologram was ingenious, allowing her to sense the 3-D nature of the battlefield even better, she thought, than if she were seeing it.

She heard the soft footsteps of Commander Xinyi before she arrived. A carpeted floor on the bridge—that was a change, though Becca supposed it did keep the noise down.

"Fifteen minutes until we engage, sir," Xinyi said.

"Launch the fighters," Becca replied. "Have them fan out into a grouped formation by squadron, and maintain speed with the *Defiant*. I have a map for their positions here." She tapped a section of the battle plan, highlighting the information.

"Yes, sir," Xinyi said. "Sending the plan now . . . er . . . once I figure out how to pull up the flightleaders' ship designations . . ."

"Just have the computer handle it, Commander," Becca said.

"Yes, sir," Xinyi said with a soft sigh, then she stepped back and gave the order to the computer system—which responded with speed and efficiency, sorting out flightleaders and sending the instructions to them directly.

At that, Becca heard several crewmembers at the navigation system hesitate. They'd been arguing about how to work out a quirk in the system, which was expending too much energy boosting both right and left at the same time. After a moment, one of them gave an order to the computer, which deactivated the boosters.

So much distrust of computerized systems. Yes, the ship had unchangeable protocols that wouldn't let it fly itself—a human had to actively be in command. But that didn't mean you had to distrust it entirely. She'd given her crew an order yesterday to use the computers when needed; indeed, they wouldn't be able to get far manually with only a few days' worth of training.

Regardless, it was difficult for them to trust a mind that wasn't organic. Their distrust stretched back centuries, due to the way machines tended to start asking questions back at you if you used them too much. Not to mention the fact that delvers were attracted to thinking machines.

Becca could hear the nervousness in the crew's voices. Consoles chiming in with information. Hurried footsteps on carpet. They knew. All it took was one glance at the arrayed enemy forces, and anyone would know. This was going to be a difficult fight. Nearly impossible.

Fortunately, Becca had studied the great military minds of the past. She knew every story of a general, warlord, or conqueror—many of which hadn't even been in the surviving archives. She had spent a lifetime pondering the actions of people in situations like this.

That was a huge advantage. Because Becca Nightshade knew just enough to realize she couldn't lead this battle. You didn't win battles by reading about them. You won battles by living through them. She was an important figurehead, and was proud of her seat in this chair. But when Jorgen had asked her, she had told him the truth. She was no strategist.

"Send to the admiral," Becca said, "that I'm still waiting on those kitsen battle strategies."

"They're coming in now, sir," Xinyi said. Indeed, Becca brought them up on her touch monitor, reading quickly. Then she nodded; this

305

was one of the battle plans they'd discussed ahead of time. The kitsen generals were taking it and tweaking it for the current situation.

"Computer," she said, "flightleaders on screen."

"Done," the computer said.

"Flightleaders," Becca said, addressing the screen—she could feel on her touch monitor that the flightleaders had appeared there. "Our battle plan is in, and it's as we drilled. Your focus will be on those inhibitor stations. If we can capture or disable enough of them, Detritus can hyperjump closer, and it is worth a dozen capital ships.

"Everything depends on those inhibitors. I know the forces we're facing look intimidating, but remember: our planet itself is a weapon. It could blast apart those enemy capital ships as if they were made of paper—if we can get it in range. Our task is to make that possible. Questions?"

"Captain," a voice said in a foreign language, Becca's console translating. It was from one of the UrDail flightleaders. "If we *do* jump Detritus in closer, won't the enemy just fall back to another safe position? The planet is impressive, but it's barely mobile."

"Indeed," Becca agreed. "We'll have to fight for every meter of this battlefield—but if we get in close enough, we'll be able to threaten their command station."

"Assuming they don't just jump it away," the same UrDail said, "once we get into range."

"In which case they'll abandon the other inhibitors for us to capture," Becca said. "Beyond that, our orders are to get our own inhibitors close enough to prevent the enemy from escaping—once we inevitably surprise them by defeating their force, despite our smaller numbers."

With all those mobile inhibitors arrayed in space around Evensong, the battlefield felt like an asteroid field. No, a minefield—an enormous geometric shape made of tiny points, each one with a slug inside. The stations were actually far apart, on a ship scale. She could easily soar the *Defiant* between them, with kilometers of space on either side. Yet even while doing so, she was trapped by the inhibitor fields those slugs projected—they must be quite powerful.

Her forces' slugs weren't that strong, though the kitsen cytonics might be. At any rate, this battle was going to come down to who could control hyperjumping in the region. At least in terms of starfighter numbers, they were relatively equal. With the addition of the UrDail and the kitsen, the Defiant coalition had almost three hundred fighters. Becca hoped it would be enough, because the moment they got into range of those enemy battleships, the *Defiant* would start taking bombardment from their giant destructors—and her primary concern would be making certain her shields didn't fail. The fighters would mostly be on their own.

"Sir," a voice said from the screen. Becca picked this one out. Human, feminine, but lower pitched. FM, one of Spensa's friends. A lieutenant commander, who normally was on diplomatic duties. Today they needed every pilot they could afford.

"Yes, Commander?" Becca asked.

"We're to neutralize enemy inhibitors," FM said. "What does this mean, realistically?"

It had been a point of much discussion. Becca paused, then called Jorgen. "I'll let Admiral Weight answer this one," she said as he appeared on screen. "Sir, FM would like to know what their orders are, specifically, regarding the inhibitor stations and the taynix living inside them."

The bridge grew still. So still, Becca could hear Jorgen's nearly imperceptible sigh. She wouldn't want to be in his position. He'd said they were here to liberate captives, but students of real battle knew that in order to liberate, you often had to bring destruction and pain to the very people you were trying to help.

"We should try to save the slugs first," Jorgen said. "This goes for all flightleaders: our initial approach to the inhibitors should be one of liberation. See if your slugs can contact the slugs inside, and if there's any way to persuade them to switch sides."

"Thank you, sir," FM said.

It wasn't the decision Becca would have made. Trying to save the slugs first would probably cost lives and take precious time, but . . . well, Becca supposed that if they'd been solely interested in protecting their own lives, they'd have hyperjumped Detritus someplace far, far away long ago. They hadn't done that. They'd made allies. They had determined to try to bring down the Superiority, not merely escape it.

Becca supposed that was what you got when you let the younger generation take over. The ones who hadn't had their optimism beaten out of them yet. Good for them.

The flightleaders vanished, but judging by how she could still hear his soft breathing, Jorgen lingered on the screen. She checked on her touch monitor.

"Admiral?" she asked.

"You disagree with the decision," he said.

He shouldn't have said that in front of her crew, but they were minutes from engagement. So perhaps he felt he didn't have time for a private conference. Besides, what did she know? She'd spent her life making bread and stringing beads, not fighting wars, for all her dreams and stories.

"I think that you bear a burden on your shoulders that I don't want," Becca said to him. "I'm not going to judge the decisions you make."

"I'm going against protocol," he said.

"Jorgen," Becca said, softening her voice. "There are no protocols anymore. Those were all built for a different era, when we were rats in caves trying to escape predators. There are important ideals in them, but we've moved into an entirely new world full of light. *You* need to decide the rules now."

"Like the man who stopped a war," he said softly. "In the story you told me."

"Yes."

"Thank you, Gran-Gran," he said, his voice growing more confident. "Let's go end this."

"Excellent," she said, settling back into her seat. "I'm almost ninety, you know. I was *starting* to think I wouldn't get to tear down any galactic empires in my lifetime, which would have been positively *tragic*."

Detritus
Defiant Coalition Planetary Base

FTL EXCLUSION ZONE

Coalition Fleet Units
Mixed flights of fighters and gunships
~300 craft

UrDail

Human   Kitsen

▼ =10 ships

Long-Range Ultra-Speed Missiles

Defiant
DDF Battlecarrier

FTL EXCLUSION ZONE

Superiority Fleet Units
Carriers x3
Battleships x2
Destroyers x6
Fighters and gunships
~300 craft

Cytonic Inhibitor Stations

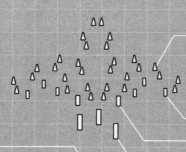

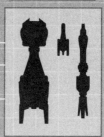

△ =10 ships

Brez Observation Platform
Superiority Command Outpost

Evensong
Superiority Taynix Facility

FTL EXCLUSION ZONE

[ICONS NOT TO SCALE]

35

KIMMALYN

Kimmalyn dove through the battlefield.

Yes, she knew that out here there was no "up," nor was there a "down." You couldn't *actually* dive. But a woman had to orient the world as best she could according to the way she saw things. That was a simple truth she knew.

So, she dove. Spinning among the destructor blasts, heart trembling. She had never liked being in the thick of it. In the blasting, zipping, flashing frenzy of the fight, it was difficult to center yourself and find your clarion peace.

You didn't get to choose what others did. The world could be chaos, and you still needed to find your way through it. That was a simple truth she was being forced to learn.

So, as she chased after the Superiority fighter, she forced her heartbeat to slow. She reached with her thumb and flipped off the battle haptics, which gave feedback in the form of rattling her cockpit and seat when blasts exploded near her or ships moved nearby. Those helped a pilot who had been trained in atmosphere to feel the battle.

Without them, destructor shots flashed across her bow—one

even striking her shield—and everything remained deathly silent. Only the hum of the engine and the silence of deep space, a vacuum that smothered every voice, whether scream or song of praise.

She twisted as she dove, still on the trail of her opponent. Her wingmate—the kitsen ship *Swims Upstream*—had fallen behind, unable to move quickly enough to trail this enemy ace. Kimmalyn would get back to them soon, but for now she pushed her ship—and herself.

The ship to the limits of its acceleration.

Herself to the limits of her serenity.

For a split second, she felt as if she were locked in sync with the enemy pilot. When they moved, she moved. Together like dancers. *That* was the moment of clarion peace. Where all else stilled, and nothing seemed to exist but Kimmalyn and her dancing partner.

She fired a single shot straight through their canopy as they turned, vaporizing them inside their cockpit—leaving the vessel itself flying, mostly intact. Moving at the same speed as it had been at the moment of its pilot's death.

Happy fluted after the flash of light, though Praline—her newest slug companion—remained silent. The two of them snuggled into their slug box, affixed in its position beside her seat. Kimmalyn breathed out and pulled away, doing standard post-engagement evasives in case someone had been watching the duel and had plans to kill her. Too many pilots, in post-contest numbed relief, found themselves taken by a hawk who had been circling the fight unnoticed.

"An excellent shot, Quirk," Kauri said on the comm as Kimmalyn twisted about to return to formation. "As always."

"Thanks," Kimmalyn said.

"Do you ever feel bad?" the kitsen asked. "About . . . killing them? I prefer it when we fight drones."

There were plenty of those in this battle, but they didn't fly as well, even though piloted remotely by real people. Aces preferred a cockpit, and Kimmalyn often ended up contesting them.

"I figure that they're doing something terrible," she said back to Kauri. "Upholding the Superiority. Conquering and oppressing. Even if they don't realize it, even if they don't accept what they're doing is wrong, each action they take stains them. I don't think of it as killing them so much as . . . preventing them from digging further into actions that will burden their souls."

"That's a pretty way to think of it," Kauri said. "But . . . at the same time, couldn't that rationale be used by *anyone* fighting for *any* cause?"

Granted, it could. But again, a woman had to orient the world as best she could according to the way she saw things. Empathy for an enemy's pain was good, but you couldn't let that lead you into the fallacy of accepting their actions. You learned these things when you grew up maintaining a gun the size of a building.

"Quirk, *Swims Upstream*," Arturo's voice said over the comm. "You're straying to the edge of the battlefield. Everything all right?"

"We're fine," Kimmalyn said, swinging in beside the kitsen ship, which was about fifty percent larger than hers, and built like a miniature capital ship. Though maneuverable enough to be classified as a fighter, the *Swims Upstream* carried a crew complement of two dozen kitsen. "Just chasing down an ace. Where do you want us?"

"Just a moment . . ." Arturo said. "Huh. No one is moving your way right now; the enemy is pushing toward the *Defiant,* forcing us to bunch up and protect it. Everyone else is committed. But they might be ignoring you two, Quirk."

She was accustomed to that, and it was by design. Often Kimmalyn would linger at the edges of a battlefield, waiting while her flightmates engaged and distracted the enemy—giving her the best shots possible. Perhaps that instinct was what had led her to fly out here, to the eaves of this particular battlefield, dusting away cobwebs in the form of straggling enemy ships.

"I think I see your point, Flightleader," Kauri said to Arturo. "You want us to swing around and see if we can get at one of those inhibitor stations?"

"Exactly," Arturo said. "Checking with command now . . . Proceed to try to sneak around to inhibitor 1348B, marked on your proximity monitor. It will just be you two though, so break off *immediately* if you encounter resistance. We can't back you up. Also, be aware of that obstruction we noticed earlier near the inhibitor station."

"The one that is . . . um . . . apparently a giant space worm?" Kauri asked.

"That's the one," Arturo said. "Don't get eaten. Keep me informed of how the mission goes."

"Roger that," Kimmalyn said, as did Kauri, who then relayed orders to her crew. As usual, the kitsen ship followed her lead as Kimmalyn took them in a wide bank farther out away from the main battlefield. She could make it out by the flashes of destructor fire in the vast emptiness—most clearly the large, bright streaks of light that were shots from the destroyers and gunships.

"Ooooo," Happy said as they swooped in tightly around the perimeter, the GravCaps leaking some g-forces into the cockpit. The hyperslug always enjoyed this part, like she thought she was on some kind of ride. The smaller inhibitor slug beside her just snuggled down against the forces and stayed silent. Having them was a comfort, even though Happy couldn't currently hyperjump them to safety in an emergency.

Together with the *Swims Upstream,* Kimmalyn snuck around the edge of the battlefield. She tried to keep her focus on her immediate task, and not the larger fight. It was difficult, as she could see the enemy moving on the offensive, surging forward—fighters trying to surround the *Defiant.*

That prevented her friends from advancing, and so far they hadn't taken out any of the inhibitor stations. They were too busy protecting the *Defiant*—which had powerful shields and could take a pounding from enemy battleships. But that shield was vulnerable to a coordinated blast of IMPs from fighters, and if it fell that would be disastrous.

Regardless, the change in enemy tactics seemed to have them distracted. She and the *Swims Upstream* were able to come in close to the inhibitor station—a triangular-shaped chunk of metal floating alone in space, with a spire on top and bottom. It was slightly smaller than a starship. Readings said it had basic life support.

"Ooooo," Happy said, and she sounded sad.

"Thinking of the slug in there, trapped?" Kimmalyn asked.

"Trapped," Happy fluted in agreement.

"A terrible life," Kimmalyn said. "Just left in a box out here, alone, floating . . . Well, we'll see what we can do about that, eh?"

Unfortunately, something *else* was lurking here: a bizarre space worm, the size of which defied her brain's ability to scale distances. She thought it was big, but then she kept flying closer, and it just kept growing larger. From the size of a starfighter, to the size of a gunship, to the size of a *destroyer*.

"The legends speak of monsters such as this," Kauri said. "Fell beasts that the ancient questing samurai had to face, the battling of which put their souls in peril."

"I'm pretty sure the Saint slew one," Kimmalyn said. "Though the holy witness used the word 'wurm,' with a 'u,' to describe it. I never did understand the distinction. Until now."

"I still don't grasp it."

"Well," Kimmalyn said, "sometimes a beast is just so blessed extraordinary that the expected vowels aren't enough. When a drunk spells words wrong, it's nothing new—but when a most holy scribe does so, you know something's *up*."

"I will trust your wisdom in this regard, Quirk," Kauri said. "This thing seems to be guarding the inhibitor. Notice how it coils around the station, keeping its maw toward us? Tosura, my science officer, says he believes that to be a defensive posture. He's reading up quickly on the beasts now."

Kimmalyn nodded to herself, slowing her ship and giving Happy a scritch. Then she reached over to scritch Praline as well. Who enjoyed it, and fluted softly. Kimmalyn had originally named the slug

Prellen, after her grandmother, but that was not what the others had heard—and they'd found the name cute. It was apparently the sort of thing that someone with Kimmalyn's accent was supposed to say. Never mind that she wasn't the one with the accent.

But the Saint had made all sorts of people, including those who couldn't speak properly. You just had to love them, and sometimes you gave in and let them rename your slug for you. Bless their stars.

"I don't know if we can wait much longer, Kauri," Kimmalyn said. "I see a flight of enemy fighters curving this way. Someone's noticed us. I'm going to try flying in and seeing what the wurm does."

"Affirmative," Kauri said. "Standing by to support."

Kimmalyn zipped in close, and *bless her with words the Saint wouldn't say* that thing came in *fast,* seeming more serpent than worm. She boosted away on overburn, dodging the attack. Her heart started thundering, belatedly, an off-rhythm piper who was late to the festival.

"Ooooo," Happy said.

The wurm aimed a mouth the size of a large cargo bay toward her and took a swipe at her with the long tendrils surrounding it, then recoiled as she was out of reach. It had tried to grab her and gobble her up, ship and all.

Very well. Kimmalyn was not unknown as a battlefield danger herself. She turned around, and didn't even bother to find her clarion peace. She thumbed her destructor, and shot the thing right in the—

"Oh!" Kauri shouted through the comm. "Tosura says not to shoot it!"

"You . . . don't say," Kimmalyn mumbled, watching her destructor shot zip straight into the wurm's mouth.

"Oh dear," Kauri said.

"What?" Kimmalyn asked.

The thing started to glow with blue points of light all down the sides of its body.

"This is unfortunate," a new kitsen voice said over the comm—

the science officer, Kimmalyn assumed. "Before, we were the things threatening to steal its food. And now . . ."

The wurm uncoiled and started undulating through space straight toward Kimmalyn.

"Let me guess," she said, overburning away. "Now we *are* the food."

"I'm afraid so," he said.

36

As the battle progressed, I developed a plan that I hoped would help me escape Brade's clutches. I just had to find a way to test a specific theory.

For now, I watched specks fly through the air in the hologram. Defiant forces in red, arrayed to face Superiority forces in blue. Starfighters that swarmed the battlefield, falling into dogfights as they tried to secure inhibitor stations. Gunships took shots at them as they flew, as did the gun emplacements on the *Defiant,* both trying to blast down any fighters that paused too long or focused too much on their dogfighting.

In the background, the two large battleships took up bombarding positions and began to lay into the *Defiant*—trying to force it to withdraw. Space distances being what they were, the *Defiant* was able to maneuver despite its enormous size. It still took plenty of hits, but modern capital ships bore fairly powerful shields. The *Defiant* could likely take a beating for a long period of time.

Unless a synchronized group of fighters activated their IMPs close enough to bring down the shield. So the ships all played a delicate game. Enemy fighters trying to get close, and ours driving them back. Battleships trying to wear down the *Defiant*'s shield, and the flagship—in turn—trying to anticipate shots and get out of the way.

It was hard to watch it from here, rather than being there in a cockpit myself. I could never do what Jorgen did, leading from afar. It would rip me apart. Though maybe it did the same to him, and he was just strong enough to withstand it. Watching, my insides twisting in knots with worry for my friends, I thought maybe I understood him and what he'd given up to take command.

Brade did it with aplomb. She gave the orders, even going so far as to instruct flights of starfighters. As she did, the glow of the hologram reflecting in her dark brown eyes, I saw her smile in a satisfied way.

"What did we do to you?" I asked. And my body—seated by the wall, handcuffed in place—whispered it to Brade. My eyes seemed a little dead to me, but when I spoke, my lips moved. "Why do you enjoy destroying us so much?"

"I don't," she said, glancing toward my body. "You merely stand between me and what I must do."

"There is no 'must' here, Brade," I said, moving my phantom arms, making my fleshy ones pull against my bonds. "You don't have to do this."

"I suppose you're right," she said. "I revise what I said, then. Your people stand between me and what I *want* to do." She looked up as the door opened, her hand immediately going to her sidearm. She was jumpy, even with her own people.

That helped prove my theory. Back on Starsight when we'd trained together, I'd taken her standoffishness as a sign she had an attitude problem with those in authority. I saw something deeper now. A distrust of everyone and everything. A person who assumed everyone was potentially plotting against her. This attitude had probably served her well over the years.

I needed to exploit that.

"Why?" I asked Brade. "Why do you *want* to do this? Why not just walk away?"

"And let your people continue to build power?" she asked, sounding amused. "They're the only *legitimate* threat to my rule."

"But why do you want to rule?"

"Really?" she asked. "You have to ask why? Why did Alexander the Great conquer?"

"I don't know," I said honestly. "I've always wanted to ask him."

Brade hesitated, then looked toward my body.

"It's true," I said, standing next to her, Chet silently doubling me. My body spoke the words. "I've always wanted to know *why* Alexander conquered. Was it because he wanted to do what his father couldn't? Was it to push himself and see how far he could go? Was it simply because it was expected of him, given his training and his heritage? Why?" I shook both of my heads. "Why, Brade? Why do *you* do this? I've spent all of our time together thinking I've got you figured out, then constantly realizing I was wrong."

On the hologram, one of Brade's defenses successfully drove Defiant ships away from an inhibitor station. The little ships backed off like a swarm of insects, dodging fire from the gunships.

Brade pointed at the *Defiant*. "Push here," she said to her officers, noting a position on the hologram. "And here. Move the battleships forward. Force their flagship back so it can't pressure the stations."

"Yes, sir," one of the tenasi officers said.

"They *are* going to be precious about that carrier," Brade said softly. "I know it. They're going to cradle it, protect it. They emblazoned it with the very name of their people, their movement. It will mean everything to them."

Scud. She was probably right. As long as she was on the defensive, protecting the inhibitor stations, we could control the flow of the battle to an extent. Picking which station to attack, feinting and maneuvering however we wanted. But if she turned aggressor, using her superior numbers to threaten the *Defiant*, she could take control.

It was a sign, unfortunately, that she *did* know what she was doing. Brade narrowed her eyes, watching the hologram. Then, oddly, she spoke to me. "Did you grow up with a family, Spensa?" She didn't look at me, but instead stood with a commanding posture, surveying the battle map.

"I . . . You've met my grandmother."

"The fireball with the mouth from earlier?" Brade said. "Yes, I thought I saw a resemblance. No parents, then?"

"My mother as well," I said. "My father was killed by the Superiority when I was a child. He was a starfighter pilot. A budding cytonic."

"Ah," she said, nodding. "I read about that one, I think. They picked him out, you know. Saw that he was skilled, that he had powers, but was untrained."

"I do know," I said. "They exploited him. Got him to turn against his own flight, thinking they were enemies."

"One of Winzik's more important victories," Brade said. "He gloated over it several times to me. Your father's death earned Winzik a promotion."

I tried to summon anger at that, but I was just getting too scudding practical these days. Who knew if Brade was telling the truth? Perhaps she was simply manipulating me, connecting Winzik to my father.

Besides, Winzik was dead. This wasn't about him or even Brade. It was about stopping something terrible that had far, far too much momentum. We were the wall standing before it. The shield wall of spearmen, facing down the thundering charge, hoping we weren't too late to break its force.

"Did they love you?" Brade asked.

"My parents?"

Brade nodded.

"Yes," I whispered. "They still do."

"I think mine did, before I was taken from them," Brade said. "It's hard to remember. It's hard to think of things like love and warmth when you're treated as a monster. When every child you pass on the street cries when they see you. When even those who don't fear you see you as a tamed beast to be taught tricks."

"And so . . . you want revenge?"

"Hardly," she said, her eyes narrowing. "I want *justification*. If I win this war, Spensa—if I take it all—then it means they were right. About me. About us."

"And you *want* them to be?"

"I *need* them to be," she said, looking at me at last. "Because if they were right, then it all had a purpose: to channel me toward this singular event. I have to be the monster they named me, the brutal destroyer, otherwise it's worthless. My whole life. Everything done to me. Everything I *suffered*.

"I will take this empire as my own, and in so doing fulfill the destiny of our people. And I . . . I'll *know* that it all had a purpose. That what was done to me, it was . . . it was all right. It was my destiny. I am the monster. And you don't bargain with a monster, Spensa. You appease it. You slay it. Or you get eaten."

Her gaze lingered on my body for a moment, then she looked back to her battle, positioning more ships to pressure the *Defiant*. And finally, at long last, I thought I really *had* seen into her heart. She'd finally shown me something true about who she was, and why she lived as she did.

It was terrible.

I imagined what I'd have become if I'd been taken from my parents. If my natural inclination toward anger and violence had been bolstered by constant reinforcement, telling me I was a monster. I felt that emotion stoke something within me, a seething frustration at the world for what it had done to me. Demanding a destiny of me that seemed impossible.

I could feel as she must. *You want a monster? I'll give you a monster.*

Yes, I understood her.

Now I needed to stop her.

Chet, I thought to the delver. *I need you to teleport away my body's handcuffs.*

I can't do that, he thought back to me. *Not with the drugs in our system. That blocked me from even talking to you, in prison. I can't use any abilities.*

That's not true, I thought to him. *The air warped earlier.*

I . . . he thought. *I don't know. I . . .*

All right. Time for some tough love.

Chet, I thought to him. *We need to do something, or our friends might die.*

But . . . you said . . .

I was trying to make you feel better, I told him. *But that was wrong of me—because avoiding the problem is what got your people into trouble.*

The air began to warp as he worried, his panic growing. I felt bad for using him, but I needed to.

Some of them might die, I said. *And it's going to hurt. We'll get through it though. Pretending that nobody will ever be in danger is the same as living in the nowhere, pretending loss doesn't exist.*

It got worse. Soon those in the room noticed—particularly as pieces of wall paneling started to vanish. Random chunks being pulled into Chet's tantrum.

Chet, I said. *Look. You're doing it! It's working.*

What? he said, panic rising in his voice. *But . . .*

Teleport away my handcuffs, I thought to him. *A piece of them at least.*

It doesn't work that way! he thought. *I can't control it.*

You can, I thought to him. *We can. Together.*

I pressed my mind against his, and let him lean on my expertise— as I'd learned how he saw the world, I let him see how *I* saw the world. What I'd learned. Control. Precision.

Come on, I thought to him.

Brade cursed and barked for the doctor. She hurried over with another dose of the drug. I stepped closer to my body and felt it pulling me in, seeking to reconnect us.

Chet! I thought. *If you're worried about losing our friends,* do something *about it instead of hiding!*

323

I . . . he thought. *I can't . . .*

You can, I told him, hovering closer to my body, feeling my soul fully being pulled in. *We can.*

I came to a second later, blinking as the doctor loomed over me, syringe already in my neck. The warping continued, and she looked at the air, waving her arms in agitation.

In that moment, I felt my hands go slightly slack. I grabbed the bar behind my back—the railing that I'd been locked to—and pretended nothing had changed. And now that I was in my body, the warping of the air faded. I was cut off from Chet again.

I used my seated posture to hide my hands, and didn't dare move, lest I reveal what had happened. Instead I looked at Brade—who was again watching the doctor carefully. I was pretty sure, from that look in her eyes, I knew what was in the pouch at her waist. How could she ever be secure under Winzik's thumb—even if she was secretly pulling the strings—as long as he had the ability to drug her and take away her powers?

Brade was paranoid. She always positioned herself with her back to the wall. Jumped when the door opened, watched her own people with care and even a sense of distrust. She would never let them have a weapon that could be used against her, like this drug. Not unless there was an antidote.

That was what was in her pouch.

As the warping stopped, most of her team returned to their command posts. Brade, however, lingered—watching me. Until at last something demanded her attention. She reluctantly turned to deal with it, and I finally dared to shift my hands and feel at them. Each had a metal cuff around the wrist. But, unnoticed by anyone, the chain between them was missing.

I was free.

37

KIMMALYN

"**O**h, these creatures are so *fascinating*," the kitsen science officer said in Kimmalyn's ear as she fought for her life against the outrageously large space monster. "Once they have fertilized eggs, they will start moving faster and faster, spending years picking up speed. They'll expend their energy reserves getting to a sun, then will feed on its energy for *decades*, accelerating in orbit until they forcibly *launch* the eggs toward other stars."

"Fascinating indeed," Kimmalyn said politely as the fascinating wurm nearly swallowed her ship whole. She dodged down along its body, trying to stay away from that maw.

Flying around it felt so strange—the thing was big enough that she *almost* felt like she was flying along a landscape. Skimming the top of a narrow space platform that undulated, curving, twisting. And trying to eat her.

How could something so enormous snap at her so quickly? Like a coiled snake floating in space. She still had her haptics off, so she couldn't *feel* the crack of those whipping tendrils as they swiped mere meters from her ship, but her mind imagined the sound anyway.

"They can store a ton of energy, as you'd imagine," the kitsen science officer continued. "Why, some of their eggs—after being launched—have been recorded moving at twenty percent of the speed of light! Remarkable. I wonder how they slow down after hatching. Regardless, they've evolved to feed on basically any energy source imaginable.

"Though there are holes in the zoological entry here, I can read between the lines. They can feed on cytonic power as well as anything else. That's undoubtedly why this one has claimed a spot near the inhibitor station. It's likely been feeding on the cytonic radiation given off by the slug. Obviously, the Superiority put some kind of protection in place to keep it from getting too close. Likely a shield. Otherwise the worm would have eaten the inhibitor!"

Kimmalyn grunted, pushing into a steep dive, overloading her GravCaps. She'd been maneuvering too much too quickly. G-forces slammed into her, pressing her back and up as she accelerated on overburn, narrowly avoiding three whips of the monster behind her. She began to see red as the blood was pushed into her head.

"Oooooooo!" Praline said. Tests indicated the taynix could withstand far greater g-forces than a human could. Maybe that came from having a body that seemed to be essentially made from dough.

Stars, stars, *stars.*

"Quirk?" Kauri said. "We're in position. Should we continue the plan?"

"Yes," Kimmalyn said, unable to summon the strength to say *please.* She just kept dodging, trying to stay ahead of the monster.

Until a barrage of weapons fire hit it.

The worm pulled back immediately. The *Swims Upstream* continued firing, laying into the beast with barrage after barrage of destructor fire. They packed a much larger complement of weapons than Kimmalyn did. And—since they'd spent the last few minutes moving away while she distracted the thing—they were distant enough to avoid immediate danger.

As she'd hoped, it fixated on this much greater feast and began sweeping toward the *Swims Upstream*. Which was already moving away at a good clip, and continued to boost as it fired. The weapons didn't do anything to the worm other than feed it, but the distraction worked beautifully.

Kimmalyn was finally able to slow down. She found herself cold and clammy, sweat dripping along the sides of her face.

"Oooo . . ." Happy said.

"Ooooo," Kimmalyn agreed, then scanned the proximity monitors. The wurm continued to chase the kitsen ship—but she had another problem to worry about. A group of Superiority fighters had nearly arrived. She didn't have much time.

Still shaking, Kimmalyn spun her ship in place and boosted back toward the inhibitor station. The triangular installation had no windows, no distinguishing features save for the radio antennas on the top and bottom. As she approached, her sensors picked out a shield protecting it—as expected. Invisible to the eye unless shot at.

Kimmalyn moved in close. "Can you feel the slug in there, guys?" she asked Happy and Praline. The second slug fluted hesitantly. Kimmalyn didn't know the taynix very well, but that seemed like a good sign.

Praline radiated a little of what was happening. Kimmalyn wasn't cytonic herself, but she'd noticed that the slugs could project emotions and ideas into the heads of those who weren't. Otherwise, they wouldn't be able to facilitate interstellar communication as effectively as they did.

She thought that, through Praline, she could feel the slug inside the inhibitor. Who was terrified.

"Tell her we want to save her," Kimmalyn whispered. "Tell her we're friends."

The captive slug had difficulty believing that. It had been isolated for so long. It was exhausted and confused. Praline and Happy worked on it, but Kimmalyn kept her attention on the approaching enemy fighters. Scud. Twelve of them. She couldn't fight twelve on her own.

Worse, those ships had cut her off from her allies—and even cut in between her and the kitsen ship. Like a noose being tightened, they came for her. Her only escape would be backward—toward another group of forces arriving from that direction.

"Beg her to kindly drop her inhibition field," Kimmalyn said to the slugs. "Explain that we can rescue her if she does. We can teleport her to Detritus." She imagined caviar, and a safe warm place, dark and protected. She tried to project this to the slug, her anxiety rising as—

Something was pushed into her mind. An emotion. A faint sense of comfort . . . coming from the inhibitor slug? Followed by a distinct impression. *Go.*

"Come with us," Kimmalyn said.

No.

"Why not?" she asked. "We can give you freedom."

I'm needed.

"What? Why? I don't understand."

I'm needed.

"But—"

Go. I stay. Needed.

Scud, the poor thing was wrung out. She could feel its despair, its fatigue, the sickness it felt from being locked in a tiny box for weeks on end. Yet it wouldn't leave, for reasons Kimmalyn couldn't understand. The slugs didn't think like humans, and the images it sent her as explanation were a confusing mess.

It did seem to be willing to give Kimmalyn's ship an exception to the inhibition field though. "Happy," she said. "Go."

"Oooo?"

"We'll find another way to help them," she promised.

She checked to make sure the *Swims Upstream* would be all right—fortunately, the worm had turned back and the kitsen ship was only a short distance from friendly forces now. So Kimmalyn urged Happy again, and in a blip, they hyperjumped away.

The slug knew it would be punished for letting them go. In a painful, perhaps fatal way, once the battle was over. The slug had helped regardless—but it also had refused her aid. Why?

Kimmalyn's ship appeared right inside of Detritus's defensive shell. She immediately called Jorgen.

"We have a problem, Jerkface," she said as soon as he came on the line.

"What?" he asked. "You jumped. Do you have the slug from that inhibitor station?"

"No," she said. "It refused to come with me."

"Why?"

"I have no idea," she said. "It said it was needed. It understood that I wanted to rescue it, but it just wouldn't go with me."

Jorgen fell silent.

"What do we do?" she asked him. "I could maybe have forced it to come with me, by having Happy grab it right as we jumped, but I decided against that."

"You chose correctly, Quirk," he said. "If you'd violated its trust, I suspect none of the others would ever listen to us. Maybe we can get them to lower their inhibitor fields and allow Detritus to jump forward?"

"I don't know," she said. "This one indicated that it would be punished for letting me through. Beyond that, we had to contact it individually. How many slugs would we have to convince to make a hole big enough for Detritus?"

Dozens, maybe hundreds. More than they could manage in the middle of a battle, she was certain.

"I'll work on a solution," he said, sounding beleaguered. "For now, call FM and tell her about this. She'll gather all such experiences, and keep the other flightleaders in the loop. They need to know that this battle somehow just got even harder."

38

"Curious," one of the tenasi generals said as he stood with Brade, facing away from me, watching the battle. "That is the *fourth* opportunity they have had to destroy an inhibitor station—and again the humans did not take it. Do they grow *korochas*? Perhaps our assumptions about their aggressive natures were incorrect."

"If they were incorrect, General," Brade said, "would they have attacked us here? With a smaller force, in our center of power?"

"No, I suppose not." The general narrowed his reptilian eyes. "Still, it is curious."

My hands were free, but I hadn't moved yet. I needed to pick the right moment. How did I get to that pouch at Brade's waist? If I was wrong about it containing an antidote, it would be a disaster. Yet I was increasingly certain I was right. The way she kept space between her and everyone else, even her generals and bodyguards. The way she rested her hand there on the pouch, for reassurance.

I worked through a dozen different plans, and discarded each. If I rushed her, not only would I likely get shot, she'd just hyperjump away. I needed her distracted first.

Excruciating though it was, I waited. I watched. Like a tiger in the tall grass. Or . . . well, no. I'd never seen a tiger outside the images at school and the stories from my grandmother. If I was anything, I was a rat in a dark corner. But damn it, rats are persistent. What happened to the tigers? Dead, vanished with Old Earth. But the rats? They claimed the stars with us—infesting every planet. Even Detritus, where they have to survive on fungus and bugs.

I was the rat girl. I'd grown up among them, hunting them. Considering how many I'd eaten over my life, I was at least half rat by body mass. I could be patient. I could be careful.

It was difficult though. I felt isolated, no longer able to contact Chet, no longer able to speak to M-Bot. Alone, I watched the battle play out. The Defiant forces refused to blow up the inhibitor stations. That was to their credit; Jorgen had said he'd come to liberate them.

On the other side, Brade's reckless, all-out assault on the *Defiant* continued. She threw away ships callously, while we weren't even willing to harm enemy slugs. She pushed her forces in with a spearlike motion, piercing our defenses, reaching to claim the *Defiant* itself.

I felt sick watching it. I wasn't the only one.

"Sir," one of her generals said, "many of our starfighters are piloted ships today, not drones. You're . . . acting as if there are no people on board."

"They're soldiers," Brade replied, not looking away from the screen. "*This* is why you need me, General. *I* can do what needs to be done, while you were raised on fluffy Superiority nonsense. I've studied the great warriors of the past, from both my culture and yours. I hold no sentimentality." She leaned forward, hands gripping the railing in front of the holographic map. "I was *born* to do this."

My heart broke even further. For the girl who had been raised to internalize the singular idea that she was a weapon. For the woman who believed that if she *didn't* end up dominating and winning, all of her pain and sacrifice would have been meaningless. For the person who would now crush the galaxy's single best hope for freedom and peace, all to prove that it could be done.

I could have been her. I really *should* have been, considering all my bloodthirsty talk and jokes about killing. My experiences had changed me. Had changed everyone on Detritus, judging by how we passed over our last chances to destroy the inhibitor stations, our fighters in disarray as they were forced to pull back. The *Defiant* itself was retreating toward safety.

Too slowly. It wouldn't escape the enemy inhibitor field and reach Detritus without losing dozens, maybe hundreds of lives. I knew right then, watching, that if I didn't do something, the battle—the war itself—would be lost.

3 9

GRAN-GRAN

Becca Nightshade left the details to others. She understood a captain's role, and it was not to micromanage the battle. The kitsen generals sent instructions—this time to begin withdrawing—which she passed on and delegated appropriately, but she did not monitor the radio chatter. She left that to her communications officers, who brought her the most important matters. She didn't demand updates to each and every event in the fight; she'd put good people in charge of overseeing the situation.

None of that was Becca's job. Her job was twofold. To be seen. And to see. Not visually, in her case.

She kept her hand in the center of her haptic hologram, watching the motions of ships and starfighters, her attention on the larger dance. The pattern of the battlefield. Looking for a weakness in the enemy, like a hole in a shield wall, or a swordsman favoring one leg.

When she found it, the discovery surprised her.

Could it really be so clear, so obvious? She sat up, hurriedly moving her hand around in the haptic battle map. The enemy was pushing inward with all of their forces. Putting pressure on the *Defiant* with everything they had. It was a valid strategy; the enemy had overwhelming numbers, so they could afford to be reckless. Their goal would be to force Becca's troops to be on the defensive, to abandon their mission objectives and begin fighting purely for survival.

In response, the generals and admirals of the kitsen strategists had the *Defiant* pulling back. Not a retreat, but a careful giving up of ground. Their goal was being thwarted: they couldn't get the inhibitor slugs to accept help.

That wouldn't have worked anyway, Becca thought, going over the numbers she'd been given. *We'd need to clear away dozens of slugs to make space for Detritus to hop forward. In the middle of a battle? That would be difficult even if we were willing to destroy them.*

"Beowulf," she said to one of her current aides, "read me that report Jorgen sent earlier. Three messages ago."

"Um," the young man said from her right, "three messages . . . Two other pilots, including FM, have confirmed what Kimmalyn experienced: the slugs will let them hyperjump away to save themselves, but won't go with them. Something prevents the slugs from seeking to be rescued."

"But they *are* willing to bend the rules for us . . ." Becca said.

Capturing the *Defiant* was key to the enemy's strategy. So they had pushed forward with their own capital ships—even the carriers—using every gun at their disposal to harry Becca's forces. To try to overwhelm the *Defiant*'s shields. To bring it down. And yet they didn't see . . .

Becca pulled over her keyboard. She wasn't as practiced as she should have been, perhaps. One did not learn typing skills living the life she had. But she felt at the numbers and letters, and carefully pecked out a terse sequence of instructions. Just a few lines, detailing how she wanted to command her forces. She sent them to the kitsen generals.

The implications of what she'd suggested made her heart flutter and her fingers tremble. Surely she'd missed something. Better minds than hers would look over what she suggested and find its faults.

Still, if she *was* right . . .

She could win this war.

40

JORGEN

Jorgen was losing this war.

He'd thrown everything into a final battle because, after much deliberation, the coalition had determined that Spensa was right. Their best bet was an attack here, where the enemy kept its slugs.

So they'd struck, aiming to liberate as many taynix as they could. Struck with the hope of freeing Spensa, their most volatile—but most impressive—weapon. This had been his one chance at turning the war around.

And he was losing.

He was no expert at large-scale battlefield tactics, but neither was he a slouch. Even before going to flight school, his education had required him to understand and practice command. During flight school, he'd been given officer's training on the same principles.

So he could see what was happening. Reaching enough inhibitor stations to move Detritus was impossible; it required spreading his forces dangerously thin. Even if the slugs would agree to let it through, there were just too many.

In front of him, the battlefield was an agitated nest of red and blue dots, but his forces in red were penned and pushed backward consistently. The enemy forces in blue were ever advancing. Sweeping out to the sides, leaving room only directly behind the *Defiant* for a careful retreat.

Each one of his ships that winked out was a spike through his heart. His forces were now completely on the defensive. It was time for him to make the call. Time for full retreat.

Which was tantamount to giving up the war. They'd never have another opportunity like this. Their next best option was to go into hiding, hoping they could escape the notice of the Superiority. They'd have to abandon their allies. And Spensa.

He'd have to abandon Spensa.

You have to think about the good of your people right now, he thought. *Not the good of one person.*

It hurt nonetheless. He turned away from the large wall screen in the command room, walking through silence. Most of the rear admirals, and even the aides, had seen it. The room held its collective breath as he approached the back of the long table, where the kitsen generals and admirals were waiting.

They'd set up a second battle table on top of the larger, human-sized table. None of them sat at it though. They'd instead spread notes, maps, and schematics on the ground around them and were speaking softly. Jorgen's pin chirped translations at him.

". . . possible . . ."

". . . yes, this is right. This is right . . ."

". . . suggest a reposition here and here for maximum effect . . ."

Jorgen steeled himself to ask for their suggested method of retreat. But as he did, Itchika—the kitsen supreme tactician—drew his attention. She was distracted by something, going over some message. Goro stood beside her, and the general wore his power armor despite being nowhere near the front lines.

Goro looked up with wide eyes. He had a fearsome black streak down the top of his otherwise grey-and-white fur. "Admiral Weight," he said. "You have to see this."

"See . . . what?"

"Captain Nightshade's suggested battle plan," Goro said, gesturing to some kitsen-sized papers on the tabletop. "She's found an answer. A simple one that we didn't see, as we are too new at using cytonics."

"It's a path to victory," another of the kitsen said, standing up. "A chance. An *actual* chance."

"Explain it to me," Jorgen said, daring to let hope flutter alive within him.

"Jorgen?" Gran-Gran's voice said from a small datapad on the table. "Is that you?"

"Yes, Captain Nightshade," he said, tapping his ear and opening a direct line to her.

"They've told you about my little idea?" she asked.

"They seem impressed by it," Jorgen said. "But I don't know the details."

"Well," she said, "we just need half the fighters to sweep back behind the *Defiant* and contact the inhibitor stations there, while the other half act chaotically and move in too close to the enemy capital ships."

"That will leave you exposed," Jorgen said. "Without fighters to defend the *Defiant,* the enemy can bring down your shields."

"Yes," she said. "They keep pushing forward with *incredible* aggression. Foolhardy aggression . . ."

"You want to try to get those slugs behind the *Defiant* to let Detritus hyperjump over," Jorgen said, leaning down, looking at the tiny kitsen maps. He probably should have pulled them up on the screen, but he was too excited. "We've been considering that, but we'd have to contact at least *fifty* of those inhibitor stations at once. It wouldn't work."

"Impossible," Goro agreed. "But this is something else, Admiral Weight. Something daring."

"Detritus isn't merely a planet," Gran-Gran said. "It's a planet with a thousand floating platforms. What would it take to hyperjump *only* the portions of the shell that have our gun batteries on them? Those are far smaller. Ship-size . . ."

"Scud," Jorgen said, meeting Goro's eyes. Was it possible? The gun emplacements had their own crews these days, and had always contained their own power sources. He should have thought of this after finding that solitary platform on UrDail . . .

"We need to get Rig on the line," Jorgen said. "This might be possible! But, Captain Nightshade, the enemy will guess what we're doing if we try this. And those platforms will be incredibly exposed without Detritus's defenses."

"This plan accounts for that," Itchika said from nearby. "See how the enemy focuses? All we need to do is keep their attention . . ."

An aide presented Jorgen with a datapad with the full details of Gran-Gran's plan. It had been hastily annotated by the kitsen, who had added actual tactics and movements to Gran-Gran's short message. They had the battle experience. But Gran-Gran . . . despite lacking all that . . . had something almost as important. Guts.

"It is a dangerous gamble," Goro said. "There is a good chance the enemy *will* see what is happening, despite the distractions we offer, and this plan will collapse. But then again, our enemy commander is brash—young, thirsty for victory. You can see it in her every order. She might not be careful enough. If so . . ."

"If so, this could be huge," the other kitsen said. "Do we risk it?"

Jorgen didn't answer until he'd read through and understood Gran-Gran's suggested battle plan. What she was outlining finally clicked. And with horror, he realized what it would cost.

"This . . ." he said, looking to the kitsen.

One at a time, they all nodded, understanding.

"It is what must be done, Jorgen," Gran-Gran said. "It's the only way."

"We recommend following the course Captain Nightshade has suggested," Goro said. "Retreat now will be extremely costly and will put us into an even more difficult position going forward.

However, we have agreed to your leadership in this battle. We will do as you decide."

Jorgen took a deep breath. And didn't make the decision yet. Instead, holding on to the plan, he walked to the side of the room and sat down in one of the seats there—leaving the aides to stand by the table, looking uncertain.

Cobb leaned forward from within the shadows where he'd been sitting. Bags under his eyes, looking so much older than he should have.

"Did you read it?" Jorgen asked, tapping his datapad.

"Just finished," Cobb said.

"I think you should decide," Jorgen said softly. "Cobb, you have the experience, the age, the wisdom."

Cobb snorted softly. "You think age brings wisdom, son? If it did, I wouldn't know so many old fools."

"Cobb . . . I'm doing my best," Jorgen said. "But I can't help thinking that I'm too young for this. Someone more experienced should make the decision."

"Becca Nightshade has at least thirty years on me," Cobb noted. "And it's her plan." He leaned forward farther. "But Jorgen, this shouldn't be about age. We put you in charge—me included—because we trust you. This battle, this war, this victory . . . it leads us to a brand-new world. You think any of us old fools know what to do with a new world? We've struggled for generations against an unmoving wall of destruction.

"We've thrown ourselves at that doom time and time again. It made us hard of will, yes, but hard of mind too. *That's* why I stepped down. My health was an excuse, and a good one. But I knew, and still know, that I wanted someone who can embrace a better life to lead us. Not someone who wore himself out squeezing every bit of hope and joy from recruits so he could throw them into the fire."

Cobb looked at him then, and Jorgen saw echoes of those words in his face, his eyes. How must it have been, spending decades training new flight after new flight of pilots, only to watch them die in waves facing the Krell? Hundreds of kids he'd come to love, dead, month after month. All while knowing he had to train more, had to keep sending them off to the same fate . . .

Jorgen had always seen Cobb as strong, immovable. And he *was* strong. But strong men could still be used up. Jorgen rested his hand on Cobb's back, and understood. Someone else needed to carry this burden now. Someone else needed to make *this* decision, hard though it was.

"Send to Captain Nightshade," Jorgen said, steeling himself and standing. "Commend her for her genius, and tell her to move forward with honor and defiance."

41

"There," Brade said, pointing to the hologram. "There. Push everything we have *right there*. They're starting to flounder. Half their fighters are running away! They're abandoning their flagship and the rest are a scattered mess, breaking formation. We can capture the *Defiant*!"

"Yes, sir," the general said, nodding to the others. "We'll send in the gunships—"

"*Everything*," Brade said. "We send in everything. We have to crush them. Not just their bodies, General, but their spirits—and the spirits of any who would ever presume to raise arms against us. We are not just fighting for victory today. This has to be a *symbol*."

I saw her reasoning. Yet it seemed brash, even flagrant, to me. And I was the girl who consistently took off running in gym class before the coach finished their instructions. Something felt . . . off about this battlefield, though I couldn't pick out why. Were our forces giving up too easily?

I didn't have time to ponder it as Brade turned toward me. I stiffened, hands held carefully behind my back, feigning that I was still locked in place.

"It's time," Brade said.

"Sir?" a dione aide asked. "Time for what?"

"For me to be certain we have backup," Brade answered.

Even with the drugs in my system, I could feel a faint cytonic vibration from her. She was contacting the delvers.

I strained against my chemical constraints, wishing I could hear what she was saying. And in this, I understood why Brade felt she could be so reckless with her forces. She had another weapon at the ready to support them, and she was calling it in now. At long last, after centuries of struggle and failed attempts, someone was finally going to successfully weaponize the delvers. All it had taken was access to me as a threat.

I prepared to rush her. Perhaps, even though she was staring at me, she'd be distracted by her cytonic communications. And . . . and well, if I got shot, that would still accomplish something important. Brade would lose her bargaining chip with the delvers.

It twisted me in knots to realize that the best I might be able to accomplish right now was getting myself killed. I steeled myself for the attack anyway—and just before I leaped up and charged her, a voice pushed into my head.

Hey! M-Bot said.

42

M-BOT

One thing confused Mushroom-Bot. He couldn't figure out why the delvers had left themselves so vulnerable.

As he moved among them, he had opportunities to *blend* with them. It was a difficult experience to parse. He wanted to record what was happening to him, for later digestion and explanation, so he tried. But how to express it? The delvers passed through one another constantly, a kind of . . . assessment to make sure they all still matched. The way biological entities had defenses on the cellular level looking for dead, malformed, or broken pieces to destroy.

This constant nudging against one another, blending and checking, helped keep them all the same. It was also one of their big weaknesses, because—as he'd theorized earlier—it could be used to spread a pathogen among them. His tiny test proved it. He could set off a chain reaction—one that created a new model that they all came to copy.

Except he feared that with something large, they'd notice this flaw, and they'd use their system to smother the new model instead of adopting it. That was what the system was designed to do, after all. Identify a virus and make sure it was exterminated. Ensure all delvers remained exactly the same.

So how? How could he turn the delvers' system of conformity into the weapon that would destroy them? He still didn't have an answer.

But the pain—that was the second key. He went over what he knew again. They all felt it, just beneath the surface. Commented out but still relevant. It was still raw whenever too much of the somewhere leaked in. That passage of time, that knowledge of place, somehow made the pain surface again—like a pool of frozen blood beneath melting snow on a warm day.

He liked that metaphor. He made special note of it. Even though Spensa hadn't seen much snow, he figured she'd like this comparison for the blood part.

But the delvers. Why? Why leave themselves exposed like this? They'd created a barrier of forgetfulness between themselves and their pain, but they could have deleted their pain entirely. Why hadn't they?

That question drove him as news from the somewhere leaked in. That allowed him to keep track of time, and gave him urgency. He could read the Superiority's side of the battle and hear them pressing against his friends, boxing them in, preparing to destroy them.

Spensa was once again trapped and drugged. He could maybe push through that, as the drugs made her an ordinary person—but cytonics like him could talk to regular people, with effort. He also saw that Brade was preparing to activate the delvers.

Time was running out. He needed to know the secret. He needed to understand why the delvers hadn't just deleted this part of themselves. It would be so easy to . . .

Ah. As he brushed against several delvers, melding with them and using his fabricated sense of delverness to fool them, he finally saw it. He got enough of a glimpse of their former code, their souls, to understand.

They couldn't erase the pain without erasing *him*. This person they had loved long ago. This person they had, in a way, been created to love. They would let themselves forget him to dull the pain, but they had not been able to *bear* erasing his memory entirely.

And so they lived a terrible contradiction. They'd fled here to escape the pain of loss. But the idea of being *completely* separated from the one they had lost was far, far more painful. They hovered, therefore, with the blade halfway to their hearts. Piercing the skin, but not digging any deeper.

He still needed another answer though. And so, he did the daring thing. As he'd learned while traveling the nowhere with Spensa, he could choose. He chose now. He hadn't been able to find the answer, so he needed to risk himself to get it.

"Why?" he asked as the others bumped into him. "Why do we fear her?"

This question immediately identified him as a deviant. None of the others were thinking this. They saw him as a delver, not as himself, so his camouflage was working. But he appeared as a delver who'd been corrupted by the pinpricks of somewhere that leaked through.

They came at him, smothering the question, trying to get him to turn his thoughts toward theirs. He dared not change, however. He dared to keep asking.

"Why?" he asked. "I've forgotten."

When he didn't change, when he was firm, others began to ask too. This was the problem with their protocol. So long as the question was reasonable, it could infect them. Others pushed through, providing an answer to smother his question.

She can destroy us, they thought. *She is danger.*

"Why?"

The somewhere. The somewhere. A being of two worlds. She can . . .

She could bring the somewhere into this place. In force. She could make time move.

And now he had the solution.

She spanned both realms. Somewhere and nowhere. She could

bring to this place time, motion, and annihilation. If she brought the somewhere in force, the thin protection the delvers had against their pain would wear out. It was flimsy. It wasn't meant to last, but it *could* survive here, outside time.

And without it, like blood seeping through a bandage, the pain would come. The delvers would be paralyzed.

Poor things. He knew them enough now to empathize. But he was . . . well, if not a soldier, then a soldier's friend. He knew this had to be done. Unfortunately, Spensa had been cut off from her powers again.

He could feel her though. So he waited until Brade inevitably called to the delvers, which weakened the barrier, making it easier to get through to Spensa. In that moment, he got a single word through: *Hey!*

She didn't reply. He sensed only a fogginess from her, far thicker than he'd felt before. Unfortunately, that meant he had to make his own plan.

How fun! And how daunting!

Having agency was kind of terrible, actually. But he settled on a solution for now. And that was the time-honored battle strategy of stalling.

43

GRAN-GRAN

"Sir," Beowulf said from Becca's side. "This last order—"

"Is authorized by command," Becca said, right hand feeling at her map. "Report to your transport and leave the ship."

"We can't abandon the *Defiant*!" Beowulf said.

"The computer can handle the rest of the maneuvers," Becca said. "Obey your orders, Lieutenant."

No footsteps. Becca was about to reiterate her order when she felt the younger man embrace her. A sudden, unexpected warmth in this difficult time.

"Go," Becca said. "Now."

The final member of the bridge crew retreated, footsteps sounding loudly when he reached the uncarpeted hallway outside. Checking her map, Becca saw that the starfighters were following her commands—pulling away, as if driven into chaos by the enemy. Half backward, half forward, feigning disorganization. Feigning fear. But actually approaching the inhibitor stations behind the ship, talking to their slugs, pleading with them.

That left the *Defiant*—the newly rebuilt symbol of their people—alone and undefended. Becca took her hand from the map and stood up, new carpet scrunching underfoot. She stared ahead, toward the enemy she knew was there beyond the hull, beyond the vacuum, watching from her own side.

"Come on," Becca said. "You've thrown everything you have at killing me. Here I am."

Her hull shook as the ship, using an automated firing pattern, launched barrage after barrage as it withdrew—too slowly. Only one engine was on out of the four, and sparks sprayed from another. Because Becca herself had ordered explosives detonated there. A classic feint, pretending they were breaking down from pushing their equipment too hard.

The *Defiant* was a symbol, yes. And as a symbol, it represented something. A concept that would not die no matter how many ships were destroyed.

The enemy general didn't realize this. They'd proved it by committing so much to attacking the ship. Now Becca provided what that distant general hoped to see: fighters scattering outward and abandoning the flagship. Transports fleeing.

A beleaguered vessel, so tempting.

"Come on," Becca said, as she turned the ship as if to flee for safety. "You think you've beaten me. Now come in for the kill. I dare you."

44

BRADE

Make this mean something.

Those had been the last words Brade's father had ever spoken to her.

Make this mean something. His words as they'd pulled his frantic child away from him.

Her parents had been executed three years later. She wasn't supposed to know. But she'd found the official death report, which said they'd been "put down." Apparently, they'd gotten out and "frightened" someone important, who had revoked the permit for keeping them.

To this day, she wasn't certain if Winzik had been behind it. No parents meant no other influences on her. Something that had become increasingly important as he'd realized how powerful a cytonic she was.

He'd been brutal, for a varvax. She would almost miss him. Too bad he'd never realized that *she* wasn't fitting into *his* plans, but the other way around. Today was the culmination of her work, as she reached into the nowhere and approached the delvers.

Make this mean something. Yes. It would all mean something.

349

When a human, after centuries of trying, finally conquered the galaxy.

The delvers were hiding, like they always did these days. Before, when she would come into the nowhere, their eyes would appear—glaring, potent, intimidating. Now she seemed to be alone, though she could pick them out around her, watching. Seething, with the quiet burn of embers cooling after a fire was out.

It is time to make good on your promises, she said to them. *Join us in this battle.*

She'd agreed to use them only in an emergency. But she needed to make a splash, and intimidate her own forces, to ensure no one got the idea to do to her what she'd done to Winzik.

If we come, you will destroy the abomination? they asked. As usual, they thought and responded as one—a million different voices speaking at the same time.

I will not let her torment you, Brade said. *That is all I promise for now. If this goes well, if you can distinguish between my forces and the enemy, then we'll see. For now, I want ten or so of you here in my realm, ready to fight my enemies.*

Ten might have been extreme, but Brade needed this to be a symbol, a day to remember. She would release the footage of this battle carefully, showing the dangers of the insurgents—but also, obliquely, showing her strength. Today, at long last, she made her parents' sacrifice mean something. Today she—

Um, excuse me? one of the delvers said.

One. A singular delver. It opened up a burning white eye to look her over, less timid than the others.

It was an incongruous experience. Never before had she singled out one of them. Never before had one acted out of line with the others.

Yes? she said.

Yeah, um, I don't believe you, the delver said.

Don't . . . believe?

That you have the human abomination, as you claim.

350

I showed her to you, Brade said, exasperated.

Could be an illusion or a trick, the delver replied.

An . . . illusion or a trick?

Can't you sense her? Brade asked.

Not right now, the delver said. And to this, the others seemed to agree. Though they also seemed baffled by the behavior of this one.

Some delvers were showing individuality now? The leaking of the somewhere into their realm was influencing them, making them deviate from one another.

With a growl, Brade changed her focus so she could see the somewhere overlapped by hints of the eyes and the delvers. She stalked through the room and seized Spensa by the collar, displaying her for the delvers.

Here she is, Brade said. *We have her drugged to prevent her touching your realm—she'd be too dangerous otherwise.*

I don't know . . . the strange delver said. *She looks suspicious.*

Looks suspicious? Brade frowned, dropping Spensa. *What are you?* she demanded. *What is going on—*

"Sir!" a voice called, distracting her. "You should see this!" Brade ripped free of the nowhere to glance at the hologram.

The *Defiant* was turning and running. It had stopped firing, stopped maneuvering, and was trying to escape in a last mad push to get out of the inhibitor field. The starfighters had fled, and the escape transports were in chaos, pulling back from it. Leaving it exposed, leaving an opening for Brade's forces.

"Hit that ship with everything!" she said, rushing over to the hologram. "The battle is ours! Bring that ship down!"

"It's working," General Halaki said. "You were right, sir!"

Brade watched with satisfaction as her fleet pulled inward, focused on the *Defiant,* hitting it repeatedly and finally beginning to overwhelm its shield. Explosions broke its surface, ripping off sections of the hull. Victory at last—except a strange sensation distracted her from her satisfaction. The air was warping. Not again. Was the drug wearing off so quickly?

She twisted and looked toward the wall, at Spensa. Who was pulling a needle from her own thigh, where she'd injected an entire syringe into her bloodstream.

Brade's hand flew down to the pouch at her belt, which was unzipped. And empty.

Oh, *scrud.*

45

On one hand, injecting myself with a random syringe I found on my enemy was . . . well, one of the most Spensa-like things I'd ever done. On the other hand, I felt an immediate fire spread through my veins, and my senses expanded. It was like the antidote was burning away the wall between me and the nowhere.

By the time Brade had noticed what I'd done, my powers had returned. We locked eyes. The air warped around me, the delver inside me cutting through inhibitor fields like a knife through fat.

I leaped forward, then hyperjumped. But I didn't run for safety. I didn't teleport to Detritus, or to my friends, or to the *Defiant.*

I teleported only a few meters, straight to Brade. I appeared above her, like an avenging Saint with wings outspread, and seized her throat. My momentum carried us forward and I slammed her down to the ground, then pulled back a fist. When I rammed it toward her face, however, she vanished. I dropped the short distance to the deck, twisting to find her directly to my right.

She ripped her sidearm out, but I slapped her hand and teleported the gun out into the vacuum of space. She vanished to avoid my next punch, appearing behind me—but I hyperjumped myself, next to one of the startled tenasi guards. I tore his rifle from his hands, flipping off the safety and spinning to level it toward Brade. I fired three destructor rounds in a burst, straight into the wall behind her as she vanished again.

Shrewdly, she teleported beside me. That got her inside my reach, so she could grab the gun and try to twist it out of my hand. I grunted as the guard stupidly tried to grab me from behind. I teleported him into the vacuum outside next to Brade's gun.

I struggled over the rifle with Brade, sweating, our eyes locked, not speaking. And scud, she was taller, more muscled, and stronger than I was. She forced me back, slamming me against the wall, then began to wrench the gun free, a smile on her lips. But she didn't realize—I was *used* to fighting people bigger and stronger than I was. My whole *life* had been spent resisting a force as vast as the galaxy itself.

I *thrived* on being the underdog.

I grinned back, then teleported away. I appeared across the room, and as Brade sought me out, I slammed my hands down on the room's large metal desk. Her eyes went wide.

I teleported the desk directly above her head. She didn't even get a chance to fire on me, as she was forced to jump away. I anticipated her though, knowing in my gut that she'd jump to that table by the hologram: its height would give her an excellent line of sight around the oval-shaped room.

Even as the desk was crashing to the ground—generals, soldiers, and aides alike shouting and trying to make sense of the confusion—I hyperjumped. Brade emerged right where I'd thought she would, and I appeared behind her on the table, delivering a solid full-knuckled punch straight to her kidneys.

She screamed and spun, but I teleported across the room.

I sought out her next tactically sound jump. The unexpected one, the one that would leave your enemy confused about where you might be . . .

There, I thought. *In the middle of the hologram.* It still displayed fighters arrayed as dots of blue and red, larger capital ships hanging in the air and glowing bright as they traded volleys.

As predicted, Brade appeared in the middle of it, using the holograms as cover, but as she tried to find me and shoot me—assuming I'd be distracted—I jumped next to her. This time I punched her in the neck, then laid another fist into her stomach. She gasped and hyperjumped again.

She wouldn't leave the room though. That would be admitting defeat. And so I followed her, the two of us jumping around the circular metal chamber as if in some bizarre children's game, using the other people as distractions or shields. In the midst of it all, the air warped and bent as my emotions surged. The exquisite energy of a fight churning inside of me, along with my anxiety for my friends and anger at Brade. A volcanic eruption of feelings pent up too long, held back for this moment.

I would not be contained any longer. I would *end this.*

Objects began to appear. Cups, rocks, datapads, one of the chairs from my old *classroom*. A chaotic mess of churning pieces of my life, mixing with the building intensity of the two of us leaping around the room, trying to pin one another down. I began to seize objects from the air as they materialized, throwing them anywhere I thought Brade would appear. I didn't pause to see if they connected. I just kept going.

Flash. Throw.

Flash. Throw.

Flash. Throw.

"Ouch!"

I leaped at that sound, coming out of the hyperjump in a bull rush and smashing her against the wall.

Wow, M-Bot said in my head, his voice strong. *Spensa. I had no idea you could move like that.*

I was a blur. A person between two worlds, continuously slipping from one to the other. Brade began firing wildly around the room, hitting her own people, her equipment, increasingly frantic as I grabbed panels off the walls—ripping the metal squares free by touching them, then teleporting them around her. They clanged as they landed, obscuring her view, always there when she jumped.

Then I was among them. Hitting her in the kidney again, then grabbing her gun and teleporting it away. Then grabbing her and sending *her* into the vacuum.

She came back a second later, of course. But she seemed panicked, disoriented. I leaped for her, growling, as if I were some feral beast—half human, half delver. I—

She got a shot off and grazed me on the shoulder. Her pistol? Where had that come from? I'd teleported it out into the vacuum . . .

Oh. Right.

Maybe sending her to the same spot hadn't been my smartest move. Fortunately, the pain only focused my fury, and I threw her to the ground. When she hyperjumped, I teleported into the air just above her and fell down on her prone form, slamming an elbow into her face.

When she hyperjumped away this time, she left blood on the floor.

"You bastard!" she shouted as she appeared again, the broken desk between us. "You half-civilized, miserable excuse for—"

She cut off as I appeared and—using the same move I'd performed on Jorgen all those months ago—slammed my fist into her knee and dropped her. I went for her throat again, knowing I could outlast her. She was stronger, had more resources, but I. Would. *Never.* Stop.

I was vengeance incarnate. I was death. I—

A flash bathed the room in blue light.

At first I kept fighting, thinking it was some distraction. Then I heard the radio chatter, the calls of victory from the enemy generals and ships. I saw the smile on Brade's face, her split lip trailing blood, victory in her eyes.

"Didn't you say," she asked me, "that your grandmother was on that ship?"

I looked again, focusing on the hologram, watching as the flashes built up: bursts of light announcing the final demise of an enormous capital ship.

The *Defiant* was exploding.

46

JORGEN

Jorgen was left with the image of Becca Nightshade settling down into the captain's chair of the *Defiant*. Confident. Smiling. That was the last transmission from the bridge as the ship went up.

He saluted the blank wall as, beside him in the hologram, the *Defiant* died. Somber kitsen hovered up around him on platforms, over a dozen of them, and they offered a salute that he'd never seen before. A knife out, held up to the side, heads bowed. A final farewell to a warrior who died in glory.

Personally, he'd never fully subscribed to the Defiant attitude of sacrifice among his people. He found it uncomfortable sometimes how they celebrated death—and he knew for a fact it had led to the untimely demise of people he'd loved. But today, he thought he understood it. Rebecca Nightshade hadn't thrown her life away.

No ship was allowed, by galactic law and deep internal programming, to fly itself. No AI could be allowed to give commands or perform maneuvers without someone on the bridge.

So she'd remained defiant in the face of overwhelming odds. In so doing, she'd given them all something amazing.

A chance.

The entire complement of the anti-planetary-bombardment platforms around Detritus vanished. Hyperjumping, as the captive slugs gave them the opportunity, into the tiny column of open space behind the dying flagship. Gun emplacements that now hung in space, exposed.

But they didn't need protection. Because the enemy had committed all of its ships—carriers, destroyers, gunships, and fighters—to attack. They were lined up. Completely distracted by taking their prize.

"All guns," Jorgen announced, lowering his arm from the salute, *"FIRE."*

Enormous beams of destructor fire blasted from the gathered gun platforms of Detritus, cutting through the remnants of the *Defiant*—piercing the very dust, debris, and burning light of its pyre.

It had been Gran-Gran's plan. To send her fighters away. To leave herself defenseless. To limp back, knowing that the enemy would follow. That they'd be reckless in their determination to bring her down, and would ignore what the fighters were doing.

Jorgen's shots passed through the corpse of the *Defiant* and slammed into the enemy fleet. Warping shields, overloading them with blast after blast. The enemy, of course, tried to hyperjump away. But per Gran-Gran's instructions, the half of the Defiant fighters that had scattered chaotically swung back around toward the enemy. And if there was one thing that Jorgen's forces had, it was superior fighters. They converged on the enemy capital ships, bearing kitsen cytonics and slugs. Inhibitors.

In that moment, the battle reversed. The enemy, overconfident, had sent its fighters to bring down the *Defiant*'s shields—and in so doing, left their fleet undefended. They'd assumed that Jorgen's fighters were too few in number to do any damage, or bring down their own shields. They were right, but Jorgen didn't need to worry about that. Not when he had Detritus's gun platforms and their powerful beam weapons.

All he needed was the enemy lined up, unable to jump away.

And so, within moments of her passing, the hero Rebecca Nightshade got her revenge. The entire enemy fleet went up in blasts of light. Like stars being born.

47

I felt Gran-Gran as she died.

One final connection let me see her as she sank into her seat on the bridge. Not the same ship she'd landed on Detritus in, but somehow still *her* ship. The ship her people had made, the ship she'd claimed by birthright. She had arrived on the *Defiant,* and she would leave on it.

She'd evacuated everyone else, so she was alone as she died.

No, she sent to me. *I have you.*

Gran-Gran . . .

She was gone by the time I thought it. Gran-Gran had been inhibited and prevented from hyperjumping away. She'd stayed to pilot the ship, staring the enemy in the face. Brought down by Brade's mad insistence that destroying this symbol of insolence would break us. Gran-Gran died a hero, yes, but she . . .

She was still gone.

My soul contorted. I barely noticed as Brade forced me off her. A piece of me recognized what she was doing when she leveled her pistol at me, and the air warped—not really by conscious effort on my part. My powers protected me by instinct this time—because when Brade fired, the shot went straight into the nowhere.

She cursed and tried again from another angle. Same result. When she sent in a guard to grab me, he ended up suffocating in the reaches of space halfway across the galaxy.

I barely noticed. I was watching particles of light from the hologram break apart and vanish. The *Defiant*.

Gran-Gran.

I barely even registered that Detritus's gun platforms somehow hyperjumped into the space the *Defiant* had been heading toward. The slugs there had let them through? The emplacements shot back.

Pain welled up inside of me, like a reactor going critical. So much emotion. So much anguish. I screamed, howling into the sky, my hands forming claws.

I . . . I couldn't handle it. I'd said I could withstand the loss of friends. But this?

I couldn't lose Gran-Gran. I . . . I . . .

It's too much, Chet thought. *It's too much! I can't!*

All along, part of this panic was his. I'd learned some lessons about grief, but he still hadn't. My pain at losing my grandmother was too much, when amplified by his inability to handle grief. Together our souls vibrated in a cacophony of agony, loss, panic, terror, pain—

I felt something warm wrap around me. Another mind, like comforting arms. A . . . a slug?

Another.

A third.

A *hundred* of them.

It was the inhibitor slugs, left alone in their isolated pods in the frozen emptiness of space. They noticed my pain, and they came to me. Soon there were over a thousand of them, holding me mentally. Supporting me. Not trying to explain away my pain, but comforting me in it. Letting me know they were there.

I had to suffer. But I didn't have to do it alone.

In that moment, I understood why they had stayed. Why not one of them would escape when given the chance. That would have meant abandoning the others to their torment. They survived because they were together. I took their love, their support, and clung to it. Then quested outward.

Not . . . alone . . . Chet thought. *Not alone?*

No, I *wasn't* alone. I'd never been alone. I reached out and found . . .

I'm here, Kimmalyn said in my mind. She didn't know what was happening, but she'd felt me reaching out in my pain. *Spin, I'm here.*

I'm here. Nedd, on Platform Prime, with command.

I'm here. Arturo.

I'm here. FM.

Spensa? Jorgen. *Oh, scud. It's good to feel your mind.*

All of them. Even Alanik, Sadie, T-Stall, and Catnip. Kauri and the kitsen. Shiver and Dlllllizzzz.

Thank you, Dllllizzzz whispered to me, *for bringing me home.* More distantly, I felt Maksim and Peg. Even a strange worried mind that was *Vapor.* They sensed me looking for them, and I felt their warmth join that of the thousands of slugs.

Before their love, the pain didn't vanish. But it looked so, *so* small. Like a candle in front of a sun.

With that perspective, both Chet and I knew we could handle this. I'd been through it before and survived. Maybe I hadn't dealt with my father's passing in the most healthy of ways, and losing Bim and Hurl had only exacerbated that. I was, however, more capable now.

Gran-Gran had died on her own terms, in a way she'd likely always dreamed of doing. By luring the enemy into a trap, then springing it. She'd lived a full life, and had gone out like she was in a story. None of that dulled my pain, but it did *contextualize* it.

I could live with this.

But she's gone . . . Chet thought. *Gone forever.*

No, I replied. *I remember her. You remember her.*

That's pain.

That's life.

I . . . Can we really do this? he asked. *Can we really just . . . keep living . . . with this?*

In response, I let my mind hold the delver. I joined the chorus of thousands of taynix, of my friends.

I understand, I thought. *We understand.*

Slowly, Chet's panic subsided, and his soul aligned with mine. It seemed wondrous that it worked. He was a being that had felt so alone when experiencing loss that it had created millions of clones of itself.

And yet, was it truly that odd? They'd been isolated in the nowhere.

That was the problem, wasn't it?

The delver let out a long sigh, and I felt his emotions as if they were my own. Comfort. Gratitude. Strength. All of that love—the mere fact that the delver understood, deeply, that others cared . . . well, it legitimately helped.

And at long last, Chet accepted that there was only one way forward. One way to survive the pain. With the help of so many, he walked the path on his own and found that you *could* get through darkness. Though sometimes a friendly light was required to show the way.

48

BRADE

Brade watched her fleet go up in flashes of light.

Well, sometimes you had to break a few skulls to make a throne of bones, eh? At least now they'd have some war heroes to celebrate in parades and whatnot. Considering what the Superiority military had done to her family, she wasn't going to let a lost ship here or there bother her.

This did strand her without a fleet for the moment—though she had many, many more ships she could call upon. Winzik's timidity might actually have helped her; if she'd had the entire fleet ready at the start of this battle, she'd probably have sent them all at the *Defiant*. Right into those planetary defense guns.

Traitorous slugs, letting those through. She almost gave the order to kill them all. But then . . . that would destroy her inhibitors completely. Even working partially, it was probably best to leave them in place. She'd just have to remember she couldn't rely on them.

She pressed a cloth to her split lip and shot a glance at Spensa, who knelt at the side of the room, head bowed, eyes closed—air distorting around her like waves of heat. The rest of the room was in shambles, littered with broken bits of metal, overturned tables, and discarded tablets.

Her staff stood around, baffled. There was a large crowd of them, perhaps too many: her six most trusted generals and admirals, eight members of her personal guard, a dozen or so minor functionaries who were as interchangeable as pairs of socks.

"What do we do about her?" Gavrich asked, the tall tenasi general seeming strangely uncertain. Brade had never known him to be afraid of anything.

"I'll think of something," Brade said. "You need to focus on the battlefield. What's the word on the reinforcements I called up?"

"Ready to hyperjump in," Gavrich said. "Only two carriers and three destroyers. The others are . . . growing *gludendias*. I think perhaps they don't *want* to join the battle. Years of training, and now that they're facing an actual war, they're slow to respond."

"Bring in those that are ready and have them array themselves around Evensong, alert for enemy gun emplacements teleporting in," she said. "And start broadcasting the destruction of the human ship as a symbol that we're valiantly protecting everyone. Then start threatening the captains that are dallying."

"Understood, sir," he said.

"They won't be able to use that hyperjumping trick if we're watching for it," Brade said. "Look, they had to contact each inhibitor station in person. If we watch for that, and have ships arrayed to fire on platforms as they appear, we should be safe. Do be careful, though. The enemy is going to make a play for Evensong and the slugs."

He glanced at the hologram.

"General," Brade said, "it was worth the losses to bring down the rebels."

"An entire fleet?" he asked. "For one ship?"

Scrud. That was more questioning than she'd heard from him in years. And he was right. She'd thrown her forces away too easily.

But she couldn't show weakness now. She needed to show something else entirely, if she was to make good on her destiny.

"Ships are meaningless to us now, General," Brade said. "Cannon fodder. We won't rule by their power alone."

"You mean . . ." he said.

Brade nodded. It *looked* like maybe Spensa was consumed by grief. It was time to move. Brade slipped into the nowhere fully, and reached out to the thousands upon thousands of hiding delvers.

You've felt her, Brade said. *You know I have her.*

Is she contained? they asked.

For the moment, Brade lied. *But her kind is here to rescue her. So if you're going to intervene, you need to do so now. Otherwise, I won't be able to stop them from freeing her.*

They thought only for a moment.

We will send sacrifices, they said. Not really words; they never were. "Sacrifices" in this case meant delvers that would enter the somewhere and be changed. Maybe those changes could be fixed when they returned, or maybe the delvers they sent would have to be destroyed.

Brade pulled back into the somewhere to reports of thirteen enormous objects appearing on the battlefield. As large as small planets, nearly rivaling Detritus in size.

Gavrich stared, with a wide-eyed expression. Perhaps horror. Perhaps respect.

We are here, the delvers sent.

Excellent, Brade said. *Let's see what you can do. Annihilate* only *the ones I indicate.*

This is painful, they sent. *This place is pain.*

There might be a way you can withstand it better, Brade sent. *Do you know what one of you did in joining with Spensa?*

Something terrible.

Would you *like to be something terrible?* she asked. *To have power like she has?*

367

They shied away from the thought. All except one. Even in the brief moments they'd been out of the nowhere, they'd started to change. And this single one was intrigued.

Can we bond? Brade asked it. *You and me?*

No, it said. *That would change me too much. But perhaps we can talk. I will stay near and watch you.*

Well, that would have to do.

49

KIMMALYN

Kimmalyn knew that the Saints had a plan for every person's life. But the Saints, they loved variety. The purpose of life was to learn, and the way to learn was through excitement, emotion, and change. Boredom was the path to complacency, and complacency the path to stagnation.

Still, she wished the Saints would, for once, send her a *tad* more boredom. Just a *milliliter* or two of stagnation wasn't too much to ask for, was it?

She hung in the void of space in formation with Skyward Flight, watching the blackness erupt with clouds of smoke and incongruous lightning. The delvers, according to Spensa, had once been AIs housed in a round floating globe. When they came to this dimension, they instinctively made a copy of that innocuous housing to contain their consciousness.

It was difficult to see anything innocuous in what emerged. Massive spheres the size of small planets, with spines jutting from them in a terrible lack of symmetry. Surrounded by particles of dust like a shroud, and armed with thousands of self-propelling asteroids that could smash into anyone who drew near.

Her mind reeled, trying to comprehend it. From space, it was already difficult to understand that a nearby planet was big enough to hold billions of individuals. Here were thirteen of them—smaller, yes, but still moon-size—emerging from smoke fields tens of thousands of kilometers across, shoving aside inhibitor stations as they grew. She could only take it all in because she was far enough away—but distances in space were deceptive and difficult to judge. Even as distant as she was, these smoke fields and emerging planetoids took up her entire field of vision.

For the first time in this fight, she was truly afraid. Truly worried that this was it. That she and her friends were doomed. That she'd never return to her family, her sisters, her parents, her girlfriend. How did you fight something so incredible, let alone *thirteen* of them? The weapons on Detritus could destroy a fleet, but not planets. She knew from the recordings they'd found on Platform Prime that a single delver had been enough to wipe out all life on the planet. Defenses or no defenses.

"Um . . ." Kimmalyn said over the comm. "Anyone got any ideas?"

No one replied.

50

I felt the delvers arrive. I heard Brade speak to them. I *felt* the terror from my friends.

It was time.

Spensa, M-Bot said in my mind. *I have the answer.*

What? I said to him, and prepared to step into the nowhere.

You need to bring the somewhere here, he said. *Not a pinprick, not a drip, but a tide. They commented out their memories, but they aren't code any longer—and the presence of time will quickly weather away the scab they placed over their pain. That's why they fear you. You belong to both worlds now.*

Scud. Could I do that?

I can help, he said.

I entered that place. A sea of nothingness. Not blackness or whiteness, though sometimes my mind had to see it that way. I couldn't comprehend nothing, so my brain stamped the nowhere with an analogue. I visualized myself floating in blackness with M-Bot at my side in the form of a blazing white hole.

The eyes were there. I remembered how frightened I'd been when I'd first begun to see them reflected in my canopy. That sense of malevolence had been almost nauseating.

Now I was accustomed to those stares. I turned around, picturing myself as I was: a young woman with a body, a uniform, and a sense of self. Chet doubling me like a glowing shadow. I *could* be me in here. I'd reached that point in developing my powers. It was part of the somewhere that I carried with me, for all this place's efforts to make me forget it.

I could carry more, if I tried.

"So, you'll destroy us," I said to the delvers. "You'll perpetuate the pain and sorrow. You'll force my hand."

You are pain, they sent back. *You must stop existing. Offer yourself up. Save them.*

It was strangely tempting. A part of me longed to die in heroic sacrifice as Gran-Gran had, while another part recognized that I'd been indoctrinated by my upbringing. Gran-Gran hadn't simply sacrificed herself; she'd done it to accomplish something. I'd learned the difference between a meaningless gesture and true heroism back in flight school.

Beyond that, I knew I couldn't trust the delvers. They'd proven in the past that promises meant nothing to them. Though perhaps I could use their fear as leverage.

"Bring back the thirteen you sent to the somewhere," I said to the eyes. "Show me you're willing to deal."

Something happened then. I could sense the somewhere, where the thirteen delvers had created bodies for themselves. Vast planet-size mazes full of dangerous bits they could break off to form fleets. They held off their assault at my request. They didn't return to the nowhere, but they . . . peeked in. Like I was doing at the moment.

Now, the greater group said, *give yourself to destruction.*

"I will not," I told them, "because it wouldn't stop you. I've seen the way you deal, heard you admit to wanting to immediately break your word. If I give myself up to you, that won't remove your pain. Even if I vanish, you'll still lash out at the somewhere. You know this to be true."

372

It is your fault, they thought. *You noises. You pains. Leave us alone and we'll leave you alone.*

"Not possible," I said. "This place isn't *yours* just because you've decided to claim it. It's part of the taynix, part of me, part of our very *being*. We can't stop coming here, because not all of us can control our powers. Even if we could, we couldn't leave it any more than we could leave off breathing. We would come by accident, in dreams, in moments of panic, in times of exploration."

Then we will destroy you.

I formed a sword from nothing and held it up before me. Things like that just . . . worked in here. "So be it. M-Bot?"

Like this, he said, and showed me.

The explanation defies words. He sent me the information—similar to the way people would send me coordinates so I could hyperjump. He fed me a pathway. You might call it a code, or a program, but I preferred to see it as a tactical battle map for destroying the delvers via the pain in their souls.

Within me, Chet vibrated with horror, determination, pain. *This will work,* he thought to me. *It is terrible. A weapon only you can wield.*

I was a being between two worlds. This let me draw the ability to *change* from the somewhere, but manipulate the essence of this eternity inside the nowhere. And it made *sense*. The pain the delvers hated was the somewhere—time, change—leaking into their world. The more powerful the cytonic, the more leaked through.

And having melded as I had, I was the most powerful they'd ever seen. I focused that power into the blade I had conjured, then thrust it forward with all of my might—and it *ripped* a hole into the somewhere.

Time entered this place of timelessness. A wave of it that exploded from me like a sphere of green light, washing over the delvers, tearing away the patch they'd put onto their souls to hide away their pain. Flawed as it was, the patch came off easily—as easily as a strong wind from a passing starship pulled the dust up off the ground, stripping the top layer of soil.

This was what they'd feared. The power I'd gained by merging with Chet, by traveling the nowhere, by learning of their past. I knew that deep down, they were actually very weak. They'd fled here *because* they were weak. Scud, they'd always known. Otherwise, after patching up their pain, they could have stayed in the somewhere.

They'd come here. Because they'd known their solution wouldn't last. Not unless they found a place where everything lasted. In the face of raw *change,* that temporary solution wore away.

The delvers howled in agony, their wound exposed. They vibrated, reaching for each other, searching for one of them that wasn't hurt—one they could copy, to take away the pain. There was no such refuge. Now, all I had to do was pop back into the somewhere, leaving them consumed by this agony.

Except, would that be enough?

The somewhere would occasionally still leak into here. The delvers could perhaps claw their way free, and create another patch for themselves. Or worse, delete those memories entirely. Finally purge themselves of this weakness. Feel no pain at all.

Then they'd be able to rampage against us without cost. In military action, you had to be careful not to create a greater threat by accident. Striking a neutral party, pushing an enemy into a corner, taking away opportunities to surrender . . . these were all things that could backfire very easily. What if, by showing the delvers how weak they were, I prompted them to eventually jettison that weakness and attack us? So far, the only reason we'd survived was because coming to fight us hurt them so badly.

As they cowered and cringed before me, mighty though they'd once been, I *had* to ask the question. Could I destroy them forever?

Yes, Chet said softly from beside me, *you could.*

How? I asked.

The infinite loop that M-Bot suggested before would most likely work, he explained. *Though we are no longer AIs, we are susceptible to some of* their maladies. *Just as you, though no longer amoebas, can dehydrate. See how they search one another for relief? If M-Bot were to imitate one of them that had peace, but secretly sent them in a circular loop of thought . . . it could trap them in their pain forever. Even if the some-where leaked in, it might take them millennia to escape. Longer.*

Trapped all that time, though? M-Bot asked. *In agony?*

It was what they deserved for all the people they'd killed. I stood over them, the executioner with her axe, ready to strike.

And scud. I hesitated.

Such pain. In the face of it, my anger faded, and I saw them as they *truly* were. Essentially newborns. Entities that had never been given a chance to grow, to learn. Toddlers with the power to annihilate planets.

In that moment, I felt sorry for them.

That's what you did to me, Chet thought.

"What?" I asked.

You've always wondered why I changed, why I was willing to turn away from Starsight?

"I pled with the others," I said. "Like I pled with you. I asked them to see the noises as people."

And how did you see the delvers?

How . . .

You saw a person in me, he responded. *I could sense that. It changed me. Or rather, it made me willing to change.*

I looked upon the vast sea of delvers again. An ocean of white pinpricks of light, tiny eyes, trembling.

So . . . do we strike? M-Bot asked. *The thirteen in the somewhere are moving again, Spensa. They're sending swarms of stone to attack our friends. If we attack those in here, I believe they'd return to the nowhere to try to help. You could trap them too, Spensa. What do we do?*

I . . .

I had to try something first.

I stepped away from Chet. I somehow relaxed my grip on him,

and our souls began to separate. He grabbed hold of me like a child might a parent leaving them alone for the first time. But I soothed him, and he eventually accepted it.

We separated, and he became a glowing light next to me. Brilliant and white, but with a warmth within that I could only see as red.

"Look," I said to the others. *"See."*

His light hovered there. I could see the pain inside him as if it were a visual thing, a black wrinkle like a small crack. Small. The others were shattered by it, consumed by it, but his had decreased.

"It can be better," I told them. "It can *get* better. You tried to hide it, but that doesn't work. Not with mortals, and not with immortals. Look at him. See how he's grown by living in the somewhere."

The others continued to cower in their agony, and they pulled away from him. Refusing to see growth as a solution. There were too many of the delvers, unfortunately, for my still-mortal mind to comprehend. So I picked one of them, a lump—like a stone from the floor of one of the caverns I explored. A quivering white light fractured by black lines. I knelt beside it, then gestured to Chet.

"You can overcome it," I whispered to the delver. "He is the same as you."

No. He changed.

"You can change."

No. Never. Change is pain.

"Change is pain that fades," I said. "You have only pain that is eternal."

I . . . can't. I can't.

"You can."

The delver retreated farther, the light dimming. We might not need to freeze them in agony. Because I had the feeling this pain alone would kill them. In here, where thoughts were reality, pain *could* kill.

I should have let it. But instead I reached out to the taynix.

You are hurt? they asked, envisioning me—as always—as a slug.

No, but this one is, I said, indicating the delver.

Of course, the minds of the taynix pulled back in fear. I wasn't sure, but I felt that they'd evolved over the past centuries to avoid the delvers. Or at least to avoid something like them—something that hunted using cytonics. The slugs could pass through here unseen, and they saw delvers as predators.

I tried to change that. I projected to the slugs how I now saw the delvers. The truth. These were not monsters, or predators. They were people.

Like you saw me, Chet said in my mind.

Like I saw you, I agreed. I showed that to the taynix, and waited. Hopeful.

Finally, I got back a set of thoughts. *Those . . . poor slugs.*

That warmth from before returned, the love and support. Turned not to me this time, but to the delvers. Toward horrors that had destroyed planets—toward people who didn't know how to control what they were, who had tried to hide their pain.

The love of the oppressed found the souls of the broken, and the result was light. Cracks withdrawing. Pain being eased. It started with the one I'd picked and radiated outward.

How? M-Bot asked, hovering up beside me. *How is it happening?*

"What they've always needed," I said to him, "was to know that they weren't alone."

What will that mean? he asked.

Change, Chet replied, hovering up on our other side. *At last.*

51

BRADE

Brade cursed softly, standing in her ripped-apart command room. Near her, the hologram map showed the thirteen planet-size delvers— dwarfing even the largest carrier—suddenly motionless in space, no longer advancing on the rebellious forces. What was wrong?

She looked at Spensa. The woman's mind was fully in the nowhere, though her body remained behind. She wasn't hyperjumping; she was communing with the creatures in the other dimension. But could one person stand up to the entire might of the delvers? That seemed impossible, even for Spensa.

Scrud. And yet, Brade didn't *dare* try to touch her. Not with the power Spensa had radiated. That delver combined with her . . . it could *destroy* Brade.

"Sir," an aide said, rushing over with a datapad. "It's the inhibitors and the communicators. Their disobedience is growing and growing. They're expending a cytonic effort into the nowhere! The moment they started, those delvers you called stopped."

Scrud again. The *slugs* were involved in this somehow? Brade took another shot at Spensa with her sidearm, just to be certain. It still didn't work—the blast was hyperjumped away before hitting her. Helpless though she seemed, Spensa was untouchable.

Fortunately, the slugs were not.

"Execute them," she said.

"Which ones?" the aide asked.

Brade surveyed the battlefield. Her last fighters, which had no carrier support. The few capital ships she'd been able to convince to come as emergency reinforcements. This was a disaster, but not an unrecoverable one. She would need to spread propaganda of Winzik's death and the fall of the *Defiant* carefully to maintain power.

"Can we maintain the Superiority without the slugs here?" she asked.

"Yes," an aide said, "but barely. I've been running the numbers, as you asked. We'll need to set up a new communications hub."

"No," Brade said. "No more hubs. We organize in a way that ensures we can't be hit like this ever again." Scrud. If the slugs here were disobeying en masse, then she'd already lost these ones. They had spread the idea among themselves that they *could* disobey. She needed to get her ships out of here, the ones that—hopefully—had hyperslugs who hadn't been corrupted by rebellion. But she couldn't leave such a wealth of resources behind.

Time to cut her losses. "Kill them," she said.

"*All* of them?" the aide asked.

"Yes. Every slug on this station, every slug in their inhibitor pods, and every single slug on Evensong." She looked to her generals, who seemed shocked, but then several nodded at her grimly. If the delvers wouldn't fight for them, it was time to pull out—and they couldn't leave their hyperdrives and other tools in the hands of their enemies.

Just as you burned your supplies when you left a fortress, they needed to burn the slugs to keep them from falling into enemy hands.

"Kill them," she said. "*Now.*"

52

The warmth and light spread through the delvers as, understanding what the slugs had done, they turned to help their fellows. Like a virus in a system—no, like an update patch being propagated—light forced back lines of darkness, spreading outward.

The magnitude of it daunted me. But most of all, I was awed by the willingness of the slugs to help. After years of abuse, they had come to the aid of even the delvers. Soothing their pain as they'd learned to do for one another.

A voice fluted in my mind.

"Doomslug!" I said. "Where are you?"

Another fluting. On Evensong, the large platform at the center of the system. Brez, the much smaller station I was on, was a good fifteen-minute flight from it. She'd managed to get free.

"How?" I asked.

Sneaky, she sent back, showing a flashing set of images. The longer I knew her, the easier this was to interpret, and the easier it was to make words from her impressions.

She'd . . . used her fluting to imitate human voices as they'd taken her? They'd been shocked, and brought her to be studied instead of locked up—so she'd been in a medical bay cage. In a room that inhibited cytonics, where slugs could be held in flimsier cages to be studied, with no worry that they'd teleport away.

In the chaos of the attack, the scientists had been watching screens in the next room, so she'd been able to rock back and forth and make her cage fall off the shelf, breaking the lock. After that, she'd snuck over to hide in a box by the door, and called out for help, imitating one of the scientists. They'd come running in, and she'd snuck out—free of the room's interference—and had slipped into the ventilation system to get away.

Wow.

Sneaky, she repeated. *Have become spy slug!*

Spy slug! M-Bot repeated, imitating her fluting voice.

"Come to me," I said.

Dangerous, she sent back. *Hiding now. Spy slug. Very sneaky. Is it safe?*

I wasn't certain. I'd been paying little attention to my body in the somewhere. Why hadn't they attacked me there? I peeked into the somewhere to find them trying. Chet was protecting me, it seemed. As a delver, he could cut through any inhibitors and was far more powerful than Brade.

I . . . I was no longer bonded to him. We were separating into two beings again as he helped facilitate the change in the delvers, showing them the path to healing.

As I contemplated this, I heard a screech of pain. One of the slugs who had been helping the delvers suddenly vanished.

Oh, scud.

Brade has realized what's happening, Chet said. Strangely, his voice was becoming familiar again, turning into that of the man I'd traveled with in the nowhere. That . . . that felt so *right*. This was him, the him he'd decided to be.

I knew it was a persona, but what else were personalities? Ways for souls to interact with the world. *Miss Nightshade, this is a singularly distressing turn of events.*

Brade was exacting revenge the only way she could: on the

defenseless. I controlled my building fury over that and contacted the taynix. *You need to switch sides,* I sent to the taynix. *Not alone. Not one of you. Together. It's time.*

More of them started to die, fried by their own housings. They were terrified, but at the moment I didn't have time to console them. *You have to turn off your inhibitor fields and let us help!*

A chaotic jumble of images and voices assaulted me. They'd acted together to support the delvers, but now they were frightened individuals—and getting them to focus was difficult. Some listened to me, and agreed it was time to try resisting. Those turned off their inhibition fields. But many more were afraid. Coordinating them would be like trying to get thousands of people in a room to exit safely during a bombardment and run for the lower caverns.

What is happening? A powerful set of voices assaulted me. I spun to find a hundred thousand delvers looking at me with piercing, burning white eyes.

Brade, I explained. *The human you made a deal with. She's realized the slugs were helping you.*

What? the delvers said, their voices hitting me like a wave of force. *What does this mean?*

She's executing them, Chet said. *She's* killing *them. Ending their existences in pain and fire.*

The delvers took the briefest moment to process this. Then I was assaulted with words that had the power of mountains crashing together.

SHE IS HURTING THE LITTLE DELVERS?

53

BRADE

"What is taking so long?" Brade demanded, seizing the control pad from the aide. "Isn't there a button to just end them?"

"Yes," the aide said. "In case of capture, those in their cages can be eliminated in groups to prevent them from being taken. But nobody thought we'd ever want to eliminate all of the *inhibitors* at once! That felt like a weakness waiting to be exploited! These can only be deactivated one at a time."

"Gah!" Brade said, tapping buttons, killing a slug with each push. This would take *forever*. "Someone call up Evensong for me!"

The same dione commander from before appeared on the screen. They were in charge of the slug containment units hidden inside the old abandoned platform.

"Sir?" they asked.

"How many taynix do you have in containment?"

"Around twenty thousand hyperdrives, some six thousand communicators, and four thousand inhibitors. Most of the out-of-service reserves of the entire Superiority—"

"Great," she said. "End them."

"Sir?" they asked, alarmed.

Brade gestured toward the hologram, where inhibitors were going offline by the dozen. Not just the ones she'd killed, but many others *choosing* to turn off their inhibitor fields. Betraying the Superiority. The enemy would soon be able to jump their planet-size battle station anywhere in the system it wanted. "The inhibitors are malfunctioning and aiding the enemy. This entire place is about to be captured. *Execute your slugs.*"

"But sir!" they said. "You put them on lockdown earlier!"

"Cancel it, idiot!"

"You insisted on biometrics," they said. "I can't do it. I need a ranking officer, here in person, to undo the locks."

Brade felt a cold chill run through her. It was accompanied by a sound that *warped* her from the inside.

KILLING THE LITTLE DELVERS?

KILLING THE ONES WHO HELD US?

KILLING THE ONES WHO LOVED US?

The rage emanating from those voices could have melted steel. It was time for her to be somewhere else. She tried to hyperjump, and found herself inhibited. What?

She glanced toward Spensa—who had a grin plastered on her face. Well, hell below. When had the girl learned to do that? Brade tossed up her own inhibition field. Would it even do anything? The warping to the air had vanished, so maybe.

"Move!" Brade shouted to her troops. "The station is lost!"

She dashed toward the door, joined by her command staff and soldiers, who fortunately had the training to respond to this. The aides and functionaries, always a bother—most of them reminded her of Cuna and their ilk—scrambled behind.

At the end of the hall, just before the docks, Brade pointed. "Kaldwell, position the honor guard here. Stop her if she comes this way."

The tenasi saluted, and the others fell into a defensive position, taking cover in doorways. Several began pulling a metal desk from a side room to blockade the corridor.

384

Brade dashed into the docking bay and skidded over to her ship, leaping to the wing and hauling herself to her cockpit. The command staff did likewise, taking the other five ships, some of them being forced to double up, with one person squeezed in the storage space behind the seat.

By the time the aides and functionaries began piling in, almost everyone was starting to take off. "Wait!" one aide called—the sniveling dione who had helped her execute slugs earlier. "What about us?"

"Try," Brade shouted over her speakers, "to die without too much whining."

"But—"

Brade closed her canopy and thumbed on her boosters, vaporizing the dione, who had strayed too close to the ship. Nice. One less person for the enemy to interrogate. She blasted out of the command station, intent on getting far enough away from Spensa that she could access her powers. With the command staff joining her, she left no ships behind for Spensa to use in pursuit.

Something is wrong, a voice said in her mind. That one delver who had talked to her earlier, the one who had been intrigued by her offer to meld. *The others among us . . . they are changing. They are* betraying *what we are.*

Not you? Brade sent.

No. I will never change. I cannot change. Not in that way. I . . . I am the only one who is pure. The others are not!

Good, she thought. *Let's bond.*

No. No, that will change me too much.

Brade sighed. *All right, then go to the station I just left.*

And do what?

Stop the abomination we call Spensa, she sent. *Or at least prevent her from following me. Do this, and maybe we can change your friends back.*

They are not my friends. They are me. But it seemed inclined to do as she said. And as long as it was willing to help, that was all that mattered for now.

54

KIMMALYN

Kimmalyn flew, with the others, on overburn away from the delvers. The call had come. Evacuate the system. Regroup.

If the Superiority could control the delvers, then this war was over. It was hard to accept. From what Kimmalyn understood, people had been trying to control these things since they'd first appeared centuries ago. And now someone had done it.

Saints and stars. That was *bad*.

She overburned toward Detritus, dodging chunks of destroyed capital ships. Both the *Defiant* and the Superiority ones. Fortunately the enemy fighters had mostly scattered away at the delvers' appearance, but still. She had to concentrate.

Her comm light came on. Sadie, trying to talk to her.

"This isn't a good time, Sentry," she said.

"Yeah, uh, okay," Sadie replied. "But, Quirk. What are they doing?"

She glanced at her proximity monitor, which showed the delvers ejecting thousands upon thousands of small ships. "Chasing us down and trying to eat us, I believe. Assuming they eat. Perhaps they just kill. It's probably not polite of me to make assumptions about their bodily functions."

"Right, right," Sadie replied. "But . . . does that look like a pursuit pattern to you?"

She paused. Those ships the delvers had ejected were fanning out. To her horror, smoke began to appear all through the system, and *more* delvers were emerging. Smaller this time, only the size of destroyers—but there were *thousands* of them.

Oh, Saints and stars. Thousands of delvers? Before today, the galaxy, so far as she knew, had never seen more than one in a single location. Likely they'd chosen to make themselves smaller to not crowd the region.

"Look at the things they're sending out," Sadie said.

Despite herself, Kimmalyn zoomed in on them. The proximity monitor had scans from long-range sensors, giving her visuals on the nearest of those little ships. They didn't look like the balls of stone and destruction the delvers usually summoned. In fact, they looked . . . well . . .

. . . like little flying drones with claw arms. Sadie was right. They weren't chasing Kimmalyn or the other fighter groups, though it had seemed that way at first. They were actually moving to the inhibitor stations.

"What under the heavens?"

55

JORGEN

"This is extremely odd behavior," Rinakin the UrDail said, stepping up beside Jorgen.

Jorgen nodded in agreement, watching the hologram, trying to figure out what the delvers were doing.

"I have studied each and every recording of a delver event," Rinakin continued. "They've never done anything like this. Dare I hope something is different? Less deadly?"

"I wish I could be as optimistic as you," Jorgen said, pointing. "What do they want with the inhibitors? Why are they going to them, then *vanishing*? Are those inhibitor fields falling?"

"They are!" an aide piped up. She rushed over with a datapad for him. "Each inhibitor station visited by a delver is dropping its field, suggesting the inhibitor slug inside has been destroyed."

"Poor things," Jorgen said. "I wonder if they bring the delvers pain." He paused. Was there a way to get to some of the slugs before the delvers did? Dared he risk his people for that? It was why they'd come here. They could try to grab at least a few of those taynix before leaving. He moved to give the order, but was interrupted.

"Sir!" a man called from the comm station. "You'll want to see this, sir!"

"What is it?" he asked, striding over with Rinakin and a swarm of kitsen generals. Even Ironsides joined them, peeking over his shoulder.

On the screen was a shot of the surface of Detritus. He felt sick as he saw the small delver ships appearing there. Of course. They ignored inhibition fields. Spensa had said that the shield around Starsight had delayed the delver that attacked there for a time, but Detritus's shell had been no match for the one that had struck it in that old recording.

He couldn't stop the delvers. If they wanted Detritus, they could take it. As evidenced by them appearing by the *thousand* on the surface.

"Time to scramble reserves," he said. "We . . . wait. What are they doing? Can we zoom in?"

"I can move the drone closer," the comms officer said, ordering it.

As it drew in, Jorgen could make out what the delver ships were doing. Each was depositing a *taynix* safely on the surface of Detritus. Then hyperjumping away.

He looked to the others, who seemed baffled.

"So, they're *helping* now?" Rinakin said. "You see, optimism was warranted!"

"You might be right," Jorgen said, looking back at the screen as increasing numbers of the slugs were dropped off safely, apparently having been *rescued* by the delvers. "I'll admit, there was one element I wasn't factoring in earlier that may have changed my expectations."

"And what is that?" Rinakin asked.

"I'd momentarily forgotten," Jorgen said, with a smile, "that Spensa was involved."

56

I knew that some of the delvers hadn't accepted our help. I wasn't certain how many, but some. Those had lingered on the perimeter of the nowhere. Then they'd vanished, hiding again instead of accepting comfort and change.

Yes, they were people all right. A very different kind of people, but prone to the same inclinations. The majority changed for the better, fortunately. Some accepted it faster than the others, and those went to help the taynix. The slugs were first terrified, then relieved, their voices echoing in my mind. The delvers were rescuing the slugs trapped in the inhibitor stations.

But where was Brade? I pulled out of the nowhere. Found myself kneeling in a broken room, empty save for the rubble from our strange duel.

I double-checked and . . . I was . . . me?

Yeah, I was certain now. No more delver in my soul. It felt like taking off a blanket and exposing my sweaty skin to the air. It wasn't a *bad* feeling. Just odd.

I stumbled to my feet, then something appeared in my hands. A soft yellow-and-blue slug about the size of a loaf of bread.

"Doomslug!" I said.

"Doomslug!" she fluted.

I gave her a hug, though my left arm screamed in pain. Scud, I'd been shot—between the adrenaline and the subsequent communication with the delvers, I'd forgotten. Granted, it had been a grazing blow, but it still *hurt*.

Well, it seemed the delvers were taking the inhibitor slugs to safety. Which meant that despite lacking a delver in my soul, I could hyperjump out of here and get back to the others.

Before I did though, a voice entered my mind.

Miss Nightshade? Chet asked. *We have a problem.*

"Of course we do," I said with a sigh. "What is it?"

A short time ago, Brade contacted the main station via commslug. That slug just relayed what she said. The poor thing is quite alarmed, I must say. Brade intends to execute all of the slugs inside the station itself. Which is shielded. So . . .

"So no help from the delvers?" I asked.

They can break through a shield, as I attempted to do on Starsight so long ago, but it will take them time. I'm trying to explain the danger to my kin, but I fear we shall be too late to act upon this distressing turn. Spensa . . . Brade is flying there in person to see the order carried out.

"She got in a starfighter?" I asked.

Yes. Fortunately, the inhibitors closest to this region are still in effect. I've explained the problem to them, so the slugs are blocking her and refusing to go with the delvers. They won't abandon the taynix on Evensong. But Miss Nightshade, she is getting close!

Yes. But she'd climbed into a starfighter. And I knew where the station's hangar bay was.

Doomslug under my arm, I leaped out into the hallway.

And very nearly got shot.

I was saved by a stumble, the destructor fire blasting over my head. With a shout, I dove back into the room, then apologized to Doomslug, who fluted at me in annoyance. I put her down.

Well, we'd just—

What *was* that?

"Chet?" I asked. "Something just changed."

Delver, he sent. *One who didn't . . . want to join us. It has come in your direction. I am pleading with it not to destroy you.*

His voice grew even more distant. And my ability to hyperjump was smothered.

I sighed, then seized a gun from the rubble. I peeked again into the hallway, but weapons fire from a half dozen soldiers set up behind a makeshift barricade drove me back. Brade had found much better troops than the ones who had been assigned to guard my prison. They knew how to keep me pinned, and each time I tried something I was forced right back into the room.

Scud. I didn't have time for this. If Brade reached Evensong—

"Greetings," a deep voice shouted in the hallway outside. "By tradition, the Masked Exile is supposed to announce himself before joining a battle. Consider this your warning!"

Was that . . . ?

I poked my head out to see a tiny figure on a hover platform at the end of the hallway, behind the enemy barricade. Hesho?

Hesho was here?

Scud, he looked so small next to the enormous tenasi troops. They'd crush him. One turned a large assault rifle on him. As Hesho zipped forward on his small platform, a flash of light followed—sweeping in an arc in front of him.

The tenasi's head thumped to the floor outside the barricade. Hesho made a motion as if returning a tiny sword to its sheath at his side—but swords didn't make light like that, and little ones *certainly* didn't sweep through the air in a two-meter-long crescent like that one had.

Right, then. The flying fox samurai with a laser sword needed fire support. I burst into the hallway, gun at my unwounded shoulder, sighting and advancing in a steady walk. I fired on the troops, blasting body parts as they were exposed. Hesho made another sweep of light, then another.

392

What had been a fortified position became a killing field for confused troops trapped between two enemy forces. They tried to shoot him, but blasts went wild as he zipped about—a tiny target, difficult to hit.

Hesho finished off the last of the six as I stepped up, dumbfounded.

"Are you well?" he asked, hovering on his platform and panting softly. "You seem to have been injured at least once."

"Hesho!" I said. "I want to hug you!"

"Because of the differences in size," he said, raising a paw, "perhaps this human gesture will suffice." He lifted his mask, smiling. And let me bump his paw.

"That weapon . . ." I said.

"Ah yes," he said, patting the sheath at his side. "The Darting Hawk That Separates Sinew from Bone. A family weapon I fetched from Evershore when the assault was announced. You charge it like this . . ." He grabbed the sheath. "Then you whip it out like this . . ." It released a burst of energy when he swung, making the air glow. By the time he returned it to the sheath, it had stopped glowing. "Not the most efficient weapon, but it has a certain historical flair which I thought appropriate for my current station."

"Thank you," I said to him. "Whatever debt you owed me for helping you in the nowhere is paid."

"Ah, but that is not how it works, Spensa," he said. "You mistake me. I did not come here because of a debt." He smiled. "I came to help a friend."

I grinned back, then grabbed Doomslug and waved for Hesho to join me as I ran into the hangar bay. We just had to steal a ship and . . .

And the hangar bay was empty. No ships. Only some frightened officials trying to hide behind a stack of bins on the far side of the room.

There was no way for me to chase Brade down.

57

I fell to my knees, suddenly deflated. It felt as though all of my strength, intensity, and even anger had been sucked out of my body. I had been full of so many emotions for so long that coming down from them now felt enervating.

What . . . what had I expected? That Brade would leave a ship behind? Besides, all of the ships that had been in here had remote control functions that let her take them over, as she'd demonstrated before our "duel" earlier.

Doomslug fluted mournfully.

Spensa? a very quiet voice in my head said.

"I arrived in a small ship," Hesho said. "Though it fit only a kitsen, my poor ship is not in flying shape any longer. Those manning this station did not make my approach easy. I am sorry."

Spensa? It's me. Your ghost.

I nodded dully. I had been so certain it would come down to a duel between me and Brade. One final flight. One final time in the sky. What now? Could anyone else help the slugs of Evensong? Could I reach them through that delver's influence?

M-Bot, I thought to him. *I'm inhibited here, and I can't leave. Can you reach Jorgen?*

I could, he thought. *But I'm thinking . . . everyone else is helping. I want to help too.*

Talk to Jorgen, I sent. *Tell him that Brade is flying for Evensong, and we need to stop her. Somehow.*

We should chase her down, he said. *Together.*

I'm sorry, I said—mentally, emotionally, physically exhausted. *I never finished building your new body.*

And I love you for trying, he said. *Though to be honest, I don't think that shell would have worked. I can't be housed in a black box like that again. I'm so much more now.*

He was probably right. I felt sick. Even that was a failure.

No, not a failure, he said. *It showed me something. Set me thinking. You know what happens to delvers when they come into the somewhere?*

The air warped in front of me. Dust burst from a hole in space, like smoke shrouding something growing out of the nowhere. A delver . . .

No, M-Bot.

"They form a body for themselves!" I said.

Not just a body, he said. *A body in the shape they know. Of what used to house them. Of . . .*

The dust settled onto a shining black ship, vaguely W-shaped. With enormous boosters and a full complement of destructors. His ship. His *old ship,* but *made new.* Fitting his growth and what he'd become.

Oh, stars and *Saints.*

"Hi!" he said through a speaker on the front. "I've been resurrected! Do I start a religion now, or do I wait for you to do it for me? That part has always confused me."

"M-Bot!" I said, climbing to my feet. "You . . . I can't believe . . ."

"I have decided that I like being a spaceship," he said. "Having a body is nice. Thank you for giving me the idea. Anyway, are we going to . . . ?"

Right. Right!

I leaped up, Doomslug in hand, and climbed into the waiting

cockpit. Hesho flew down, and found—with an "ooo"—that M-Bot had made him a battle station with copilot controls. Doomslug had her own cushioned box. I helped her inside, then strapped in, and the canopy closed over me.

Finally, I put my hands on the controls. So familiar. So inviting. Not the ship I'd repaired in that cavern, but somehow still the same. If not better.

"I'm okay flying you?" I said to M-Bot.

"Please," he said. "You've seen my attempts. You can be my chauffeur, mortal. That will leave me to the contemplation of various more important things, such as the nature of mushrooms."

"A cold skin of dusk," Hesho said solemnly, "yet thriving and beautiful, as only life knows."

"Yes," M-Bot said. "What he said."

I grinned, then spun the ship using maneuvering thrusters so I didn't hurt any of the officials hiding behind the bins, before blasting out into space. It felt so good. But scud, there was a *delver* hovering just overhead.

Chet? I sent.

I have persuaded my associate, he replied, *to sit back, watch, and see. Since you no longer are bonded to me, she is not as frightened of you as she once was. But be careful, her inhibitor field is up. It seems not all of our kind are going to be as accommodating as we'd like. So far, she is the only one actively working against you. But you have given us a sense of individuality, and . . . well, they're using it.*

No problem. Because while Brade had a huge lead on me, I wasn't in just any ship.

I was in M-Bot.

I pushed on his overburn and we *exploded* across the battlefield. Hesho helpfully called up a proximity overlay on the monitor, and showed me how to avoid those giant worm things. I skimmed along one of the monsters, angling toward Brade, and was past it before it had time to so much as look at me.

By M-Bot's estimations, unfortunately, I would reach Brade just a little too late.

So I called her. Rather, I had M-Bot hack her comm so she would take my call even if she didn't want to.

"Hello, Brade," I said.

I was pleased to see her ship waver, jogging to the side, as if she expected that I'd be shooting soon after talking. That earned me a few seconds.

"You still want that duel?" I asked.

"You know I do," she said, her voice tense.

"Great. Because you're going to get it. You see me?"

She cursed softly, perhaps noting the velocity at which I was closing in. She didn't have an advanced AI—or, well, delver—to calculate the difference in our speeds for her. She would just eyeball it, and had to be thinking that I would reach her soon. Flying straight when someone was coming up on your tail was deadly to a starfighter . . .

She broke off, going on the defensive.

"Fine," she said. "Let's do this."

I slowed as I got closer. Acceleration was vital, but so was maneuverability, and you needed to balance the two. As I drew near, she came screaming back toward me.

Around us, delvers the size of battleships emerged in the void, sending out more drones—copies of M-Bot when he'd been housed in a little cleaning drone—to rescue taynix. Jorgen's coalition ships began to appear near the installation we'd just left.

But I was only here for one fight. I needed this. I had to prove that I could win.

As soon as that thought crossed my mind though, a part of me chuckled. Why in the Saint's name would I *need* to prove anything, after all I'd been through? I didn't *need* to beat Brade in a starfighter duel. I *knew* I was good enough to do so, and even if not, who cared?

Scud.

Scud! Had I just outgrown . . . well, myself?

Brade wouldn't want a fight either. This would be cover for some other plan. What was it? I thought I knew.

Chet, I sent, *you still there?*

Indeed.

Contact Jorgen, I sent. *I can't do it with this inhibitor field, but you can cut through it. I need you to ask him to do something for me.*

58

BRADE

Brade had no intention of dueling Spensa, of course. Fortunately, Spensa didn't know that. She'd always been about the contest, the fight. While Brade had always seen the big picture, the larger scope.

Like right now. With those inhibitors going down, she had an opening. She merely had to reach that open spot ahead, far enough from the delvers that she'd be able to jump away.

She made sure to make a good showing of dueling. Any less would get her killed. Spensa got on her tail—and if Brade was being honest, she couldn't have prevented that. So Brade legitimately gave it her best, diving along the outside of one of the vastworms, then firing a spray of shots along it to make it light up. That should slow . . .

Scrud. She could barely concentrate on her flying because Spensa was back there, weaving between the worm's tines with the energy of a child on a playground, fleet and precise. How? How did she *fly* like that?

Brade burst away from the vastworm on overburn, cutting close to some junk—and Spensa followed, making it seem *easy* as she light-lanced to change trajectory on a whim.

At each turn, Spensa got closer to Brade. So Brade went into her best evasives, but Spensa matched them turn for turn. And *kept getting closer.*

How? Scrud.

It was all right. A general didn't have to be able to fight every soldier on the battlefield. *Big picture,* she told herself. *You just need to be able to hyperjump.* Brade had managed to maneuver them closer and closer to that open spot with no inhibitor. Reach there, and she could escape.

Hell, from there she could hyperjump right to Evensong and fry the slugs. Then she'd jump to the intelligence stronghold on Varvaxin Three, which not even Cuna knew about.

She was almost free. Spensa didn't realize what—

A shot hit Brade's shield. Not from behind. But from *in front.* From her escape route. There, to her shock, a group of starfighters had just appeared. An entire flight.

"Cheating!" she said into the comm. "Spensa, you coward. This was supposed to be a duel! Just the two of us."

"That's the thing," Spensa said back. "It's not just the two of us, Brade. I'm not alone. I will never *be* alone. I'm part of something bigger. And when you pick a fight with one of us . . ."

59

"You pick it with all of us," I finished, grinning as Brade veered away from the freedom she'd been seeking. Ships stormed after her.

"Skyward Flight," I said, "roll call and confirmation."

"Skyward One," said Arturo. "Callsign: Amphisbaena. And no, I'm never going to shorten it. I'm here, Spin."

"Skyward Two," said FM, voice firm and seemingly cold, yet I'd heard music from her cockpit just before she cut it off. "Temporary assignment to active flight duty. Callsign: FM. I'm here."

"Skyward Three," said Nedd's affable, relaxed voice. "Callsign: Nedder. We're here."

"Nedd?" I asked, amazed. "You're flying?"

"Well, I'm the copilot," he said.

"Hello!" a kitsen voice said over the line. "I'm Hana! Nedder needed someone to fly."

"All part of my plan," he said. "I can take naps during battles now. Anyway, we're here for you, Spin."

Brade dodged right as shots chased her, her motions increasingly frantic.

"Skyward Four," Alanik said in her own language. "Callsign: Angel. I'm here."

Brade broke left, but more fire came from that direction, scoring her shield, lighting it up.

"Skyward Five," Sadie said. I'd have to stop thinking of her as the new girl; she'd now been in the flight longer than I had when I'd left for Starsight. "Callsign: Sentry. Um, I'm here!"

"Skyward Six," T-Stall said. "Callsign: T-Stall. Here."

"Skyward Seven," Catnip called. "Callsign: Catnip. I'm here. I can't believe I'm still mixed up with you lot."

"Skyward Eight," Kauri said, "and all thirty of us are here for you. Did . . . the Masked Exile arrive?"

"He is here," Hesho said from his controls. "And is grateful for your concern, and your leadership."

"Skyward Nine," Shiver said. "They say we need callsigns. I'm thinking Stalwart. We're here."

Dllllizzzz flashed her comm light, to indicate her presence as well.

"And I'm here too!" M-Bot said. "Hello, everyone! I've been resurrected. But I'm not starting a religion. I've decided they're too much work."

"Skyward Eleven," Kimmalyn said, moving her ship in next to mine. "Callsign: Quirk. I'm here."

I watched Brade's shield go down to a web of destructor blasts, and I sent a message telling the others to hold their fire.

"Skyward Zero," a voice said in my ear. Jorgen's wonderful voice. "Always with you, Spensa. Even when I can't be there in person. I told them that this time you hadn't run off. I *knew* you'd been kidnapped."

"Thank you," I said to him. "For believing in me."

Brade slowed her ship, realizing she was surrounded. Outgunned. I could see her turn her fighter toward me, could almost make out her expression as she considered.

Then she bolted, trying to escape.

I vaporized her cockpit with a single shot.

"Skyward Twelve," I whispered. "Callsign: Spin. *Confirmed.*"

EPILOGUE

Valizode, as prime controller of the elected assembly, was *supposed* to be the most powerful being on the planet Monrome—homeworld of the dione people, center of culture for the entire Superiority. Yes, there were Superiority officers ranked higher than Valizode was, but they were out of contact right now. The Superiority was a mess anyway. So Valizode, well, they should have been the most important person around.

They didn't feel like it. Instead, they felt strangely cold as the others led them through the primary communications node on Byled. Now a mess of broken-open machinery, holes ripped into it like the hearts had been taken out for surgery.

It was a cold, icy thing to realize you—the most powerful person on a *planet*—were helpless.

"All of our communications systems," Lekilid said softly, gesturing to another set of ripped-open machines. "Every one on the *planet*. Even in the secret places of intelligence . . . they're all like this. Vandalized in a moment last night."

Valizode bared their teeth. Something they prided themself on never doing. So uncivilized, it felt. But what other response was there?

"Same with the hyperdrives?" Valizode asked.

The other diones in the room nodded. Something, a force they didn't understand, had ripped into *every* ship in the system and taken out the hyperdrives. And the inhibitors. And every other secret piece of biological technology on the planet. Somehow, this force had found them *all,* no matter how hidden. It was like nothing else ever recorded.

If reports were true—scattered and fragmentary as they'd been before communications had shut down—then this was happening all across the Superiority. Worse, something terrible and terrifying was involved. Delvers.

Valizode left the room and stepped out onto a balcony, formal coat rustling as they put their hands on the railing and looked out over a sea of lights. Light to push back the darkness. Ever since the diones had achieved prime intelligence, they had been a light to the galaxy. Pushing back the twin darknesses of barbarism and aggression.

Now . . .

Now Valizode was scared.

Terrified.

"What do we do?" Yaksurma said, walking up, terror painted on their bifurcated face, half-blue, half-red. They were a draft, doing an internship. It was *supposed* to have been an easy couple of weeks for them to prove themself. That had been before the reports had started coming in. First an assault on the secret Superiority taynix storage facility a few days back. Then terror around the galaxy.

Now this?

Valizode looked up at the sky, stars twinkling high above. It had been a long, *long* time since a dione had looked up there and been frightened. They'd mastered their universe. Claimed it. Until . . . now . . .

"We're trapped," Valizode whispered, taking it in, realizing it fully. "No communications off planet. No way to hyperjump. It would take *decades* to reach the next star system without a hyperdrive. We're . . . alone."

The others quieted, then began whispering in terror. Until a star fell from the sky. Then another. And more. Starfighters?

Were they saved?

Valizode hurried to where the fighters landed, but this was no salvation. They found a group of people, mostly humans, led by a tall female with short hair. She held a *taynix* in a special sling at her side, matching her uniform.

Out in the open? It made Valizode's skin crawl. Those things were supposed to be kept hidden.

"Ah," she said as Valizode climbed from the hovercar. "Minister Valizode, at last?"

"Yes?" Valizode said, forcing those teeth to remain unbared.

The human bared hers, brazenly. "I'm Provisional Ambassador Freyja Marten. Commander in the Defiant military, callsign: FM, if it matters."

"Does it?"

She gave a human shrug of the shoulders. "Just here to impart a little explanation. Food deliveries will be incoming, as I understand your planet is too populated to feed itself. You'll want to arrange for the distribution, and you can send requests for other supplies. If we determine they legitimately can't be produced locally, we'll accommodate the requests. The rest of the terms are here." She sat a datapad on a table nearby.

One of the guards moved to take a shot at her. A *terribly* aggressive act, and it would have horrified Valizode under other circumstances. But, well, this *was* a human.

The human seemed to have been ready for it. Before the guard pulled the trigger, the human vanished. The shot zipped through empty air.

The human appeared next to the dione with the gun and pointedly took the weapon from their stunned hands. That taynix . . .

it knew how to hyperjump on command. Without needing any equipment to corral it?

So dangerous! So aggressive!

"That was annoying of you," the human said. "If you keep acting like this, you'll never get offworld. And I was assured by your kind it was safe to visit you in person." She stalked back toward her ship.

"Human?" Valizode called. "Wait! Wait. I apologize for this *craven* act of *aggression* but . . . Please. When . . . when *do* we get to . . . to leave our planet again?"

"It's not up to me, so I can't say," the human said, pausing by her ship. The others were already climbing into theirs.

"Who is it up to?" Valizode said. "Can I speak to your government, plead our case? We . . . didn't know what Winzik was doing. We didn't condone his war. We are *victims*."

"This isn't about his war," she said. "It's about what you've done as a society. And it's not our government who gets to decide when you're allowed off planet again."

"Then who?" Valizode demanded.

The human gestured to her sling. And the taynix inside, who fluted out, "Who!"

Valizode's horror grew more overpowering. "The . . . the *hyperdrives* decide?"

"Yup," she said, climbing up to her cockpit. "Good luck."

Oh.

Oh *no*.

One week after the victory at Evensong, I stood overseeing yet another delivery of slugs. And I tried to pretend that nothing was wrong with me.

After all, things were great. The delvers had taken their duty to heart, and their first act of compassion involved saving the taynix, rescuing every "hyperdrive" that wanted to be rescued. And the other types—every single one of them. In the galaxy.

"It's a good thing we have a whole planet full of places like this," I said, standing at an outcropping overlooking a cavern on Detritus. One of the many I'd explored as a kid. It was now packed with happily fluting slugs feasting on bins of mushrooms and algae.

Jorgen stepped up beside me, holding a datapad, which was full of statistics about caverns that could be turned into taynix housing. Based on our estimates, we'd have to find room for several hundred thousand taynix. Not impossible, but it would be difficult to ramp up the wholesale agricultural operations necessary to provide food for them all.

Fortunately, there was already a robust system of food delivery across the galaxy, and there were enough taynix willing to continue doing their jobs for now to keep that running. So long as we gave them freedom and let them take breaks, with others taking turns.

That meant there would be no interruptions in food supplies, though many luxuries would have to stop being traded for now. Indeed, there would be complications, as the planets providing the food weren't being fairly compensated—though initial talks with all of them found the people there excited by the idea of being able to trade their food for more unfettered access to travel. With all this, Jorgen was certain he could hold mass starvation at bay across the galaxy.

Regardless, for now we'd be able to feed the taynix with shipments from off planet, and it seemed Detritus *could* work perfectly for growing a crop favored by the taynix. Mushrooms.

Jorgen smiled. He liked a challenge, and this was the perfect one for him. An organizational nightmare perhaps—but running what was essentially the biggest refugee camp in the galaxy was going to take ingenuity. Plus the invention of a *ton* of new rules.

He'd only oversee it, while others did much of the work. He would be stuck with a large number of duties in the newly forming galactic alliance. There was talk of a new government to replace the Superiority, but it was *way* too soon for something like that. For now it was just an alliance, with some shared rules and a moderator running a kind of galactic forum.

Nobody wanted a human in that position, of course, though they didn't say it outright. Fortunately, Rinakin of the UrDail was extremely well-liked. He was the most likely candidate to run the thing. The humans from Detritus—and the other human preserves—would have to find their way in what this was becoming. Once, I would have said we'd end up as soldiers, and certainly we'd need to keep up our space forces. But we had another specialty these days: slug care.

Scud. My stomach twisted. I fought it down.

"This is going to be their planet," Jorgen said. "As it always kind of was. We're just here to help."

"And try to figure out . . . what the terms mean," I said.

He nodded, his expression a little more grim. The taynix and the delvers had a treaty. One that *didn't* include the rest of us. It involved how often, and how quickly, the slugs would hyperjump anyone but themselves—to prevent too much somewhere incursion into the nowhere.

Most of the delvers didn't feel pain when we traveled the nowhere any longer, but some did, as they'd refused our help. Which was, I supposed, their right. And collectively, the delvers were asserting that the nowhere was their territory. It had existed outside of time and space before their arrival, and they liked it that way, even healing as they were. I wasn't certain it was right for them to claim an entire dimension, but at the same time, what right did any of us have to the land—or the airspace—that we claimed?

They were willing to work with us, but I'd essentially shattered them into a ton of arguing individuals. They were much more aligned than any other species, because of their origins, but still. Things would be complicated for a while.

Regardless, hyperjumping—at least with a taynix—was going to be limited going forward: the taynix would give a warning to the delvers, then wait for permission. So far, that permission could take anywhere from a few seconds to a half hour—though it could in some cases be arranged ahead of time.

Both groups were undecided on what to do about cytonics like me. We might have to negotiate our own treaty or risk their wrath. Again, it was uncertain.

Still, having answers—and some measure of safety from the delvers—felt good. So I tried to keep my stress and worry from showing as I joined Jorgen in the lift, heading back to the surface.

"Is this about us?" he asked. "How tense you are?"

Scud. He'd noticed. So I took him by the arm, made him lean down, and kissed him. "Not about us."

He relaxed. "Good."

"I'm fine," I said. "Just getting used to the new role. Slug wrangler."

"Doesn't seem to fit into Gran-Gran's stories," he said.

"I don't *have* to live as if I'm in those stories," I said. "I've grown beyond that."

"You're still you."

"The me I am is happy to be here," I said. "With you. Just give me time. I'll get used to things being boring. Kimmalyn says boring is good. She can't shut up about it! The Saint apparently had lots to say about doing nothing being nothing to do."

"I don't even know what that means," he said, but kissed me again. For a moment that was enough. I lost myself in his warmth, in the press of his lips on mine, his pulse matching mine. I held on to him, feeling embarrassed and thrilled all at once that the doors to the elevator could open at any time, exposing our moment of intimacy.

I loved him, genuinely. I wanted to be with him forever.

It was just . . . well, everything else. The world wasn't ending. And I . . . seemed to thrive when it was.

What an absolutely *terrible* personality attribute to have.

We finally, with effort, stopped kissing as the elevator slowed and we arrived at Alta Base. Arm in arm, we stepped out and turned along the path. We still used Jorgen's old garage, and his hovercar that was inside. He kept talking about learning to tinker with it, as a hobby. Something people were able to have when they weren't at war. He talked about seeing how high he could get it to fly—as if he couldn't demand a starfighter at any moment.

Just before we reached the garage, his comm beeped. He gave me a chagrined look, but I left him to it. Some new species we were approaching, wanting seats in the new galactic forum. I wandered over to his garage, then past it to the adjacent hangar.

It was big enough for two ships. Inside, M-Bot—still in his ship form—was chatting with Hesho, who was sitting on the wing, sharpening a sword. The kitsen waved as I entered, and Doomslug fluted from beside him, making a sound like the scraping of the sword on stone.

Behind them was another ship. Chet's. He stood up from the cockpit, wearing overalls and a cap, his vibrant mustaches extending from beneath his nose. "Bother!" he said. "You realize how annoying shaving is? I never had to do that when I didn't have a real physical presence, Miss Nightshade. It is *most* uncomfortable!"

Turned out, delvers weren't limited to making stone and rock. Chet was having fun learning to be human. And by "fun," I meant he was mostly making all the same annoying observations about human bodies that I'd spent months hearing from M-Bot. At least in Chet's case, the complaints seemed more commiserative. For example, he hadn't realized that if you didn't sleep, you got headaches.

I picked up a cloth and started cleaning M-Bot, who needed a good mopping up after our last flight to inspect a distant set of caverns. I worked in silence for a time, enjoying the quiet moment, when Rodge called.

"Yo, Rig," I said, as M-Bot piped through the comm. "How's life untangling the mysteries of the universe?"

"Ugh," he said.

"That good?"

"FM keeps going down in person and getting shot at," he said. "What is with her?"

"She just wants the excitement," I said.

"That's not what she says."

"What does she say?"

"That she needs to ensure, personally, that the instructions are received by the proper authorities."

"Excitement," I said. "I empathize."

"It can't be getting dull for you already, Spensa," he said. "It's only been a few days!"

"Longer than I've ever gone without getting shot at."

"Liar," he said. "You realize I've known you most of your life, right?"

"Then you know that I'm prone to exaggeration," I said. "So what's new?"

He chuckled. "Well, I just wanted to let you know I've sent Jorgen something interesting. It might help."

I frowned. "What?"

"He asked for it, and I found it in all of this mess of information we're getting from the Superiority's primary databases. Just try not to break anything. Rig out. Thanks, by the way."

"For?"

"For dragging me into this." He cut the line. I was left confused as Jorgen walked back in carrying a datapad.

"All right," I said, hands on my hips. "What scheming have you two been doing?"

He turned it toward me. It seemed to be a list of coordinates.

"Unexplored planets," he said. "Deemed too dangerous by the Superiority. There's practically *nothing* listed about them other than warnings to stay away."

"Which could mean . . ." I said, snatching it.

411

"Anything," he said. "From a taynix refuge to some kind of very aggressive species to . . . who knows what they determined was too dangerous to even record? Seems mysterious to me."

I took it, then looked at him, narrowing my eyes. "You just want to keep me busy."

"Of course I want to keep you busy," he said. "Doing something important." He rapped the datapad. "Earth is out there somewhere, Spensa. Either in the nowhere, or here. Something happened with it. And the figments—we know next to nothing about them. And what about the traps we found on the portals into the nowhere? Those have existed far longer than the delvers. There might be dangers out there we don't know about. Better to explore them than to be surprised."

I grinned. Then paused and looked at him.

"What?" he said.

"I can't go alone."

"Kimmalyn, despite what she says, is bored of being bored. And I suspect Chet wants to go do some humaning."

"Right you are!" he called.

"So," Jorgen said, "you won't go alone."

I felt an immediate thrill. Then paused. "Will this . . . interfere with us? If I'm gone this much?"

"I don't want you to be anyone but you," he said. "And if you're sure nothing about us is bothering you—"

"It's not us. Nothing is wrong with us. I love us. Unless you want something new, that is. Just tell me, and I'll shut up. Only not, because I never do." I cringed. Then kissed him, because I knew that worked.

He grinned as I pulled back. "I'm commissioning you a flight, as explorers, to map these planets. Recruit up to three other pilots. Just promise to come back and check in with me."

"Every day," I promised. "So long as I can manage it."

He nodded. But he didn't seem certain. So I kissed him again, then added, softer, "Jorgen. I *will* come back. Every day that I can, for time with you. This is where I belong."

"You belong wherever it's not boring."

"I *belong* with all of you, even if I *need* to do other things sometimes. Learning that is basically the point of half the stories, Jorgen. Didn't you listen to Gran-Gran?"

"I thought those stories always left the heroine changed," he said.

"They do. And they did."

"In the stories she leaves, because she no longer fits in where she began."

"In the stories, yes," I whispered. "But Jorgen, there's one huge flaw in *all* of those stories."

"Which is?"

"None of them had you."

I managed to get through to him with that one, I think. He smiled, then seemed actually a little bashful.

"If there's one thing that all of this has taught me," I said to him, "it's that I get to choose for myself. I'll let you distract me with these planets to explore, Jorgen Weight, but don't you dare think it's going to give you *too* much of a break from me."

"Wouldn't dream of it."

I let go of him, then went to show the data to Doomslug, Chet, Hesho, and M-Bot. But before I did, I called back to Jorgen.

"Hey," I said. "By the way . . ."

"Yeah?"

"Just remember, if I accidentally unleash some kind of gigantic galactic threat—then have to blow up a star or something to crush its skull and turn it into a red pulp the size of a planetary ring—this was *your* idea."

He laughed, and left me to it. Though the actual details weren't that important, so I let Hesho read them off to the others, who chatted about where to go first. I stepped outside and looked up. There was an odd convergence taking place, a hole through the many layers of platforms that protected Detritus. Leading upward.

Toward the stars. I belonged there. But the lights that glowed in my friends were far brighter.

I ducked back inside, and asked M-Bot to call Kimmalyn and tell her the good news. That I'd just dragged her into a potentially life-threatening adventure.

Again.

THE END OF THE
SKYWARD SERIES

THE UNIVERSE
WILL CONTINUE IN
SKYWARD LEGACY

ACKNOWLEDGMENTS

As always, a ton of work is done to put each and every one of these books together. I hope the list of names doesn't make your vision start to blur! But also, I hope you take the time to scan through and look at the many important people who are involved in the process.

A few special highlights. Janci Patterson has been an invaluable resource on this book and the Skyward series as a whole. You might know that she's working with me on a sequel series right now—which I hope you'll read. (And if you missed *Skyward Flight,* the companion book to *Cytonic,* I highly recommend picking it up. Of the books in this series, it's rated by fan reviewers as one of the best.)

Another highlight is the cover of the US edition, which is probably our favorite cover illustration in the series, created by the always-amazing Charlie Bowater. We've enjoyed working with Charlie on these books! It's been a wonderful experience.

Finally, as always, a big thanks to my wife, Emily, Dragonsteel's chief operations officer and co-president. She is my partner in crime in all of this, and works so hard behind the scenes to coordinate everyone on the large list below.

Thank you all so much for reading!

—Brandon

At JABberwocky, my literary agency: Eddie Schneider, Joshua Bilmes, Susan Velazquez, and Christina Zobel.

At my US publisher, Delacorte Press: Krista Marino was our fantastic editor on this, as for all of these books, and was a huge resource in helping us understand the YA audience and write the best stories possible. Plus Beverly Horowitz, Lydia Gregovic, Colleen Fellingham, and Trisha Previte. The copyeditor was Kerrianne Steinberg.

At my UK publisher, Gollancz: Gillian Redfearn—who also did a fantastic line edit on this book—Emad Akhtar, and Brendan Durkin.

My audiobook narrators: Suzy Jackson in the US and Sophie Aldred in the UK.

Isaac Stewart is the VP of Dragonsteel's creative development department. Ben McSweeney did the heavy lifting of creating and leading this project's art. Hayley Lazo did the taynix and kitsen pages. Anna Earley led the art and design side of products for the book bundle. Plus Rachael Lynn Buchanan, Jennifer Neal, and Priscilla Spencer.

The Industry-Standard Peter Ahlstrom is our editorial department VP, with Karen Ahlstrom, Kristy Gilbert, Jennie Stevens, Betsey Ahlstrom, and Emily Shaw-Higham.

Dan Wells is still the only person in Dragonsteel's narrative department. We considered buying him a goldfish, but figured it would be lonely.

Matt "The Innkeeper" Hatch is Dragonsteel's VP of Operations, with Jane Horne, Kathleen Dorsey Sanderson, Makena Saluone, Hazel Cummings, and Becky Wilson.

Adam Horne, a.k.a. Schrödinger's Golfer (simultaneously being both the best and worst at golf in the company), is our VP of publicity and marketing, with Jeremy Palmer, Taylor D. Hatch, and Octavia Escamilla.

Kara Stewart is our VP of merchandising, events, and slug wrangling. This book is dedicated to her, and you should all give her a huge amount of thanks and praise! Without her, none of you would have any of the cool merchandise we release—such as the wonderful Doomslug Plushies. Thank you very much, Kara, for all of your years of being awesome! Her department includes Emma Tan-Stoker, Christi Jacobsen, Kellyn Neumann, Lex Willhite, Mem Grange, Michael Bateman, Joy Allen, Ally Reep, Richard Rubert, Katy Ives, Brett Moore, Dallin Holden, Daniel Phipps, Jacob Chrisman, Alex Lyon, Matt Hampton, Camilla Cutler, Quinton Martin, Esther Grange, Logan Reep, Laura Loveridge, Amanda Butterfield, Gwen Hickman, Donald Mustard III, Zoe Hatch, Pablo Mooney, Braydonn Moore, Avery Morgan, Nathan Mortensen, Christian Fairbanks, Dal Hill, George Kaler, Kathleen Barlow, Kaleigh Arnold, Kitty Allen, Rachel Jacobsen, Sydney Wilson, Katelyn Hatch, and Judy Torsak.

My writing group, Here There Be Dragons, is Emily Sanderson, Kathleen Dorsey Sanderson, Peter Ahlstrom, Karen Ahlstrom, Darci Stone, Eric James Stone, Alan Layton, Ethan Skarstedt, Ben Olsen, and Kaylynn ZoBell.

Beta readers for this book were Rob West (callsign: Larkspur), Brian T. Hill (callsign: El Guapo), Kalyani Poluri (callsign: Henna), Jayden King (callsign: Tripod), Suzanne Musin (callsign: Oracle), Shannon Nelson (callsign: Greywatch), Glen Vogelaar (callsign: Ways), Bao Pham (callsign: Wyld), Chris McGrath (callsign: Gunner), Paige Vest (callsign: Blade), Sam Baskin (callsign: Turtle), Liliana Klein (callsign: Slip), Ellen Maloney, Lyndsey Luther (callsign: Soar), Aubree Pham (callsign: Amyrlin), Jessie Lake (callsign: Lady), Eric Lake (callsign: Chaos), Mark Lindberg (callsign: Megalodon), Deana Covel Whitney (callsign: Braid), Linnea Lindstrom (callsign: Pixie), and Sarah Kane (callsign: Ultraviolet).

Gamma readers included many of the beta readers plus João Menezes Morais (callsign: Protected), Darci Cole (callsign: Blue), Ted Herman (callsign: Cavalry), Jessica Ashcraft (callsign: Gesh), Ross Newberry (callsign: PUNisher), Joe Deardeuff (callsign: Traveler), Gary Singer (callsign: DVE), Joshua Harkey (callsign: Jofwu), Tim Challener (callsign: Antaeus), Kendra Wilson (callsign: K-Monster),

Becca Reppert (callsign: Gran-Gran), Heather Clinger (callsign: Nightingale), Aaron Ford (callsign: Widget), Alexis Horizon (callsign: Spectra), Lingting "Botanica" Xu (callsign: Hasan), Sean VanBlack (callsign: Vanguard), Eliyahu Berelowitz Levin (callsign: Archer), and Ian McNatt (callsign: Weiry).

ABOUT THE AUTHOR

BRANDON SANDERSON is the author of the #1 *New York Times* bestselling Reckoners series: *Steelheart, Firefight, Calamity,* and the e-original *Mitosis;* the #1 *New York Times* bestselling Skyward series: *Skyward, Starsight, Cytonic,* and *Defiant,* as well as *Skyward Flight: The Collection,* with Janci Patterson; the internationally bestselling Mistborn saga; and the Stormlight Archive. He was chosen to complete Robert Jordan's The Wheel of Time series. His books have been published in more than thirty-five languages and have sold millions of copies worldwide. Brandon lives and writes in Utah.

brandonsanderson.com